Power Unleashed

By

Mickey P. Jordan

1663 LIBERTY DRIVE, SUITE 200
BLOOMINGTON, INDIANA 47403
(800) 839-8640
WWW.AUTHORHOUSE.COM

First published by AuthorHouse 01/28/05

ISBN: 1-4184-9174-8 (sc)
ISBN: 1-4184-9173-X (dj)

Library of Congress Control Number: 2004096102

Printed in the United States of America
Bloomington, Indiana

This book is printed on acid-free paper.

ACKNOWLEDGMENTS

To my lovely wife, Diane, who read and reread my manuscript over the years and was not afraid to offer suggestions for fear of offending me.

To Christina Turner, my former assistant, who helped with the tedious task of first-round editing and correcting my many grammatical and punctuation errors and who was always there with a suggestion for improving the flow of the book.

To my two lovely daughters, Christina and Mikki, who influenced my desire to want to write in the first place. With their love for the arts and their own imaginations and abilities, they inspired me to stretch myself into areas I would have never otherwise ventured.

To my brother, Larry, and his wife, Marilyn, and my sisters, Sharon Thompson and Wanda Procaccio, who read the early drafts and were honest in their assessments and gave me ideas for improving the book.

To all the people who read the first draft and gave me their feedback as well as ways to improve the book. Thank you.

To those in the government and at the IRS who helped me get my facts right to make the book more believable and interesting.

To my editor who corrected so many of my errors and contradictions to help me look good to the public that reads this finished product. Thank you for stretching my writing abilities and me.

To my associates and staff at the office, Pat, Sunny, Kendra, Kiffani, Tom, Jed, Shannon, and Stephen, who run our tax service, mortgage company, insurance agency, and financial planning firm, for allowing me the freedom to travel and write. Thank you; I couldn't have done this without you.

DEDICATION

I am dedicating this book to my wife of thirty-eight years, Diane, who has been my partner in life as well as my partner in business. Throughout this entire process of writing this book (over ten years), she continued to encourage me to write and thrilled me with her excitement as she read each new chapter as soon as it would come off the printer. When I didn't want to write, she was there challenging me. When I was ready to give up, she motivated me to move on, and when I thought I'd never get this published, she gave me the encouragement to move forward. Thank you for being my inspiration in everything I do in life, and for being the person who loves me enough to challenge my thoughts.

PRELUDE

Linda Daniels stood gazing out the kitchen window admiring the majestic snowcapped mountains miles away. It was still dark outside, but the morning sun was beginning to crest over the distant horizon. Holding her coffee with both hands wrapped firmly around the large mug, using the mug as a hand warmer, she let the aroma of the coffee fill her nostrils as she took a deep breath. This was her daily ritual and the moments she cherished. This was her alone time. On warmer days she would sit out on the deck, but this morning was one of the colder days.

"What was that?" Linda mumbled to herself as she caught the sight of a large dark object moving past the kitchen window and disappearing behind the garage. She looked closer but didn't see anything. *It was probably just a dog*, she thought as she continued her morning routine. She sat her coffee on the counter and began fixing her family's favorite breakfast, bacon and eggs.

"Honey, would you make sure the boys are getting up? I woke them once, but I'm not sure they're moving yet," she yelled to Nathan, while putting another slice of bacon in the hot skillet, avoiding the grease as it splattered on the stove.

"I'll see what I can do," Nathan yelled back.

As he walked past the bedroom window, he noticed a light coming from a strange van parked on the street in front of the house. Moving closer to the large bay window, he pulled back the sheer curtain to get a better look. He was wearing only his boxer shorts, but he knew, with the lights off, no one would be able to see him.

As he peered through the window, several men were standing around a large black van. Another van pulled up to the curb, and more men got out. His heart raced faster as he turned, grabbed his trousers, and began pulling one leg on, while at the same time hopping on the other as he tried to move into the hallway.

He yelled downstairs to Linda, who at this moment was placing the bacon strips on a paper towel, "Linda, they're here! Whatever you do, don't answer the door!"

She knew by the tone of his voice that he was upset and something was wrong, but she hadn't heard exactly what he had said. She ran toward the stairs and shouted back, "What did you say? What's wrong?"

Nathan disappeared into the boys' bedroom. "Get up! Now!" he commanded.

Matthew and Allen began to stir, rubbing their eyes and asking, "What time is it, Dad? It's still dark outside."

"Quick, get dressed and come downstairs," Nathan yelled and began throwing clothes at them as they both sat on the side of the bed rubbing the sleep from their eyes. He was trying to be firm without alarming them.

"Come on, hurry up about it!" he shouted louder. He ran out of the room. They knew that tone of voice and quickly jumped out of bed. The boys could see that their dad was not his usual self and wondered what was happening.

Linda had heard him yelling at the boys and ran up the stairs. They nearly collided as he came running into the hallway. She whispered so the boys would not hear, "Would you mind telling me what is going on here? What's wrong? What is it?"

"I think they're here! I can't be sure it's them, but I have a feeling. If it is, I want us to get out of here, fast. Grab some clothes, and let's get in the car and get out of here, now!"

"Who is here? You're scaring me, Nathan. Talk to me!"

Nathan paused for a moment, took her by the shoulders, and looked her in the eyes. "We'll talk about it in the car." He turned her and shoved her toward the bedroom. "Quick! Go get dressed. We're getting out of here!"

Nathan ran out of the bedroom, not waiting for her to ask another question. He took the stairs two at a time. At the bottom of the stairs, he could smell the bacon burning on the stove and went into the kitchen only to find it filling with smoke. He quickly shut off the burner and tossed the skillet in the sink, and more smoke filled the room.

Running into the living room, he stopped at the large picture window and ever so gently pulled back the curtain just enough so he could see the street. He slipped his brown loafers onto his feet while never taking his eyes off the street. His heart was pounding faster, and he could feel his pulse racing. There were more cars pulling up, and men in dark suits were moving slowly toward the house. He wondered what he could do; *I won't answer the door. I'll make them get a search warrant. That'll stall them a couple of hours.* He realized how futile that sounded. *They probably already have their search warrant.*

But there was no knock on the door. Without warning, there was a loud crash at the front door, and three men lunged through it, splintering the frame and destroying the door completely. At the same exact moment, five more men broke down the back door. Within seconds, the room was full of a dozen men armed with automatic rifles. They were wearing dark-blue jackets with the letters ATF on the back. "Place your hands over your head, turn around very slowly, and face the wall!" one of the men pointing a rifle aimed right at Nathan's heart commanded.

Though Nathan had served in the Marine Corps and was trained in combat, he knew that it would be useless to fight back, especially when he was outnumbered twelve to one.

He reluctantly obeyed the orders and put his hands behind his head. "Who are you? Am I under arrest?" Nathan could barely manage to get the words out.

Some of the men fanned out and moved through the house, each knowing exactly where to go. As he stood, frozen in his tracks, he heard Linda scream.

Nathan yelled, "Leave my wife alone!"

"Just shut up, Mr. Daniels, and you won't get hurt!"

One of the men shouted from upstairs, "We have secured the house! We have his wife and children with us."

The leader downstairs answered back, "Fine, bring them down here and join us."

One man held both boys securely by the arms and dragged them down the stairs. Nathan could tell by the looks in their eyes that they were horrified. He tried giving them a reassuring smile, but he knew he could not hide his own fear. The man holding Linda yanked her toward him. She fell forward, in the direction of the stairs.

The moment Nathan saw her begin to fall he lunged toward her, only to be met with a blow to the chin by the stock on the rifle. He fell to the floor, grabbing his jaw.

The man holding Linda lost his grip and could not keep her from falling, but did attempt to catch her with his foot, but instead, he accidentally kicked her, thrusting her headfirst down the long flight of stairs.

"No!" Nathan screamed. He jumped back to his feet and charged the stairs toward the aid of his wife before two men grabbed him. He received two hard punches in the stomach and doubled over in pain. One of the men hit him in the back of the skull with the butt of his gun, cutting a large gash in his head. Nathan could feel the warm blood running down his neck and onto his back.

Matthew and Allen were crying, screaming, and kicking, trying to get loose from the man who was holding them. Neither could wiggle free from the man's strong grip.

When Nathan went down the second time, he completely lost control. Forcing himself to his feet, he began swinging in a fit of rage like a madman. He connected a solid blow with his right fist to the man on his left, sending him backwards and crashing onto the coffee table, shattering it into a thousand pieces. With that one small step of victory, the adrenaline flowed through his veins, giving him extra strength, and he headed for the strong, burly man on his right. The man simply stepped aside like a bullfighter would with the bull charging at him and gave him a kick in the stomach and a hard blow to the back of the neck. When Nathan collapsed on the floor, the other two men stepped up and began kicking him in the ribs to make sure he stayed down this time. He felt like he was going to pass out and could feel the pain shooting through his rib cage.

Linda was lying at the bottom of the stairs, bleeding and groaning. She reached her hand out to try to touch him, only to have her fingers stepped on by one of the men. "If you move again, lady, I'll break all of your fingers." He applied more pressure, making her scream with excruciating pain.

Nathan couldn't tell how badly she was injured, but he knew he was not in very good shape. He managed to lift up his finger to give her an indication he was all right. She did the same.

"Tag everything," one of the men commanded, "even the cars outside. All of it is being seized."

Nathan raised his head slightly to look around the room, and he couldn't believe what he was seeing. Not a single man made any movement to help either him or his wife. He couldn't believe it. *Is this the United States government doing this? Is this just a bad dream, or is it really happening?* The pain in his chest told him that this was indeed real.

The boys settled down and stood in stunned silence weeping quietly, too afraid to move. The men moved about the house carrying on with their business, totally ignoring the two bodies lying on the floor by the staircase.

How had it come to this? Nathan thought to himself. *Where did things go wrong?* As he lay there in a pool of his own blood, he thought back over the events of the past few weeks that had led up to this moment. Then he lost consciousness.

CHAPTER ONE

Nathan Daniels was in his late thirties. He was handsome with his short light-brown hair and brown eyes. He had always kept himself in shape by exercising and loved outdoor sports. Nathan had everything a man could possibly want. He had a great job that he loved, a beautiful wife, two great boys, a nice comfortable home, no debts, and a great salary.

After his tour in the military, he attended college using his V.A. benefits. He chose computer science as his major, though at the time, many thought he was limiting his career choices. Over the years, it proved to be the right decision for him; even in the sagging economy, he had survived the layoffs of the high-tech industry.

With hard work, diligent study, and dedication, he managed to become top in his field and was sought after by every major company that manufactured computers or software. He decided on Micro Tech, not so much because of their salary package, but because of their location in Colorado Springs, Colorado. He had been with them for almost twenty years and was currently providing a very comfortable living for his family.

He met Linda at Micro Tech just a couple of years later when she began working there. She was working in one of the labs. The first time he saw her, Nathan knew he wanted to get to know her better. She had soft features, a light complexion, and auburn hair. Her body was perfect in every way, and she had gorgeous legs.

As a matter of fact, that is precisely what he noticed first about her. The partitions in the labs were about eighteen inches off the floor. He and his buddy, Ray Phillips, loved to watch the legs behind the partitions. They were known throughout the company for their antics with the ladies, and they had built quite a reputation for themselves of which they were both very proud.

"Hey, who do those beautiful sticks belong to?" Nathan asked as they strolled through the lab one day. "I don't remember seeing those magnificent legs before."

"I don't know, but I'll be more than happy to find out for you," Ray said as he bent down to get a better look.

Nathan pulled Ray up by his ear. "Uh, no, that won't be necessary. I just want to look for a while."

A few days later, they were sitting outside eating lunch when this beautiful woman came walking toward them. She was wearing high-heel shoes and a skirt that fell just above the knee. Both of them glanced down at her legs, while at the same time pointing at them, and cried out simultaneously, "It's her!"

"Excuse me! Is something wrong with my dress?" she asked, feeling somewhat embarrassed by the sudden attention.

Ray spoke first, "No, not at all. You see, my friend and I, well … we … uh …"

Nathan interrupted and jumped to his feet, "What my tongue-tied friend is trying to say is, we were admiring your legs in the lab a few days ago and wanted to meet you then." Ray admired how smooth the words came out of Nathan's mouth. "Hi! My name is Nathan Daniels, and this is Ray Phillips." They both stuck their hands out at the same time, and she reluctantly shook them, awkwardly balancing her tray with one hand while shaking with the other.

"My name is Linda. Linda Saunders." She felt her face turning red.

"You're new here, aren't you?" Ray said, proud to get a complete sentence out.

"Yes, I transferred here from our L.A. office just a few weeks ago."

"Do you like it here?"

"Oh, yes. I love it out here. I requested the transfer."

"Would you like to join us for lunch?" Nathan asked as he began to clear a spot on the table to make room for her lunch tray.

"Yeah, we always like to make the new people feel welcome," Ray quickly added.

"No, not today, thank you. I'm supposed to meet some of the other gals from the lab in a few minutes; maybe some other time."

They watched her walk away, and both began singing a Roy Orbison song just loud enough so she could hear, "Pretty woman, walking down the street; pretty woman, the kind I'd like to meet." Linda looked back smiling and gave them a wave using only her fingers.

Nathan hated the cliché love at first sight, but knew the moment he met Linda Saunders that he was in love. She was everything he had ever imagined having as a wife—auburn hair, gorgeous figure, and a wit that he just loved. She didn't even like him initially. It took a while to convince her that he was her man, but his persistence paid off.

After many encounters and chance meetings, Nathan finally got her to agree to go out with him, and after their first date, she was hooked. He was such a gentleman. No one had ever treated her like that before. She found him to be funny and very interesting to talk to as he knew so much about everything. The more Nathan got to know Linda, the more he couldn't stop thinking about her. Not only was she the most beautiful woman he had ever met, she was one of the most intelligent. A lot of the women he had dated in the past were very poor conversationalists, but she could debate any issue with him, challenging his thoughts and ideas. They dated for almost a year before he finally proposed to her.

It wasn't the most romantic proposal ever given, but it certainly was up there with being original. She had planned a business trip to New York City, where she was also going to meet up with her parents to spend the weekend. Nathan had called her father two weeks earlier and asked if he could have his daughter's hand in marriage. He immediately agreed, and they devised a surprise.

He would set up a carriage ride in Central Park, and since it was right around the holidays, her father had agreed to put her on a carriage and videotape her while asking her one question, "What is your Christmas wish this year?"

She didn't hesitate as she had thought about it often. "To live happily ever after with Nathan." She smiled and posed for the video camera as she said it. Just then, Nathan jumped in beside her on the carriage. She was in total shock.

The driver was signaled by her father to take off, and as they rode through Central Park, she still didn't know why he was there. She thought he had come just to visit with her, but her suspicions grew when he asked the driver to pull off to the side.

Nathan took Linda's hand and helped her down. They walked out into the grass. Nathan kneeled down on one knee, still holding her left hand. "Linda. You mean everything to me. You are my life." He took a deep breath, fighting back tears of joy. He could feel his hand trembling. Linda looked into his eyes in total shock.

He continued, "You have brought more joy in my life in this past year than all of my previous twenty-four years combined. I don't want to live without you. Linda, will you marry me?" The words were blurted out. There had been so much he had wanted to say, but he knew he totally lost his thoughts. He opened a little box, revealing a beautiful three-carat diamond ring.

Linda was speechless but managed to get the words out, "Yes! Yes!"

He stood up and wrapped his arms around her, and they kissed. Some people in the park had been observing and listening. They all applauded. Nathan slipped the ring on her finger, and they kissed again.

They were married in June the following year in a very elegant outdoor wedding in Vail, Colorado. The ceremony was everything she had ever dreamed about.

It was five years before they had their first baby. Matthew Allen Daniels was born in June, just seven days after their fifth wedding anniversary. Two years later, on August 15th, Allen Nathaniel Daniels came along.

Now, some thirteen years later, Nathan had climbed the corporate ladder and had become the star player at Micro Tech. Linda had quit when the boys were born so she could be at home being a full-time mom, which she loved and cherished.

Micro Tech worked with many different clients in helping them develop software to accommodate their needs. One of their major accounts was the United States government. Nathan and Ray had the highest security clearance, but neither of them had ever seen anything they felt would be considered top secret. All of that was about to change.

Nathan often worked late hours, and this night was no exception. While checking his e-mail, he noticed an unusual e-mail from an unfamiliar source with a subject line that read, "Someone needs to Read This." He moved his cursor toward it. Nathan double-clicked on the e-mail, and the computer took on a life of its own. At first, he thought he had downloaded a virus, but knew that with all the firewalls in place, that was nearly impossible. The computer calmed down, and a bar appeared on the screen.

"Hey, Ray, you need to see this." Nathan was leaning back in his chair watching the line bar on his screen slowly increase, showing that something was loading onto his computer.

Ray looked at the screen. "What is it?"

"I'm not sure. I just double-clicked on this e-mail, and it began downloading." The download bar indicated that it was only 30 percent complete. They both stared at the screen, watching the download bar slowly fill in with a dark line.

Finally, after what seemed like forever, a message popped up on the screen, "DOWNLOAD COMPLETE," and an icon appeared on his screen.

Nathan moved his mouse to the new icon that now appeared on his screen. The icon looked like an unrolled scroll, like a Bible scroll, with words on the front in bold letters:

YOU MUST READ THIS!

Ray watched intently as Nathan moved his cursor over the scroll and then hesitated. They looked at each other speechless with expressions on their faces that could be clearly read by the other, wondering if they should proceed but knowing full well that neither would be able to resist the temptation to find out what had just been downloaded onto his computer.

Ray broke the silence, "What do you think it is, and where did it come from?"

Nathan could only shrug his shoulders as his cursor circled the tiny icon. He could feel his heart pounding, and his hand was visibly shaking. Ray reached down and placed his hand on top of Nathan's, then pushed his forefinger down, double-clicking on the icon. "There, now we've both done it," Ray said as he gave Nathan's shoulder a squeeze with his other hand.

The computer screen came alive again as a Word document began to open. In moments, a 110-page document was on Nathan's computer. Both of them leaned forward and began reading. At first, it just seemed like legal double talk, but the more they read, the more they began to decipher what it was saying.

Page after page, they scrolled through the document, pausing only to wait for the next page to appear. Nathan looked up at Ray. "Are you reading what I'm reading?"

Ray nodded his head affirmatively. "Yeah, and it doesn't sound good to me at all."

Nathan continued to scan through the document on the screen. "Wait till you see this part."

As Ray continued reading, his expression slowly changed to shock. "They can't do this, can they? This is the United States of America!" Ray was yelling now, "What are they thinking? Do they really believe that they can get away with this?"

Ray walked around to the front of the computer facing Nathan and continued, "We have to do something. We can't just stand by and let the government do this to people."

"Whoa, Ray. Slow down." Nathan stood up to face him. "Let's think about this. This is evidently a top-secret document. We were not supposed to have seen it. Someone probably screwed up and forgot to lock the file. This was obviously only meant for certain people to read, and you can be certain it was not meant for us."

"Or, someone sent it to you wanting you to get it," Ray added. "Remember, there was a message that said, 'YOU MUST READ THIS.'" Ray emphasized the four words. "Someone is trying to tell us something. They want us to read it. Let's print the document and then delete it from the computer system," he suggested.

Nathan raised his voice, "Are you crazy? What are we going to do with it once we print it? This is dangerous stuff. You don't go around printing top-secret government documents without getting into a lot of trouble."

"Let's just print it and show it to someone who can do something about it. The government can't do this to the American people. What they are proposing here is wrong. It's absolutely, positively wrong, and I for one am going to try to do something. Are you with me or not?"

Nathan hesitated, then reached over and pushed the command key that told the computer to print the document. The laser printer warmed up and began printing the large document.

Nathan and Ray stood over the printer watching it intently like two school kids fascinated by an unusual bug. Slowly the printer spit out the pages, and Nathan picked up one page after another, placing them neatly in his hand. Neither of them had any idea the dangers that lay ahead for them nor that what they were holding would change their lives forever.

CHAPTER TWO

Howard Baskins had been with the U.S. Treasury Department since he was twenty-eight years old. He joined the force as an auditor and worked his way up in the organization. Howard had been in his new position for just over two years. He sat at his desk, reading over all the material that had been given to him outlining some changes to be made in the service over the next few years. He was very comfortable in his position and would do anything to impress the higher-ups. The job was extremely demanding and consumed most of his free time. He had recently been given a goal of increasing revenues in his department by 30 percent over the next year. This was not going to be easy since the president's tax cuts over the past couple of years had been reducing taxes for the average American. Congress continued passing legislation sending out bigger checks to stimulate the economy, while at the same time increasing government expenditures, requiring a need for generating more revenues to cover the deficits. But there were a lot of deadbeat taxpayers out there, and Baskins was determined to do everything in his power to find them and collect the money.

Without warning, an alarm on his computer went off, bringing Howard forward in his chair. Glancing up from his paperwork, he noticed large letters flashing on his computer screen: "**SECURITY BREACH!**" He quickly pressed some keys on his computer, and a message came on the screen, "**CODE BLUE: TOP-SECRET DOCUMENTS BEING PRINTED AT UNAUTHORIZED LOCATION. TAKE IMMEDIATE CORRECTIVE MEASURES.**"

Howard spun his chair around and picked up a book labeled *Security Measures*. He found the section marked "Code Blue" and read rapidly. He dialed the number given under that heading.

"Security, Calvin Davis here."

"Davis, this is Howard Baskins. I just got word someone is printing a sensitive document at an unauthorized location."

"Yeah, we've received the same message down here just awhile ago. I was just getting ready to call you," he lied. "I'll check it out and get back to you."

"Thanks. Any idea what document is being printed?"

"Not yet, but we'll track it down."

"Let me know as soon as you find out something."

Howard hung up the phone and turned back to his computer. Staring at the screen, he wondered to himself, *Why did this have to happen now? Things were going so well for us.*

He stood up, took some change from his pocket, and began to pace across the office floor pouring coins from one hand to the other, a nervous habit he had been doing for years now.

His mind began to drift, and he began to think back over the past few years and how he had finally arrived at this new coveted position. It was the longest day in his life, the day the news finally came of his promotion.

****

"Here's your coffee, Mr. Baskins." His secretary carried in a paper tray with his coffee and a Danish. She was well aware of the women's movements and how others criticized her for serving him they way she did, but she was from the "old school" where women still catered to their bosses and addressed them formally. It did not bother her to serve him coffee and to take care of his every need. Occasionally, she would even run personal errands for him, buying gifts, picking up his cleaning, or running to the bank. She was truly an all-around assistant.

"Thanks, Sheila. I'll call you if I need anything else."

After ten years of working with Baskins, Sheila knew all the signals. She could read him like a book and knew something was up, but wasn't quite sure what. She had watched him go through similar crises before, but today he seemed even more nervous. She suspected it had to do with another promotion.

Howard had given up smoking cigars, which he had loved dearly. It had gotten to the point where he could not enjoy them anymore because everyone complained about the disgusting odor, and every building posted "No Smoking" signs. To Howard, the aroma of a good cigar smelled wonderful, and he could not understand why it bothered people so much.

Cigarettes, on the other hand, were disgusting, and he certainly understood why smoking was banned in all public places, but cigars were another story. Howard could still taste the tobacco of a good cigar and still savored the smell of the high-quality tobacco burning. It had been five years since he stopped cold turkey.

His new habit was just as disgusting to those around him. Instead of smoking the cigar, he would simply chew on it, moving it from one side of his mouth to the other. He would constantly have to spit little pieces of tobacco out of his mouth, not caring where they landed. He would chew a cigar down until it was a soggy mass of unraveling tobacco leaves.

Another habit that was equally as annoying was when he was nervous or just thinking; he would pace back and forth across a room, while taking a handful of change and pouring the coins from one hand to his other. Back and forth, the jingling of the coins could drive a person in the room insane. He always made sure he had plenty of change in his pocket. It was a silly habit, but it helped him to think.

Baskins stood five feet, ten inches tall. He weighed about 250 pounds and knew he was overweight but just didn't care anymore. He had tried all the fad diets, tried the exercise routines, but nothing seemed to help. The moment he stopped dieting, his weight would bounce right back to where it was. Now, in his mid-fifties, he gave up all hope of ever being slim and trim.

He paced back and forth across his office, pouring change from one hand to the other as he waited. He picked up his wet cigar and began chewing on it nervously. It was the waiting he couldn't handle. This would be the biggest promotion of his career, and he knew three other men were being considered for the job. Today a decision would be made, and he was told he would be called.

Finally, at three o'clock in the afternoon, Sheila's voice came over the intercom and broke the silence. "Mr. Baskins, you have a call on line one."

Howard leaped across the room and grabbed the phone. His heart was pounding; he could feel his pulse quickening and his palms beginning to perspire. He put the change back into his pocket, placed the cigar gently in the ashtray, took a deep breath, and said, "This is Howard." He was trying to sound calm.

"Good afternoon, Howard. Hope we didn't keep you in suspense too long." The voice on the other end gave a forced laugh.

"No, Commissioner, I have plenty to keep me busy." Howard could only hope there were no hidden cameras watching him pace the floor all day long.

"Well, I just wanted to be the first to call and congratulate you on your new promotion. Starting next week, you will be head of the Collection Division in our national office. You're coming to Washington DC."

Even at his age, Baskins felt like a school kid who had just gotten the lead part in the school play. He tried to keep his voice calm, but inside he was jumping up and down for joy.

"Thank you, sir. I'll do a good job for you."

"I know you will, Howard. We'll be sending you a briefing packet by courier. I want you in my office in Washington on Monday morning. I'll see you then."

"Thank you again, sir, and I'll …" The phone went dead on the other end.

Howard opened the door of his office, and Sheila was looking at him but didn't have to ask the question. It was written all over his face. He grabbed and hugged her as he often did when he received good news.

"Are you ready to move to Washington D.C?" Sheila had been with him for over ten years. She was single and was free to move with him and had done so two other times. Each time her boss was promoted, she received a pay raise and moved up the ranks with him. She loved being able to live in and see different places. The only problem was that every time she was promoted, she had to apply for the position, as it was a government rule that openings were open to all. She couldn't prove it but knew in her heart that Howard had to be pulling strings for her to land the job each time. She could only assume that a door would open up for the capital job as well.

"I've already begun packing. I had a hunch you were getting another promotion. I held my garage sale last Saturday."

A week later, Howard and Sheila entered the boardroom in Washington and were immediately greeted by a room full of familiar faces. These were men and women he had come to know over the years but spent very little time with, except at meetings. The Service, as it was often called, was so big it was possible to go for years without seeing the same person twice, even if you were in the same rank and attended the same meetings.

"Good morning, Howard," the commissioner spoke first, and the others nodded a silent hello. "Hope you had a good flight and your accommodations are satisfactory. This must be Sheila." He got out of his chair, walked around the table, and gave her a more formal greeting. Smiling and admiring her, he said, "Howard has spoken so highly of you, but he never told me how beautiful you were."

Sheila blushed slightly. "Thank you, sir." Howard had warned her to watch out for the commissioner, who was now in his late sixties. Though married for over forty years, he still considered himself a real ladies' man and would put the make on anyone in a skirt.

The commissioner continued, staring deep into her eyes, making Sheila very uncomfortable, "Howard, you have been keeping her a secret from me all these years. Shame on you." He pulled out a chair and motioned for Sheila to sit down. He walked back to the head of the table and began addressing the group. "Gentlemen and ladies, I want to formally introduce you to our new national director of collections, Howard Baskins, and his assistant, Sheila Anderson."

Howard and Sheila both waved to the group casually and smiled.

The commissioner addressed the group, "Howard begins today as the executive director of our National Collection Division. This is a new position we have created. As most of you know, ever since the Revenue Restructuring Act of 1998 our collections of delinquent taxes have dropped considerably. We used to have over ten thousand revenue officers out there in the field, and now we are down to around three thousand. Well, the kinder, gentler IRS is going to be a thing of the past. We are reinstating many of our old policies, and we are under strict orders to increase revenues over the next ten years, and that is what we're going to do. We don't have the budget to get ten thousand revenue officers out into the field again, at least not right now. So, with the staff we do have and with your leadership, we're going to get tougher, meaner, and more aggressive. The new fight on terrorism in our country has opened the door for us to have more access to information and thereby more power than we've ever had before. But enough from me. Howard, these are your regional directors of our National Collection Division and their assistants. Your job is not going to be an easy one, but it will be rewarding, knowing you are helping your government raise the necessary funds to meet our constantly increasing budget."

As the commissioner spoke, Howard looked around the table at his two dozen directors and their assistants. There were eighteen men and six women. He guessed they were all in their late forties to early fifties. All of the assistants were female with the exception of two. They appeared much younger and probably averaged about thirty years of age. They came from all over the country, and all of them were new to this position. The directors were all Grade 14, while the assistants were Grade 12.

The commissioner continued, "You will spend today being briefed on your new assignments. You have all received a briefing packet, and we will be going over this in detail. I hope you have read it thoroughly. I must remind you, everything you read and hear today is strictly confidential. I look forward to working with all of you. We are depending on you for the next five years, and most of all, your country is depending on you too. Mr. Baskins, perhaps you would like to address your troops."

Howard wasn't much for giving speeches or pep talks and had not come prepared to speak now, but figured he probably should say something. He stood slowly, cleared his throat, then spoke in a loud voice, "I'm not one to mix words or beat around the bush. I say what I mean straight out. I expect you to follow orders. I expect you to do your job superbly. I expect you to give me 110 percent, no less. I don't like excuses; I only want results. If you are fair with me, I'll be fair with you. If you cross me, write this down, I'll cross you. I expect complete loyalty from my people, no questions asked. You must trust me and know I am receiving my orders from someone else. If you have a problem with this, let's talk about it up front—see me after the meeting. If you can go along with this, then I look forward to working with each of you in the future."

Howard sat down, and there was polite applause. He wasn't pleased with what he said, but he never was and just hoped it sounded okay. He liked to operate and manage from fear. Sheila reached under the table and gave him a pat on the knee to assure him he sounded okay.

****

Howard came out of his daze and back to reality. He looked at his watch and noted that it had been two hours since the alarm on his computer had gone off, and no one had yet called him back. He grabbed his phone again and dialed security to see if there had been any change in the status. There wasn't. Still no news as to what document and where it had been printed.

CHAPTER THREE

Ray and Nathan had read through the 110-page document at least twice. Neither of them could believe what they were reading. They sat nervously at a local Starbucks sipping their lattes with the document hidden in a black leather case.

"This sounds like something from a John Grisham novel or a Hollywood movie script. I can't believe our government would be doing anything like this," Nathan whispered, shaking his head from side to side.

"What are we going to do with this information?" Ray asked.

"Shh! Keep your voice down." Nathan glanced around to see who might have overheard Ray. The patrons seemed oblivious to their conversation. "I have no idea. What are your thoughts?"

Ray moved in closer across the tiny round table lowering his voice. "My gut instinct tells me to forget all about it and mind my own business, but my heart tells me this just isn't right and we should let the people know what is going on with our government."

Nathan nodded his head in agreement. "I have the same mixed feelings. You do know that we may lose our jobs over this. You know that, don't you?"

Ray had really never thought of that consequence. "You think so? Just because we printed some top-secret government document and showed it to the whole world?" His voice revealed his sarcasm.

Nathan snapped his finger and thumb together. "Hey, why don't we call Maxwell? Maybe he could give us some ideas."

"I don't know, man. Do you think we can trust him with this information?" Ray was skeptical about bringing another party into all of this.

"He's a lawyer. He has to keep it confidential, and besides, he's our old buddy."

Ray didn't have a better idea. "I guess …"

"Okay, I'll call him right now and see if we can get in to see him on Saturday. Can you make it then?" Nathan took out his cell phone and began dialing information for the number.

"Sure, I'll just cancel out my weekend to Jamaica with Madonna and put a hold on my meeting with Donald Trump." They both laughed.

CHAPTER FOUR

Maxwell Rosenthal had gone to school with Nathan and was now one of the most prominent lawyers in Colorado. It was rumored he was a likely candidate for the next Senate race on the Republican ticket. He had connections, and if anyone would know what to do with the document, it would be Maxwell. Nathan was convinced of that.

Nathan and Ray walked into the plush office. The floors were all polished marble in the foyer. The furnishings were red leather chairs with maple wood tables. The young, petite, and very lovely receptionist greeted them as they entered, "Good morning. You must be Nathan Daniels and Ray Phillips." She smiled at both of them as she glanced down at her appointment pad.

"Mr. Rosenthal is on a long-distance telephone call but will be with you shortly. Just have a seat and make yourselves comfortable. Would you care for some coffee?"

"Yes, please, that sounds good," Nathan spoke first.

"None for me, thank you."

"How do you take it?"

"Just black."

"I'll be right back with it." Both of the men could not resist the temptation of watching this beautiful woman walk out of the room.

Nathan was wondering if Ray was as nervous as he was. His palms were sweating, and he kept wiping them on his pants. He couldn't figure out why he got nervous in lawyers' offices and in banks. He believed they purposely over-decorated to intimidate the clients. This office definitely had an aura of success about it.

"Nice place, huh, Nathan? It sure beats the pigeon hole we work in, doesn't it?"

"Oh, I don't know, Ray. Don't you think you would get kind of tired of all this space after a while and just want to be cramped up in your little cubicle?"

"Here's your coffee. Can I get you anything else?" The receptionist sat the coffee down on the table and laid a napkin alongside of it. The coffee was served in a china cup with a saucer.

"No, this is great. Thank you." Nathan lifted the cup, hoping he would not spill it on the carpet. Sitting in the big leather chair made him feel like a little school kid, waiting for the principal to come out of his office.

Twenty minutes later, Maxwell's door opened. "Good morning, Nathan. How have you been?" He took Nathan's hand and shook it like an old friend. He turned to Ray and shook his hand. "It's been a long time since I've seen you two. Come into my office." He motioned them both to follow him down the hall. Rosenthal stood at his office door and ushered both of them inside toward his desk. "Have a seat."

The office was lavishly decorated. A huge window faced the mountains and overlooked the downtown area. One wall was decorated with pictures of Maxwell Rosenthal posing with various stars and dignitaries from around the country. Nathan and Ray glanced at the wall and recognized many of the faces—politicians, movie stars, recording artists, as well as some television personalities. The other wall held a massive bookcase filled with volumes of what appeared to be legal books. In the center of the wall was a full bar.

"You have moved up in the world since we saw you last. Getting to be quite the big shot around the state," Nathan remarked, very impressed with the surroundings.

Ray joined in, "Yeah, I hear you might be running for United States Senator in the next race. Is that true?"

"You know you can't believe everything you hear on the news. Let's just say I've been approached and leave it at that for right now. Besides, it's still two years away." Maxwell took his place behind his expansive mahogany desk. Nathan and Ray sat down in the high-back leather chairs on the other side of the desk. "So tell me, what is so urgent that you just had to come to see me on Saturday and pay double my regular rate?" He forced a chuckle and then held up the palm of his hand. "Just kidding."

Ray looked at Nathan, giving him a nod to talk first.

Nathan's expression turned serious. "Before I tell you, I need to know that everything we say here today is completely confidential and you will tell no one about our meeting. Do I have your word?"

"Yes, of course; that is understood with all of my clients." Maxwell leaned back in his chair. "Now you've really got my interest. What is it?"

"Well, a couple of days ago, we were working, and by accident, we ran across this." Nathan opened up his briefcase and pulled out the document. When you read it, I believe you'll know why we are here."

Rosenthal took the document and began reading it over. It appeared to Nathan and Ray that he was merely scanning it, but Maxwell had learned the art of speed-reading in law school. When he finished the first twenty pages in just seconds, he looked at them both. "Where did you say this came from?"

"Right out of my computer. Someone sent it to me via e-mail. When I opened the e-mail, this began downloading. Once we read it, we knew we had to do something. Our question to you is twofold. First, are we in trouble for having it, and second, do we have some moral obligation to let the people know what our government is up to?"

"Those are not easy questions. Now I know why you needed to see me today. Do you have other copies of this?"

"No! Just this one copy for you, and we have the original locked up in a safe place."

"I'm not so sure I want a set, and I'm not sure I want anyone to ever know I even saw this one. This is heavy stuff."

"Do you think they would actually do something like this?" Nathan asked, leaning forward and tapping his forefinger on the document.

"You never know what our government will do. I certainly wouldn't put it past them. The real question is, does Congress know anything about it? And if they do, why aren't they stopping it?"

Nathan and Ray nodded in agreement.

"Look, do I have your permission to make a couple of calls to Washington about this matter? I won't use your names; I'll just make a few unofficial inquiries."

Nathan looked at Ray, questioning with his eyes. "Yeah, I guess so, if you need to."

"Sure, why not," Ray echoed.

"Good, then I'll do that and get back with you by next week some time. It may take a few days to get in touch with the right people. I'm not that important that my phone calls are always returned promptly."

After some informal instructions, Maxwell stood up to indicate the meeting was over. Nathan and Ray both shook his hand and thanked him again for his time. In a moment, they were out the door.

"What do you think, Nathan? Is he going to be able to help us?"

Nathan replied as they stepped into the elevator, "Right now, he's all we've got."

"Can we trust him?"

"Yeah, I think so. I've known him for twenty years, and he has always been on the up and up, morally anyway. Let's go get some lunch; I'm starving."

"You buying?"

"No. Let's go to my house; we'll find something to eat there."

"Will Linda mind?"

"No, she can't wait for us to get back and fill her in on what Maxwell said. She wants you there so she can ask you questions."

Linda had been waiting to hear from them and was surprised to see them so soon. "That was fast. Did you see him already? What did he say? Is he going to take the case?"

"Hey, slow down. How about a kiss hello and some lunch? Then we'll fill you in on all the details."

"I've got lunch all ready to serve on the patio. Ray, would you like iced tea or lemonade?"

"Iced tea for me. Thanks, Linda."

Linda poured the drinks and then hurried outside to join them. As they began eating, Nathan told her everything that was said and brought her up to date.

"It's going to be a long week, isn't it, guys?"

"You know it, honey. But all we can do is sit and wait patiently for the phone to ring."

CHAPTER FIVE

The Treasury Department in Washington DC was on full-alert status ever since the security leak had taken place. So far, they hadn't been able to track down exactly where the printing had taken place, but Howard Baskins was well aware of what document had been printed. No amount of money or manpower was to be spared to get this document back and find out who had breached their security system. Howard had made that clear to his entire staff as well as the security team.

"Mr. Baskins, there is a call on line one for you. It is Davis, from security. He has some information for you on the Code Blue."

"Thanks, Sheila."

"Davis, what's the good news?"

"I'm afraid I've got some rather bad news mixed with some good news; which do you want first?"

"Give me the bad news first. I'm a glutton for punishment." Howard picked up an old cigar he had been chewing on all day and placed it between his lips.

"The bad news is, we still don't have any clue as to where that document was printed. We think it's somewhere on the West Coast but have been unable to pinpoint the exact location. We do know it was not one of our offices. It was printed from outside the agency."

"Is that the good news?"

"No, sir. The good news is, we've been able to track the source of the document, and I have the name of the person who's responsible for leaking the file."

"Who is it?" Baskins stood up straight and stiffened his entire body.

"It is one of your own men, a George Shanks. He lives here in Washington and works in your building. Do you know him?"

"Yes, I know him." Howard lied, not knowing why, though he had seen his name before. "Can you tell if he sent it on purpose, or did someone breach his system?"

"Sir, so far we've been unable to ascertain that, but I'll keep you posted of further developments."

Howard's mind was racing, trying to place who this person was and how the document got out of his control. "I appreciate the information, Davis. I'll take care of it from here. Do you have anything else for me?"

"No, sir, my people are working around the clock but are making little progress. I'll keep you informed."

Howard hung up the phone, and the recorder stopped automatically. He was in the habit of recording all of his calls. In his line of work, he couldn't be too careful.

Baskins hit his intercom button and yelled, "Sheila, get on the phone and find out everything you can about a George Shanks." He spelled out the name so there would be no misunderstanding. "Obtain his employee performance folder for me and have him summoned to my office as soon as possible. I don't care what he's working on or how busy he may be. I want him here. If he's not in the building, find out where he is and send a car for him if necessary."

"Yes, sir. I'll get on it right away and let you know what I find out."

"Bring his file to me as soon as you get it."

"Yes, sir."

Howard assumed the natural position he always took when no one was in the room and he wanted to read or think. He leaned back in his chair and propped both feet on his desk, placing his hands behind his head. As he leaned back, he stared out the window toward the Washington Monument, which could be seen in the distance.

He had not gotten to this position without hurting people along the way. It didn't bother him to step on people's feelings and put them in their places when needed. He was a master at intimidation and loved to watch strong men back down in his presence. Now, with his new position as national director of collections, it was easier than ever to humiliate people and to crush their egos. As he sat there, he contemplated just how he would handle the situation with George Shanks. As far as he was concerned, there were no excuses for such an error. It was a stupid thing to do, and he would see to it that it would never happen again on his watch.

There were too many people involved in this program and too much at stake to have it sabotaged by an insubordinate techie. It had taken years to get these plans in place to implement, and Howard wasn't about to let George Shanks blow it all with a temporary lapse in security. If he had leaked this document, he would have to pay the price for his sins.

Thirty minutes later, Sheila walked into the office. "Here's the EPF on George Shanks."

"Do you know this man, Sheila?"

"I believe I met him once. He works on the twenty-fifth floor. But no, sir, I don't know him."

Howard reached out and took the file from Sheila, signaling her that she could leave. He opened it and began reading:

Name: George W. Shanks   Age: 54
Wife: Molly S. Shanks   Age: 49

He scanned through every detail of the file. It seemed George had an impeccable record and had moved up the ranks during his thirty years of service. It was not what Howard had wanted to see. He was hoping there would be something in his record that could be used, added to this incident, to fire him, but there was nothing.

At 1:00 PM exactly, Sheila came over the intercom, "Mr. Baskins, Mr. Shanks is here for his appointment."

"Send him right in, Sheila."

The door opened, and a thin, balding man entered the room. His large black-rimmed glasses practically covered his face. The short-sleeve white shirt with a pocket protector full of pens completed his ensemble. *Yep, he is a computer geek all right. He doesn't look anything like the picture in his file*, Howard thought. *I'm going to enjoy this.*

Howard barely looked up from his file and motioned George to have a seat in front of his desk. George was smiling, though inside he was nervous because he had an idea of why he was being summoned into the director's office.

Howard spoke in a very pleasant yet condescending tone, "George, you've been a very busy little man during your years with our service."

"Thank you, sir. I try to stay on top of things."

"How is your family? Everyone well?" Howard was pretending to look through the file.

"Yes, sir. My wife is well. My kids are grown and gone as you can see from my record there. One lives in Seattle. He's an accountant. The other one, my daughter, lives in Chicago with her husband." George realized he was probably rambling needlessly and decided he had said enough.

"Interesting. Tell me, George, do you have any financial troubles?"

"No, sir. We're in good shape. The service has been real good to me during the years."

"Do you gamble, George?"

"No, sir ... well ... I have gambled, once, when we went to Las Vegas. I liked the slot machines. We played them all night long. I think I lost twelve dollars that night. I played the nickel slots. But, no, sir, not regularly, I don't gamble." George could not imagine why he was being asked these kinds of questions.

"Have you ever seen this document before?" Howard handed him the document in question.

George squirmed uneasily in his chair. "Yes, sir. Just the other day, I was working on some things, and it crossed over my computer screen."

"Are you aware that this is a top-secret, classified document?"

"Yes, sir. I saw the code on top."

"Did you open it or read it?" Howard sat on the edge of his desk looking down at George, holding the document in his hand inches from his face.

"Oh, no, sir. I don't have clearance to open this classification. No, sir."

"Is it your practice to leave classified documents unlocked in your computer so anyone can access them?"

"No, sir, not at all. I always lock my files when I'm finished working with them. It's a habit of mine."

"Well, Mr. Shanks, perhaps you could explain to me just how this document, which, according to records, was on your computer at 5:05 PM, got printed at an unauthorized location at 8:15 PM, over three hours later."

George had no idea how this had been tracked back to him but knew that he needed to lie and stick to his story. "I don't know. I'm sure I locked the file. I ..."

"Well, Mr. Shanks, obviously you didn't lock your computer down because we have a major security breach, and this document is now in the wrong hands. If this is leaked to the press, it could hurt us all." Howard stopped himself, knowing he was probably sharing too much, and decided to change the subject.

"I'm holding you personally responsible for this incident. I can't fire you on suspicion, and believe me, I would if I could. But I'm ordering a full investigation, and until it's complete, you are hereby suspended, effective immediately."

George was devastated but knew that he had it coming. When he had seen the contents of the document, there was only one thing on his mind, and that was to let someone know what was about to happen. He had done it without fully thinking through the consequences of his actions. He deliberately had chosen people off site and not involved with the service, as he didn't know whom he could trust.

He was speechless and sat there in stunned silence. George felt the tears welling up in his eyes but managed to force himself to look at Howard directly in the eyes. Still playing the innocent victim, George stuttered, "I'm sorry, Mr. Baskins. I don't know how this happened ... I thought—"

Baskins interrupted, "There are two things I hate: people who screw up, and men who cry. Get out of my office, out of this building, and out of my sight! I don't want to see you again. You'll be hearing from our attorneys on this matter, I'm sure." Howard scribbled some notes in George's file and grabbed the phone. "Security, please meet Mr. George Shanks at his office and see that he is escorted out of the building." He spoke loud enough so George could hear him as he was leaving the office.

CHAPTER SIX

Maxwell Rosenthal had made many friends throughout his career. They were the right friends, the kind who could help a person rise in the political ranks. Maxwell's practice was very lucrative, and he really didn't want to give it up, but something inside him kept moving him toward the political arena. There was even speculation by some that he could be the first Jewish president if he so desired, which flattered him greatly.

He was young looking and carried his forty-five years well. His wife was attractive, and they had no children. Both he and his wife, Judy, had dark complexions and had Arabic features. His hair was jet black, and he was short in stature, standing about five foot six in his stocking feet. He wore expensive shoes with special heels to help compensate for his height.

Judy was taller, about five foot nine, and was a strikingly beautiful woman with dark skin and also very dark hair. Though she was naturally beautiful, she did everything she could to make herself even more so and had numerous surgeries to enhance the beauty. She hated when people referred to it as a nose job. To her, it was cosmetic surgery, and it helped with her self-esteem. Of course, it hadn't hurt that at the same time she also had her breasts enlarged, which gave her an all-new look and even more self-confidence.

It was 7:00 AM in Colorado, and Maxwell was having his coffee on the patio by the pool.

"Would you eat some breakfast if I asked Vicinta to cook it for you?" Judy asked.

"No, I don't think so. I have a luncheon appointment, and I'll eat then. Coffee is just fine."

31

Judy joined him on the patio with her coffee. They used to treasure these few moments each morning just to be together in the quietness of the hour. Judy still did because she knew that once Maxwell left, he might not be home until eight or nine in the evening. And if there were anything political taking place, it would be even later.

She loved her lifestyle, but did not like giving up her husband. She always felt guilty when she complained because she had so much. Their home cost them over a million dollars. They had several boats, a cook, a maid, and every material thing she would ever need. The only thing that was missing in her life was Maxwell. He was seldom around, and she missed him. She knew they were growing apart but couldn't seem to get him to deal with it. She had long ago stopped bringing up the subject and had decided to just accept her life the way it was.

"What are you working on today?" she asked, just trying to get him to talk to her and put his newspaper down.

"Nothing much, mostly just corporate stuff. You know, the boring legalities of the corporate world."

She could tell he was holding back. She had known him too long. "You told me last week that Nathan Daniels was coming to see you. What did he want?"

"Not much. Just some routine legal matters." Maxwell turned the page of his *Wall Street Journal* and tried to find an article that would be interesting to read. He really did not want to talk about his newest case, even with his wife.

"You know, Maxwell, I'm seeing another man."

"Uh, huh," Maxwell said routinely, then it sank in what she had said. "You're what?" He put his paper down and looked at her.

Judy smiled. "Good, now that I have your attention, would you mind talking to me?"

"I was talking to you."

"No you weren't; you were talking at me, not with me or to me. There's a difference."

"Are you?" Maxwell was really interested at this point.

"Am I what?"

"Are you really seeing another man?"

"Yeah, my hairdresser. Today at three." She reached over and took his hand across the table. "No, there is no other man. But I feel like I need one sometimes. You just don't seem to ever be here anymore. And when you are here, you're not here. Do I make any sense at all?"

"Look, I'm sorry, but I have a lot of pressure on me lately. I promise you, as soon as I get my caseload cleared up, I'll be around more.

Promise." He stood up and took a final sip of his coffee. He walked around to her side of the table and bent over to kiss her. "I have to go now. We'll talk more about this later. Okay?" He kissed her.

She grabbed him behind the neck, pulled his head to hers, and kissed him hard on the lips. There was no doubt what she wanted. When she finally released him, she whispered, "Couldn't you be just a little late for a change?"

He rose up and straightened his tie. "I'm afraid not. I'll be home early tonight." He turned and picked up his briefcase, winked at her, and headed for the door.

He slid into his BMW convertible and decided to put the top down. It was a cool, beautiful morning, but he loved to feel the morning breeze blowing against his skin and hair. The biting cold air invigorated him, getting his blood flowing. Turning the radio up to blast his favorite country hits, he turned onto the expressway and headed for the office.

With very little traffic at that hour of the morning, he arrived earlier than usual. "Good morning, Janet. It's a beautiful Tuesday morning, isn't it?"

"If you say so, Mr. Rosenthal."

Maxwell was walking by her desk smiling. "Would you continue trying to get Senator Tom Haden in Washington DC on the phone?"

"Yes, sir. I left several messages yesterday, but no one ever called back. I'll keep trying today."

Maxwell closed his office door behind him and went to his locked file cabinet. He unlocked it and pulled the file, which he had labeled "**THE DOCUMENT**." He took it over to his desk and opened up the file and reread it for the fifth time.

"Mr. Rosenthal, I have the senator's office on the line. His secretary will transfer you."

"Thanks, Janet. Good work. Hello, Senator Haden?"

"One moment please."

The senator's voice came on the phone, "Maxwell Rosenthal, it's been a long time. How have you been?"

"Doing pretty good actually. I can't complain," Maxwell said, wanting to take the conversation away from himself.

Tom persisted, "I understand you might be giving my colleague a run for his money in the next election."

"It's premature to say anything like that, Senator, but I have been approached by our party, and there has been some talk."

Senator Haden turned on the charm. "Well, I'm just glad that you're not running against me. You'll be hard to beat."

"Thank you; it is nice of you to say, Senator."

Tom interrupted, "Please, Maxwell, we've known each other much too long for such formalities. Please just call me Tom, like the old days."

"Okay, Tom, if you insist. But when you become president, I'll insist on calling you Mr. President."

They both laughed. "That's a deal, but until that time, I insist on Tom."

Maxwell cleared his throat. "Okay, Tom." For some reason, that sounded strange to him, but he forced himself. Maxwell's voice changed and took on a more serious tone. "So, Tom, I wanted to talk to you about something else."

"Sure, Maxwell, what is it?"

"Well, it's hard to explain, but let me just ask you this, has the Senate or House gotten wind of anything unusual coming out of the Treasury Department?"

"What do you mean, unusual?"

"I can't explain fully, but has there been any rumors about anything the IRS is doing or might be getting ready to do to generate more revenue?"

Tom stood up behind his desk to stretch his legs. "We are always getting information about what they are doing, and God only knows we need to get more revenue, but I don't recall anything unusual. I know there has been a shift in emphasis lately from service to collections, but that just comes from having a new commissioner on board. What are you driving at, Max?"

"I can't tell you yet. But I have a client who found something interesting the other day about the IRS, and I was just doing a little snooping."

"What did he find?" Tom's interest was high now.

"It is a document of some sort."

"What kind of document is it?"

Maxwell felt silly for not giving more information but knew he'd better not. "I can't tell you that either, but let's just say that if what's in this document is half-true, we have some serious problems with our system. Maybe you could just ask around and keep your ears open for me. If anything at all comes up, let me know. Okay?"

"Yeah, sure, but it would help if I knew what I was listening for." The senator sounded perturbed.

"Trust me, Tom; it's better if you don't know anything about this at all. If this ever comes out, you'll thank me for keeping you in the dark.

But do keep an ear open for anything unusual coming out of the Treasury Department."

"Okay, buddy. I'll keep my eyes and ears open and let you know if I hear anything. Tell your lovely wife I said hello and give her a big kiss for me."

"Yeah, I'll do that, and you do the same. Keep in touch." Maxwell hung up the phone, disappointed nothing had been discovered. Tom was his best contact in DC, and if anybody could find out something, it would be him.

****

Across town from the senator's office, in a small room full of electrical gadgets and computers, a young man in his thirties took off his headset and dialed out on the telephone. "Yes, connect me with Howard Baskins' office; this is security."

"Howard Baskins' office," Sheila answered.

"Yes, this is security calling for Howard Baskins. Is he in?"

"Just a moment, I'll connect you." Sheila punched the intercom button. "Sir, I'm transferring a call to you from security."

Howard picked up the receiver. "This is Howard Baskins."

"Sir, this is Billings in security. Mr. Davis told me to call you if I heard anything at all on the security leak."

"Do you have something?" Howard's voice was anxious.

"Well, I don't know, sir. We are monitoring the offices on Capitol Hill, and a call came in from a Maxwell Rosenthal, an attorney in Colorado, to Senator Tom Haden. He's the senator from Colorado. Here, I'll play the tape for you."

Though it was highly illegal and unauthorized, Baskins' team had ways of finding out information they desperately needed and would on occasion monitor, from a van outside the Capitol Building, conversations and calls to and from the offices of the congressmen and senators. Howard considered it a necessity and just never worried about the consequences of his actions if ever caught. After all, someone was probably watching everyone in Washington, he thought, and even considered himself a target of such actions.

Listening to the tape, though he could only hear one side of the conversation, Howard had a hunch about this and decided to follow through with it. After it was over, he said, "Find out all you can about this Maxwell Rosenthal, and let's assume he knows who has our document. Keep me informed of your progress."

"Yes, sir. We'll get on it right away, sir."

CHAPTER SEVEN

Returning to his office, George Shanks felt devastated that he had been discovered. He had given his whole life to the service and had an impeccable record. "How did they find out it was me? I had been so careful and thought I'd covered my tracks quite well. I can't believe this," he mumbled to himself. He didn't relish his new role as a government whistle blower and had hoped that he would remain anonymous. He had read too many stories about those in Corporate America who had blown the whistle and lived to regret it, and he knew this target was far more dangerous than any corporation.

George picked up the phone and dialed home. "Hi, honey. How is your day going?"

"Well, surprise, surprise. You don't usually call me this time of day. What's going on?"

He wasn't about to tell her at this point. He would wait until he arrived home. "Oh, nothing. I'm just calling to let you know that I'll be home early for supper."

"Really? Are you sick?" Molly knew her husband would never just take an afternoon off unless something was wrong.

Shanks forced a grin. "No, nothing like that. I'm just going to come home early. I haven't done that in years. I should be home in about an hour or so, depending on traffic. I've got to go now though."

"Oh, okay. I'll have an early supper ready for you, and maybe you can tell me what is really going on with you."

He almost laughed when he thought about what he was going to have to tell her. "Okay. I love you. See you soon."

"I love you too." The phone was silent.

George began gathering up his personal items. There wasn't much, but he had some pictures of his family, a few certificates on the wall for outstanding service, as well as some items on his desk that had been gifts to him. He placed them all gently in his briefcase.

Almost with perfect timing, two uniformed men entered his office. "Mr. Shanks. We're here to escort you from the building."

George looked up and saw two large security officers whom he didn't recognize. "Yes, I'm just about finished up here."

"Sir, we will need to inspect your briefcase before we leave."

"Sure, no problem. I'm done; you can look at it now." He felt like such a criminal. He wondered what his colleagues were going to think, seeing him escorted out by security. What would they be told?

He closed the briefcase once they had approved of the contents. Then each of the officers took him by an arm, one on each side. "Let's go."

"Is it really necessary for you to handle me like this?"

Neither of them acknowledged his question but simply moved him forward and began to escort him out of the office. George was humiliated and just wanted to die right there on the spot. He held his head low. The guards opened the stairway door, and one of them said, "We'll take the stairs; it will be better." George was relieved.

Moments later, an object fell past the windows like a meteor heading toward earth and landed on the roof of a new Jeep Cherokee parked in the street. The startled driver jumped out of the car to find a body sprawled on top of his car. In minutes, the police, fire department, and EMS were on the scene. The crowd grew larger as people came out of the offices to discover what had happened.

A search of the rooftop of the building uncovered a briefcase belonging to George Shanks. Among the contents in the case was a neatly typed suicide note, signed by George. There were no witnesses. The guards that had escorted George out of his office could not be located.

****

Molly Shanks stayed busy all afternoon since the phone call from George. She wanted this dinner and evening to be extra special. She knew George was upset about something and wanted to try to make him feel better. The table was set for two with candles. She had put out her best china, and the meal was ready to be served. She waited patiently in the living room. She looked at her watch. *Six o'clock; he said he would be here at three. Where could he be? He must be caught in traffic*, she thought to herself.

A car pulled into the driveway, and she jumped up out of her chair and went to the kitchen. She wanted dinner to be on the table when he came in the door. She ran and lit the candles; she had rehearsed this in her mind several times. As she heard footsteps coming up the walkway, she struck a seductive pose by the table. The doorbell rang.

She buttoned the top button on her blouse and walked to the door. When she opened it, two strange men were staring at her; one of them had a badge opened up so she could see it. "Mrs. Molly Shanks?" one of them asked.

"Yes, that's me." She was puzzled.

"Mrs. Shanks, I'm Detective Golden with the Alexandria Police Department, and this is my partner, Detective Jacobs. May we come in?"

Examining the badge closer, she then opened the door and motioned them to step forward. "Sure, what is this about?" She could feel her pulse quicken, and she feared the worst. "Is something wrong?"

The two detectives stepped into the home and looked around. "Could we sit down somewhere?"

Molly was now in a state of shock and could tell from their expressions that they had some bad news. "Sure, I'm sorry. Yes, come on in the living room."

Each of the officers took a seat, sitting upright in a formal position.

The detective began talking in a monotone voice without emotion as if he had done this many times before, "Mrs. Shanks, I'm afraid I have some bad news." Molly could feel the tears welling up; she fought back with all of her strength and continued staring at the officer while waiting to hear.

"Your husband committed suicide this afternoon at about three fifteen."

The emotions took over, and Molly let them go. She pulled both hands toward her face, trying to fight back the tears.

"Why? I mean how?" she managed to ask.

"He jumped off his office building. I'm sorry. Is there someone we can call for you?"

By this time, Molly was visibly shaken and sobbing uncontrollably. She couldn't respond to the question. She just shook her head, indicating there was no one.

"Is there some place we can take you?"

She caught her breath. "Can I see him? I mean his body?"

"Yes, ma'am, if you would like, but we—"

"I don't care. I have to see him. Please!"

"No problem, we'll take you down to the morgue."

"I'll only be a minute; let me grab my purse." Molly walked slowly to the dining room table and blew out the candles. She paused for a moment and just stared at the table. Tears continued rolling down her cheeks as she thought of how it could have been. After what seemed like several minutes, she took one last look at the table set for two and moved away, clutching her purse tightly in her arms.

She sat in the back seat of the unmarked patrol car, and her mind was flooded with thoughts: *Why did he do it? He had so much to live for. He was only a few years from retirement.* The one question that kept going over and over in her mind was, *Why George? Why?* She wanted to find out the answer.

CHAPTER EIGHT

Senator Tom Haden picked up the morning newspaper, and the headline jumped off the page at him: **"TOP IRS OFFICIAL COMMITS SUICIDE."** As he read the rest of the story, which speculated that the reasons were job-related problems, he could not help but recall his conversation with Maxwell Rosenthal the day before. A top government official was quoted as saying that Shanks had been suspended from the service and was under investigation.

Tom had not had time to make any calls or talk to anyone about Maxwell's concerns. But after reading the article, he immediately picked up the phone to call one of his old friends just to see what he could find out.

"Verlin, this is Senator Tom Haden. How in the world have you been?" He used his title out of habit and hadn't meant to refer to himself as senator.

"Great, Tom. Same old routine; you know nothing ever changes at the Treasury Department. Just the same old mundane, bureaucratic garbage happening day in and day out. What have you been up to? I haven't spoken to you since you were reelected almost two years ago."

"Yeah, sorry about that. Time does slip by, especially when you're having so much fun."

"Don't tell me; let me guess. You're calling about the story in this morning's paper. Right?"

"Well, not entirely ..." Tom felt embarrassed. "I was wanting to invite you to lunch today, my treat."

"Sure, I'm always available for a free lunch. What time and where?"

"Let's say twelve noon at the Blue Moon Diner on Pennsylvania Avenue. Do you know where it's located?"

"Sure, I used to eat there all the time. I'll see you at noon."

Haden had known Verlin Chapman for over twenty years, and they used to be old buddies. Life had taken them on different paths, but they somehow had managed to stay in touch over the years, at least periodically. One reason they didn't see each other more often was because their wives didn't get along. When Verlin remarried, Tom's wife just could not adjust to the new wife, so they drifted apart. Tom and Verlin stayed in touch and would occasionally get together for breakfast or lunch. He hadn't realized it had been over two years since he had last seen him.

Tom turned on the television to CNN to see if anything else was being said about the suicide. Nothing. He flipped to a local news channel and watched it for a while, and there was only a brief mention of it, nothing more than the newspaper had carried.

The Blue Moon Diner used to be the hot spot in Washington for all the government officials. But like all of the hot spots, it was a fad, which soon faded. Five years ago, you couldn't get near the place at noontime, but today you had your pick of choice seats as trendier restaurants opened all around. It was a small family-run business, and there were still quite a few loyal patrons that came in to enjoy the food, but most came because they liked the conversation. Tom knew the owners and all of the waitresses, and they knew him. They liked him because he treated them like real people and would converse with them, asking them about their personal lives. He acted like he really cared about them, and he did. Of course, it didn't hurt that he was a great tipper and would often leave an amount equal to the check if it was a small tab and fifty percent if the check was larger.

"Good morning, Senator Haden," one of the waitresses said. "Do you want your usual table?" Tom nodded, and the waitress led him to his seat. "How have you been? We haven't seen you around for a while. Have you been cheating on me and eating lunch somewhere else?" She acted like she was going to scold him.

Tom opened his arms and gave her a sisterly hug. "You know I would never do that. I've just been busy, making new laws for you to live by and keeping our country safe for democracy."

She gave him a funny look with her eyebrows raised. "Yeah, right." She patted him on his chest. "You just keep right on believing that, darling." They both laughed.

"I'll just have coffee now. I'm waiting on someone to join me. You'll recognize him; he works for the Treasury Department and will have that look about him." Tom grinned and winked at her as she headed toward the kitchen.

Tom pulled out his pad on which he had scribbled some notes and began to write down some additional questions and thoughts. Ten minutes later, Verlin Chapman walked over to the table. "Sorry I'm a little late; I got held up at the office."

Tom stood up and greeted his old friend with a hearty handshake. Normally, he would have hugged him, but he felt a little self-conscious in such a public place. "That's all right. It's good to see you again. How is your lovely wife?"

"She's great. She's as stubborn as ever, but we are getting along super. How is your family?" Verlin asked.

"They're all doing okay. Our oldest, Michael, is a junior in high school, and our other son, Mark, is trying to get on the baseball team at his junior high school. Melissa is all girl and is trying everything. One week it is ballet, and the next week it is theater. She's seven now and keeps the two older boys on their toes."

They each shared some of their personal experiences over the past two years. They talked for twenty minutes, until the food arrived. When they began eating, Tom diplomatically changed the subject. "That was something about the guy from your office who jumped off that building. Did you know him? What was his name?" Tom couldn't recall the man's name from the paper.

Verlin shifted the food in his mouth, chewing and trying to talk at the same time. "George Shanks, and yes, I knew him. We weren't close, but we worked on the same floor and saw each other from time to time."

"The newspaper said it was because he was depressed over some sort of investigation and that he had been suspended; is that true?"

Verlin guarded his words. "No one really knows for sure. That was some reporter's speculation. He was a quiet man by nature."

"Was he doing well with the department?"

"He was doing great, at least up until recently."

"What do you mean?" Tom leaned closer, anxious to hear more. "What happened?"

Verlin took a sip of coffee, ignoring Tom's last question. "Say, what is your interest in all of this? Why are you asking so many questions on the subject? Are you guys on the hill trying to dig up something?"

"I'll tell you in a minute. What happened recently?"

"Well, that's just it, no one really knows for sure, but he had just been called into the director's office. Rumor has it that even if he survived the investigation, he would have been demoted and shipped off somewhere to never be heard from again."

Tom took another bite of his sandwich. "And?"

"Security had been summoned to his office. When they arrived, he had already left the office. They were there to escort him out of the building. I guess he decided to take a different route."

"Do you have any idea as to why he was suspended?"

"No. That's the funny thing about the whole matter. He had an impeccable record of service and was probably due for a promotion soon, at least until all of this came up. It took everyone off-guard. You still haven't told me why a United States senator is so interested in this suicide."

Tom looked around the restaurant to see who might be close by, then lowered his voice. "You're going to have to swear to me that you'll keep our conversation confidential. Can you do that?"

Verlin nodded his head. "Sure, no problem, but now you really have my attention."

Tom almost whispered, "I had a call a couple of days ago from an attorney in Colorado. He wouldn't tell me much but asked if I had heard about anything unusual happening at the Internal Revenue Service. I told him I had not, so he asked if I would make a couple of calls. Then today, I saw this and was wondering if the two were connected in any way."

"What was this attorney referring to?"

"Well, that's just it. I don't know specifically. All he said was he had a client who had found something which was very revealing about something the IRS was planning on doing."

"More coffee, Senator?" the waitress interrupted.

"Not for me; how about you, Verlin?"

Verlin gestured by covering his cup with the palm of his hand and shaking his head. The waitress walked to the other tables.

Verlin spoke softly, "So, you think there might be some connection between this phone call from Colorado and George Shanks jumping out the window?"

Tom raised his voice to a more normal level. "I really don't know anything for sure, but I think it's quite a coincidence, and I'm just wanting to play detective. Do you have wind of anything which is a bit unusual in the IRS or that is being kept unusually quiet?"

Verlin wiped his mouth with his napkin. "In my department, it's so routine and boring I would more than welcome something out of the ordinary just to put a little excitement in my job. No, I'm afraid there's nothing at all."

"By the way, what is your title in the department now? The last I heard you were running some department."

"My position is not a public one; let's just say that I work behind the scenes and leave it at that." Verlin looked straight at Tom and smiled.

"Would you keep your ears open and ask a few questions? If you hear of anything, anything at all, give me a call."

"Yeah, I guess I could do that for an old friend. I mean, after all, we are all on the same team, right?"

"Let's hope so, my friend, let's hope so."

They finished their lunches, and the waitress brought the check. The tab came to $12.78. Tom handed her a twenty-dollar bill and said, "Keep the change, but give me a receipt showing the twenty dollars," and winked at Verlin. "Got to keep the IRS happy."

As Tom and Verlin walked out onto the sidewalk, neither of them noticed that across the street in an alleyway stood a man dressed in a raincoat with a small camera. He took picture after picture of Tom and Verlin standing on the sidewalk talking and watched them as they went their separate ways.

CHAPTER NINE

Howard Baskins was just beginning to eat his lunch when a knock came on the door. "Come on in; the door is open!" he yelled with his mouth half-full of a roast beef sandwich.

The door opened slowly, and Calvin Davis, a tall, heavy-set man with an overgrown mustache, entered the room. "I'm sorry to barge in on you, sir, but your secretary wasn't out here, and I wanted to get this to you as soon as possible."

"That's quite okay, Davis; what do you have?"

"We just received these pictures and thought you might want to see them. We're not sure if there is a tie-in yet, but one of our men, a Verlin Chapman, just had lunch today with Senator Tom Haden, the one who received a call from that attorney in Colorado."

"What did they talk about?"

"We didn't get in on the conversation. We were just following the senator to see whom he might contact. It may just be a coincidence, sir."

"Coincidence, my ass!"

Davis interrupted, "They've known each other for over twenty years."

Howard had just taken another big bite out of his sandwich and was talking with his mouth full, waving the sandwich in the air. "A senator gets a call from an attorney in Colorado just a few days after we have some top-secret document printed. The attorney asks him to keep his ears open for any news, and then suddenly, we have this same senator having lunch with an old friend from the service. Trust me, Davis; this is no coincidence. And this is not just two old friends having lunch. This senator knows something." He reached for his Diet Coke and took a big drink.

"Yes, sir, I tend to agree. I just didn't want you to jump to any conclusions."

Howard raised his voice and looked Davis directly in the eye. "Don't worry about what conclusions I jump to. You just keep bringing me this kind of information, and we'll solve our little mystery."

"Yes, sir. I'll do that, sir." Calvin Davis turned to leave.

"Have we contacted this Maxwell fellow yet? Do we have the name of his client?" Howard asked.

"No, sir! Not yet, but we are working on it."

Howard stood up. "Is there anything else?" he asked as he took another bite, roast beef dropping onto the desk.

"No, sir, that's all for now." Davis moved closer toward the door. "I'll keep you informed, sir."

When Calvin returned to his office, he immediately called his contacts in Colorado and gave them the pertinent information.

****

Maxwell Rosenthal was busy preparing for his next court case. His client was suing a storeowner for negligence for two hundred fifty thousand dollars. The store, a gift shop in the mall, had waxed their floor, and his client fell and hurt his back. He was certain the case would be won and had hoped to settle out of court, but the owner's insurance company only offered fifty thousand, so it appeared they would be going to court next week.

"Mr. Rosenthal," his secretary's voice came over the intercom, sounding a bit nervous, "there are two men from the U.S. Treasury Department here insisting that they must see you. They say it's urgent, regarding one of our clients."

"Okay, send them right in," Maxwell closed up the folders on his desk and tried to straighten it a little.

When the two men walked into his office, they looked like something right out of the old television show *The F.B.I.* They wore black suits, had narrow black ties, and wore the same type of wing-tipped shoes. They walked into his office and began looking around. The taller one flashed his commission, which identified him as an employee of the Treasury Department, at Maxwell and said, "I'm Agent Miller, and this is my partner, Agent Anderson. We're with the Internal Revenue Service, Security Division. We're doing a little investigation and were wondering if you would cooperate with us by answering a few questions?"

"Sure, have a seat. What's this all about?" Maxwell pretended not to know the purpose of their visit but suspected it had something to do with his friend Nathan Daniels. "By the way, don't you guys usually make an appointment first?"

Anderson spoke for the first time, "No, sir, not usually. We find the element of surprise works to our advantage most of the time." They both chuckled as if it were an inside joke. Maxwell wasn't laughing but forced a grin.

Miller opened up a notebook and glanced at it, getting right down to business. "Did you make a call a few days ago to Senator Thomas Haden in Washington DC?"

Surprised that anyone knew of such a call, Maxwell replied, "As a matter of fact, I did. Why? Is that a federal offense?" He couldn't resist the sarcasm.

Ignoring Rosenthal's last two questions and looking back at his notes, the agent continued, "You mentioned in that conversation that you thought maybe something was going on at the IRS and wanted him to ask around to see if he could find out something for you. Mr. Rosenthal, just what is it you are looking for from him?"

Maxwell could not believe that these men had every small detail of his conversation. He wondered whose line was tapped, his or the senator's. "I don't believe I really have to answer any more of your questions, gentlemen. Now, if you will excuse me." He stood up. "I have an appointment in a few minutes."

Neither agent moved but continued to probe, "You mentioned you have a client who, and I quote ..." Miller looked down at his pad. "'Found something interesting about the IRS' end of quote. Mr. Rosenthal, we would like the name of your client and exactly what it is he found."

"I'm sorry, but that is privileged information."

"Mr. Rosenthal, do you understand that we are dealing here with a person who may be classified as a traitor to this country? And under the new Terrorism Act, you could be considered an accomplice to the fact and be charged with treason."

Maxwell was irate. "There is something in this country called attorney-client privilege, and I cannot give you any information even if I wanted to. I cannot release his name to you or anyone else. I'm sorry, but I'm afraid I can't help you and must ask you to leave." Maxwell walked to the door, opened it, and made a sweeping gesture with his hand toward the exit.

As Maxwell was talking, Miller was writing in his little black notebook but was not moving. Finally, both of them rose out of their chairs slowly and moved toward the door. "Mr. Rosenthal, we will be back, and you will cooperate with us." As Miller spoke, Anderson placed his hand under the desk, attaching a small listening device. It went unnoticed by Maxwell.

"Not without a court order, I won't." He slammed the door behind them as they walked through it. He would not be intimidated by the government.

Maxwell was now more convinced than ever that he was on to something big. He knew now that the government wanted this document, and they wanted it badly. He also knew the reason they wanted it. They feared someone might make it public before they had a chance to implement it. He reached into his pocket, pulled out his keys, and unlocked a drawer in his desk. Pulling out the heavily underlined document, he glanced through it one more time. *Maybe I'll be the one to pull the plug on their little scam. Who knows, I could become a national hero for this. Maybe even become president of the United States*, he was thinking. "Or I could be electrocuted for treason!" he mumbled to himself, snapping out of his daydream.

He reached over and dialed the phone. "Hello, Nathan? This is Maxwell. We have to talk and not on the phone. Can I come by your place tonight?" Suddenly, fear came over him, and he slammed down the receiver with his heart pounding. *What if they have my phone bugged? Then they will know who my client is. At least I only said his first name. But what if they follow me now?* Maxwell grabbed his coat and ran out of the office toward the elevators. "Hold all my calls; I have to go out for a bit." He glanced at his watch. "I should be back in about an hour or so."

He was beginning to feel like he was being watched. He looked at the man on the elevator and then at the woman accompanying him. *Maybe they are both agents. What if they are? I'm not doing anything wrong. Just going out for a bite to eat, that's all.* He stepped off the elevator and watched as the man and woman both went their separate ways. They seemed to care less about him.

He knew enough not to use his cell phone as anybody could easily listen in on that conversation. He knew what he had to do.

Maxwell walked out into the Colorado sunshine and could feel the crisp, cool air. He walked briskly, not noticing that a black car two blocks away was slowly moving forward, staying close to the curb. Someone was watching his every move. Maxwell walked into his favorite eating spot, went to the back of the restaurant, and found a pay phone.

"Hello, Nathan?"

"Yeah, what's going on? You sounded funny a minute ago, and then you just hung up on me. What happened?"

"Hey, I'm at a pay phone now. Don't call me at my office anymore. I just had a visit from the feds, and they want your name."

Suddenly, Nathan became very nervous. "Did you give it to them?"

"No. But it's just a matter of time before they track you down. I came to a pay phone to tell you that I will not meet you at your home tonight. I wouldn't doubt that I am being followed. Just stay cool until I get back to you. Okay?"

Nathan's mind was racing with all sorts of scenarios, but he managed to ask, "Have you found out anything yet? What should we do with the document?"

"I haven't gotten that far yet, but we know one thing; we can't trust anybody with this information. Call Ray and tell him to keep his mouth shut and to lay low too."

"You got it. Tell me truthfully, are we in danger?" Nathan's nervousness could not be concealed in his voice.

"I have no idea; I don't think so. I believe they just want to know who has the document. They're afraid it will get into the wrong hands." Maxwell didn't want to tell him about being called a traitor. He felt like it was just a scare tactic and didn't want to make Nathan more nervous than he already seemed.

Nathan's voice sounded calmer. "Yeah, like the American people might find out what they are really up to."

"I've got to go now. I'll get in touch with you later."

After hanging up the phone, he walked back into the restaurant, looking over all the patrons to see if anyone was following him. He couldn't tell; they all looked so normal. He didn't feel like eating and decided to go back to the office. As he walked outside, the car that had been following him was parked across the street. He didn't notice it and walked back to his office.

CHAPTER TEN

The two men called themselves the A-Team, after the popular television series of the same name back in the seventies. They were for hire by anyone, to do anything for a price. Unlike the television series, there were only two of them; Big Al and Sergio, they called themselves. Neither of them used their real names. Different government offices used them from time to time to do things that were illegal or bordered on being illegal. This way, the government could deny any involvement if something went wrong. The A-Team had received a call from their usual contact at the IRS for this latest job. Neither had any idea who this contact was, only that his code name was The Shark.

Tonight they were city workers with the Colorado Power and Light Company. Walking up to the security desk in the lobby, Big Al spoke, "Yeah, we're doing some work out on the street, and we need to check out your building. We may need to turn some power off."

The security guard, an old man wearing thick glasses, looked them over carefully. "Sure, go ahead. Just sign in here." He pointed to a guest book. "Do you know where you need to go?"

"Yeah, we've been here before," Sergio answered as he picked up the pen and acted as if he was going to sign the guest book.

They made their way through the building and found the office they were looking for. "This is it, Maxwell Rosenthal, Attorney-at-Law." Big Al placed his lock pick in the door and, after a couple of jiggles, turned the knob and smiled at Sergio. "Works first time, every time."

They opened up their toolbox and went to work taking the mouthpieces off all the phones and placing a bugging device in each one. In addition, they placed some in other places so as to not miss a single conversation, including the conference room.

They then moved to the file cabinets in the reception area. Again, Big Al just picked the lock, and the cabinet came open. They spent the next sixty minutes taking pictures of the files; just the names and addresses were all they were told to get.

When they completed their task, they left, making their way quickly past the security guard and waving. "Everything looks okay. We won't have to shut anything down, after all. Have a good evening."

The security guard looked up and yelled, "Hey, you guys didn't sign in or out of my book. You have to sign it."

They both turned around and waved. "Sorry, no time now; so long, old man," Sergio yelled.

The security guard shook his head and recorded the time in and out in his book so it would be noted. He prided himself in keeping good records.

When they got to their van, they took off the coveralls they had worn, tossed them in the back, and placed the toolbox in there as well. Big Al threw the keys to Sergio. "Here, you drive. I'm tired."

Sergio caught the keys with his left hand and climbed behind the wheel. "Where to now, boss?"

Big Al looked at his watch. "It's about nine o'clock now. This Maxwell was supposed to have left his house by eight thirty. Let's go on up to Majestic Hills subdivision and see if he's gone."

Majestic Hills was one of the most prestigious areas in Colorado Springs. The streets were lined with homes that cost five hundred thousand and up. Maxwell's home was a two-story brick home with large white pillars on the front. The lawn was professionally manicured, as were all the homes on the block. They drove past the house a couple of times just to check and make sure there was no sign of life. There wasn't. Sergio pulled the car into the circle driveway. "Who is this Maxwell anyway?" Sergio asked.

"He's some uppity lawyer our client wants to investigate. Seems he has gotten on the wrong side of some people. They want to nail him for something."

"Who hired us?" Sergio asked.

Big Al didn't answer him. They got out of the van, took the toolbox out, and walked around to the back of the house.

As they walked, Big Al answered Sergio's question, "It's the same guy we've worked for in the past, code name Shark. He isn't fooling anybody; he's with the CIA or the FBI, and I'd bet my life on it. I don't really care; it's an easy ten thousand dollars, just for planting a few bugging devices and listening in on some conversations. They said we only had to stake him out for a week or so. We get an extra ten grand as a bonus if we find out who this client is."

They stood at the back door. Big Al looked around the doorframe. "We got us an alarmed house here."

"I'll take care of that." Sergio walked around to the side, following the wires to the main box. He opened up the electrical box, took out his screwdriver, and disconnected some wires. "Go ahead, Al, I got it taken care of now."

Al took out his picks and found the right size. After several attempts, the door opened. They both stood there to wait for any sign of an alarm. There was silence. Moving through the house, they first bugged all of the telephones and then continued putting listening devices in all the rooms.

"Here's a good place for it." Sergio pointed to an air vent. They removed the screws, and Big Al reached into the toolbox, lifting out a small camera. He placed it inside the vent so it would be aimed right at the front door. He turned on a small, handheld television monitor and kept adjusting it until the camera was in the perfect position. He put the vent back in place, checked for dust on the floor, and moved to the next spot.

"How many cameras are we going to put in the house?" Sergio asked.

"We only need the one, just to monitor the front door, but as always, I like to have a little excitement of my own, so let's go check out the bedroom." Big Al was grinning a big smile.

"What do you think, Sergio? Can we get one in there aimed just right?"

Sergio jumped onto a chair and took the screws off the vent. "Give me the camera." Big Al handed him another camera, and Sergio placed it in a prominent position, again checking it on the little monitor until they had just the right view of the entire bedroom.

"This should give us a pretty good show, don't you think?" he said, showing Sergio the screen position.

"I think that'll do it. Let's just hope they give us something to watch." Sergio tightened up the screws on the vent and dusted off his footprints from the chair. They checked out the room to make sure there was no sign of their being there.

They slipped out the back door and locked it securely. Sergio went to the electrical box and secured the alarm system, making sure not to touch the wrong wires, which would accidentally set it off.

They left for the evening but would return with the monitoring van the next day to begin their surveillance. Big Al contacted Shark per his instructions. "Everything is in place. We should have something for you shortly."

"Any problems or complications?"

"Not at all; we'll get you the film on the files and keep you posted if anything else develops."

"Good work, A-Team. I knew I could count on you."

The man with the code name Shark wrote a message on his computer:

Top Priority
To: Howard Baskins
From: Shark
All stations are now secure.
Will begin following up on client list.
Stay cool. All is well.

CHAPTER ELEVEN

Howard Baskins chewed on his unlit cigar, moving it from one side of his mouth to the other. He paced the floor in his spacious office, pouring loose change from one hand to the other. It had been over a week since the document had been printed, and he was getting nervous that it might soon leak to the press. The publicity of George Shanks' death had not helped any either, and he thought for sure some investigator would discover his secret, a secret that only he and a few others knew. But now someone out there in the world knew it too, and it made him very nervous.

"Sheila!" Howard shouted in his intercom, "Get me Stevens in our Colorado office on the line."

"Yes, sir; right away, sir." Even Sheila was not fully aware of what was happening. She knew something unusual was going on with her boss. He was more irritable than he usually was, and there were strange messages coming in and different people showing up at the office all the time. There were also more closed-door meetings than normal. When she tried to probe for information, he would quickly change the subject by saying, "This does not involve you. I'm sorry, but I can't discuss it with you."

The buzzer sounded in Howard's office. He picked up the phone receiver. "Yeah, this is Howard Baskins. How you doing out there, Stevens?"

"Just the usual, Mr. Baskins. Trying to get the collections up and keep the folks out here honest."

"I've got a favor to ask of you, and we need your help."

"Sure, anything. What can I do?"

"I've got a list of people I would like for you to call into your office for a routine audit. I want your best people on them, and I want them to go through their past three years' returns, conducting a thorough audit."

"No problem, but our people are a little jammed up right now. I'm not sure when I can get to it."

Howard raised his voice, showing his irritation. "Stevens, this is top priority. Nothing you are doing is more important. I want the notices sent out today to these people, setting up immediate appointments with each of them. Don't allow any of them to reschedule or put it off. Tell them to bring in what they have ready, and they can always bring the rest in later. Are you getting my drift? Also, if you have the manpower, drop in on a few of the clients and conduct field audits. That is always effective."

"Yes, sir, I understand. Send me the list, and we'll begin the process. How many are there, sir?"

"Just a little over two hundred."

"Two hundred? We can't—"

"Stevens, there is no such word as *can't*. It does not exist in my vocabulary. May I suggest to you that if you can't do this, then I will find someone who can!" Howard shouted.

"Uh, yes, sir. I didn't mean we couldn't do it ... I was just—"

Howard interrupted, "I want a complete report of each one as the auditor compiles the information. Send it through the system. I want to see daily activity on this project. Oh, and by the way, Stevens, this is top secret; you're to tell no one about this project. As far as the auditors are concerned, it's just routine. Understand?"

"Yes, sir. May I ask what is going on, sir?"

"Sure you can ask, but it's better if you don't know. One last thing, if a Maxwell Rosenthal contacts your office, direct his call to me personally. Thanks, Stevens, for your cooperation. We appreciate your help."

"Anytime, sir."

Howard slammed down the phone and mused to himself, *Now, Mr. Rosenthal, we'll tighten up the net a little bit, and you will be talking soon. One way or the other, we will find out who your client is, if we have to pull in every single one of your clients and harass them. We will find our man.*

CHAPTER TWELVE

Family and friends had surrounded Molly Shanks for the past few days. She was glad the funeral home had been able to fix George up to look better. When she saw him at the morgue, he looked pretty bad. Molly thought she would have to have a closed casket funeral, but they had done a great job.

Molly didn't know what she was going to do now that she was alone. Her grown children were trying to get her to move out to the West Coast to live with them or at least to be in the same area, but she wasn't sure yet. She needed time to think. She was actually glad they were gone. It wasn't that she didn't get along with them, but they were just too nosy and bossy, trying to act like a parent instead of her children.

She thought she would just stay in her house for a while until she had time to think through all of her options. Fortunately, George's life insurance was paying off even though he had committed suicide since he had owned the policy beyond the two-year limit. He had taken out a two-hundred-fifty-thousand-dollar term policy on himself five years earlier. This, plus the one hundred thousand from the government, would help her make the transition to being a widow. She was glad now they had not canceled the term policy. The ninety-five dollars per month for the premium seemed like a waste at the time, but now she was so thankful George had listened to her.

In addition to the life insurance money, she would also receive a small government pension from his retirement plan. She knew, however, even though this sounded like a lot of money, that it would have to last her the rest of her life. They had not been able to accumulate anything else over the years, and they owed a lot of money. Her first priority was to get all the bills paid off, just as soon as the insurance money was received.

She sat down at her desk in the den and began going through the stacks of papers. This was where George had worked. He would sit there at night, paying the bills, looking over the mail, and just reading through stacks of papers. Sometimes he brought work home with him and would stay up all hours of the night.

She closed her eyes and remembered the good times. She thought about their first date, how George was so shy and bashful. She laughed to herself when she remembered how he finally got up enough nerve to ask her out.

"Gee whiz, I don't suppose a girl like you would ever consider going out with a guy like me, would you?" he asked as he kicked the pebbles in the driveway one day after school, never looking up to see her face.

"Well now, that depends on whether a guy like you would ask a girl like me to go out with you," she replied.

He quickly glanced up with one eye. "Well, does that mean you would?"

"I might if I were asked properly."

George Shanks fell down on one knee and took her by the hand and said, "Molly Miller, will you go out with me this Saturday night?"

Molly blushed as kids were staring at her but quickly responded, "Why, George Shanks, I would love to," as she batted her eyes like a movie star.

She remembered their first kiss, their first fight, and then after their marriage, their first time to make love. As she thought through their early life, looking at his picture on the desk, she asked out loud, "What happened, George? Where did we go wrong? When did we begin drifting apart? Why did you have to leave me?"

She began to cry as she gripped the picture and held it close to her breast. She screamed louder, "It's not fair, George. You cheated me. We can't work it out anymore. You took the easy way out just like you always did." Her crying turned to anger, and she threw the picture across the room, sending it crashing to the floor. The glass broke into a thousand little pieces. She sat in her chair sobbing.

The phone rang, and Molly came out of her trance. She quickly began to sniffle and wipe her eyes. Trying to sound normal, she answered it, "Hello."

"Is this Molly Shanks?"

"Yes, it is. Who is this?"

"You don't know me, Mrs. Shanks, but I'm Senator Tom Haden. I would like to talk to you about your husband's recent death. I know it might be difficult, but I really need to see you."

"Did you know him?" Molly asked.

"No, ma'am, not really. Could we meet somewhere, or could I come over? I'll bring my wife along if it will make you feel more comfortable."

"No, I mean, sure, if you'd like to bring her, but it's not necessary." Molly was actually honored that a United States senator would have the time to pay her a visit.

"Good; when would be good for you?" Tom asked.

Molly glanced at the clock on the wall and said, "How about this afternoon at about four thirty?"

"Sure, that will be fine. I'll look forward to meeting you then."

"Do you know where we—" Molly caught herself. "Do you know where I live?"

"Yeah, I think so. I'll get directions off of the Internet. Thanks. I'll see you then."

When Molly hung up the phone, she looked at the broken glass shattered on the floor. She walked across the room, knelt down, and began slowly picking up the pieces. She was sorry she had thrown it, but she just had to let out her anger somewhere.

Molly looked at her watch and decided she had better get dressed for the day if she wanted to run her errands before the senator arrived. She couldn't imagine what he wanted from her. She tried not to think about it as she went through the mundane routines of her day.

****

Tom Haden had been in politics a long time. For a young senator from Colorado, he was very experienced. He was forty-five and had managed to keep his youthful appearance. Unlike former Vice President Dan Quayle, his youthfulness had always been an asset to him. Tom was a model family man with a wife, Lucy, and three children: Michael, age sixteen; Mark, age twelve; and Melissa, age seven. They had not intentionally named each one beginning with an M; it just worked out that way. All three attended a private school in Colorado and lived with their grandparents while Tom and Lucy stayed in Washington parts of the year.

Lucy was a real asset to him and had helped him tremendously in his campaigns. She practically ran his last campaign, supervising everything from advertising to organizing the volunteers.

Unfortunately for Tom, Lucy could not make the four o'clock appointment, so Tom had decided to go alone. He had not wanted to because he felt a married man, especially one in politics, should not be going to a widow's home alone. It could look wrong to someone if it were to get out. However, he decided this was an exception and he would take his chances. Lucy had given him the go-ahead.

At four o'clock exactly, he pulled into the driveway of the Shanks' two-story colonial home. It was in a quiet suburb in Alexandria, Virginia. All the homes had the colonial look, and theirs was red brick. He rang the doorbell and waited, having no idea what he was going to say; he only knew he had to talk with her.

Molly Shanks looked younger than she was. She carried her age very well, and Tom had expected a much older woman.

"Hi, I'm Tom Haden." He extended his hand to hers.

"I'm Molly; it's nice to meet you. I've seen you a lot on television."

"I'm sorry my wife couldn't make it, but she had some pressing appointments this afternoon and couldn't get away."

"That's okay. Come on in. Could I get you some coffee or something cold to drink?"

"Yes, a glass of water would be wonderful."

"I have some iced tea if you would prefer."

"Yeah, that sounds better. Thanks."

"I'll just be a minute. Make yourself comfortable," she said as she led him into the formal living room.

Tom tried to get comfortable on the overstuffed couch with pillows all over it. He was certain some couches were made for looking at and not for sitting. If he leaned back, he would look too relaxed, and if he sat forward, he appeared too formal.

Molly came back in with the tea. "I hope you like sweetened tea. That's the only way I make it."

"That's exactly the way I like it."

Tom didn't know exactly how to broach the subject, but thought it best just to jump right in and blurt it out. "Mrs. Shanks, first of all, let me say how sorry I am about your husband's death. I know it must be hard."

Molly agreed, nodding her head and closing her eyes for a moment. She took a deep breath. "It's okay. I'm doing fine."

Tom smiled, cleared his throat, then asked, "Were you aware of anything your husband was working on, any special project, a special assignment or anything?"

Molly set her tea down and folded her hands in her lap. "No, not really. He didn't talk much about his work. His division was usually working on classified stuff, and he wasn't allowed to talk to me about it."

Tom tried to adjust his position on the couch. "Did he ever bring work home with him?"

"Oh, yes, a lot of times. Sometimes he would stay in the den working at his desk until one or two in the morning. That usually happened when he was working on a specific project that was not considered classified."

"Was he working on something just before his death?"

Molly had to think back over the course of events of the last few weeks. "As a matter of fact, he was. Every night the week before, he worked late. Sometimes at the office and sometimes here at the house."

Tom took a sip of his tea. "And you have no idea what the project was or what it was about?"

Molly shook her head. "I really don't. Do you think there is some connection between what he was working on and his death?" As she said the word *death*, she felt a lump in her throat but managed to suppress it.

Haden tried to be sensitive to her feelings. "I may be way out in left field here, but something keeps telling me that there is a connection between a phone call I had just the day before your husband's suicide. Don't ask me what it is; I don't know yet, but I just had to come by and talk with you about it."

"A phone call? What kind of phone call? Who from?"

"An attorney friend of mine called about a client of his and was asking questions about the IRS, and then almost the next day, your husband jumps ..." Tom stopped in mid-sentence, rethought how he was going to say it, and continued, "There may be nothing to it, but I wanted to find out for sure. I used to be a district attorney in Colorado, and it may be the attorney in me that is curious."

"Well, Senator Haden, I wish I could be more help to you."

"You said your husband brought work home sometimes. Did he ever leave papers lying around on his desk?"

"Yes, occasionally he would, if he was working on something on the computer and felt like he didn't need—"

The senator interrupted, "Your husband had a computer here at the house?"

"Yes, he would carry his disks back and forth from the office and oftentimes work on things."

Tom could feel his pulse quicken. He sat straight up and leaned forward. "I'm sorry to keep interrupting you, Mrs. Shanks, but have you had a chance to look on the computer to see if there is any of his work on there?"

"Me? Not hardly. I don't know the first thing about how to work that thing." She pointed toward the office. "I'm scared to death of those things. I don't even know how to turn it on and off."

"Could I take a look at the computer and browse through his files? Would you mind?" As Haden asked the question, the words felt awkward coming out of his mouth.

"Sure, I guess so, if it will help in finding out why George did this." Molly stood up and began walking toward the study, motioning for the senator to follow. "It's right in here."

"I can't guarantee that there is any connection, but I won't know until I look," Tom said as he followed closely behind her.

Tom reached down, turned on the computer, and waited impatiently while it warmed up. A menu screen popped up, giving several options. Tom began opening up file after file, but nothing was there. After about twenty minutes, he opened a directory that had been labeled "personal" and found a file entitled "**OPERATION: REVENUES.**" "Bingo!" he yelled.

"Did you find something?" Molly leaned closer, trying to see the computer screen.

When he tried to open the file, he received a message asking for a password. "Darn! Do you have any idea what password he might have used to lock a file?"

"No. I didn't even know he had any of his files here at the house. As I said, we never talked about his work."

Tom continued looking through the various files and found nothing. He was convinced that if he could just get this file opened, there would be something related to his death. "Do you have any blank disks?"

Molly opened a top desk drawer. "Here are some; will these do?"

"Will it be okay if I copy this file and take it with me?"

Molly hesitated. "Sure, if you think it will help."

Tom placed the disk in the computer, formatted it, and then asked the computer to copy it. After a few minutes, a message came on the screen: "LOCKED FILE! UNABLE TO COPY!" "This isn't going to work. I'll have to come back here and work on it. Will it be all right if I bring a computer friend of mine tomorrow and try to get into this file?"

"Sure, I guess so …" Molly wasn't sure about this. "But what if this is a government file? Won't we get into trouble?"

Tom held up his hand to assure her. "I am the government, remember? Besides, this is your property, not theirs. I just want to read it, and then you can do with it whatever you want. But first, we have to get the file opened."

Molly felt more assured. "What time would you like to come by?"

"I don't know yet. I need to talk to my friend and see when he's available. I'll call you later this evening or in the morning. Will that be all right?"

Molly smiled. "Sure, just let me know when you want to come, and I'll make plans to be here."

Tom shut down the computer using the proper commands then turned it off. He stood up and turned to Molly. "I really appreciate your letting me come here today. I hope we can find something. By the way, is there anything I can do for you, anything at all?"

"No, I'm fine. Thanks anyway." They both walked toward the door. The moment the door opened, a man in a dark sedan parked up the block began taking pictures using a telephoto lens. He was not noticed by either of them.

Power Unleashed

CHAPTER THIRTEEN

Ray had been out of town for a few days, backpacking and camping in the mountains with some of his friends, and had not talked with Nathan. Nathan had been trying unsuccessfully to reach Ray since the conversation with Maxwell. Ray walked into his apartment and sat his backpack down in the living room. *It's always good to get back home*, he thought. He loved getting up into the mountains, away from the hassles of life, away from responsibilities, away from the phone. He reached for the phone beside his bed and dialed Nathan's number. After several rings, he hung up before the answering machine picked up. He hated talking to a machine. He decided to call Maxwell at his home. He looked up the number in his directory and dialed it.

"Hello, Rosenthals' residence." It was a woman with a heavy Spanish accent.

"Yes, is Maxwell in please?"

"Yes, he is; who may I say is calling?"

"This is Ray Phillips."

"Just one minute please; I'll get him." Pressing the hold button, she dialed the intercom to Maxwell's office.

"Señor Rosenthal, there is a Mr. Phillips on line one."

Maxwell grabbed the phone.

Down the street, inside a van disguised as a city electric truck, Big Al spoke, "He's got an incoming call." Sergio put on the headset and listened.

"This is Maxwell. Hey, Ray, did Nathan talk to you yet?"

"No, I tried to call him, but couldn't get in touch with him. I was just wondering what was happening, if anything. I've been away for a few days taking a much-needed vacation."

"A lot has happened. I got a visit from our government friends, asking for your name and Nathan's as well."

"Did you give it to them? Are we in trouble?"

"No, I didn't give it to them, but we need to be careful. You obviously have something they want."

Big Al and Sergio were hanging on every word. They were watching the television monitor but could only see an empty room. Occasionally, the maid would walk through the foyer. Mrs. Rosenthal walked out of the bathroom in her nightgown, and Sergio caught the picture out of the corner of his eye. He began pointing to the monitor, trying to get Big Al's attention. "Wow, she's gorgeous," Sergio said while making a gesture with his hand as if he were throwing her a kiss, Italian style. "She's something else. This may be a job worth doing for free."

"Yeah, let's just hope the entertainment gets more exciting than it's been lately."

"Hey, listen to this." Big Al got serious and pressed the earphones closer to his ears.

"Do you have the document in a safe place?" Maxwell asked.

"Yeah, it's tucked away."

"Don't tell me; I don't need to know. Look, get it out of your possession completely. These guys aren't playing games. They mean business."

"How long before we break the news to the press or tell someone?" Ray was sounding perturbed about the delay. "After all, it's been a week now."

"I don't know yet. You'll just have to sit tight. Until I have something legal to stand on, we'll have to wait."

"Are you going to contact us when you find out something, or do we call you?"

"I'll call you as soon as I know something. Don't call me at the office. I don't trust it. They may have bugged it. I can't take any chances."

"Thanks, Maxwell. I'm sorry I called, but I just thought maybe you found out..."

"No problem. It's okay. I'll be in touch in just a few days."

"Thanks. Good night."

"Good night." Ray hung up the phone.

Sergio turned to Big Al. "Do you think he's our man?"

"Duh? What do you think, stupid? Didn't you hear him? Of course he's our man." The recorder automatically clicked off when the lines went dead.

"But more important," Big Al continued, "if he has the document, we might be able to get the ten-thousand-dollar bonus."

"Let's go for it. I could use the cash." Sergio took off the headset and rubbed his ears.

Big Al pointed to the monitor. "Looks like we might see some action, after all." Maxwell was sitting on the bed, kissing his wife.

Sergio put his headset back on and turned the volume up on the video monitor just in time to hear her ask, "How much longer are you going to work tonight?"

"I've got to finish these briefs. I'll probably be up for several more hours."

"Oh, honey, you've got to get your rest. You can't keep pushing yourself this hard."

"I know, I know, but this has to be done." He leaned down and kissed her again. "Good night, sweetheart. I love you."

"I love you too."

Sergio reached up, turned the volume off, and threw the headset down. "I don't believe this. If I had a babe who looked like her, I'd forget my work. This guy needs to get a life."

Big Al interrupted, "You would never have a classy lady like her, Sergio, and you know it. All of your women usually stand on street corners when they are not with you."

Sergio glared at Big Al. "What do you say we find this Ray fellow and check him out some more?"

"Let's tell Shark what we've got so far and ask him how he wants us to proceed."

They contacted Shark from a pay phone.

The Shark spoke, "Excellent! I knew I could count on you to get our man."

"We found out there is another one out there too," Big Al boasted. "His name is Nathan. Don't know his last name yet."

"Go ahead and check out Ray Phillips and see what you can find out. Get a little rough with him and see if you can find the document anywhere. Scare him a little, make him talk."

Big Al was smiling, showing his excitement. "Okay, but we get another ten grand for rough stuff. You understand that, don't you?"

"Yeah, yeah, no problem. You get me the last name of this Nathan fellow and the document, and I'll give you an additional ten grand; that's $30,000 more." The Shark always used money to entice. It was his power to get what he wanted. Besides, it was tax dollars anyway; if he didn't spend it, then the government would.

69

"You got yourself a deal, and we'll get back to you as soon as we find out something." Big Al hung up the phone.

He turned to Sergio, sitting in the car, and gave him an okay sign. "What is it?" Sergio asked when Big Al returned to the van.

"We just got us a green light and an additional twenty-thousand-dollar bonus if we get both the document and the last name of this Nathan guy."

Big Al decided not to tell Sergio about the other ten grand. He needed the extra money, and he figured he deserved it. After all, he reasoned, he was the leader of the A-Team. No sense in getting into an argument over money, when he could just take the additional ten thousand off the top and pocket it. Sergio would never know. He had done this before on several jobs and gotten away with it. Big Al figured as long as Sergio was happy, it didn't really matter.

Sergio started the van and drove to the address the computer had given them, the only Raymond Phillips listed. It was an apartment complex.

"There it is." Big Al pointed to an upstairs apartment in a small apartment complex.

"Are you sure?" Sergio asked.

"The computer printout shows him as apartment twenty-two, and there it is. Let's go ahead and drive around the complex, just to check it out."

Sergio drove slowly as both of them scanned the area for private security or police. They were professionals and didn't like the idea of being caught, so they worked cautiously.

Sergio parked the van in the street. "What's our game plan?" he asked. "Are we going to be nice or rough?"

Big Al was thinking of the bonus. "Let's go in rough and not waste any time. I would love to call Shark back in an hour to tell him we got the information. That would be a feather in our cap."

"Yeah and twenty thousand bucks in our pockets."

They worked on their approach and decided to knock on the door and go in through the front. The element of surprise was always on their side, and they knew how to use it.

Sergio opened a small closet in the back of the van and began locating his clothes. He dressed, putting on a black suit. They had decided to use the detective approach, except they would pose as government officials. Maybe that is why they liked this work so much; they both loved acting and pretending to be other people.

70

Big Al opened a drawer and began rummaging through it, looking for his identification. "Sheriff, detective, private investigator." He threw each one to the back of the drawer. "There it is, U.S. Treasury." He picked it up out of the drawer and threw Sergio his badge.

"How do I look?" Sergio asked.

Big Al looked him over and laughed. "Like an agent who forgot to change his sneakers."

Sergio looked down, and sure enough, he had almost forgotten to change his shoes. "It's the newest in government fashion," he said, striking a pose.

When they stepped out of the van, each double-checked his gun in the holster, giving it a secure pat.

Ray finished his shower, dried off, put on his robe, and sat down to catch up on the news. When the doorbell rang, he clicked off the television with the remote control, looking at the clock in the kitchen. "Who could that be at eleven thirty?" he mumbled to himself. He walked to the door and looked through the peephole. *These things are totally useless*, he thought. *All I see is a big blur; I don't even know why I bother looking through it.*

Ray opened the door. The moment he saw them, he knew they must be the FBI, but for some reason they didn't seem to fit. They looked like two construction workers dressed in black suits. "May I help you?" Ray asked with a puzzled look on his face.

Big Al took out his badge from inside his coat and flipped it open so Ray could see it. "I'm Agent Ricco, and this is Agent Sutherland. Are you Ray Phillips?"

"Yes, I am, but …"

Big Al continued, "We're with the U.S. Treasury Office. Could we come in and ask you a few questions?" He didn't wait for a response but stepped forward into the doorway.

"Yeah, sure, come on in. I don't understand why—"

Big Al interrupted, "I'll come right to the point. Our office has information that you and a friend named Nathan have something of ours, and well … we would like it back."

Ray began to fidget. "I really don't know what you're talking about. I don't have anything of yours."

"What is Nathan's last name?" Sergio asked.

"If you found me, I'm sure you could find him if you look hard enough," Ray said, trying to sound at ease.

"We're just trying to save both of us some time, and we thought we would try the easy way," Sergio said, beginning to move further into the apartment.

71

Big Al motioned for Sergio to begin looking around. "But since you aren't going to cooperate, we'll take a look around for ourselves."

Sergio went to a desk, opened a drawer, rummaged through it, and then threw the contents onto the floor. Items on top of the desk, he also threw to the floor one by one as he picked them up and glanced at them.

"Hey, wait a minute! Do you guys have a search warrant?"

Big Al ignored the question. "We know you or your friend have a document of ours, and we want it back. Give it to us, and we'll leave you alone."

Sergio held up an expensive gold clock high in the air, watching Ray's expression.

"Hey, don't break my clock; it cost a fortune!"

Sergio threw the clock to the floor, shattering it in a million pieces, and said, "Oops, it slipped."

Ray's mind was flooded with thoughts. Something was wrong with this whole picture. Then, he realized Sergio was wearing black leather gloves.

"You're not from the Treasury Department, are you? Who the hell are you?"

Big Al just grinned, and Sergio responded by picking up another item off the desk and hurling it through the living room.

"If you're so smart, Mr. Phillips, why don't you cooperate and give us what we want?"

"I don't think so. I don't know who you are, but you can't come barging in here in the middle of the night without a search warrant and begin destroying my house. I haven't done anything."

"This is my search warrant!" Big Al drove his fist into Ray's stomach, forcing all of the breath out of him. Ray doubled over, gasping for air, but Al met him with a blow to the face that lifted Ray off the floor and sent him backwards about three feet.

Big Al walked over to where Ray was lying and stood over him. Still smiling, being ever so polite, he spoke in a soft voice, "Mr. Phillips, we wanted to do this the easy way. We don't want to hurt you or destroy your home, but we have to have that document, and we also need the name of your friend. Now, what will it be: the hard way or the easy way?"

Ray licked his lips; he tasted the warmth of blood with his tongue and knew it was a deep cut. He tried once again to catch his breath. "I'm not going ... to help you even if you ..."

Sergio walked over to Ray, took him by his collar, picked him up off the floor and gave him another severe blow to the stomach, and then hit him with his left fist on the other side of his face. The leather gloves made the blows hurt even worse. "Are you sure you wouldn't like to reconsider, Mr. Phillips?" When Sergio let go of Ray's robe, he slumped to the floor.

As Ray lay motionless, Big Al and Sergio went through every drawer, pulling them completely out and dumping the contents on the floor. "Look behind all the pictures too!" Big Al shouted into the living room.

Ray could hear the items breaking. *They're destroying my place. These are criminals. I have to stop them,* Ray thought to himself. He spotted his backpack still sitting where he had laid it from his camping trip and began to slide across the floor to get to it. He looked to make sure that neither of them was watching him and crawled closer. It hurt every time he moved. *I bet I have more than one broken rib,* he thought. *God, it hurts.*

He reached the backpack and slipped his hand inside one of the pockets and found it. He always carried it with him on trips, just in case. He placed his fingers around the handle and pulled out his little .22 revolver. *I have to do this right the first time. I won't get a second chance.*

Ray had never aimed a gun at a person before, except in the military. The only thing he ever did now was target practice at a shooting range. He was a fair shot and knew if he could get the drop on them, he would have a chance. He placed the gun under his stomach and lay face down, waiting for the perfect moment.

Big Al came back into the room and spoke to Sergio, "I didn't find anything. How about you? Any luck?"

"Yeah, I found a nice black book full of names of some broads." Sergio laughed as he held it up to show Al.

"It figures you would find that." Al grabbed the book.

Neither of them noticed that Ray had moved and was now lying in a different spot from where he had originally fell. Ray watched out of the corner of his eye until both of them had their backs to him. At the precise moment, he jumped to his feet, taking a police stance, just like he had seen on television so many times and rehearsed at the target range. "Freeze, you two. If you move, I'll put a bullet through you." The pain in his side shot through his entire body, causing him to double over.

Big Al started to turn around. "I said don't move!" Ray yelled again, regaining his posture. "Put your hands in the air where I can see them."

"You can't shoot both of us before one of us takes you out," Sergio said.

"Yeah, but which one will it be?" Ray replied.

"You wouldn't shoot a government official now, would you?" Big Al asked.

"You're no more a government official than I'm Santa Claus. And even if you were, you're violating my rights by destroying my home. Now, get those hands in the air where I can see them." Ray cocked the pistol for effect.

Big Al began slowly raising his hands but suddenly moved his right hand toward his shoulder holster. At the same moment, he jumped to his left, drawing his gun. Sergio responded by jumping to his right. They looked like a well-rehearsed team. The two had done this many times before.

Ray fired, hitting a lamp. Sparks flew, and the room was darker. Big Al and Sergio fired simultaneously at Ray, hitting their mark every time. Ray's body twisted and fell backwards with each shot, and he collapsed to the floor in a pool of blood.

"Let's get out of here," Big Al commanded.

Several neighbors had heard the gunshots and came running out of their apartments to see what was happening. Two men in dark suits were seen jumping into a van and speeding away, but no one saw their faces.

Later that same night, Shark was notified, and he sent a message to Washington through a secured server.

TOP PRIORITY
TO: HOWARD BASKINS
FROM: THE SHARK
ONE WITNESS IDENTIFIED!
DOCUMENT NOT LOCATED.
HAVE LEAD ON SECOND WITNESS.
KEEP ME INFORMED OF PROGRESS ON YOUR END.

CHAPTER FOURTEEN

"Mr. Rosenthal, I believe we have a serious problem. Can I see you for a moment?" Janet's voice came over the intercom.

Maxwell had only slept two hours the night before, and that was in his chair in the den. His back was stiff, his head hurt, and he could barely keep his eyes opened. Janet's shrill voice coming over the intercom didn't help matters any.

"Sure, come on in," Maxwell answered back. He yawned and rubbed his eyes, hoping to look more awake.

Janet walked into his office and took her place in her usual chair. She held a wad of phone messages in her hand and lifted them toward Max so he could see them. "It seems we're being flooded with calls this morning from clients who are suddenly being audited. So far this morning, we have received fifteen calls."

"Fifteen? What the ..."

"Yes, sir. There doesn't seem to be any connection or pattern. I told them you would get back to them later today."

"Today? I can't possibly ..."

"Sir, there's one other very strange thing." Janet sounded nervous.

"What's that?"

"The audits are all being scheduled for this week." She made a face that was apologetic and handed him the pile of messages.

Maxwell read the first name, then went to the next, looking at each one, hoping for some connection. There was none.

"This is bizarre. I've never seen anything like this in my life." He shook his head, going through the pile of messages a second time. The phone rang.

Janet reached over to answer the phone. "Maxwell Rosenthal's office. May I help you?"

Maxwell was watching her as she listened to the person on the other end. She nodded toward him, letting him know this was number sixteen.

"I'm sorry, but Mr. Rosenthal is in a meeting right now. He'll call you back just as soon as he's free. Can you be reached at your home? Very good then, he'll be in touch. Goodbye."

She hung up the phone, and Maxwell stared at her in disbelief. "Get me the Internal Revenue office on the phone. I want to talk to somebody over there who is in charge."

"I'll buzz you as soon as I'm able to get through." Janet walked out of the office and shut the door behind her.

Maxwell sat in his chair, turning it to look out the window. He couldn't believe this was happening. "It's that document! They're putting the squeeze on me," Maxwell mumbled out loud.

"Mr. Stevens from the local IRS office is on line one, sir."

"Thanks." Maxwell pushed the button under the flashing light and reached over to turn on a tape recorder. "Mr. Stevens, this is Maxwell Rosenthal. I'm an attorney and was wondering if you could help me."

"I'll sure try. Rosenthal, is it?" Stevens asked, pretending like he had never heard the name before.

"Yes, Maxwell Rosenthal. So far today, I have had calls from sixteen of my clients who are being called in for an audit tomorrow by your office; can you explain to me what is going on and why my clients are being targeted?"

"Mr. Rosenthal, I'm afraid I can't help you. I've been instructed to have you call Howard Baskins in Washington DC. He's the national director of our collections division. I'm sure he can explain everything."

"Could you at least tell me why these clients are being called in so suddenly, without advance notice?"

"I'm not at liberty to discuss the matter with you at all, but I'm sure Mr. Baskins can answer all of your questions."

Maxwell displayed his anger and frustration in saying, "Thanks for nothing!" and slamming the phone down.

He quickly dialed the number given to him and waited for an answer. "Yes, Howard Baskins please."

"I'm sorry, Mr. Baskins is in a meeting at the moment. May I take a message and have him return your call?"

"Yes, please. This is Maxwell Rosenthal, and a Mr. Stevens in your Colorado Springs office referred me to him. Tell him it is urgent."

"Mr. Rosenthal, can you hold just one minute?"

"Yeah, sure."

Maxwell listened to the music play through the telephone and was thinking to himself, *This can't be happening to me. There has to be some mistake.*

Minutes later, a man with a deep, gruff voice came on the line. "Mr. Rosenthal?"

"Yes, Maxwell Rosenthal; who is this?"

"This is Howard Baskins. I'm glad you called. We have a little business to take care of today, don't we?"

"Are you aware of what is going on out here?" Maxwell didn't try to hide the anger he was feeling.

"Oh yes, I'm very much aware of it. You might even say that I'm the cause of it," Howard said calmly. "You should have cooperated with us when we asked you for the name of your client. It would have been a lot easier on you. By the way, before I forget, would you mind turning your tape recorder off?" Howard didn't know for sure Maxwell was recording, but took a guess that he probably was.

"What makes you think I'm recording this conversation?"

"Let's just say I know you and leave it at that."

Maxwell turned off the recorder. "Okay, it's off."

"Thank you. Now, Mr. Rosenthal, we can stop the process of auditing your clients if you will just cooperate with us. All I want is my document back and the names of the people who have it as well as the names of everyone who has read it. You do this for me, and I will make life so much easier for you and your clients."

"How did you get the names of my clients?" Maxwell asked.

"We have our ways. As you know, the government knows everything. We're like Santa Clause in that respect." He laughed at his own little analogy. "Are you going to cooperate, or do we continue our audit procedures?"

"I'll have to think about it and get back to you."

"I assume, Mr. Rosenthal, you have read our little document and you are aware of the dangers of something like this leaking to the press."

Maxwell wanted to guard his statement carefully. "Why don't I just agree that I'm aware of a document and leave it at that."

"You should know this ..." Howard's voice took on a more serious tone. "The document you have was not ready for release and certainly was not being circulated to our field offices. We were still working on it when it was leaked."

Maxwell was silent on the other end.

"So, Mr. Rosenthal, why don't you think about it a little longer. But you better keep the next few weeks open, because you're going to be a busy little lawyer trying to help your clients on their audits. There is one other thing you should know."

"What's that?" Maxwell asked.

"We're explaining to all of your clients that they are under investigation because you are under investigation."

Maxwell blew up. "You can't do that! That'll ruin me!"

"Exactly, Mr. Rosenthal, exactly. You have a good day." Howard hung up the phone and smiled. *I can be so pleasant when I really want to be.*

Maxwell was furious. He wasn't sure what he should do. The IRS could literally put him out of business. *How did they get my client list?* he thought. Suddenly, he had an idea. He jumped out of his chair, ran out of the office, and shouted to Janet as he ran out the door, "I'll be back in a few minutes."

Downstairs in the lobby, he walked over to the security desk. "Good morning, Bill. How are you doing today?"

Bill stood up; he could tell something was wrong. "Not bad, Mr. Rosenthal. I can't complain. What can I do for you?"

"Could I see the log for people coming in after hours?"

"Sure, it's right here." Bill put the book on the counter and opened it to the proper page.

Maxwell began to scan the past several evenings. "What is this?" he asked, pointing to an entry.

"Oh, that …" Bill bent over to read the entry. "Looks like the guys who came in from the electric company to work on the power."

"They were in this building for over an hour working on the power?"

Bill looked at it again. "That's what it says."

"Thanks." Maxwell walked away.

"Is anything wrong, Mr. Rosenthal?" Bill yelled.

Maxwell waved his hand back at him and shook his head to let him know nothing was wrong. When he got back to his office, he stopped at Janet's desk and said, "Get the electric company on the phone and see if they have any information on some work being done on this building or around this building in the past few days, specifically this past Tuesday evening at around eight PM."

Maxwell knew what the answer would be, but he just had to double check to be sure. *That was how they obtained my client list; they literally broke into my office and got the names*, he thought. *They could destroy me by harassing my clients.*

His thoughts were broken by Janet's voice coming over the intercom. "Mr. Rosenthal, your wife is on line one. Do you want to take it, or shall I tell her you'll call her back?"

"No, that's okay. I'll talk with her."

"Hi. What do you need?" he asked rather abruptly.

"I don't need anything," she said, emphasizing the word *need*. "Why does Janet always act like I'm intruding when I call?"

"She's just doing her job. Don't be so sensitive. Now, what do you want?"

She could tell he must be having a rough day and decided to drop the matter. "Have you read the paper today?"

"No! I've been going nonstop since six. Why?"

"Well, your friend Ray Phillips is on the front page of the local section."

Maxwell sat straight up in his chair. "Why? What does it say?"

"It seems he got shot last night, six times ..."

"What? How? Why?" Maxwell was in shock and grasping for words.

"They're not sure, but they suspect robbery was the motive."

"Is he dead?"

"No. He's in the intensive care unit at St. Mary's Hospital. They don't think he's going to survive. He's in a coma."

Maxwell just sat in silence.

"Was he a client of yours too?" Judy asked, trying to get Maxwell to discuss it with her.

"I can't talk about this now. Look, I have to go. I'll be home late tonight. All hell is breaking loose around here, and I've got to—"

"I understand. I'll have Vicinta keep your dinner warm for you. See you whenever."

"Bye ..." He paused, then added, "And thanks for calling." He hung up the phone and stood up to walk. He had to walk, move, do something. His insides were churning, and he could feel his anxiety level increasing. He knew his blood pressure was up. He took a couple of deep breaths; *I'll be all right. Just relax. There's nothing to worry about. It was probably just a robbery like they said.* He knew he was lying to himself. *But why would they try to kill him? Maybe I'm next. Or Nathan. My God, I have to call Nathan and warn him.*

****

Nathan heard something on the radio about a shooting and robbery that took place as he drove to work but didn't catch the details. When he arrived at the office, he found out it had been Ray who had been shot. He tried to get more information from some people in the break room who were gathered around the coffee machine. "Is there any clue as to who is responsible?" he asked.

"None at all," one of the workers replied. "They say it was robbery, but nothing was taken."

"Yeah, according to the newspaper this morning, they didn't even take his wallet," another worker added.

"It just doesn't make any sense at all. Why would a person break into a house, shoot someone, and then not take the wallet?" the first worker asked.

Nathan cut in, "Does the newspaper say anything about his condition?"

The second worker held up the newspaper for Nathan to read. "Yeah, it says here he's in critical condition. They're not sure if he is going to live or not."

"Let me read that." Nathan grabbed for the paper. He read the entire article. It didn't really say much. He decided to call Maxwell to see if he had any additional details.

Nathan found a secluded phone. He thought of a way to get a message to Maxwell and hoped it would work.

"Maxwell Rosenthal's office," Janet answered.

"Yes, I would like to leave a message for Mr. Rosenthal. This is an old friend of his. Tell him our luncheon has been changed to 1:00 PM and to wait for me in the lobby of the Sheraton Hotel downtown."

Janet glanced at the appointment book and didn't see any luncheon appointment written in. "I'm sorry but I don't—"

"You probably don't have it in his book. Just give him the message; he'll know all about it."

"I'm sorry, but I didn't catch your name," Janet persisted.

"Just tell him it's his old college buddy. He'll know." Nathan hung up quickly and could only hope his scheme would work.

****

Big Al and Sergio listened from the van parked across the street from Maxwell's office.

"What was that all about?" Sergio asked.

80

"Could be our man," Big Al replied. "We'll follow him at one o'clock and see who he meets."

****

When Janet showed Maxwell the message, he knew exactly who it was but didn't want to let Janet know. "Oh yeah, I forgot to tell you. I ran into him a few evenings ago, and we made tentative plans today for lunch. Thanks."

"You have a one-thirty appointment with Mr. and Mrs. Cleveland," Janet reminded Maxwell, pointing to his appointment book on his desk.

"I know, I know. I'll be back. If not, just keep feeding them coffee until I get here."

Janet gave him a dirty look. "They don't like waiting. You made them wait last time, and both of them kept complaining."

"I'll try to be back on time. I won't eat lunch. Promise." He smiled, trying to reassure her, then held up his right hand. "Promise!"

At one o'clock, Maxwell was waiting in the lobby of the Sheraton. People were walking everywhere, and he could only assume Nathan would be smart enough to disguise himself. His only choice was to stand in the lobby and wait for Nathan to reveal himself.

Big Al stood by the gift shop looking at magazines, keeping one eye on Maxwell. Sergio stood at the front door watching people come and go. Both were hoping this would be the big payoff.

A bellhop walked over to where Maxwell was sitting. "Are you Maxwell Rosenthal?"

Maxwell looked up startled. "Yes, I am."

The bellhop continued, "You have a call on the courtesy phone right over there," and pointed toward the white phone on the wall.

Maxwell walked over to the phone and picked up the receiver. "Hello?"

"Maxwell?"

"Nathan?"

"Yeah, I'm sorry about the cloak-and-dagger stuff, but I needed to talk to you and I'm—"

Maxwell knew what Nathan was about to say and interrupted him, "I understand, and I'm sure it is. Where are you?"

"I'm in room 1025. Are you being followed?"

"I have no idea, but I'm sure I can get to the room without being tailed. Is your room close to the elevator?"

"Yeah, it's the second door to your left."

"I'll check it out, and if it's okay, I'll be up in a minute."

Maxwell was nervous. He looked around suspiciously at everyone in the lobby. He saw a man in the gift shop who looked like a businessman. There were a few people milling around the lobby. *How would I know if one of these people were tailing me? They all look like normal people.* Sergio had slipped outside to get some fresh air.

Maxwell headed for the elevator. Several others got on with him, so he pushed the button for the eighth floor. Big Al darted onto the next available elevator.

Sergio stood in front of the elevator, watching the numbers of the elevator move, then stop at eight. He lifted his radio, "Try the eighth floor."

People on the elevator with Big Al heard the voice over the radio. He smiled at them and said, "Security. Just routine." He stepped off the elevator moments after Maxwell had stepped off. "Hold that door," he yelled to the others. He looked up each hallway and saw nothing. "He's not here," he spoke into his radio.

"The elevator has stopped at the tenth floor now," Sergio spoke. "Try it."

Big Al stepped back onto the elevator and pushed ten. He was getting impatient at the slowness and kept pushing the button, hoping it would move the elevator faster. As the doors slowly opened, he squeezed out, repeating his routine from the previous floor. "Still nothing."

Out of breath from climbing two flights of stairs from the eighth floor to the tenth floor, Maxwell opened the stairwell door to see if the coast was clear. He noticed the elevator opening and watched a man with a two-way radio in his hand step off. *I bet that is him,* he thought. He closed the door quickly, making sure it made no noise, hoping he hadn't been spotted.

"The first elevator is coming back down now!" Sergio yelled into the radio.

Big Al stepped back into the elevator and rode it up to the next floor where everyone got off. He pressed the button for the lobby and held the radio up. "I guess we lost him."

Sergio responded, "Yeah, come on back down, and we'll wait for him down here."

When Maxwell heard the elevator door shut, he opened the door again, but this time just a crack to look. *It looks like the coast is clear.* He slipped out of the stairwell and walked to room 1025 and knocked on the door, anxious to get inside.

Nathan opened the door, and Maxwell darted past Nathan. "That was close. I was followed, but I think I threw them off. I got off on the eighth floor and walked up."

"This is getting a little out of hand. I never dreamed we would be running and hiding. Who are these people anyway?"

"I guess they're government agents, but the guy I saw sure didn't look like one." Maxwell made his way into the room and found a chair. "Are you renting this room by the hour?"

Nathan smiled. "No. I had to pay for the whole night, but I really needed to see you, and this is the best way I could think of to do it. Besides, I may call Linda in a little while and have her join me for a romantic afternoon interlude." They both laughed. Nathan had said that to try to break the tension in the room. He was obviously in no mood for romance right now.

Maxwell's facial expression changed. "I'm sorry to hear about Ray. Have you seen him yet?"

"No. I was afraid to go or even call the hospital for fear this may be connected to our deal. Have you?"

"No, and for the same reasons. There's no doubt, at least in my mind, that it's connected. But I can't figure out why the government officials would shoot him. It just doesn't fit."

"I'm scared to death. What should we do with this document? How can we get rid of it?"

"I'm afraid getting rid of it is not the solution. The problem is, you've seen it and so have I. They want the document, but they also want assurance it will not show up again somewhere at a later date."

"If Ray is an indication of how bad they want this thing, they've got my attention," Nathan responded.

"We have to come up with a plan which will protect you and, at the same time, clear your name."

"Clear my name? I haven't done anything wrong. It's not like I stole the document. It just appeared on the computer screen one day."

"I didn't tell you this before, but the last time I spoke with someone from the government, he used the term *traitor* to describe the person who printed the document."

"Traitor? I'm no traitor!" Nathan became frantic and began to shout, "If anybody is a traitor, it's the person who wrote that … that …" He got up and began pacing the small area in front of the beds.

"If you want to, I'll call the IRS and tell them we want to sit down with them and explain the whole story. We'll try to reason with them.

We'll negotiate a deal which says you will give back the document in return for them leaving you alone."

"But what about our responsibility to the American people? If they go through with this plan, it will bring needless pain to a lot of people."

"You're right. That's exactly the choice we must make. I say we, because I'm in this too deep to get out now."

"What do you think we should do?" Nathan asked, hoping for a solution.

"You want my honest opinion, or do you want my gut reaction?"

"Both."

"My instinct says get out of this mess any way we can, then flee the country. But my conscience says stay and fight the rascals, exposing them for what they are."

"Has anyone ever fought the IRS and won?"

"There are several court cases where the little guy has won the battle. They almost always have to go to court and have a jury listen to the evidence."

"Are you saying we take them to court?"

"We may not take them to court, but we threaten them with court action. We file a class action lawsuit, based on the evidence we have, on behalf of the American people to stop this action from ever taking place. Once it's made public, I doubt they would kill either of us then. They would have too much to lose if they were caught."

Nathan stood silent, pondering Maxwell's last remark. "Do you think it would work?"

"We won't know until we try. Even if it doesn't work, we'll both be safer." Maxwell paused. "At least I think we will be."

After a few more minutes discussing their game plan, Maxwell looked at his watch. "It's one thirty. I've got to run. Listen, Nathan, I'll call you the next time. If you must call me, use this code word." He scribbled a phrase on the hotel stationery.

Nathan took the piece of paper and read it. "Are you serious? You really want me to say this?"

"Only if you want to stay alive," Maxwell said emphatically.

Nathan walked him to the door. "Be careful out there."

"Yeah, you too." Maxwell opened the door and looked both ways cautiously. He slipped into the hallway, shutting the door behind him, and walked to the elevator. He thought for a minute and decided to take the stairs.

At the basement, he went out the back door to a side street. He hailed a cab and returned to his office. When he walked in, his one-thirty appointment was waiting, and Janet pointed at her watch, scowling at him.

"Sorry I'm late," he said to the couple. "I'll be with you in just a moment."

He needed a couple of minutes to pull his thoughts together. It had been a long day already.

CHAPTER FIFTEEN

Senator Tom Haden made the appointment to return to Molly Shanks' home at 5:30 PM. This time, he brought his friend Douglas Preston, a computer expert. Doug owned his own company and primarily helped individuals and small businesses with their computer needs. He had once worked for a major computer firm but grew tired of the long hours and the corporate hassles. He enjoyed his freedom of being independent. The money wasn't as good, but he sure had a lot more free time than he used to. And for a single man in DC, that was a good thing. Tom knew that if anyone would be able to unlock this file, it would be Doug. He also knew that Doug could keep a secret and that he wouldn't have to worry about this information being blabbed all over Washington.

"How are you?" Tom asked as Molly opened the door. "This is my friend Doug Preston."

Doug stepped forward and extended his hand.

"This is Molly Shanks," Tom continued.

"It's nice to meet you. Would you two care for something to drink? I have tea or soft drinks," Molly asked, as she escorted the two men to the study.

"No thanks, none for me," Doug said.

"I'll have another glass of your good, old-fashioned, southern iced tea, if you have it already made," Tom responded.

"One iced tea coming right up."

Tom led Doug into the office and turned on the computer. When the menu screen lit up, he clicked on the correct directory, and then pointed to the file that he wanted Doug to open.

Doug began hitting keys so fast that Tom couldn't keep up. Doug inserted a disk and opened up a file, explaining as he went, "If I'm right, this program should take us in the back door and around the locked program."

"Why have locked programs if people can get into them anyway?"

"Keep in mind that locking a file is for the purpose of keeping the average person out of it. They aren't designed to keep us pros out, at least not at this level of security. Besides, most every locked program has to have a way to get around it in case the password is lost. If you know what you're doing, or if you have a program that knows what to look for, then it's fairly easy to get into the program through the back door."

Molly walked into the room carrying a silver tray. "Here's your tea, Senator. I hope it's sweet enough for you. Let me know if you need more. Are you sure you don't want something, Mr. Preston?"

"No, thank you. Please, just call me Doug." His fingers never missed a stroke on the keyboard. "I think I've got it!"

"Let's take a look." Tom took a sip of tea. "This is great tea, Molly. It's perfect."

Doug pointed to the screen. "Here's the file." The computer screen filled with words.

Molly and Tom leaned over Preston's shoulder to begin reading it. The expression on each face slowly changed to shock as they read.

"This must be it," Tom said. "It must be the same thing the attorney in Colorado Springs found."

"Now we know why they don't want this to get out," Molly said.

Without warning, something exploded, and there was a flash of light. All three of them jumped into the air, Doug coming out of the chair. "What in the sam blazes was that?" Doug yelled, guarding his language.

"It sounded like a bomb!" Tom replied.

They all ran to the window to see if there was any sign. There was another loud rumble, then a flash of lightning. "Look, it's pouring outside," Molly said.

The thunder rolled a third time, and another streak of lightning appeared to strike the house. They all moved back from the window, and suddenly, the lights in the house flickered then went off for a few seconds. Tom and Doug quickly looked at the computer, and the screen went black.

"Let's hope we didn't lose it," Doug said as he walked over to unplug the computer. "I think we'll just leave it off until the storm passes."

"Do you think we lost it?" Molly asked.

"You never know; sometimes when a computer crashes like this, anything can happen. An electrical surge from lightning can wipe out the entire hard drive. We won't know for sure until we open it back up."

The thunder rattled the windows in the entire house, and the lightning continued as the wind blew the rain against the windows.

****

Howard Baskins answered the telephone, "What do you have for me, Davis?"

"I thought you would like to know, sir, Tom Haden has returned to Molly Shanks' home this afternoon. He's there right now."

"Why would he keep going over there?"

"We don't know, but he's not alone, sir."

"Who went with him?"

""It's a guy by the name of Doug Preston. We're still trying to get a rundown on him. We're running his tags through the DMV and hope to have something shortly."

"Are we getting any communications from the house? Did you bug it or anything?"

"No, sir, we didn't …"

"Give me one good reason why we're not listening to conversations from her house."

"Well, sir, we thought …"

"You idiot, I don't pay you to think. I pay you to get information. The only way to get information is to listen to conversations."

"Yes, sir. I understand, but …"

Howard shouted into the phone, "Get a car over there immediately and see if you can get something on the listening device."

"Yes, sir. I'll see what I can do."

"One other thing, Davis. Have we received any new information from the Colorado project?"

"Just what I already sent to you yesterday."

Howard glanced at the latest report from Shark on his desk:

To: Howard Baskins
From: Shark
Priority Code 1
Still looking for lost file.
With no cooperation,
but are moving closer to final solution.

Net is being tightened, and we
should have something in 48 hours.
Stay calm; this will be over soon.

Howard took the document and placed it in the shredder. The message was torn into hundreds of tiny pieces of paper in a matter of seconds. He didn't like leaving a paper trail of any kind.

****

The rain stopped almost as fast as it had begun. Tom cautiously plugged the computer back into the electrical outlet. Doug hit the on switch and said, "Cross your fingers and pray it's still there."

The computer lit up. Doug scanned through the menu screen. "Here it is. I think it's okay."

Molly and Tom stood by him, looking over his shoulder. Molly had her fingers crossed.

"Yes! It's all here. Let's print it before we lose it again," Doug said, breathing a sigh of relief.

Tom turned on the printer, and the three of them stood by, watching it print the mysterious pages that had turned Tom and Molly's world upside down. Little did they know that things were about to get a lot worse for both of them.

****

Across the street from the house, an unmarked car pulled to the curb. The photographer jumped into the back seat. "I'm glad to see you two. I was wondering if they were going to send some backup. There is only so much information you can get with a camera."

"Davis sent us over. Said he wanted us to try and tape some of their conversation. Did you get any good pictures?"

"I tried to get a few close-ups by the house, through the windows, but it started raining hard, and I backed off."

The two men in the front seat were busy assembling what looked like a miniature satellite dish.

A voice came over the car radio, "Central to 479, come in."

The driver of the car picked up the microphone. "This is 479, go ahead."

"This is Calvin Davis here. Do you have anything yet?"

"No, sir, we just got here. We're setting up now. Should have something for you in a few minutes."

"Keep me posted. I want to hear from you the moment you know what they are up to. Over."

"Yes, sir; we're ready now."

Each of the men placed an earplug in his ear so they could both listen to the conversations. The man on the passenger side of the car picked up the communications disk and pointed it toward the house. They could hear faint voices. He turned the dish to his right; the voices faded. He turned the dish to his left, and the voices became stronger.

"There! That's perfect," the driver commanded. They could hear everything clearly. He adjusted some controls and turned on a tape recorder.

****

As the three of them read through the document that had been printed, they stood there in shock and total silence.

Molly spoke first, "Is this why George committed suicide? Is this why I had to become a widow?" Her voice became stronger and louder. "Is this why I have to face a life of loneliness, so the government can make more and more money?"

Tom reached over to comfort her and to calm her. "Maybe George wasn't involved in this. Maybe he was trying to expose it. That is a possibility, you know."

Doug cut in, "How can they get away with this? Can't the Senate or Congress stop them?"

"You have to understand something," Tom answered. "We've tried in the past to slow them down, but we're often powerless. Do you remember what Ronald Reagan said in a speech once: 'The power to tax is the power to destroy.' The Internal Revenue Service has the power to destroy. If someone tries to fight them, be it Congress, a group, or an individual, they can just harass and beat them down until the person or group surrenders. As the old saying goes, you can't fight city hall."

"But if they get away with this," Molly added, "we'll be living in a country where freedom is lost. The American people can't sit around idly and watch this country be brought down by this group of thugs. We must do something to stop them."

"You of all people, Molly, should understand their strength. The IRS is the only government agency that can attack 100 percent of a person's wages and property without first proving just cause. They can invade the privacy of any citizen without due process. They are also able to legally subject citizens to surveillance without a court order. Furthermore, with the IRS, a taxpayer is always guilty until he or she can prove themselves innocent."

"Why can't the United States Senate or the Supreme Court do something to change this?" Doug asked.

"We have let them get out of control over the years. Their power has increased, and if anyone in Congress tries to interfere, then we get audited and harassed, and none of us can afford or want the close scrutiny of all of our financial information."

Molly shook her head. "So we just let them get away with murder?" She emphasized *murder*.

Doug added, "If they get by with this plan, it will be worse than Nazi Germany in World War II. The Gestapo acted in the same manner, and no one was able to stop them."

"It's funny you should say that because the IRS has been compared to the Gestapo on more than one occasion."

"I just can't believe that my George would be involved in such a thing. He believed in the system. He was honest and law abiding all of his life." Molly paused in deep thought. "He would have done something to stop this, I'm sure."

Tom nodded his head in agreement. "Maybe he did, Molly, maybe he did."

Molly's face questioned Haden's last comment. Tom placed his arm around Molly's shoulders and continued, "And maybe he didn't commit suicide."

Molly had never thought about the possibility that he had been murdered, but that suddenly made more sense to her than George jumping off a building.

Doug looked at his watch. "I really must be going. Is there anything else I can help you with?"

"No. You've been a great help." Tom reached in his wallet and pulled out five twenty-dollar bills. "Here, take this for your troubles."

Doug pushed the money away. "No. I can't take money from you. I came here as a friend, to help another friend in trouble. Keep your money."

Tom put the bills back into his pocket. "Well, thanks for all of your help."

Molly walked him to the door. "I also want to thank you for your help, and it was nice meeting you."

"It was a pleasure meeting you. I hope this helps you find out why your husband had to die. By the way, I'm sorry." There was an awkward pause.

"Thanks again." Molly smiled and shook his hand.

"I'll call you later!" Tom shouted as Doug walked to his car. As he sped away, the photographer took several pictures of Preston's vehicle. He had taken quite a few close-up shots of Doug standing on the front steps.

CHAPTER SIXTEEN

Linda opened the letter frantically. Her hands trembled, and she could barely get the letter out of the envelope. Her fear was confirmed as she read the first few words at the top of the letter: **NOTICE OF AUDIT.**

They were being instructed to bring in their past three years' tax returns along with all of their receipts and other pertinent tax records. The audit was scheduled for the next day at 2:00 PM. "We can't possibly make it tomorrow!" she screamed out loud.

She ran to the telephone and dialed the number on top of the letterhead.

"Good morning, Internal Revenue Service."

Linda was nervous. "Uh, yes ... I ... we ... received a notice today ..."

"Is this about an audit?"

"Yes, it is, but we can't make it ..."

"Could you read me the reference number at the top of the page please?"

"Yes. It's P-401785."

"I'm sorry, ma'am, but those appointments cannot be changed. If you do not show up, then you will be assessed the taxes due as if you did not have receipts to prove your deductions."

"But we can't possibly get all of our records ..."

"Just bring in what you have, and we'll go from there. It is imperative you keep this appointment."

"Okay. Thank you." Linda's heart sank. She had to call Nathan. She dialed his work number, and in a few minutes, he came to the phone. "Nathan, it happened today," she spoke fast, and her voice was raised. "I called them, but they wouldn't listen."

"Calm down," Nathan said. "What happened today? Who did you call about what?"

Linda began to cry as she explained about the letter and the phone call.

Nathan tried to comfort her. "It'll be okay. We don't have anything to hide about our tax returns. I know exactly where the receipts are, and we can prove everything. We don't have anything to worry about at all."

"Are you sure? What about … the … document you found? Do you think …"

"No. I'm sure these two things are not related. It's just a coincidence, I'm sure. Don't worry about it. I'll come home early tonight, and we'll discuss it then."

Nathan hung up the phone and stared at it for several moments. He only wished he could be sure the two were not connected, but he was almost certain they were. He felt lying to Linda was better than telling her the truth, at least until he arrived home to see her face to face.

On the drive home, Nathan thought about calling Maxwell, but knew it would not help. *Besides, what good would it do to drag him into this? He is already in deep enough,* he thought. *No, I'll go alone to see what they say. If I need help later, I will ask for it then.*

Linda greeted him at the door with the letter in hand. They kissed, and she said, "I can't believe this is happening to us. Why don't we give them the document back?"

Nathan looked at her. "It's not that simple anymore. We've read the document and know the contents. They have to be sure we don't tell the press what we know."

"So they'll shut us up like they did Ray!" Linda screamed.

Matthew and Allen came running into the living room. "Hey, Dad, come see what we built today," Allen shouted.

"Yeah, it's super cool. It's our own skateboard jump." Matthew grabbed his father's hand to lead him to the backyard.

Linda followed along. "I told them they couldn't use it until you inspected it."

"Hurry, Dad!"

"Wow, it looks like you two have been busy." Nathan felt the wooden ramp. He stepped up on it, jumped a few times up and down, and then walked to the top of it. "It feels safe. You two did a good job. Let's see it in action."

Matthew and Allen jumped with excitement. "All right!" they both yelled and grabbed their skateboards.

"Put your helmets on," Linda called out.

"Oh, Mom!" Matthew jerked his helmet off the ground. "Watch this, Dad!" He went to the far corner of the driveway and began to skate toward the ramp. He built up speed, hit the ramp, and went flying through the air, landing five feet on the other side, almost losing his balance.

Nathan and Linda applauded. "Yea! You did good!"

Allen was in position and yelled for their attention, "Watch me now!" He skated toward the ramp. When he hit the ramp, he lost his balance and went flying through the air without his skateboard. He landed on his head and was stunned by the fall.

"Are you all right?" Linda screamed as she ran toward him.

Allen looked up at her, wiped the dirt off his mouth, and said, "Aw, Mom, I'm not hurt." They all smiled with relief.

"You two be careful on this thing and wear your knee and elbow pads when you jump on this," Nathan said.

Nathan and Linda left the boys playing with their skateboards and returned to the house. They stood for a moment with their arms around each other, watching as the two boys took turns jumping the ramp.

"What will it be like for them?" Linda kept her eyes on the boys. "How will it be when they grow up?"

"How will what be?"

"Everything. The government, IRS, everything."

"I would imagine ..." Nathan turned her toward him. He placed his finger under her chin and lifted it up, and looked directly into her eyes. "That there will be good things and bad things in tne world in which they live, much like it is today. Some things will get better and others will get worse. Hopefully, somewhere along the way, many of the things that are wrong today will be fixed for them."

He encircled his arms around her waist and held her tightly. "As long as they have someone to hold and to walk through life with, it won't really matter." He kissed her, and she kissed back.

She needed to be lost in his love right now. She closed her eyes and imagined they were on a faraway island in the middle of nowhere. She thought of the sand, the beach, the palm trees, and the bright-blue waves beating against the shore. She could see herself running partially naked in a bikini across the sandy beach without a care in the world. She would meet Nathan, and they would spend hours frolicking in the ocean until they fell, exhausted, on the shore. There was no IRS, no audit, and no government document on this island paradise. There were no problems here, just peace and tranquility.

As the boys continued to play outside, Nathan took Linda by the hand and led her to their room. For the next forty-five minutes, Linda and Nathan were in their own place of paradise, forgetting all about the problems confronting both of them.

****

The next day, on schedule, they drove downtown, pulled into a parking lot, and let the attendant park the car. They walked slowly toward the government building. Once inside, a sudden fear came over them both. Nathan took Linda's hand as they rode the elevator to the fifth floor. "It's going to be okay," he whispered. "I've got it all figured out in here." He motioned toward his briefcase.

They walked slowly off the elevator and saw the sign with an arrow under it, **AUDITS**. They followed the arrow, and just before opening the glass double doors, they both took a deep breath as if to say, "Here it goes."

The woman behind the reception desk looked up, forced a smile, and said, "You here for an audit?" Without letting them answer the question, she continued, "Your names please."

"Nathan and Linda Daniels."

She looked through her appointment book. "I don't have a Nathan Daniels. I have an Alexander Daniels; is that you?"

"Yes, my first name is really Alexander, but I don't use it except on my tax return," Nathan explained.

The lady barked an order like a drill sergeant, "Have a seat over there, and your auditor will be with you momentarily."

The waiting room was full, but Nathan found two chairs together. No one was smiling. A few acknowledged their presence with a nod and a knowing smile. The room had a gray tone, and the metal chairs made the room feel cold and uninviting. It was definitely a government building and brought to mind his military days. Nathan couldn't help but wonder if this was all by design.

Nathan couldn't remember the last time he had felt this nervous. It was probably back when he had a root canal in the twelfth grade. When he was in high school, he had to go to the principal's office a lot, but he was never this nervous. "Why do we fear these people so much?" he asked Linda. "I mean, what is it about the IRS that is so frightening?"

"I don't know, but it is worse than going to the dentist's office." They continued talking in whispers.

An hour later, Nathan had looked through every magazine in the place and was beginning to read IRS rules and regulation procedures on audits. Linda was engrossed in a women's magazine, reading an unbelievable article about how to feed a family of four for just $50 per week. Finally, an older woman, heavy set, with her hair pulled up into a bun, came out. "Mr. and Mrs. Alexander Daniels," she spoke so everyone in the waiting room could hear.

Nathan and Linda stood up and walked slowly toward her. Nathan started to extend his hand to greet her, but she turned quickly and said, "Follow me please."

They walked down several corridors, past cubicles where taxpayers were busily working, frantically trying to support their deductions while the IRS was trying to get more money.

She opened the door. "Have a seat in there. I'll be right back." She closed the door. Nathan and Linda looked around nervously. Linda sat down first; Nathan explored the tiny cubicle a bit, glancing over the items on the desk to see if he could see anything important.

In another room, the woman auditor, Stevens, who was head of the branch; and two other men stood around a television monitor, watching it closely. "Is he our mysterious Nathan?" one of the men asked.

Stevens motioned them to be quiet. "Listen, and we might find out. Is this recording too?"

"Yes, it is."

Nathan fidgeted. "I'm tired of this waiting game. I don't believe they are this busy. Where did our auditor go, anyway?"

"Just quiet down. Maybe she had to go use the bathroom or something. Maybe it's her lunch break." Linda sat quietly looking through the glass at all the auditors at work. "Do you think they know about the document?"

"I doubt it. If they did, why wouldn't they have just come out to our place like they did Ray's?"

Inside the monitoring room, Stevens said, "Bingo! He's our man." Stevens turned to the auditor. "Okay, here's our orders. Go after him with all you've got. Don't allow canceled checks, demand receipts. Disallow as much as possible on all three years. We are to get him in a position where he's begging for mercy."

The auditor returned to the cubicle. "I'm sorry you had to wait. I'm Angela Carter." She extended her hand to each of them and continued, "I had an unexpected emergency. Let's get started and see if we can get you out of here by suppertime."

The auditor was ruthless, going over every aspect of the past three years' tax returns. She demanded receipts for every little deduction. Nathan kept immaculate records, but unfortunately, a lot of his documentation was with canceled checks.

Meanwhile, Stevens picked up the phone. "Get me Howard Baskins in our Washington office."

"Yes, sir, right away," his secretary answered.

"Don't let them put you off or take a message; tell them it is urgent and top priority."

"Yes, sir."

Stevens felt proud of himself for having made the discovery. He still didn't know what it was all about yet, but he knew it was a major event. He felt that this could be the ticket to get him his next promotion.

"Howard Baskins is on the line, sir."

"Hello, Mr. Baskins. This is Stevens in Colorado. I believe I might have some good news for you, sir."

"What is it, Stevens?"

"Well, sir, I believe we found the Nathan fellow you were looking for. Listen to this." He reached over and turned on the tape recorder to play it for Howard. He could feel the pride swell up as he sensed Howard's pleasure.

"Stevens, you did good. I'm sure a promotion is well overdue for you, and I'll see to it a good word is put in for you. Now, listen, do exactly like I tell you. Do you have a pen?"

"Yes, sir; I'm ready."

"First of all, ship all their tax records including the receipts to me. We'll take over the audit and send out any future notices from here. Second, if Mr. or Mrs. Daniels contacts you for any reason, refer the call to my office personally. Do you understand?"

"Yes, sir; I've got it."

"There's one more thing, Stevens."

"What's that, sir?"

"You are to tell no one about this procedure. This is a high-security program and has top priority. You don't have the security clearance to be privy to this information, so if anyone asks you, and I mean anyone, you refer them to me. Got it?"

"Yes, sir. Is that all, sir?"

"Yeah, keep up the good work out there."

"Sir, I do have one question. Do you want us to continue auditing those other two hundred clients?"

"Yes. It is imperative that we keep applying pressure to this situation. We can't let up, at least not yet. I'll talk to you later."

****

100

After four hours of arguing back and forth, the auditor finally sat back in her chair and said, "Mr. and Mrs. Daniels, I'm afraid you do owe us some money."

"How much?" Nathan asked.

"Well, I won't know for sure until I calculate it all up. I'll need to keep your receipts and finish this up at a later date. No sense in keeping you folks here another hour or two."

"Leave you our receipts? But this is all the proof we have," Linda protested.

"Yeah, what if you lose them?" Nathan didn't like the idea either.

"I'll give you a receipt showing that you gave all your receipts to our office. If something happens to them, your receipt proves you had all of your deductions substantiated. We never lose anything around here. Trust me, Mr. Daniels, they will be safe with us."

The auditor filled out an official-looking paper, signed it, and handed it to them. "I should have something for you in a few days. You can call me then. You may need to come back by to pick up your receipts and sign the acceptance forms. I'll let you know." With that, she stood up and extended her hand. "It's been a pleasure working with both of you. I hope it didn't hurt too much." She chuckled.

Nathan felt very uneasy about leaving the receipts but didn't know what else to do. He also didn't want to sit there for another two hours. Linda was glad that she had made plans for the boys' dinner.

As they walked out of the building, they felt worse than when they had entered.

"How much do you think we are going to owe them?" Linda asked.

"It can't be that much. We had receipts for almost everything. Even if they disallow the deductions we made that we only had canceled checks for, I can't believe that it would amount to more than a thousand dollars or so."

"I'd gladly pay them a thousand dollars just to have them leave us alone." They both climbed in the car and were silent for the drive home.

CHAPTER SEVENTEEN

Washington DC intrigued Tom Haden because not only was it the capital of the United States, but it was also the heartbeat of the whole world. He loved government work and loved serving the people who had elected him. Tom had come a long way since he first went into politics. After being a prosecuting attorney for eight years in Denver, he was elected attorney general of Colorado, where he served for four years. The Republican Party approached him about running in the Senate race. After a hard battle, he won the election.

Now in his third term as a United States senator, this made him a seasoned veteran in Washington. He often used his pull to get his bills passed. He knew when to fight, and he knew when to let something go. An old-timer had told him long before, "You can't win them all, so pick your battles carefully."

The battles he did fight usually had two things in common. First, it was good for the people, especially the people in Colorado. Second, it was a battle with national publicity tied to it.

This latest battle that he was contemplating going into over this document certainly met both of these criteria. But, he also realized that this battle was with a Goliath, and he wasn't so sure if he was a David or not. It was times like this he didn't like politics at all.

Tom sat at his desk. He studied the document in front of him. He had already read it several times, marking the major points. Quietly, over the past few hours, he had been gathering other facts and data from various sources regarding the IRS and their tactics. He wasn't pleased with some of his findings but didn't know what his next steps should be. He picked up the phone and dialed a number.

"Maxwell, this is Tom Haden in Washington. How have you been?"

"I've been fine, but before you go any further, you should know, I think my office and phones are tapped, and I'm afraid to use my cell phone. As a matter of fact, I'm sure of it."

"Okay then, why don't you call me when you get a chance."

"It'll be a few minutes," Maxwell replied.

"That's all right. You have my number?"

Maxwell hung up the phone and was going to take his usual walk to the local diner where he had been going for the past several days when he wanted privacy in his telephone conversations. The agency was bolder now and didn't even bother hiding from him. From his office window, he could see the car across the street. The man who trailed him was now very conspicuous. Maxwell hated being followed all the time but loved to play their little game. His goal was always the same: lose the tail.

This time, he didn't leave the building. Instead, he took the elevator to the thirtieth floor, got off, went into an insurance adjuster's office, and asked, "I was wondering, could I make a call? My office phones seem to be on the blink, and it's urgent. I'll put it on my credit card."

Because they knew him, they agreed. He was escorted to an empty office where he could speak in private. "Tom. Now I can talk freely. A lot has happened since our last conversation."

"Tell me about it," Tom said.

Maxwell's voice changed. "Did you turn me in or tell anyone about our conversation?"

"No, I didn't tell a soul. Why?"

"Right after we spoke, some government officials came by and paid me a little visit. They quoted you and knew all about our conversation. I thought you had …"

"No. I would never do that. Man, I'm so sorry." Tom's voice was very apologetic.

"Not only that, but now the IRS is harassing all of my clients, auditing them, telling them I am under investigation. It's really a mess."

Tom realized the ramifications of what Maxwell was saying and shouted, "Don't say another word, Maxwell!" There was a long silence on both ends, and then Tom continued, "That means my phone must be bugged too. How else could they have known?"

"We'd better end this conversation now. I'll figure out a way to get in touch with you, or you with me."

"Understand. So long, old friend."

104

Tom hung up the phone. Anger filled his face. He yanked the telephone out of the wall and threw it across the room.

His secretary heard the crash and burst into the office without knocking. "Senator, are you all right in here?" She saw the phone lying on the floor and Tom staring at it, her presence unnoticed by him. She gently closed the door, deciding not to ask any additional questions. "Sorry."

Tom realized for the first time what he was up against. If he pursued this, he would be bucking the whole system. It could mean sacrificing his entire political career. He was well aware of the Treasury Department and their dirty tactics. They could smear a political figure's reputation and destroy him if they wanted to. The words stuck in his head, *the power to tax is the power to destroy.* He would have to find a way to reveal this plan to the public. He could only hope that he could do it without destroying himself.

As he walked out of his office, briefcase in hand, he turned to his secretary. "You might want to get someone up here to repair my phone; it seems to have broken." She gave him a knowing smile. "Also, please have my office checked for listening devices and yours as well."

"Yes, sir," she replied, picking up a notepad and jotting down every word Tom said. "I'll call right away. Is there anything else?"

"Yes, I'll be out the rest of the day."

"But, sir, what about the sub-committee report? You're supposed to give it at 2:00 PM. It's been scheduled for days now."

"Call Senator Kennedy and tell him I'm unable to be there today. Get a new date and time. Tell him something urgent came up ... tell him I had a death in the family ... tell him whatever you want." The last words trailed off as he stepped out into the hallway and disappeared.

When Tom reached the garage, he couldn't resist the temptation. He got on all fours and began looking underneath his car for an electronic tracking device. "There it is. Those spying, good-for-nothing ..." He took the device and smashed it with the heel of his shoe. *That means they know about Molly ... and Doug. I've got to warn them*, Tom thought.

He jumped in the car, threw it in reverse, and then sped out of the parking garage, squealing his tires all the way. When he reached Pennsylvania Avenue, he turned right. Instinctively, he glanced in the rearview mirror and noticed a light-blue sedan pull away from the curb. *Who do they think they're fooling? You can spot an unmarked government vehicle a mile away. Try this!* He downshifted to second gear and put the gas pedal of his little BMW to the floor. Turning across three lanes of traffic, he cut off several cars, causing them to slam on their brakes. He headed north on Fifteenth Street, hitting speeds in excess of fifty miles an hour, running several red lights along the way.

The blue sedan, which had been following him, got caught in traffic at the first turn and lost the BMW they were following. Tom grinned and felt proud of himself as he noticed they were no longer behind him. He took several more turns, just to be sure, and then relaxed, slowing down his speed.

****

Calvin Davis, head of security, paced nervously in his tiny office, waiting on a report from his men. He had been contacted just moments before and told that Tom had discovered his office was bugged and that his car had a tracking device. He knew the senator was up to something but didn't know what.

"Sir, we lost him," the voice broke over the radio.

Davis grabbed the microphone and screamed, "What do you mean you lost him? You're professionals. How could you?"

"He cut across six lanes of traffic. He took us by surprise; we're still looking."

"Okay, go back to his office and wait for him there. I'll send a car to stake out that Doug Preston's office and another to Molly Shanks' home. He'll probably show up at one of those three places sooner or later."

"What about his home? Do you want us to follow him there if he comes back to the office?"

"You follow him anywhere he goes. I have someone watching the house, so if he goes home this evening, just join up with them and watch it together."

Tom pulled into a busy mall. He parked his car and walked inside. He found the pay phones and began dialing. He knew better than to use a cell phone, which could easily be listened to if they were anywhere near him. He called Molly first, then Doug, to warn them both. He told both of them not to call him at the office or at his home. He gave them a number where they could leave a message if either of them needed anything. He pulled out his little phone directory and dialed the Colorado number. Maxwell answered. "Maxwell, this is Tom. Can't talk but a minute. Find a place to call me from and call me back at this number." Tom gave him the pay phone number where he was standing. "I'll only be here for five minutes, so hurry."

Maxwell returned to the adjuster's office and used the same phone. Tom answered it on the first ring.

"Where are you at?" Maxwell asked.

"Don't worry about that, just listen. You're right about something happening at the Internal Revenue Service. I think I found the same document that you have in your possession …"

"You've got a copy of it too?"

"Yeah, I'm sure it must be the same thing."

"Are you aware of what all is happening out here?" Maxwell asked.

"No, what?"

Maxwell filled him in on all the details, including Ray Phillips, the audits, and his meeting with Nathan.

Tom brought Maxwell up to date on the events of the past week, from George's supposed suicide to finding the document to being tailed a few minutes ago. When they compared notes, there was no doubt in either of their minds that they were in deep trouble.

Maxwell shared with Tom their plan of filing a suit against the IRS in federal court to stop the action and put the whole matter on public record.

"That might work. But it could backfire on you. They could make you look like a crackpot, some tax dodger who doesn't want to pay his share of taxes. I'm telling you, these guys can eat you up, spit you out, and never miss a beat," Tom spoke from personal experience.

"If we had your help in Washington, couldn't we possibly pull this off?"

"They can do the same thing with me. I've seen it before. Do you remember that senator from Oregon who was trying to investigate the IRS's practices?"

"Yeah, that was several years ago, wasn't it?"

"That's my point. Have you heard anything about him since?"

"Now that you mention it, no."

"Exactly. The IRS leaned on him so heavily he had to back off, and he had a stroke. Many of us think the IRS put him in the hospital by their constant badgering and harassment, but of course we couldn't prove anything."

"So what do we do?"

"I'm going to fly out there this weekend and join you. We'll discuss our plans and pool our resources. Can you find us a quiet place to meet, a place where no one can get to us?"

"I'll work on it."

"Good. Leave me detailed instructions at the Hertz desk under the name of Jeffrey Lockwood. I don't know when I'll be flying in, but it should be before Sunday."

"I'll do that. I look forward to seeing you again. By the way, I apologize."

"For what?" Tom was curious.

"All the names I've been calling you when I thought you finked on me. I would have sworn you turned me in to the feds."

"No problem. You're forgiven. Let's just hope we both live long enough to enjoy our friendship."

"See you in a couple of days."

Tom hung up the phone and looked around the mall. It was busy, and everyone looked suspicious to him. He saw a man standing in front of a store, looking in the window. *Maybe he is following me*, he thought. He saw a couple with two children, which would be a perfect cover. *Who would suspect a family in the mall?* He shook off the thought and felt he was becoming paranoid. He chuckled to himself as he remembered a quote his pastor used to share with him: "Being paranoid isn't bad when you know they're out to get you."

Tom made his way home. Lucy greeted him at the door with a kiss. "You're home early today. What an unexpected surprise!"

Tom lifted his forefinger to his lips and at the same time put his arms around her and drew her close. He leaned down and whispered into her ear, "We are being watched and listened to. Be careful what you say. I need you to play along with me." He let her go and then responded to her statement, "I needed some rest. I just wanted to come home and collapse. I'm exhausted."

As he spoke, he tiptoed to various places in the living room, looking under tables, inside lamps, feeling under furniture. He looked inside an artificial flower arrangement, and there it was, a tiny little microphone. Tom motioned Linda over and pointed it out to her. She stood in shock. Tom lifted his finger to his lips once again, telling her to be quiet.

"I wonder what's on television," Tom said as he picked up the remote control. "Do you have any idea how long it's been since I've been home to watch afternoon television? Is Judge Judy on yet?"

Lucy began to play along. "I know it has been awhile. What do you want to watch?" She shrugged her shoulders at Tom, feeling awkward and not knowing what else to say.

Tom flipped through the channels and found Oprah Winfrey. "There, this looks good. I haven't seen her in a year." Tom turned up the volume. He quietly moved toward the telephone and unscrewed the mouthpiece. Inside was another tiny transmitter. He stood up, walked out of the room, and began searching the entire house. Lucy followed along with him, but neither said a word. All together, they found fourteen bugging devices throughout their house. Tom grabbed a pad of paper and found a pen. They returned to the den and sat on the couch. He began writing notes to her, and for the next thirty minutes, they wrote notes back and forth, laying out their game plan for the evening.

Tom tried to explain briefly what was going on, why their house was being bugged, and who he thought was responsible. Lucy was furious that her privacy was being invaded, but she was even angrier that it was her own government doing it.

On cue, later that evening, Lucy announced, "Honey, I want to go visit my mother. I've thought about it and really think now would be the perfect time, before I get too involved with my committee work again. I want to go before the session is over so we will be able to spend our time together then. What do you think?" She felt stiff and unnatural, practically reading her lines off her yellow pad.

"Sure, I think that's a great idea," Tom responded. "When are you thinking about leaving?"

"This weekend sometime. I don't suppose you'd be free to go with me, would you?"

"Hmm … this weekend." Tom pretended to be thinking about it.

"Oh, please. You haven't seen my mother in months. The last few times I've gone alone. She wants to see her Senator Son-in-Law. Besides, she likes to show you off to her friends." She was ad-libbing now, but also speaking from her true feelings.

"I'll see what I can do. Maybe we could leave early tomorrow afternoon, but we have to be back by Sunday evening."

"Great, I'll start packing."

****

The van marked POOL CLEANING went unnoticed by everyone in the neighborhood except Tom and Lucy. When they went out for their evening walk, it sat there so out of place now that they knew. They wondered how long this had been going on and how long the van had been in the neighborhood, unnoticed even by them.

The report came across the computer screen in Davis's office. "SENATOR AND WIFE GOING TO HER MOTHER'S FOR WEEKEND. DO WE FOLLOW?"

Davis stared at the message. He couldn't see any need to follow him there, but wanted to make sure that he did indeed go there. He got on the radio. "This is Davis to Unit 78."

"Unit 78, go ahead, sir."

"Just follow Haden to the airport and make sure he gets on the plane to South Carolina. No need to follow him any further. Report back to me when he leaves."

"Will do, sir," came the reply from the van.

CHAPTER EIGHTEEN

Nathan was a nervous wreck. He paced the floor in a circular motion. The IRS audit had shaken him, and now he regretted leaving all his receipts. It just didn't seem right. On top of that, he felt guilty for not having visited Ray Phillips in the hospital before he died. They said he never came out of the coma, but he still felt he should have been there. The case was still under investigation, but it had been ruled as a burglary that had gone bad. The police theorized that Ray had come home and caught the burglars in action and drew his gun, and they returned fire. But Nathan had his own theory, and it made him very anxious to think about it.

He put in a call to Maxwell using the code word that Maxwell had given to him, and he was waiting for him to call. He knew it would have to be at a time when Maxwell could get away. The phone rang. Nathan grabbed the phone. "Hello."

"This is Maxwell; what's going on?"

"Am I glad to hear from you. We just spent the afternoon at the IRS in a detailed audit."

"Did they get you for anything?"

"We don't know yet. The auditor said we would probably owe something, but they wanted me to leave all my receipts with them for further calculations ..."

"I hope you didn't leave them there."

"They didn't exactly give us a choice. I was given a receipt for them. The auditor told us she would go through them and return everything to us."

Maxwell was worried. "That really doesn't sound too good. Do you think they know who you are? I mean, that you are the one who has—"

Nathan interrupted, "The document? It's hard to say. If they do, they certainly didn't let on that they did."

"When are you supposed to hear from them?"

"They didn't really say. She just said she would contact us as soon as it was all put together. I assume in a day or so."

"Okay, well hang in there. I may have something for us this weekend. I'm meeting with—" Maxwell hesitated and decided to rephrase his statement. "Let's just say I may have some news for you after this weekend. I'll keep you posted."

"Do you think our audit will turn out all right?" Nathan asked, looking for some reassurance.

"You shouldn't have any problems if you had all of your receipts. They're only auditing my clients to harass me and to get me to tell them your name and where the document is located. No, I don't think you'll have too much of a problem."

"Well, I'll let you know if I do. Thanks for calling me back. I feel better just having talked with you about it."

"I'll be in touch after this weekend."

Linda walked in with the two boys. "They didn't really want to come home. They were both having too much fun."

Matthew ran to Nathan. "Yeah, Dad. They have this huge trampoline, and I can do a complete flip."

Allen joined in, "Yeah, and I can do one backwards. It was great."

"Can we get a trampoline, Dad?" Matthew asked.

Nathan ignored the question and turned to Linda. "I just got off the phone with Maxwell. He may have some information for us this weekend. I got the impression he was meeting with someone, but he didn't want to talk about it."

"What did he say about our audit?"

"Nothing really. He thought it should turn out okay."

****

Tom and Lucy dressed casually for their trip to South Carolina. Tom put on his Redskins baseball cap and his tan jacket. They were cautious in their speech, weighing every word, but trying to sound normal and unrehearsed.

Tom loaded up the car, and they headed toward the airport. Tom could see in his rearview mirror the unmarked government car behind them. They only carried on small talk inside the car, knowing that it too was probably bugged.

At the airport, they checked their luggage, purchased their tickets, then sat down near the gate and waited. They both knew that their every move was being watched, even though they could never spot them.

The voice boomed over the loudspeaker, "Flight 409 for Charleston, now ready for boarding at gate four."

Tom and Linda stood up. Tom motioned to Linda that he was going to the restroom first. He ducked into the men's room and went to the last stall. He tapped twice on the side panel, and the return tap came back. Tom took off his cap and jacket and threw them both over to the stall next to him. The man in the stall passed over his trench coat, hat, and umbrella.

The man left wearing the brown jacket and the baseball cap, holding his head down, not looking around as he walked out. He stood beside Linda and held her arm. As she handed the tickets to the person at the gate, and they each showed their picture ID, she prayed that they would not be pulled out for a random check by security. They were waved through, and both breathed a sigh of relief as they boarded the plane.

When they settled down into their seats, Lucy smiled at the man next to her. She only knew him by name but had never met him before. She felt awkward, but whispered, "Thanks for your help. Did Tom explain any of this to you?"

"Just a little bit. I've always wanted to be a spy, so this is kind of fun. Besides, I get a free weekend in Charleston. I've never been there before."

As they talked, Linda kept looking nervously toward the front of the plane, afraid someone would come on board and spot them. She felt reassured when the large door finally closed and the plane lunged away from the gate and began moving slowly backwards.

Haden sat in the stall, pretending to have an upset stomach. He looked at his watch. It had been nearly twenty minutes. He would wait ten more before he would leave. He flushed the toilet again, slowly opened the door, and looked out. The restroom was empty. He moved toward the washbasins and looked in the mirror. He laughed when he saw himself. The oversized detective coat and hat did not go with his tennis shoes at all. He fumbled around inside the pocket and found a fake beard and mustache and placed them on his face. *If my constituents could see me now, I probably wouldn't get re-elected.* He adjusted the brim of the hat down over his eyes, took a deep breath, and opened the restroom door and walked out.

Instead of walking toward the terminal, he walked toward gate fifteen. He carried no luggage, so he was able to walk briskly. Arriving at the gate, he showed his ticket and his new picture ID to the attendant at the counter, got checked in, and then sat down to wait. His plane wouldn't leave for thirty minutes. He was nervous about waiting out in the open. He decided to go to the men's room and wait in a stall. He felt more secure there.

"Flight 157 to Colorado Springs, now ready for boarding at gate fifteen." The familiar voice came over the loudspeaker.

Tom walked out of the restroom toward the gate. He wanted to look around but forced himself not to. In a few moments, he was safe on the plane, headed for Colorado. He smiled to himself as he sat back in his seat, pulling the large-brimmed hat down over his eyes. They had pulled it off. It felt good. He closed his eyes and reflected on the day's events. *I wonder how Lucy is doing. I hope they didn't follow her. How will all of this end?* He fell asleep on the plane. He didn't even hear them serve coffee or drinks. The flight attendant woke him when they arrived at Colorado Springs.

Tom walked straight to the Hertz rental car agency. "Yes, I have a reservation for a car. Jeffrey Lockwood."

The sales clerk was a young, perky blonde. "Yes, Mr. Lockwood. Would you like a midsize or full-size car?"

"I believe a midsize would do just fine."

"We have free upgrades today and a weekend special on our Lincolns for the same price."

"Okay, then give me the Lincoln."

"I'll need to see your driver's license and a credit card, Mr. Lockwood."

Tom pulled out a driver's license with his picture and the name Jeffrey Lockwood on it. He showed a credit card with the same name. He didn't use this name often. Occasionally, he found it helpful when he wanted to travel without the press tracking him. Another senator friend, who had learned how to do it from a CIA agent, had introduced him to the idea. He never dreamed he would ever be using his second identity to hide from his own government.

"Mr. Lockwood, someone left this envelope for you also." She handed him a small white envelope with his name on it.

After the paperwork was signed, she handed him the keys and gave him directions to catch the bus that would take him to the lot. Thirty minutes later, he was on the road. The directions were specific, and it was estimated that it would take about two hours to drive to the destination in the mountains. Maxwell said in his note that he would be up the next day some time in midmorning. Tom was instructed to make himself comfortable and get a good night's rest.

CHAPTER NINETEEN

The mail came early in the Daniels' neighborhood. It was Saturday morning, and Nathan went to the mailbox to get the usual junk mail and circulars. When he opened the box, right on top, he saw it. His heart sank as he slowly reached in and pulled it out. The top left-hand corner spelled out the name in bold letters, **U.S. Department of Treasury.**

Nathan nervously tore open the envelope. It was full of papers outlining his rights and recourse. There were several pages of handwritten papers. He looked at the typed portion of the letter that stated, "As a result of your recent audit, we are adjusting your tax return as follows."

Below that were several columns of figures. He looked at the bottom figure, which showed amount due, and couldn't believe his eyes. He repeated the number out loud, "Twenty-four thousand seven hundred and forty dollars! Where did they come up with that figure?"

He ran into the house. "Linda!" She didn't respond. He walked through the house, opening doors. "Linda! Where are you?"

"I'm in here," she yelled from the laundry room.

"Come out here; we've got major problems."

Linda walked out. She was still wearing her bathrobe and had a towel wrapped around her head. "What is it? What are you yelling about?"

He didn't say a word; he just pointed at the piece of paper with the figure on it.

"What? Are they kidding? Where are we going to get that kind of money? And how did they come up with such an outrageous figure?"

"Oh my God …" Nathan looked like he had just seen a ghost. He turned white.

"What is it now?" He handed Linda two other pieces of paper. Each had a different year at the top. Each showed a similar amount due at the bottom.

"It seems they are coming after us for three years' worth of back taxes." Nathan grabbed a calculator and added the figures up. "They are showing we owe ninety-seven thousand one hundred twenty dollars and fifty cents."

Linda was on the verge of tears. "How could we owe them that much money? Where are we going to get it?"

"Most of it is interest and penalties that are tacked onto the tax due. The actual tax only adds up to a little over twenty thousand dollars."

"Oh, only twenty thousand dollars. Well, that's a relief." Linda was being sarcastic. She stared at the IRS notice. "How are we ever going to pay this?" She began to cry.

Nathan took her in his arms and held her tightly. "I'll call Maxwell today and see if he has any suggestions. Monday, I'll call the IRS office and talk with our auditor. Maybe they made a mistake." Nathan knew in his heart they hadn't.

****

Howard Baskins paced back and forth across his office. He had a handful of change, which he poured from one hand to the other as he paced. His face showed frustration. It had been nearly two weeks and still no document. He was getting more pressure every day from Shark to get this behind them. They both knew the longer this document was floating around, the more likely it would become public.

Sheila brought in the latest reports showing the collection statistics on the IRS audits. Instead of being up for the month, the stats showed they were down 10 percent. His superiors in Washington didn't like to see revenues go down. They only wanted to see them go up. Howard knew that if he didn't get the revenues up, his head would roll.

Sheila sat quietly and watched him pace. She knew he was thinking but decided to interrupt his thoughts anyway. "Do you want to send a memo or hook up a conference call?"

Howard continued pacing, not responding to her. The phone rang. Sheila answered it, "Howard Baskins' office." She listened. "Sir, it's Stevens, from Colorado Springs."

Howard leaped to the phone. "What do you have?"

"I've seen the bill you sent to Nathan Daniels, showing the amount of taxes they owe. How do we explain this to him when he calls?"

"When he contacts your office, you refer him directly to me. No one else in the department needs to talk with him. He is a very valuable taxpayer. I will handle him personally. I'm sure he'll be calling you on Monday. He should have received the bill today."

"I'll have him call you as soon as we hear from him."

"Good. Thanks for your help out there. By the way, since we have our man now, you can cut back on auditing Rosenthal's clients, after all."

"Well, sir, we've already got the notices out, and besides, the ones we've audited have proven to be very successful. Our collections should be up considerably this month."

"I hope so, Stevens. We need a good showing from your office to improve our statistics. Keep up the good work."

Howard hung up the phone. He sank into his chair, picked up a cigar, and began chewing on it. He turned to Sheila. "I think we have our man. It's going to be a good day, after all." He smiled as he sucked on the cigar like it was lit and pretended to blow smoke from it.

Sheila stood up and grinned. "I'll leave you alone now, sir, unless you have something else for me. After all, it is Saturday, and I'd like to do some shopping."

"No, you can go now. I'll just sit up here and enjoy the moment."

Sheila walked out to her office. Sometimes she felt sorry for the taxpayer. This was one of those times. She didn't know why the Danielses were receiving a bill for that large amount, but she knew Howard well enough to know that he was not above playing dirty to get what he wanted. She could only imagine what the family must be going through right now. Her heart went out to them in sympathy.

CHAPTER TWENTY

Maxwell left his home early Saturday morning. He arrived at the cottage located high in the mountains by 9:30 AM. Tom came out to greet him. "Welcome. I'm glad you could make it. I just made a fresh pot of coffee."

Maxwell climbed out of the rental car, stretched, and then greeted his old friend with a handshake and a hug. "I see you found it okay. Did you have any problems?"

"Last night in the dark, I stopped three times to get directions. I got lost once, but finally arrived here around eleven. This is a nice place. Is it yours?"

"No. It belongs to one of my clients. He lets me use it whenever I want. I've only been up here one other time. My wife and I came up here last year to get away from everything for a long weekend."

They walked to the cabin. It was a rustic log cabin with a front porch deep in the Colorado Forest. The porch looked out over the mountainside and had a spectacular view of the valley below. Behind the cabin, there were more mountains, like something out of a travel log.

Maxwell and Tom sat down at the kitchen table. Tom poured the coffee as he filled Maxwell in on the events of the previous day. Maxwell brought Tom up to date on where he was with his legal research on the case.

"Do you think we have enough proof to get a court order to stop the procedures spelled out in the document?" Tom asked.

"I won't really know that for sure until we file and get into court. The judge could throw the whole thing out if he feels that it's deficient. What I'm hoping he'll do, however, is to at least put an injunction against the IRS so they cannot proceed until a hearing."

"How long will that take?"

"It depends. It could happen quickly, or they could drag their feet and postpone it for a year or more. My intention is to get this thing into public record so the IRS cannot harass me or my clients any longer."

Tom was making notes. "You mentioned on the phone yesterday about a Ray Phillips. Is he still alive?"

"No. He died yesterday. He was in a coma the whole time. I talked to his family. They didn't believe he would survive. He stayed alive only because of the respirator. As soon as they pulled the plug, he was gone."

"I'm sorry to hear that. Was he a close friend of yours?"

"I wouldn't say we were close friends, but we were long-time friends. We went to school together."

"Are there any clues as to who did it?"

"Officially it's listed as a robbery. But I'm convinced that it was someone looking for the document. When he didn't give it to them, they got rough."

"That's too bad. How about your other client? What's his name, Nathan?"

"Nathan Daniels. He's doing okay. He's obviously running a little scared now, as is his wife. They both want to follow through with this thing on principle, especially after what happened to his best friend."

Tom and Maxwell talked for another hour about how each of them had gotten involved. Maxwell reached into his briefcase and pulled out the document. "Did you bring the one you have?"

"Yes, I thought we would compare them to see if they are the same." They laid the two down side by side. They scanned page after page. The two were identical, except for one minor difference. At the top, left-hand corner on Tom's copy were the words *From: Howard Baskins.*

"Do you know who this Howard Baskins is?" Maxwell asked.

"I know he's the head of collections at the IRS, but I don't know him personally. Do you?"

"I talked to him the other day. He basically threatened me if I didn't cooperate with their investigation. He's the one who seems to be controlling this whole thing. It's my guess that this document is his baby, and it got out of his hands before he could implement it. Now he's running scared, hoping the media doesn't get a hold of it."

Tom stood up from the table. "I think you're right. Maybe we should call and confront him first, before we go to court or to the media."

"I don't know. When I talked with him, he didn't seem very cooperative. I'm not sure he's going to back down from this that easily. I guess we would have nothing to lose by trying."

Tom walked over to the stove and poured himself another cup of coffee, offering Maxwell more. "Do you have any idea how powerful the IRS really is and all they can do?"

"I know that even as an attorney, I don't like to mess with them. My clients are scared to death of them."

"Exactly, and that is what they count on to intimidate people. They operate out of fear. Most people receive a bill from the IRS and will pay it without question because they're afraid of what might happen if they don't."

"That is what their plan is counting on, isn't it?"

"You got it. There is no telling how many billions of dollars could be raised if this plan is implemented."

"But it's not fair," Maxwell protested.

"These people don't care about fair. Did you hear about the cases that one of those news shows did about the IRS?"

Maxwell shook his head that he hadn't.

"A couple received a bill for seventy-five thousand dollars for back taxes. The IRS was garnishing his wages, taking their house and all of their possessions."

"Did they owe it?"

"Not only did they not owe the taxes, it was determined that the taxes were payroll taxes that were not paid by the corporation. The wife was the bookkeeper for this company, not a stockholder or an officer, just a paid employee. The corporation went defunct, the officers couldn't be found, and so the IRS went after her as the bookkeeper. They determined she was personally liable for the payroll taxes of the corporation even though she was just a hired bookkeeper."

"That doesn't sound legal either!" Maxwell felt the anger rising inside.

"Well, there have been several more cases around the United States with similar stories. The IRS is not backing down and feel they have a right to go after whoever they need to, in order to collect taxes owed."

"Why can't you guys in Congress stop them? Why don't we make laws to stop this harassment?"

"In 1986, we came up with a Taxpayer's Bill of Rights. Unfortunately, most taxpayers don't know what their rights are and oftentimes are too afraid to exercise them. Individuals at the IRS, on the other hand, ignore the taxpayer's rights at their discretion, so they can collect more revenues. A second problem we have is that Congress turns a deaf ear to these things because they need the additional revenues. Every time the administration has a tax cut and wants to give more money back to the people, those tax dollars have to come from somewhere. The Treasury Department appears before Congress and builds the case for collecting from deadbeat taxpayers, and we go along with it. It's a vicious circle. The whole program needs major reforms, but who is going to do it? It's a political football; the two parties just keep kicking it back and forth, and no one scores."

"This certainly gives me an incentive to run for Congress. I would love to have the opportunity to make some changes in the system."

"Maxwell, if you follow through with this thing, you may not even have a career, much less a political future."

"I've heard that before, but thanks for the warning."

The two of them talked all day and late into the night regarding their plans. It was decided that Maxwell would file a class action suit and try to get an injunction to stop the government from taking further action until a court could hear the case. This would be filed in federal court in Denver on behalf of the American people. He would file it immediately, hoping for a quick hearing, and then he would hold a press conference that same day. Tom would hold a similar press conference in Washington DC immediately following the one in Colorado. The idea was to attack fast so that the government would not have time to respond or get to the press.

Later that same evening, Maxwell left the cottage to drive back to Colorado Springs. Tom decided to stay another day and would leave Sunday, catching a flight back to Washington that evening. They set up a system for contacting each other and promised to stay in touch.

"Good luck, Maxwell!" Tom yelled from the porch.

"You too. Keep the faith!" Maxwell yelled back as he climbed into his car. In a moment, he disappeared through the woods, down the winding road.

****

Big Al turned to Sergio. "Let's stick with Maxwell. I don't think anything else is going to happen here."

"I believe you're right. I'll drive; you send in the report." Sergio started the van and drove out of the woods onto the little road. He was careful not to turn on his headlights.

Big Al sent a message via computer through the phone modem:

TOP PRIORITY
TO: THE SHARK
FROM: THE A-TEAM

COURT INJUNCTION BEING
FILED IN COLORADO FOLLOWED
BY A PRESS CONFERENCE.
SENATOR IS SCHEDULING PRESS CONFERENCE
FOR SAME DAY IN WASHINGTON DC.
WILL AWAIT FURTHER INSTRUCTIONS.

Big Al played back the tape recorder and listened to the whole conversation again. Every word came out clear and crisp. He was proud of his work since they had not had time to bug the place but only listened with a distant listening device from the woods behind the house.

They followed Maxwell to his home and stayed there for the rest of the evening. Sergio and Big Al took turns sleeping. Big Al turned on the TV monitor, hoping to see some action in the bedroom, but was disappointed again. *These two could use a little romance in their lives*, he thought to himself. In frustration, he turned off the picture and kept the sound turned on. He flipped through the latest copy of *Playboy*.

CHAPTER TWENTY-ONE

Nathan and Linda Daniels could not sleep all weekend. They worried about what would happen on Monday morning when he called the IRS. Both of them looked at the papers from the IRS nearly a hundred times in the course of the two days.

Nathan called into work and told them he would be in late. He glanced at his watch; it showed nine o'clock exactly. He dialed the number. He could feel his pulse quicken and his stomach begin to churn.

"Good morning, Internal Revenue Service," the voice was cheerful but mechanical.

"Yes, I would like to speak with Angela Carter please."

"I'm sorry, Ms. Carter will not be in today. Is there someone else who could help you?"

Nathan's heart sank. "Well, maybe. We were in for an audit last week, and we were shocked to receive a bill in the mail on Saturday. We really need to speak with someone."

"I'll see if I can get someone to help you. May I have your name please and Social Security number?"

Nathan spelled the names and gave her the numbers.

"Please hold, and I'll see if I can find someone to assist you."

When the phone operator put the Social Security number in the computer, a message came on the screen that advised her to refer all calls to Mr. Stevens.

"Mr. Stevens, there is a Mr. Nathan Daniels on the phone. They were audited last week and—"

"Yes, put him through. I'll talk with him. Mr. Daniels, how can I help you?"

Nathan stammered and stuttered but managed to explain what had taken place. Stevens let him talk without interrupting him. Finally, Nathan said, "Is this normal, to be audited on one day and then to receive such a large tax bill the next?"

"I must admit, Mr. Daniels, your case is out of the ordinary. It is actually being handled out of our Washington office. We turned everything over to them. I can give you the name of a person to contact there if you like."

"Washington DC? Why there?"

"We have our orders, Mr. Daniels."

"Who has all of my receipts? We left all of our—"

"I'm sure they have kept everything in good order. You will need to contact a Howard Baskins. He is the head of our collections division." Stevens gave him the number and then said, "I'm sorry I can't be of more help, but it's totally out of our hands at this point."

Nathan hung up the phone. He was in a daze. Linda had listened to the entire conversation from his end but didn't understand anything. "What is it? What's wrong?" she asked.

"They know."

"They know what? What's wrong, Nathan? What did they say?" she persisted.

Nathan came out of his trance. "They know about the document. They know we have it, and our case has been turned over to the collection division in Washington DC."

Linda sank back in her chair. "Did they say that?"

"Not in so many words. But think about it. We're just ordinary citizens with a routine audit. And suddenly our entire case is turned over to Washington?"

"What are we going to do?" Linda asked.

"In a moment, I'm going to call this Howard Baskins and see what I can find out. I'm going to call Maxwell and see what he has found out and see what he's going to do. Then we'll just have to play it by ear. What time is it in Washington?"

"I think they are two hours later than we are."

"Good. I'll call right now." Nathan picked up the phone and dialed the number given to him by Stevens.

"Howard Baskins' office."

"Yes, this is Nathan Daniels, and I've been referred to Howard Baskins by Mr. Stevens, regarding our account. Is he in?"

"Wait one minute please." Sheila put him on hold and buzzed Howard. "Mr. Baskins, Mr. Daniels from Colorado is on line one."

Mickey P. Jordan

Howard cut off Sheila and pushed the button on line one. "This is Howard Baskins, Mr. Daniels, and I've been expecting your call."

"Then you know why I'm calling?"

"Oh, I believe we both know why you're calling. You have something I want, and I have something you want. Isn't that true?"

"Then you can do something about this tax bill I received?"

"Mr. Daniels, if you owe taxes, you'll have to pay them. I'm afraid I can't help you there. However, if you're willing to cooperate and give me a certain piece of information, which I might add you've illegally obtained, then I might be able to adjust your tax bill downward to a reasonable amount."

"Mr. Baskins, you and I both know what you're doing, and I don't believe you can get away with it. It's nothing short of blackmail, and that is still illegal in this country. I'm going to make my information public, and when I do, the media will have a field day with you and the IRS. It will be quite embarrassing. I don't intimidate easily." Nathan's voice was tense as he spoke louder.

Howard spoke calmly and deliberately, "Mr. Daniels, I don't know why you called me then. I believe this conversation is finished. You do what you feel you must do, but I'm warning you, for the sake of your family, to cooperate with us."

Nathan couldn't stand it any longer. He hung up the phone. His heart was pounding, and sweat was pouring from his brow. He knew that he was getting nowhere with the conversation and was afraid of what he might say next. "That sorry, good-for-nothing ..."

Linda placed her arms around his shoulders. "What did he say? I take it he's not going to help us."

"Oh, he'll help us all right, if we will cooperate and give him back the document we've found."

"That's it? That's all we have to do? Let's give it back to them and forget about this whole thing."

"Linda, I'm afraid it's not that easy. If we give them back the document, they still could come after us. Once we give it back to them, we've lost our leverage. As long as we keep it in our possession, we have something to bargain with, and they'll continue to negotiate. I think he's bluffing. This whole thing is nothing more than an attempt on their part to intimidate us into giving them the document back."

"But what if they're not bluffing? Then what?"

Nathan put his arm around Linda and squeezed her tightly. "Then, I'm afraid we're in for a very rough ride. This could get real nasty."

Linda buried her face in Nathan's shoulder and began to cry. "What are we going to do?" At that moment, she thought about the boys, and that thought scared her even more. She looked up through her tears. "What's going to happen to us?"

Nathan wasn't sure he could answer that question. He wasn't even sure what he should do next. He wanted to call Maxwell. He needed some assurance that he was doing the right thing.

****

Howard buzzed Sheila. "Do you have those papers prepared on Nathan and Linda Daniels yet?"

"Yes, sir; I worked on them yesterday."

"Bring them to me along with their complete file."

Sheila picked up the three file folders of information that had been received from the Colorado Springs office and brought them in to Howard's office. "Here is everything we have on them, sir. It seems they owe close to one hundred thousand dollars."

"Yes, I know." He took the papers and began to look through them. "This date needs to be changed to three weeks ago," he said as he handed her the final bill. "I want a Notice of Levy filed, but date it last week."

"But, sir, we need to give them sufficient notice …"

"This is an exception. Open up the file. Do you see what is stamped on the front?" Sheila opened up the file and in large letters were **PDT**. She knew this was only found on files where threats had been made against the IRS. It meant that these people were potentially dangerous taxpayers. She closed the file slowly.

Howard continued, "We're dealing with criminals here. We have to get them served immediately, or our whole department is in jeopardy. We can't worry about rights at this point. This is a matter of national security. These people may be arrested as terrorists."

"Yes, sir, but we should be careful about—"

Howard interrupted her again, "I'll worry about all the details. You just make sure that this notice is dated last week. I want full collection action filed on them showing that they are refusing to cooperate. We're going to take some drastic action, and I have my orders from above."

Sheila turned to leave; Howard stopped her. "One other thing. Make sure we have all the signatures we need so we can seize their home."

"Yes, sir." Sheila left and returned to her desk. She had never seen him act this way before. He was always hard to work with, but this seemed way out of line. She couldn't help but wonder what these people had done to be labeled as terrorists. She obediently prepared the necessary papers, back-dating all of the information. She put the data into the master computer and began the process of collection. The Treasury Department had ways of collecting money that was the envy of all collection agencies in the world. The wheels were now in motion. There would be no turning back.

CHAPTER TWENTY-TWO

Maxwell worked all weekend late into the night on his briefs, preparing to file his case against the government. Monday mornings were always hectic, but today was worse than ever. Clients were calling; some stopped by without appointments, and many others had left messages all weekend. Most of them had been audited or were in the process of being audited. They needed his help as well as some assurance that things were going to be okay. He felt bad about what was happening to them but knew that what they were experiencing was just the tip of the iceberg of what many more around the United States would soon experience if he didn't do something.

Janet tried to screen the calls and only put through those clients whom she deemed to be the most important and who were insistent on talking with Maxwell. It seemed that no sooner would she hang up the phone, it would ring again. This went on all morning long.

Maxwell put the final touches on the court documents. He planned to take them to the federal courthouse on Tuesday morning and hold a press conference on the courthouse steps immediately afterwards. He looked at the final draft and smiled as he pondered the bold heading at the top, **THE PEOPLE OF THE UNITED STATES VS. UNITED STATES TREASURY DEPARTMENT.** He could only hope that it would work.

****

Tom caught the redeye late Sunday evening and arrived in Washington at 3:00 AM on Monday morning. Lucy was scheduled to arrive home in the evening. He worked feverishly in his office, trying to gather information on the IRS. Tom had asked that his office be checked for bugging devices. The FBI came in over the weekend and had found several. He was now confident that his office was clean. He would have it checked every day from now on, he decided, at least until all of this was over with.

Tom sat at his desk and dialed a number.

"Internal Revenue Service," the operator answered.

"Yes, connect me with Verlin Chapman please."

"One minute please … I'm sorry, that line is busy. Would you care to hold?"

"Yes, thank you." Tom listened to the music on the phone, tapping his feet to the sounds of an old familiar tune and mouthing the words. The phone began to ring.

"Verlin Chapman."

"Good morning, buddy. This is Tom Haden."

"Tom. How have you been? What's up?"

"Nothing much. I was wondering if you had some time to talk today, say about two thirty this afternoon?"

Verlin glanced at his calendar. "Sure, I guess that would be okay. What are we talking about this time?"

"Now, what makes you think I have an agenda? Can't two friends get together without having a reason?"

"Sure, but for some reason, I don't think you just want to get together with me because I'm good company. Where do you want to meet? Blue Moon Diner?"

"No. How about the park in front of the Capitol Building, near the fountain?"

"Sure. I know where that is. I'll see you at two thirty."

"Good. I look forward to it." Tom hung up the phone. He wondered if he was doing the right thing. Could he really trust Verlin, or was he in on this whole scheme? Tom didn't feel like he had too many options available to him at this point.

****

"Mr. Rosenthal, Nathan Daniels is on the line. He says it's urgent, and he doesn't care who listens."

"Okay, I'll take it." Max put down the brief and picked up the phone. "Hello, Nathan. I thought we agreed not to talk on my office phone."

"I know, but I figured it really doesn't matter much now. They know who I am, and they're putting the screws to me." Nathan explained all the events that had transpired over the weekend, including his recent conversation with Howard Baskins.

"Okay, just relax. Since they have just sent you the bill, we have plenty of time to appeal and work out some sort of agreement. They can't do anything to you with regards to garnishing your wages or putting liens on anything unless they send you a certified letter beforehand. This is in the Taxpayer's Bill of Rights."

"I'm not so sure that this Howard Baskins is willing to play by the rules. He didn't sound like the type who really cared about the rules and regulations. There is something about his attitude that scares me."

"He doesn't have a choice. He has to abide by the rules, or he'll be in big trouble. We'll work it out. Trust me."

"I've trusted you so far and look where it's gotten me." Nathan tried to sound like he was kidding, but he really meant it. "By the way, what's happening on your other deal? Are you making any progress?" He chose his words carefully for the benefit of those who may have been listening.

"There may be some new developments pretty soon. Watch the news the next few days. I'm sure something will develop. Meanwhile, you sit tight. Play along for right now, and I'll file the appeals for you. We'll be able to get your taxes straightened out."

****

Tom sat on the fountain, waiting. He looked around to see if he was being followed. He was. Two men, trying to act inconspicuous, sat across from him on the other side of the fountain. Verlin walked up, and they shook hands like old friends.

"Let's go for a stroll," Tom said. "I talk better when I'm walking." He decided against telling Verlin about the two men, afraid it might hinder him from releasing any information he might have.

"If you are wanting to know if I have found out anything, the answer is negative. There has been nothing new on the George Shanks' suicide."

Tom became serious. "I've found plenty. Do you want to hear?"

"Sure, what is it?"

Tom pulled a file out of his briefcase. "Take a look at this." He handed him the document that he had found at Molly's house on the computer.

Verlin looked at it. He walked over to a bench and sat down. He began to read, slowly at first, then faster, turning each page with anticipation. When he finished, he turned to Tom. "Where did you get this?"

"I found it on George's computer. This is what that attorney in Colorado was calling me about also. He got hold of the same document. His client printed it by accident when he was working in the IRS files."

"Where are the other copies? Does the attorney have them?"

"I didn't say there were more copies, but there is one other copy."

"I just assumed that perhaps more copies had been made. Anyway, where is the other copy now?"

"My attorney friend has it. He is filing a suit in federal court tomorrow morning. We're both holding a press conference to let this information out so as to protect us. We figured that once the media got news of this, we would be safe from harassment."

"What do you want from me? How can I help?"

"I thought that maybe you would be able to get me more information now that you know what we're looking for. Be my eyes and ears at the service and keep me posted of anything unusual that's taking place."

"Sure, I could do that, I guess. But I'll warn you now, my work is pretty boring, and I don't know if I'll hear anything or not, but I'll tell you if I do."

"That's all I can ask for."

"Anything for an old friend. I don't suppose I could take this document with me."

"No, I'm afraid not. I'll make you a copy and give it to you the next time we meet," Tom said, reaching out for the papers.

"Oh, that's okay. It's probably better if I don't have a copy anyway. By the way, have you shown this to anyone else?"

Tom looked at Verlin suspiciously, but decided he should trust him. "Just Molly Shanks; she's seen it and my friend who helped me obtain it."

Verlin looked surprised. "Oh, what was his name?"

"I'd rather keep him out of all of this. You understand."

"Oh, sure, no problem." Verlin looked at his watch and stood up. "I better get back to the office. Some of us government workers have to work for a living. We can't play cloak-and-dagger games all day." They both forced a laugh.

"I'll catch you later. Let me know if you hear anything," Haden yelled. As Verlin walked away, Tom looked around for the two men who had been by the fountain earlier. There was no one in sight anywhere.

I wonder where they went. Maybe I am just becoming paranoid, Tom thought.

Power Unleashed

CHAPTER TWENTY-THREE

Maxwell Rosenthal walked into the courthouse with Judy by his side holding his arm tightly. She was almost running, trying to keep up with his brisk walk. She had insisted on coming, and Max was glad to have the company. He needed the moral support that she provided. The hearing would only take a few minutes once it began, but it could be hours before their case was called. As they approached the steps of the old Federal Courthouse, reporters seemed to have come out of nowhere and converged on them like fish in a feeding frenzy, thrusting microphones in their faces. "Mr. Rosenthal, who are you representing in this case?" One of the reporters yelled.

"No comment!" Maxwell and Judy continued walking briskly, trying to get through the reporters who had now surrounded them. He stuck out his arm instinctively, making a way through the crowd, while his other arm sheltered Judy. He was surprised that there were so many reporters there and that they seemed to know exactly why he was going to court. He looked around, hoping to see Nathan Daniels somewhere but could not spot him.

"What is the suit you are filing against the government?"

"No comment!" Maxwell repeated, shouting it this time.

"Can you tell us why you are filing the suit?" another asked.

Maxwell stopped suddenly like he'd had enough and abruptly turned to the reporters, yelling so they would all hear him clearly, "I will give you a full statement in just a few minutes when I come out of the courthouse. If you'll be patient, I'll answer all of your questions, but please, I need to get into the courthouse." He put his arm around Judy and ushered her through the doors.

The reporters didn't back off but followed them into the courthouse. They were stopped by security at the lobby and watched as Maxwell and Judy went through the security clearance procedures. The elevator doors opened just as they approached. Once inside, just the two of them, they both breathed a sigh of relief.

"You are a popular man today," Judy exclaimed.

"Yeah, but there is one problem."

"What's that?" Judy huddled closer.

"I didn't tell them to be here this morning. I had set the press conference up for this afternoon back in Colorado Springs. Someone else has sent these vultures."

The elevator stopped at the designated floor, the doors opened, and Judy chose not to ask any more questions.

They found the courtroom, opened the door, and crept in quietly. The room was filled to capacity. They found two seats near the door. Maxwell leaned over to Judy. "I'm not sure when our case will be called. We could be waiting an hour or more."

They listened as the judge ruled on case after case, accepting or rejecting the documents filed. This was not a court; rather, it was simply a judge ruling on the acceptance of the filing. After they had been sitting for thirty minutes, the bailiff shouted, "Case number twenty-seven thirty-two, The People versus The Department of Treasury."

Maxwell jumped to his feet and walked toward the front of the courtroom. He opened his briefcase and took out the papers. He was nervous. Another lawyer took his place across from Maxwell. He was surprised that the government was even represented in the courtroom since he was just getting ready to file the papers. He continued emptying the contents of his briefcase.

The judge watched as Maxwell laid out his papers, putting them in order. Appearing frustrated, the judge spoke, "Is the plaintiff ready?"

Maxwell looked up from his papers, realizing the judge was speaking to him, and said, "Your Honor, I have some documents to present which were discovered recently. We are filing this case on behalf of the American people to stop any and all action by the Treasury Department to carry out this program. We are asking for an injunction to prevent them from acting in any capacity against me or my client until the case is heard in this court, and also to stop them from taking any action outlined in this document until said case is heard."

The judge began looking over the papers that had been handed to him by the bailiff, periodically looking up at Maxwell then back down at the document. The judge slowly removed his reading glasses and cleared his throat. "Do you realize, Mr. Rosenthal, what you are accusing the government of doing?"

"Yes, sir, Your Honor, I'm very much aware."

The attorney for the State Department stood up. "Your Honor, I move that this case be dismissed."

"And on what grounds would that be, Mr. ..." The judge paused, lifting his glasses to his eyes, and looked down at the petition that had been filed, searching for a name. "Mr. Jensen."

The attorney picked up some papers and began to walk toward the bench. "First of all, Your Honor, the evidence that is being presented has been obtained illegally, was actually stolen from government offices." He spun around slowly to see the reaction of the people in the courtroom. They all seemed interested. Smiling, he continued walking toward the bench. "I have here a sworn affidavit to that effect." He held it in the air to show the judge as well as his audience.

The judge was not amused. "Mr. Jensen, may I remind you that this is only a hearing, not a trial. You can tone down the theatrics and save it for a jury."

Everyone in the courtroom laughed. The judge hammered his gavel, signaling the courtroom to quiet down.

Jensen, changing his demeanor, handed some papers to the judge. "This will prove that the document which Mr. Rosenthal has obtained was done so in an illegal manner and cannot be used in this process."

The judge looked over the papers. They contained computerized printouts showing unauthorized access to files by Micro Tech. There were photographs and transcripts of conversations that had taken place between Maxwell and Nathan. There were phone logs and other various reports that linked both of them to Senator Tom Haden in Washington DC.

The judge handed the papers to Maxwell to look over.

Jensen continued, "If we proceed to trial, the State will prove beyond a shadow of a doubt that these three men mentioned in our petition committed conspiracy against the United States government, jeopardizing our national security by printing and distributing this sensitive document."

"I object, Your Honor!" Maxwell screamed. "My colleague has found us all guilty before evidence is even heard; furthermore, he has included me in his accusations."

"Objection sustained. Mr. Jensen, you will have to refrain from passing sentence in this case; that is my job. As far as your motion to dismiss the case, I find in favor of the plaintiff. The case will be scheduled for three months from today. Does that meet with both of your schedules?"

Both attorneys agreed, but Maxwell began to protest, "Your Honor, in three months, it may be too—"

The judge interrupted, "Good, then I'll see you then. As far as the injunctions go, they are denied until I have heard more on the case." The judge picked up his gavel and hit it once. Both attorneys returned to their tables to gather their papers. Maxwell knew that reporters would be waiting and took out his notes that he had prepared for the afternoon press conference as to what he was going to say. He had chosen his words carefully.

Maxwell walked to the designated spot outside the courthouse where the reporters had gathered. He stepped to the microphones that several stations had put in place. Lights were flashing, and cameras began to roll. "Ladies and Gentlemen." He held out his hands to quiet everyone down. He moved closer to the microphones. "Ladies and Gentlemen, I want to make a brief statement, and then I'll answer some of your questions. First of all, I'm not prepared today to reveal to you my client's name that brought this to my attention. Several days ago, my client discovered an IRS document that reveals some actions, which if taken, would be a direct violation of our rights and your rights as taxpayers. This document is being kept in a safe place until the court hearing that has been scheduled for three months from today. After the court date, we will make a full disclosure of the document, but not until then." Maxwell paused for breath and affect.

"Is it true that you are under investigation by the IRS for tax evasion?" one reporter yelled out.

Maxwell was startled by the question, but before he could reply, another reporter shouted, "And isn't it true that many of your clients are under investigation as well and that it has been discovered you were helping them to illegally beat the tax system?"

Maxwell was shocked. *Where did they get this false information?*

Maxwell could feel the anger welling up inside him and thought for a moment, thinking of the best way to respond. After a few moments, he said, "My clients have been under investigation, but it was the IRS's way of harassing me to get me to reveal the name of the person who originally brought the document to my attention. Furthermore, to my knowledge, I am not now and have not ever been under investigation for tax evasion."

Another reporter fired a question, "Mr. Rosenthal, we understand that your client has been served notice that he owes a lot of money to the IRS. Isn't it true that this is all just a ploy to get back at them?"

"I'm not aware of the bill you say my client has received," he lied, "and I can assure you that this is no ploy. It's real. I believe this press conference is over." Maxwell turned with his wife by his side and tried to walk through the crowd. Reporters continued blasting questions at him, shoving microphones in his face. His anger was evident, and he didn't say a word but kept making his way through the crowd, pushing anyone that was in his way so that he and Judy could get through.

When they got into their car, they both fell back in the seats, relieved to be away from the reporters. Judy turned to Max and put her arm around him, leaning over the console to get closer. "What are you going to do? Where did the reporters get all this information?"

"I'll give you three guesses, and the first two don't count. The IRS must have called them and given them all kinds of stuff on me. No telling what the press was told."

Suddenly, Max had a thought, and fear came over him. He jumped out of the car and lay on his back, flat on the ground. He slid under the car. In a second, he saw it. "Those sons of ..."

"What is it? What are you doing under the car?" Judy was standing over him, watching.

"They have a tracking device on our car." He climbed out, holding it in his hand. He started to throw it but stopped in midair. He slowly lowered his arm and began to smile. Instead of throwing it, he walked over to the car next to theirs, reached underneath and felt the magnets take hold. "There, let them follow this attorney for a while." They laughed, got into their car, and drove off. Maxwell wanted to forget about this day and decided to take a long drive into the mountains. He could only hope that Tom's press conference was going better than his had.

****

Senator Haden walked briskly into the pressroom of the Capitol Building. The room was packed with reporters, and for the first time in his life, he was nervous about speaking as he stood before the crowd. He organized his notes on the podium, took a sip of water, and began to speak, "Good afternoon, ladies and gentlemen of the press. I would like to read a statement, then I will answer your questions." He picked up the glass of water and took another drink.

A young reporter from *The Washington Post* yelled from the back of the room, "Senator, we understand that you are now under investigation by the IRS for misuse of campaign contributions. Could you comment on this?" The question took Tom completely off-guard. He didn't know anything about an investigation by the IRS and certainly had not misused any campaign contributions. "You have me at a disadvantage, sir. I don't know anything about an investigation."

Another reporter cut in, "Senator, we have information that you are also connected with a conspiracy against our government, originating out of Colorado Springs. Could you comment on this please?" *Conspiracy? Where are they getting their information?* Then it hit him. *Of course, the IRS beat us to the punch. They got to the press before we did.* He tried to speak, "The conspiracy that I'm involved in is to uncover the dishonest tactics against the American people by the United States Treasury Department in collecting taxes—"

The same reporter continued, "So you admit that you are involved in this?"

"What I came here to share with you and the American people is that the Treasury Department is about to implement a program to raise billions of dollars in revenues by ripping off the American taxpayer and making him or her pay thousands of dollars in taxes which have probably already been paid."

Another reporter stood up. "Are you saying that you have information that no other congressman or senator knows about?"

"That is exactly what I'm saying," Tom said, feeling like he was regaining control.

"Where did you get your information, and why only you?" a reporter yelled out.

"An attorney in Colorado Springs found it first. I found the same information later, on a computer owned by a former government employee. He had the document stored in his home computer."

"Is the person in Colorado Springs named Maxwell Rosenthal?"

The senator was surprised. "Why, yes, he is—"

The reporter didn't let the senator finish. "Did you know that he has been charged with misuse of clients' trust funds and is currently under investigation by the IRS as are all of his clients?"

Tom stood there numb from this new information. He couldn't believe his ears. He decided to bring the conference to a close. Without saying a word, he turned abruptly and walked off the platform, out the door. His aides surrounded him and protected him from the crowds. He returned to his office, sat down in his chair, and tried to contemplate how the press conference had gone so wrong.

He picked up the phone to call Maxwell. He tried his office, his cell phone, and his home. There was no answer.

CHAPTER TWENTY-FOUR

The evening sun burst through the window, giving the white antiseptic walls of the hospital a glow that almost made it look heavenly. A machine was beside the bed with lines and cords running in all directions.

Nathan Daniel's thoughts were fuzzy and confused as he began the process of waking up. *Where am I? What day is it?* He couldn't remember. He looked at the lines running from the liquid bag over his head and slowly followed them down to his own arm. Another tube ran from a bag beside the bed up under the covers. He lifted the blanket, almost afraid to look, afraid of what he might see. A tube ran up into his penis. *Ouch, that looks like it should hurt.* However, he could feel no pain down there. He tried to focus his eyes better, but everything was blurry. He felt the pain shoot through his body as he tried to move one of his arms. *Cold metal. I feel cold metal. What is it?* He took a deep breath through his nostrils. He couldn't place the odor. *It smells like medicine.* He forced himself up by pulling on the cold metal rail next to him. The pain intensified, and he collapsed in agony, groaning, hoping someone would hear him.

A pleasant voice talked to him in a loud tone as she walked into the room, "Now, Mr. Daniels, you mustn't try to get out of bed. You have to be a good boy and stay still."

Nathan attempted to make his mouth move, but he only grunted. His lips were dry and cracked, and he felt like he had a mouth full of cotton balls. He formed the words, "Where … where am I?"

"You are at St. David's Hospital. It seems you and your wife took quite a fall down some stairs. Do you remember?"

Nathan shook his head and groaned. He tried grabbing both sides of the rail using all the strength he could muster to force his body upright in the bed. The searing pain through his chest caused him to yell some choice obscenities.

The nurse came running over. "Now, Mr. Daniels, you have to lie still. You have several broken ribs, and that's causing your pain. Please don't move, or I'll have to tie you down for your own protection," she said, half-kidding.

He managed to open his eyes a little wider. He saw a pretty blonde nurse standing over him. He could feel her strong hands, pushing him back down in the bed. He was connected to something. He followed the tube to a needle stuck in the top of his hand with tape over it.

Nathan pointed to his mouth and grunted.

"Would you like some water?" the nurse asked.

Nathan demonstrated his excitement that he had been able to communicate this simple need. She lifted the glass to his lips and bent the straw in so he could sip it. He took a sip. The water felt good in his mouth, and the excess dripped down his chin. She wiped it with a napkin. He took several more sips and motioned that he was finished.

He was beginning to come out of the fog he was in, and reality was taking hold. He tried to talk again, "Where's my wife?"

"Oh, she's down the hall doing fine now. She's not in as bad a shape as you are. She's been asking about you. I'll bring her down here a little later if you behave yourself."

Nathan grinned and nodded in agreement.

"How about the boys?" His voice was raspy.

"I don't know. There were no boys brought in, just you and your wife. I'll check and see what I can find out." She placed a cord in the palm of his hand. "If you need anything, you press this button, and I'll come running, but don't try to get out of bed." She shook her finger at him like he had been a bad boy and walked out the door.

Nathan was trying to remember what had happened. *I don't remember falling down any stairs. What day is it? If I only knew what day it was, that would help. Where are Matthew and Allen? Who has our boys? Oh, I want to see Linda.* Nathan fell back asleep, too tired to stay awake.

The knock on the door woke Nathan out of his deep sleep. Before he could answer, the door swung open. There was Linda in a wheelchair. The male attendant rolled her to the side of the bed. "Is this okay, Mrs. Daniels?"

Linda looked up at him and waved her hand in agreement. Tears streamed down her face when she saw Nathan lying in bed, swollen and bruised. She couldn't speak. She wanted to grab him, hug him, and smother him with kisses but was afraid she would hurt him.

Nathan rubbed the sleep from his eyes and tried to focus. As she leaned forward, toward the bed, she spoke, trying to hide her emotions, "Hi there, handsome. How are you feeling?" She reached her hand between the rails to touch his and gently lifted it toward her lips to kiss it. "You look like you were run over by a Mack truck."

Nathan moved slightly, trying to shift his position, and felt another excruciating pain on his whole right side. He forced a smile. "You aren't looking too good yourself." Linda's face was black and blue. It was swollen on one side, closing her left eye completely shut. Her right arm was in a cast, broken in three places. Though her lips were swollen, she could talk in a muffled tone like she had marbles in her mouth.

Linda laughed and in her sexy voice said, "Well, sailor, are you looking for a little action?"

Nathan groaned from the pain the laughter brought on. "Not tonight, dear, I have a body ache." They smiled at each other. "How are you doing?"

"They say I'll be fine. I look worse than I feel. Do you remember what happened?"

"Not at all. They told me we fell down the stairs; is that true?"

"Oh, I fell down the stairs all right. I believe I was pushed. Remember, the men busted into the house in the early morning with guns and—"

"How about the boys? Where are they?" Nathan was beginning to remember bits and pieces. Scenes flashed into his mind, giving him split seconds of the ordeal, but he couldn't put it all together yet in his mind.

"I was told they were safe and that both of them were being held at a children's center by Social Services until we are released. They were not hurt, or so I've been told. But I'm sure they must be frightened by this whole ordeal."

The scenes became more vivid as Linda spoke. Faces were a blur, but he remembered being kicked and falling to the floor. "Why were they beating us? What did we do?"

"It has to do with our audit and that government document you found. Remember?"

Nathan looked lost in his thoughts. "Document? What document?" He paused. "Oh, the document!" He finally remembered. It was beginning to come back to him. "What day is it?"

Linda could tell that something was beginning to click in his brain. "It's Wednesday."

"Maxwell was supposed to have done something this week. He told me to watch the news. I wonder if he did anything. Do you have a newspaper?"

"No, but I can get us one." She turned her chair around and, using her good foot, began to move slowly toward the door. "It may be awhile, but I'll get there," she joked as she opened the door and scooted out into the hallway.

Nathan closed his eyes. He wanted to remember it all. Larger portions of the incident flashed in his mind. He was able to connect some of the events in random order but became frustrated because he couldn't remember the details.

Linda finally reached the gift shop. As she rolled herself toward the magazine rack where the newspapers were, her eye caught the headlines, **"PROMINENT ATTORNEY MAXWELL ROSENTHAL UNDER INVESTIGATION BY THE IRS."** She picked up the paper and began reading. She couldn't believe it. There was nothing about a document, a suit filed, or even a press conference. The only thing the story talked about was the possible mishandling of a client's trust fund, which the IRS was investigating.

She paid for the newspaper and made her way back to Nathan's room. She opened the door and scooted toward him. Nathan could tell from her expression that something was seriously wrong. "What is it?" he cried out.

"Nathan, the IRS is investigating Maxwell Rosenthal for the mishandling of some trust fund. There's nothing here about our suit or the document." She handed the paper to him. He grabbed it and began reading every word, being careful not to move too suddenly.

Nathan slowly put down the newspaper and stared at the ceiling. It had come back to him now—the finding of the government document, the death of his friend Ray Phillips, and their audit that had brought them both to this point. Finally, he spoke, "That was our last hope. Max was our only chance to get out of this thing. I don't know what we're going to do now."

Linda laid her head on Nathan's arm and began to weep silently. "When is this nightmare going to end? Oh, Nathan, I want our lives to return to normal." The tears rolled down her cheeks. Nathan could feel the wetness hitting his hand. He gently wiped her tears from her cheeks. She cried harder. "I want my boys back. I want to leave the United States. I hate it here!" She screamed the last two statements.

Nathan placed his arms around her and tried to comfort her. "We'll get out of this somehow. I promise … I promise." He couldn't stand to see her cry and wanted so much to make it right again. He was feeling responsible for all of this now, and he knew that he would need to fix it somehow.

CHAPTER TWENTY-FIVE

Howard Baskins summoned Calvin Davis to his office. He chewed on a cigar, wishing he could light it and smoke it while pacing the floor in his office. The events of the past two days had made him plenty nervous. Davis walked into the office.

"When are we going to get that document?" Baskins shouted without even saying hello.

"I don't know, sir. We thought we would have it by now. We're dealing with some stubborn people. Maxwell hasn't given in to our pressures at all. Nathan Daniels and his wife, Linda, are hospitalized from the beatings they underwent." He caught the words and corrected himself, "I mean, the accident they had, and we still can't find anything. We haven't applied much pressure to the senator for obvious reasons."

Howard took a handful of change and poured it from one hand to the other and began his ritualistic pacing of the room. He talked out of one side of his mouth, holding the cigar tightly in his teeth, "We've got to get those documents back in our possession. It's too dangerous having them floating around out there. No telling where they'll end up."

Davis walked over to a chair and sat down. "Yes, sir. We've alerted all the media people, warning them of the document falling into their hands. We've told them it is a forged document and to return it to us if it shows up."

"I saw the press conference that Tom Haden held. It was quite an embarrassing spectacle. You did good work," Howard said, giving Davis a little praise.

"Thank you, sir. I received word that Maxwell's press conference was just as embarrassing to him. I think we have been able to discredit all of them so the media will not listen to them or take them seriously."

"Okay. That's good, but now we must work harder on locating the documents and getting them back. God only knows how many copies are out there now. I want you to go to any extreme to do this. Do you understand?"

Davis squirmed uncomfortably. "You've made yourself quite clear, sir. Message received and recorded. I do have one question though." He hesitated in bringing this up.

"What's that?" Howard asked, his eyebrows raised.

"How about Molly Shanks and Doug Preston? What should we do with them? They know about the document even though they don't seem to be involved in any other way."

"I would say that Mrs. Shanks is probably very distraught over her husband's death. It wouldn't surprise me if she did something very foolish."

"You're right, sir. She's been acting very strange since her husband's suicide. I'll keep you posted of our progress."

"And Mr. Douglas Preston, well, I'll let you handle him."

Davis stood up and walked toward the door. He knew what he had to do.

Howard put the change back into his pocket and returned to his chair. "Oh, and one other thing, the Shark is counting on us to get this thing resolved and soon." He sat down and began going through his pile of papers on top of his desk. "And I don't want to disappoint him."

"Yes, sir. I understand. I'm on it." Davis closed the door.

He quickly returned to his office, picked up the security phone that was equipped with a voice scrambler, and dialed a number. The familiar voice at the other end said, "Hello."

"Yeah, this is Calvin Davis in security. I'm going to need some help."

"That's what we specialize in around here."

"First of all, do you have anything else for me from your contacts in Colorado?" Davis was hoping for an update.

"No, nothing is new there, on the home front. I know that your senator is confused and really doesn't know what he's going to do. We're going to feed him some wrong information that will send him in another direction. What can I help you with?"

Calvin cleared his throat, lowering his voice. "We have to take care of some unfinished business here in town. Do you have anyone outside the agency who can handle it?"

"You know we do. I have someone who can do anything you want. Give me the details."

"I'll get the necessary information to you. I still don't trust these phones, even if they have been checked."

Davis hung up. He didn't like this part of the job but had convinced himself it was for the interest of national security. Over the years, he had tried to distance himself from what he called the dirty work of this business.

CHAPTER TWENTY-SIX

The man was neatly dressed in a business suit. His hair was cut short, and he could pass as a congressman or senator. He walked into a pharmacy. The pharmacist greeted him and invited him behind the counter like an old friend.

He handed the pharmacist a note. He proceeded to get down a bottle of pills and counted out the number of tablets needed. He typed up the label for the bottle. Without saying a word, he handed the man in the suit the bottle, and the pharmacist received two five-hundred-dollar bills in his hand. It was amazing what could get done for just a little cash in the palms.

****

It was early in the evening, but Molly Shanks was tired. She sat in her bedroom at the makeup mirror, brushing her grayish-brown hair. She didn't like what she saw. She wished she could get rid of her excess weight and some of those wrinkles. *I think I'll join a health spa this week*, she thought as she examined herself more closely. *Maybe I'll take some of the life insurance money and get a face-lift. Yeah, that will be nice.* She leaned in toward the mirror and pulled her skin tight on her face. *They seem to be coming out of nowhere, more and more each day.* She bent closer to look at a blemish on her forehead.

The man in the suit, now wearing gloves, stood outside Molly's house. He would have no problem getting inside. The alarm had not been turned on yet according to the monitor he could see on the wall. The patio door slid open quietly, and he stepped in cautiously, listening for sounds. He heard a radio playing upstairs. He moved slowly and purposefully toward the stairs. He couldn't afford to have her scream or see him before he got the drop on her. She could lock herself in a room and call the police. Surprise was always his best weapon.

As he moved to the top of the stairs, he saw her shadow. This was a game to him. He liked to see how close he could get and how long he could watch before he was seen. He moved closer and was now looking at her. *She is pretty for her age*, he thought.

Molly stood up to look at herself. As she stood there in her silk pajamas, he could only regret having to do this to her, but business was business. The man stepped out of the shadow and grabbed her from behind, covering her mouth. She let out a muffled scream. The leather glove almost smothered her. "Mrs. Shanks, you mustn't scream. If you promise not to scream, I'll let you go."

She nodded her head in agreement. He loosened his grip on her mouth to see what she would do. He was satisfied that she was not going to scream and relaxed his hold even more, putting his arms to his side. He drew his revolver. "Now, that's better, isn't it?"

Molly's eyes widened when she saw the gun. "What do you want? Who are you?"

His voice was calm and gentle, sounding like a trained therapist. "Mrs. Shanks, I've come to help you get over your sorrow and grief."

"Help me? How?" Her voice quivered as she spoke.

The man removed a prescription bottle from his coat pocket. "Here, these are for you. The doctor's orders are to take them tonight before you go to bed. All you have to do is take twenty of these, and your worries will be over."

"Are you crazy?" she screamed.

He remained calm and composed. "No, ma'am, I'm not crazy. I believe you're the one who needs help. You see, you've been so distraught over the death of your husband that you just couldn't go on anymore. Tonight you will kill yourself."

"I'll never take those pills. You'll have to shoot me first."

"If you don't take them voluntarily, I have ways of getting them down you without leaving a mark on you. It's your choice. Now, go get a glass of water." He waved his pistol toward the sink.

Molly moved slowly. "Who are you? Why are you doing this to me? If this is about that document, I haven't told anyone. I won't tell anyone. Please!"

"I'm sorry, lady; I have my orders."

She placed her glass under the faucet and turned on the water. Instead of filling the glass with water, she slammed the glass on the counter. "No, I won't do it. If you want to kill me, then you'll have to shoot me."

He grabbed the glass and filled it with water.

"Hold out your hand," he commanded.

She hesitated. *What choice do I have?* she thought to herself. *If I don't do it, he'll force me. Maybe I could make a run for it. No. There's no place to go. He'd catch me before I got ten feet away.*

"Come on, lady, now! I don't have all night."

She held her hands in a tight fist behind her back in defiance. "Go ahead, force me. I'm not going to help you."

He knew that if he forced her, it could leave evidence that it wasn't a typical suicide. He didn't want to take the chance that there would be a struggle. He placed the gun to her head. "Mrs. Shanks, I'm going to count to three, and you had better start taking these pills, or I will blow your brains all over this bathroom wall."

"If you do that, then they'll know it was murder."

"It won't be my first. One." He cocked the pistol.

"You want it to look like an accident. You'll never pull the trigger," Molly spoke fast and could feel every nerve in her body responding. Fear had been replaced with anger and defiance.

"Two." He pressed the gun closer to her temple.

Molly stood up straight and took a deep breath, getting ready for the worst. *At least if he pulls the trigger, it will be over with fast, and there will be evidence that it was murder. I don't want my family and friends to think I committed suicide.*

"Three …" Something jumped out from underneath the bed and ran toward the bathroom. Startled, he jerked the gun away and aimed it at the target, then grinned. "What a pretty cat you have, Mrs. Shanks. Is it a Persian?" He reached down and stroked the cat with his hands. "Pretty kitty, yes, you are."

Molly relaxed with the gun away from her head.

The man gently picked up the cat, stroking it with his revolver. "I think, Mrs. Shanks, I've found my leverage." He pointed the revolver at the cat's head. "What's her name?"

"Nikko," Molly replied, "but you wouldn't dare."

"Nikko, that's a pretty name for such a pretty cat, and yes, I will if you don't cooperate. You can watch me torture your cat, and then I will shoot you, or you can obey my orders, your choice. Now, hold out your hand like a good patient, and I won't harm your precious cat."

The thought of him harming her innocent Nikko was more than she could stand. She loved her cat so much, and the thought of him hurting her was unbearable. *He's going to kill me anyway*, she reasoned. *At least this way, I can save Nikko's life.* Molly obediently, but reluctantly, held out her hand.

He poured the pills into her palm. "Now, be a good girl and take each one of these. I promise, you'll feel better in the morning," he said, holding the gun closer to Nikko's head.

She began to swallow each pill, one at a time at first, then two, then several. She lost count of exactly how many she had taken but knew that it was enough to do the deed he wanted done.

"Good! Now, let's find some paper and a pen so you can tell everyone why you did this to yourself." He continued holding the cat in his arms, placing the barrel of the gun in the cat's ear, playing with it.

Molly watched him nervously then led the way to her bedroom and opened a dresser drawer where there was a pen and paper. She sat down to write but couldn't think of anything to say.

"Just start writing; you'll think of something."

"Well, excuse me, but I've never written a suicide note before. Give me a minute to collect my thoughts."

"Lady, in a few minutes when those pills start kicking in, you won't have any thoughts left. Start writing!"

She did as instructed and wrote:

> To whom it may concern:
>
> I'm Responsible So don't blame anyone else. I just could not go on anymore without my George. I hope you understand. I didn't mean to hurt you. Please forgive me.
>
> I Recently Started to have strong bouts of depression and have never gotten over them. I decided several days ago that I'd Rather Set myself free than to go on with my life.
>
> I Respectively Submit this to you as my suicide note, written with my own hand.
>
> Molly Shanks

She handed the man the note. "How's this?" He read it and seemed satisfied with it. "You should have been a writer." He motioned for her to move. "Okay, now get comfortable on the bed." He let the cat down, and she scampered out of the room.

She walked to the bed as ordered and lay down on her back. She was beginning to feel dizzy and lightheaded. "Would you have really killed my cat?"

"I guess you'll never know for sure, now will you?" He smiled a big grin then continued, changing the subject, "You just lie down and get comfortable. You'll soon be at rest."

The phone rang. Molly sat straight up in bed and groped toward the sound, knocking items off the nightstand.

"Don't answer it!" he shouted. "Let it ring!" His gun pointed directly at her.

She stopped, looked at him, and said, "It's probably … my mother. She calls me … this time of night … to check on me. She'll keep calling until I answer." Her speech was slurred and her words unclear.

"Just let it ring," he repeated.

Molly threw her head back on the pillow. "I've got to stay awake, but I'm so tired … I'm so tired. I can't go … I must … sleep." She didn't say another word.

The man looked the room over carefully; making sure nothing was out of place. He took the bottle of pills out of his pocket and poured the remaining ones onto the nightstand, then laid the empty pill bottle beside them. Molly had knocked her water onto the floor when she grabbed for the phone. *It looks good*, he thought. *I couldn't have done better if I'd done it myself.*

He walked over to her and touched her on the cheek. "I'm sorry it had to end this way. You really seemed like a nice woman."

He took a deep breath, taking one last look around. He walked downstairs and let himself out the same way he had entered, making sure the patio door was locked behind him.

CHAPTER TWENTY-SEVEN

Senator Thomas Haden's dream of running for president of the United States was being shattered. The publicity surrounding the IRS investigation could obviously destroy his reputation and credibility and any chance he had of being nominated by the party.

Tom sat on the sofa in his living room, drink in hand and Lucy by his side. She stroked his head, running her fingers through his thick brown hair. He was still a handsome figure in her eyes. Gray hair was beginning to show, and his face displayed the tough years of politics that he had survived. They both knew that this was going to be the toughest challenge of his career.

Lucy cuddled closer to Tom, putting her arm around his neck and pulling him closer. "It's good having you home anyway. We should do this more often." Tom didn't respond. He took another sip of his drink.

Lucy knew his quiet moods. When the pressures would get too great or he would get depressed, Tom just shut down his system. He could go for hours without saying a word to anyone. Lucy wanted to know what was going on inside his brain. She wanted to be a part of this side of him, know what he was thinking and feeling. He would seldom let her inside.

"Talk to me, Tom. Please," she pleaded. "I need to hear your voice. You need to talk to someone. Let me in so I can share this with you."

Haden continued staring straight ahead. Lifting his glass to his lips, he took another drink, this time finishing it. He handed the glass to Lucy and broke his silence, "Could I have another one, please?"

Lucy went to the bar and fixed him another Scotch and soda. She stirred it with her finger. When she licked her finger, her expression revealed her distaste for liquor of any kind. "How can you stand to drink this stuff?" she asked as she walked back to the sofa.

"You have to acquire a taste for the finer things in life," Tom replied. It wasn't much, but Lucy knew that his last little remark was a major step in returning to his normal self.

"Yeah, well, I guess I'm just a simple country girl who will always believe that a tall glass of Diet Coke is one of the finer things in this life." She sat down close to him, pressing her body close against his.

Tom turned his face toward hers, and their lips met. He kissed her hard. She responded. Lucy gently took the drink from his hand and awkwardly sat it on the table. With his free hand, he began to stroke her.

Tom pulled away gently, his mind on other things. He spoke softly, "I don't know which way to turn anymore. Who can I trust?"

"Maybe you should just forget the whole thing. Pretend you never found out about it. There are plenty of other worthwhile projects you could concentrate on which wouldn't jeopardize your career." Lucy was trying to be comforting to him but was afraid she was only discouraging him more.

"I can't quit. I can't just drop this matter. It's too important. Do you have any idea what it would mean to the American people if the IRS implemented this program?"

"I'm afraid I don't."

"Well, it would cost us dearly, not only in terms of dollars, but the loss of our personal rights and freedoms are also at stake here. No, I can't let them get away with it if I can possibly help it."

The phone rang. Lucy moved toward the phone. "I'll get it. Are you available?"

Tom shook his head that he wasn't.

"Hello."

"Hello, is this Senator Haden's residence?" The voice on the other end was obviously that of an elderly woman and one unfamiliar to Lucy.

"Yes, it is. May I help you?"

"Well, I hope so. I don't know why I'm calling you. I don't even know if you can help me, but I thought I would try you first before I called the police. I just hate to bother the police if it's not an emergency, and it may not be an emergency. I don't know."

Lucy listened as the lady rambled on about one thing after another. She made a face at Tom that let him know the call was not a normal one.

"Why don't I let you talk to Senator Haden? Maybe he can help you." She quickly handed the phone to Tom. Holding her hand over the mouthpiece, she explained what the lady had said so far.

"Hello, this is Tom Haden; who is this?"

"Oh, I'm sorry; I didn't even tell your wife who I was. How stupid of me. This is Abigail Bishop; I'm Molly Shanks' mother. You don't know me. We've never met. I've read a lot about you though, and Molly has told me so much about you, how you've been helping her and all. I almost feel like I know you; that's why I'm calling. She says you helped her after George jumped out of that building. Wasn't that awful? I don't know why he went and did something like that. It just doesn't make any sense. He must have been crazy to leave his wife all alone like that. What was he thinking anyway?"

Tom interrupted, "Yes, ma'am, it was a shame. How could I help you tonight?"

"Well, every night I talk to Molly before I go to bed, and tonight she isn't answering the phone. I have a feeling that something bad has happened. You know how you get those feelings sometimes? Well, the last time I got this feeling, my dog, her name was Betsy … We called her Betsy after my grandmother; now, there was a dear old saint … never had anything bad to say about anyone. She always had a good word for everyone."

Tom held the phone away from his ear and made a motion to Lucy with his hand and mouthed the words, "Yak, yak, yak."

Tom cut in, "Abigail is it? I'm sorry to interrupt you, but I'm kind of in the middle of something here. What is it you were saying about your daughter?"

Abigail ignored Tom and continued with her story. "Well, anyway, I had this feeling that something bad had happened, and sure enough, when I got home, my dog, Betsy, she had gotten run over by a car. She was dead. Well, I got this same feeling tonight when I called Molly. She's always been home when I called. And we talk every night. She would tell me if she was going out somewhere, especially with her husband being dead and all. Wasn't that awful?"

Tom tried to reassure her. "Maybe she went out for the evening and—"

Abigail cut in again, "No. Molly would never be out this late. Besides, she isn't seeing anyone, and she don't have any friends, except you of course. If she had gone away, she would have told me she was going. Molly is like that, you know. Why, one time she called me just to let me know that she wouldn't be home until after nine at night, said she was going to a movie with a friend. No, Molly always checks in with me. Well, tonight she didn't check in with me, and she doesn't answer the phone. It's already ten o'clock, and I'm getting worried. I was going to call the police, but I hate to bother them. They are always so busy, and I would feel really

163

bad if she was okay and everything. But I remembered she had said you and her were friends, and I thought maybe you could check on her for me. Could you?"

At this point, Tom would have agreed to anything just to get her off the phone. "Yes, ma'am. My wife and I will go check on her right now. Give me your number, and I'll get back to you just as soon as we find out something."

Abigail gave him her number and began another story about the time a farmer had been trapped for several days under a tractor because no one had come to check on him. Tom interrupted her again, "Let me hang up now, and I'll go right over there to see what I can find out. Goodbye, I'll talk to you later." He eased the phone away from his ear and could hear her still talking in the background as he laid the receiver down.

"What was that all about?" Lucy asked.

"Let's go for a ride, and I'll explain it all to you in the car." Tom put on his shoes then took Lucy's hand and pulled her up off the sofa. He rubbed his ear. "How can a person talk nonstop like that? It amazes me."

Tom called the police from his cell phone and asked them to meet him at Molly Shanks' home. When he drove up in front of the house, they had not yet arrived. He surveyed the house. Tom and Lucy got out of the car and walked slowly up the front walk. "Looks like the bedroom light is on upstairs," Lucy said.

"Maybe she's home now." Tom rang the doorbell. After several times, he peeked inside the window. "Hmm, that's odd."

"What? What do you see?"

"If she's not home, why wouldn't she have turned on the security system? The light indicates it's not turned on at all."

"Maybe she's home and hasn't turned it on yet," Lucy remarked.

"Then why doesn't she answer the door?"

"I don't know; perhaps she's in the bathtub or shower."

"Would you take a shower, home alone in this day and age, without turning on your alarm?"

"Maybe she just forgot. It happens."

"Or maybe the old lady is right; something is wrong." He tried the doorknob, but it was locked. He began looking around the front porch area, feeling above the doorjamb, nothing. He stepped into the shrub area, still looking around.

"What are you looking for anyway?"

"Sometimes people hide spare keys around. I'm just seeing if I can find one. Bingo!" He stooped down and picked up a large rock. He opened the bottom, and a key dropped out.

"I'm impressed. But should we go inside? Shouldn't we wait for the police?"

Tom thought for a moment. "Do you have any idea how long that could be? Besides, we've been given permission to investigate."

He put the key in the door and opened the door slowly. "Molly! Molly! Are you home?" he yelled as they crept through the door.

There was no response. They both walked into the house. It had the appearance of someone being home, but there was not a sound. Then they both heard it, a radio playing upstairs.

"That's probably why she didn't hear us yell. She has her radio on and can't hear us," Lucy whispered, feeling very nervous about entering someone's home uninvited this late at night.

Tom moved toward the stairs and yelled again, "Molly Shanks, are you up there?"

Lucy yelled, thinking a female voice would be less frightening if she was home, "Molly, Molly, we're coming up. I hope you're decent." They were halfway up the stairs now and still no response.

Tom moved faster toward the sound of the radio. When he arrived at the bedroom door, he knocked loudly. "Molly, are you in there?" He reached down and turned the knob, slowly opening the door. As soon as the door opened a crack, something lunged at both of them. They jumped back, covering their eyes. Lucy screamed, and they both realized that the cat had jumped down toward them. She walked slowly out the door. Then Tom saw her lifeless body lying on the bed. "Oh no, Molly!"

Tom and Lucy ran into the bedroom. They saw the pills spilled out on the nightstand. He reached down and lifted her head in his hands. "Molly, wake up. Molly!" He slapped her face several times, but no response.

Lucy reached for her wrist to see if she could find a pulse. "Nothing, I don't feel anything. I think she's dead."

Tom slapped her some more. "Molly, you can't escape this easy. Molly, wake up." He turned to Lucy and shouted, "Call 911 and tell them to send an ambulance."

While Lucy was on the phone and Tom continued working with Molly, the door to the bedroom burst open. "Freeze! Police, don't move!" The voice was stern and demanding.

Tom looked up, and there were two guns aimed right at each of them. Lucy eased the phone down away from her ear. Tom stuttered, "I'm Senator Tom Haden. I called you. I think she's overdosed on these pills."

One officer turned to his partner. "I recognize him. He is the senator." They both put their guns back into the holster. "Sorry, Senator. We didn't mean to scare you."

"That's okay; I'm just glad you're here. She isn't responding. The room is just the way we found it. My wife is calling 911 for an ambulance."

The officers began the routine of trying to save Molly's life. One of them lifted her off the bed and placed her gently on the floor. They began CPR, taking turns working with her until the paramedics arrived. They were still getting no signs of life, but they continued their efforts, hoping for a miracle.

When the paramedics arrived on the scene, they took over and in a few minutes had Molly strapped to a stretcher, into the ambulance, and on the way to the hospital. They were able to get a pulse, but it didn't look good for her.

By this time, the place was swarming with police, at least ten cars. They were going through the house, looking for every detail.

One of the officers walked into the living room where the captain was standing. "Sir, it looks like a typical suicide. She left a note and everything." He handed the captain the note, holding it with a pair of tweezers.

The captain studied the note carefully. "There is no evidence of foul play or forced entry?"

"No, sir. Mr. Haden was here with his wife when we arrived. They said the front door was locked. They found a spare key and let themselves inside. There are no marks on any doors or windows to indicate that there was a forced entry."

"Okay. Thanks. Put all of that in your report."

Tom leaned toward the note, trying to read it. "Could I look at that?"

"Sure. Here, hold it by this." The captain handed the note to Tom. "Don't touch the paper. There may be prints on it."

Tom took the note and read it. Something looked strange about it. He read it again. It sounded strange. He read it a third time then handed it to his wife. "Lucy, read this." She read it over slowly.

"Do you notice anything out of the ordinary?"

Lucy shook her head no. "It looks normal to me. Why?"

"I don't know; something seems out of place. Let me see it again." He read it for the fourth time, and then he saw it. "Look. There it is. That's why it doesn't look normal. Each paragraph begins with three words which all have the same three letters." He pointed to them, showing Lucy, and began reading them out loud, "I'm responsible so … I recently started … I respectively submit. The first letter of each of these words is capitalized. I believe she was trying to tell us something in her note."

"What does it mean?" Lucy asked.

"The three letters which are capitalized are IRS. I think she's telling us who tried to kill her."

Lucy looked at him with doubt. "I believe you've been watching too many detective shows, Columbo, and are stretching a bit. Maybe it's just a coincidence."

"Okay, assuming it was a coincidence, then why did she choose to capitalize only those three letters?"

The captain interrupted their conversation, "Senator, would you and your wife mind coming downtown with us to answer a few questions and to sign our reports?"

"No, not at all. We'll follow you down."

Lucy turned to Tom. "Are you going to tell him about the note?"

"I don't think so. He would never believe me anyway. Besides, like you say, maybe it's just a coincidence."

At the police station, they were interrogated for a few minutes. They both signed their statements and an hour later left. As soon as they returned home, Tom called Abigail Bishop to let her know about Molly. In all of the excitement, he had totally forgotten about her.

The minute Tom mentioned the word hospital Abigail became hysterical. "I knew something was wrong. Oh, my God! Oh, my God! My poor, precious little girl. My baby."

Tom tried to calm her down. "Mrs. Bishop, everything will be all right. We'll call you as soon as we have some news. Don't worry; I'm sure she'll be fine."

CHAPTER TWENTY-EIGHT

Maxwell and Judy had grown closer since this ordeal had begun. The allegations of wrongdoing had hit the newspapers and television, but Judy was there by his side in full support of her husband. She believed in Max, trusted him, and knew in her heart that the allegations were false. In the words of Tammy Wynette, she had told the media, "I'll stand by my man."

They walked off the elevator on the seventh floor of the hospital and located the nurses' station.

"We're here to see Nathan Daniels."

"You can go right in. His room number is 710, down the hall on your right."

"Thank you."

Maxwell knocked on the door.

"Come in!" Nathan yelled.

When he saw Max, he smiled. "You're still alive. I thought for sure you had died and gone to heaven, or wherever it is that Jews go when they die."

"You sound like you're feeling better," Maxwell said, shaking hands with Nathan. "You remember Judy, don't you?"

Judy extended her hand and greeted him cordially, "It's been a long time. You're looking good for someone who was beat up, stomped on, and almost killed."

"Thank you. It still hurts a lot, but they say I'll be fine in a few days." Nathan was glad to see Max and had a hundred questions he needed answered. "I guess our little plan backfired on us."

Max grinned. "Yeah, I guess we didn't count on them getting to the media first, and I certainly never dreamed that they would feed out-and-out lies to them."

Nathan pointed to his beat-up face and body. "And we never thought they would beat Linda and me to a pulp. They almost killed us!"

"Sorry about that. How is Linda anyway?"

"She's okay. She has a sprained ankle and a fractured arm, but other than that, she's fine. Did you know they've taken our boys?"

"No!" Maxwell and Judy were stunned. "Where to?"

"We don't know. Social Services has them. Linda is making some calls now to see if she can get any more information. She should be here in a little while. By the way, are they still following you?"

"I haven't seen them as much, but I'm sure they're out there. I know they're still listening in on all of our conversations." Maxwell looked around the room and moved his finger in a circle, motioning that bugs could even be in here.

Nathan tried to sit up but groaned with pain. "Could you put another pillow under my back please?"

Judy reached for the pillow and gently lifted his head and placed it under his neck. He made a painful expression. "It only hurts when I move." He laughed. "Thanks, that feels a lot better. Now, Max, how do we proceed from here? What's our next move?"

Max pulled a chair over and turned the back of it toward the bed, straddling both sides and placing his arms and chin on the back. "Well, now that's our problem. These guys aren't playing by the rules. Legally, they can't serve you a Notice of Tax Due then turn around and seize everything for nonpayment three days later. I'll call them today on your behalf and see if I can find out what they are up to. I'll try to use my legal pull to bluff them."

"And if that doesn't work?"

Judy walked around to the other side of the bed. "I'll let you two talk shop. I think I'll go find your wife. What's her room number?"

"She's on the fifth floor, room 510."

"I'll be back in a little while." She walked out the door and headed for the elevator.

Nathan returned to his question. "Well … what do we do if that doesn't work?"

"We can fight it in tax court …" Max hesitated, and his expression changed.

"What is it? What's wrong?" Nathan could tell that Max was in deep thought.

"Well, before all of this began, I had faith in our system, but now, I really don't trust them anymore. The system works only if everyone plays by the rules."

"I certainly can relate to that. I don't trust the IRS anymore. Who can we turn to though?"

"Senator Haden is trying to help us, but they are smearing him too. I'm not sure if he's going to be able to rally anyone to our aid or not."

"So, I repeat my question. What are we going to do now?"

Max sat silently staring out the window. Turning slowly to face Nathan, he finally responded, "I don't know, Nathan. I really don't know."

The door opened, and Judy was pushing Linda in her wheelchair. "Well, did you guys solve all of our problems with the IRS yet?" Judy asked.

Maxwell and Nathan looked at each other and only smiled. Nathan changed the subject. "What did you find out about Matthew and Allen? Where are they?"

"It seems they've been placed in a temporary foster home. They won't tell us where, only that they are both doing fine."

Nathan forced himself to sit up but grimaced with pain. "Did they say why they took them away?"

"The lady I spoke with, a Mrs. Jacobs, said it was normal procedure when there was no immediate family to take them. She assured me not to worry, that as soon as we were out of the hospital, she would turn them both back over to us."

Max listened but kept his doubts to himself. He gave Judy a questionable smile.

Power Unleashed

CHAPTER TWENTY-NINE

Douglas Preston had not talked with Tom Haden since that day at Molly's house. He had not even thought about the document he had read until he saw Tom's name in the paper with a mention of an IRS document in the column. The article made the senator appear he was lying. Doug knew what he would have to do.

He left his office and headed for his car. He glanced at his watch; it was after eleven in the evening. *I'll call Tom first thing in the morning,* Doug thought. *Maybe I can collaborate his story.* As he started his engine, the thought hit him for the first time that he might be in some danger.

The government wouldn't do anything to me. I've paid my taxes on time. Besides, I haven't done anything wrong. As the thoughts flooded his mind, he knew in his heart, he was trying to convince himself.

As he drove out of Washington DC, he looked in his rearview mirror and could see the city lights in a distance. Doug had moved to the country three years earlier. It was a long commute, but he loved it. He would drive the curved mountain road at top speeds in his Corvette. It was a challenge for him to see how fast he could make the trip home from the city. His fastest time so far was forty-eight minutes and twelve seconds. That had scared him so badly that he swore he would never drive it that fast again. The normal drive time was one hour and ten minutes.

Once he hit the two-lane road, there were no more stoplights, just twists and turns in the road, all the way home. As he pressed the accelerator to the floor, he watched the speedometer climb, sixty, sixty-five, seventy, seventy-five. He held it at seventy-five miles an hour. He knew the road like the back of his hand.

He turned the radio to his favorite country station. Garth Brooks was singing Doug's favorite song of all time, *Thunder Rolls.* As Garth sang the chorus, Doug pressed the gas pedal further. He watched the speed climb, eighty and then eighty-five.

He loved the feeling of driving fast, and the music added to the excitement. This made a long daily drive an exciting adventure.

Police were not too much of a problem on this desolate stretch of roadway. Occasionally, a local sheriff would pass by, but there was not usually any radar to worry about, especially at this time of night. Besides, his radar detector would light up at the slightest hint of a policeman. He had them mounted on the front and back of his car.

Doug downshifted the Vette to fourth gear to prepare to go into a long curve. He enjoyed the sensation of feeling like a racecar driver as he went through the gears, hearing the roar of the engine increase with each downshift.

In third gear, he was doing sixty-five when he hit the heart of the curve. *Now, step on the gas. Give it all you got!* Doug told himself. *That's the only way to bring it out of the turn without losing it.*

When the car hit the far end of the curve, the roadway was filled with bright, blinding lights. *What the ...? I've got to stop!*

Doug swerved to avoid hitting the bright lights, which were now directly in front of him. He couldn't see the road. The lights were blinding him completely. He felt the car go off the road and hit the loose gravel. After the first swerve, he lost control, and he felt the car being lifted into the air, sailing. *There's nothing I can do. I'm going to crash.* Doug went through all his options, but he no longer had control of the vehicle. He was still blinded by the lights, which he was flying over.

The Corvette hit the ground with the hood first, shattering the fiberglass into little pieces. The entire steering column crushed Doug against the seat. The floorboard and firewall pinned his legs, wrapping them underneath the dashboard. Doug screamed as glass shattered in his face, his neck being severed at the shoulders.

****

The ambulance pulled up to the scene. The medics had been on a lot of calls, but nothing prepared them for what they saw at this one.

"What happened here?" one of the medics asked as they took the stretcher out.

"Just another fool going too fast for road conditions," the officer on the scene replied. "We figure he must have been doing seventy when he left the road."

The medics looked at the wreck. There wasn't much left. The Corvette was folded up like an accordion. It was now half of its original size.

"Somewhere inside that mass of metal is your body. You'll need more tools than we've got to get him out of there."

The younger medic was throwing up on the side of the road. "Don't mind him; he ain't never seen anything this bad before," the older medic told the officer.

"I've been on the force forty years, and I've never seen one this bad before. I don't know when these young drivers are going to learn that speed kills."

A small crowd had gathered, and they watched as the firemen, medics, and police officers worked diligently to pry the body out of the wreckage. They ended up cutting the car into pieces before the body was finally exhumed.

Watching from a distance, lost in the crowd, were two men, well dressed, about middle age. The taller one spoke, "The beauty of this method of execution is that no one ever knows. They can guess, but they can never know for sure."

"How many times have we used the bright light routine now? Five, maybe six times?"

"I don't know, pal, but it works every time, especially with those who like to drive at high speeds."

"Let's go call Shark and tell him the job is complete."

"Yeah, then let's go celebrate another successful job well done."

The men turned and pushed their way through the crowd of people, then made their way back to the city. On the long drive back, they celebrated their victory by passing a bottle of whiskey back and forth until the bottle was empty.

CHAPTER THIRTY

Calvin Davis showed his pleasure when he received word that Douglas Preston had been killed in an automobile accident. He wasn't too pleased, however, that Molly Shanks was fighting for her life in Mt. Sinai Hospital. It was suspected that she might pull through. She was still lying in a coma, but there was hope, and that was what bothered him.

Davis sat in a secluded, dark corner of a bar located in a very seedy neighborhood. A well-dressed man in a black pinstriped suit approached and sat beside him. "Do you have the rest of my money?"

Davis swallowed hard and worked up his courage. "I'm not paying the twenty-five thousand until the job is finished. The deal was half up front and the other half when she's dead, and she isn't dead," Davis whispered.

"It's just a formality. She'll die in time. I gave that woman enough pills to kill a horse in half the time. She's not talking to anyone; she'll die."

"You had better make sure of it. You'll get the other half when I get news that she is buried, and not a moment before. Are we communicating?"

The man in the suit stood up, grabbed his employer by the collar, and with a sinister grin said, "You dirty rotten …" He picked up a beer bottle and, holding it by the neck, broke it on the side of the table. He put the cut glass near Davis's face and ran it down his cheek, applying a slight pressure to the skin, making a trickle of blood drip down his cheek. "You better have my money ready when I call you in a few days. I'll finish the job, then I'll be back to collect. Don't try to renege on our deal, man. Am I communicating?" He threw Davis into the seat, turned, and walked away, waving to the bartender.

Davis picked up his napkin to wipe the blood from his face. He sat in silence and took another sip of his beer. Staring straight ahead, he didn't want to look around for fear people were staring. After about ten minutes, he paid his tab and walked out of the bar, still trying to regain his composure.

He hated this part of town and dreaded coming to it. He looked across the street and saw two men transacting business near an old building. *Drugs probably*, Davis thought. *How can these people live this way? This place gives me the creeps.*

He walked faster toward his car. He had the automatic car remote in his hand and pushed the button. He heard the familiar beep and jumped in, pressing the door locks quickly. Three young, rough-looking men began walking toward his car. He fidgeted with the key, turned the ignition on, and heard the roar of the engine.

As he shifted into reverse, a loud thud hit the hood, and at the same time, the same sound came from the trunk. Davis looked around to see that there was a young man on each end of his car. He pressed the accelerator to the floor, throwing the man on the hood to the ground.

As the car whirled backwards, laying rubber on the pavement, he looked out the driver's side window, only to see it crush in his face. The third man, armed with a baseball bat swung it full force, bashing his window and shattering it to nothing. Davis panicked, hit the accelerator again, and crashed into the wall behind him. The man on the trunk flew into the wall and onto the pavement.

Davis grabbed for his gun, but it stuck in his belt.

The man who was thrown from the car yelled obscenities as he staggered to his feet. He walked over to the driver's door, reached inside, and opened it. He jerked Davis out of the car, dragging him on the pavement. He began hitting Davis in the face and stomach. Davis instinctively responded and began returning the blows whenever he could get in a good punch. But overweight and out of shape, he was no match for these young hoodlums.

The second man came up behind Davis and held him in an arm lock, while the first man continued beating him. The man with the baseball bat struck the car continuously until all the windows were shattered. He took out a switchblade and slashed each tire, laughing as he watched them go flat.

"You are in the wrong neighborhood, mister. This is just a warning this time. We don't want your kind here. It's a good thing you're not a cop, or you'd be a dead man."

The one holding Davis let go, and he slumped to the ground. The three of them sauntered away from the scene as if nothing had ever happened. The one with the baseball bat yelled, "Get this piece of junk out of our neighborhood, man; you're cluttering up the streets."

Davis tried to move. The pain shot through both sides of his skull and throughout his lower abdomen. *What was that all about? Hoodlums, that's all they are is hoodlums.*

He forced himself up off the ground, clinging to his car. His body had taken worse beatings than this, but he was much older now, and this one hurt a lot. He wasn't sure if anything was broken, but it sure felt like it. Blood rolled down his lip as he spat it on the pavement. He tried to open his eyes, but only one could open; the other one seemed to be sealed shut.

A few pedestrians witnessed the fight and his struggle but chose to ignore them and keep minding their own business for fear the same thing would happen to them.

Davis climbed into the driver's seat, started the engine, and with four flat tires, drove out of the neighborhood to get help.

CHAPTER THIRTY-ONE

Howard Baskins called Davis into his office. The Shark had contacted Howard several times in the past twenty-four hours, wanting to know what was happening with the document. Howard's anger was evident.

"What in the sam blazes happened to you?" Baskins growled, "It looks like you forgot to duck."

Davis tried to force a smile, but his lips were swollen to twice their normal size. "I was jumped by a street gang. There were at least ten of them, but I made my mark before they fled." He couldn't stand the thought of telling Howard that three young punks, who probably were no more than seventeen, got the best of him.

"I want to know where we stand on getting our documents back. I'm beginning to feel some pressure, and to tell you the truth, I don't like it. What's going on? Why don't I have them back yet?"

"Well, sir, we haven't … I mean, I told you last week we were—"

"And I told you last week that I wanted action or else." Baskins bit off the end of one of his expensive cigars. He placed it in his mouth and began chewing. "You have to put more pressure on them. They're not going to drive over here and hand the document over to us."

"Yes, sir. We've been—"

Howard interrupted again, "You've been slipping, is what you've been doing. You've been too nice. You can't do your job and be mister nice guy to everyone. Let's tighten the noose around these taxpayers. What's the status on the other witnesses?"

"Molly Shanks tried to commit suicide and is still alive, but I expect to have word on her condition shortly. That Preston fellow met with a terrible accident. There was no hope for him at all."

"You did good on that one, I have to admit. Is anything suspected on Molly's attempted suicide?" Howard asked, taking the cigar from his mouth.

"No, police have it as a routine suicide. They've closed the investigation."

"Unless she comes out of the coma," Howard added.

"She won't, sir; I'm making sure of that."

"Good, then just get me the documents back so things can return to normal again." He turned away from Davis and pressed his intercom button.

"Yes, sir?" Sheila quickly responded.

"Sheila, could you come in here for a moment?" He looked at Davis, waving his hand at him, motioning for him to leave. "That's all. I'll talk to you later. Bring me some good news." Davis made a quick exit.

Sheila walked in carrying her pad and took her usual seat. "I'm ready when you are, sir."

"I want you to contact all the regional directors. Set up a meeting for Saturday morning. I want everyone here, no excuses. This is a mandatory meeting for everyone."

"Yes, sir; will they need accommodations?"

"I'll leave that up to them, but we'll begin at ten in the morning and will be done by about three in the afternoon. We'll bring lunch in and have a full five-hour meeting. Most can probably catch a flight back that evening."

"Anything else?"

"Yeah, call the hospital and get me a report on Molly Shanks. Call them every few hours to get an update and keep me posted on her condition. I'm really concerned about her."

Sheila stood to leave. "I'll get on this right away, sir."

CHAPTER THIRTY-TWO

Senator Tom Haden called Maxwell from a pay phone. In a few minutes, Max called him back on a phone that wasn't bugged.

Tom had urgency in his voice. "You need to know that people who have seen the document are dying here."

"Are you kidding me? How?" Max was shocked.

"One was supposedly an attempted suicide, and the other was an auto accident."

"And you don't think so, I take it." Max was hoping Tom was wrong.

"I'm afraid not. The note Molly Shanks left gave me a clue. She's still alive, in a coma. I'm hoping she'll come out of it at least long enough to talk to the police. The other one could have been a genuine accident, but in light of everything else that is happening, I have my doubts."

"Do you think we're in danger?"

"I believe we're all in danger. They obviously don't want anyone alive who has seen the document."

"Why haven't they killed us yet?"

"Probably because they know we have the document, and they can't locate it. Until they do, they can't risk taking us out, for fear the document might surface somewhere. Their first goal with us is to get the document. Once they have it, I don't believe we'll be alive long. Is your copy in a safe place?" Tom asked.

"You know it is. Now, I'm moving it to an even safer place. I'm not sure where Nathan's is. He said that the IRS agents couldn't have found it at the house, but he didn't tell me where it was hidden."

"Okay, tell him to make sure he has backup copies and not to surrender it to them."

"I don't believe he will. Did you know that the IRS came in, beat them both up, putting them in the hospital, and then took everything they own? They have nothing now."

Tom gasped. "These guys just won't quit, will they? When will they be getting out of the hospital?"

"They're supposed to be out some time today or tomorrow. There's only one problem," Max dropped his voice.

"What's that?"

"They don't have any place to go. IRS has it all. I told them they could come and stay with Judy and me. They might do that for a while. But it's just a matter of time before they come after me too."

"Yeah, and I'm sure I'll be next." Tom looked around over his shoulder, out of habit. "I think I better go now. I'll talk to you again later. Keep me posted."

When Tom hung up the phone, he turned around and thought he saw a man dart into a store. "Those guys are still tailing me," he mumbled to himself. "There's no place to hide from them."

He drove to the hospital to see Molly Shanks.

****

As the evening came, a man slipped through a side door at the hospital, unnoticed by anyone. He walked down the corridor, found a supply room, and went inside. He found a white smock, put it on and walked back into the corridor. He looked like a doctor, distinguished, well dressed, and well mannered.

He got off the elevator on the fifth floor, walked directly past the nurses' station to room 525. He opened the door, looked inside, and then walked into Molly Shanks' room.

She was lying in bed, in a deep coma. Tubes and wires hung all around her. The man walked close to her, surveying the situation. He wasn't sure what method he would use. *A pillow over the nose and mouth for a few minutes would work. At least it would be clean. Chances are no one would suspect.*

He picked up the pillow and gently laid it over Molly's face. Even in her unconscious state, her body began to wiggle as she gasped for air. *Just a couple of more minutes should do it*, he thought. "You will rest in peace now, Mrs. Shanks," he whispered.

Tom walked into the room. "Hey, what are you doing?" he shouted, startling the man with the pillow.

The intruder turned toward Tom, pushing him to the floor. Tom grabbed the man's leg, tripping him. The man fell on the floor by the door, hitting his head on the wall. Tom jumped up and grabbed him by the back of the neck, putting a chokehold on him. The man reached up to get hold of Tom, but couldn't reach him. The man then turned and hit Tom in the groin with his elbow. Tom cried out in pain, letting go of his grip. Tom received a hard blow in the stomach, and the intruder ran out the door, down the hallway, and disappeared. Tom jumped to his feet again and looked both ways down the hall but saw nothing. He shouted, "Help! Someone! Come quick!"

Two nurses came running down the hall toward the room. "What is it? What's wrong?" one of them asked.

"A man was trying to kill Mrs. Shanks. I tried to stop him, but he got away." The nurse walked to the phone and dialed security. She told them what had taken place.

Tom tried to breathe but was having difficulty. He walked over to Molly's bed to see if she was all right.

The other nurse checked Molly's vital signs. "She's still breathing on her own and seems to be fine," the nurse said. Molly's eyes fluttered. Tom held her hand tightly, and she squeezed it gently.

"Hey, she just squeezed my hand," Tom shouted to the nurse. "And look, she's trying to open her eyes."

The other nurse came to her side and began calling her name. "Molly Shanks! Molly Shanks! Can you hear us? Wake up now. You've been asleep for a long time."

Molly moved slowly, and her eyes finally came open. All she could see was a blur. Nothing made sense. Her mouth was dry and felt like it was full of cotton balls. "Where am I?" she managed to ask.

"You're in the hospital, honey. You took an overdose of sleeping pills. Do you remember?"

Molly shook her head that she didn't.

Tom took her hand and lifted it up to his chest. "Hi, Molly, remember me? Senator Tom Haden. I've come to see how you're doing."

Molly only smiled and nodded. He was encouraged with that small response.

Moments later, security arrived with the police. "We didn't find anyone. Did you get a good look at him?" one of them asked Tom and the nurses.

"No. Everything happened so fast. I walked into the room and saw him with a pillow over her face. I shouted, he pushed me, we wrestled, and then he got away and ran. The room was too dark so I didn't see him at all."

The policeman wrote Tom's statement and then asked, "Do you know what he was wearing?"

"All I saw was a white doctor's smock and dark trousers. Nothing else."

"Okay, Senator, we'll call you if we need any more information. Any idea who might want to do this?"

The senator thought and then said, "Not really." He wanted to talk with Molly before he said anything to the police.

They tried to ask Molly questions, but she remembered nothing and couldn't help them at all.

After thirty minutes, they left, leaving Tom alone with Molly.

"You gave us quite a scare. Do you remember anything about how you got in here?" Tom asked.

Molly slurred her words, but managed to answer, "I can't remember a thing. I don't even know who you are."

Tom filled her in on how they had met, about her husband's suicide. Nothing seemed to help. She couldn't remember a thing.

They visited for an hour. Finally, Tom excused himself and left. He was relieved to see a police guard posted outside the door.

CHAPTER THIRTY-THREE

Linda walked with a limp, but could get around all right. Nathan only hurt when he moved, but he could manage for himself. They had left the hospital together and were staying with the Rosenthals. Maxwell loaned Nathan one of his cars, and they headed straight for the Social Services office to see about getting their boys back.

After waiting for forty-five minutes in a dingy, filthy office, sitting on hardback chairs, someone finally came out to see them. "Mr. and Mrs. Daniels, I'm Peter Bonavich, and I've been assigned to your case. How can I help you?"

"You can help us by giving us our children back," Linda said, slightly raising her voice.

Nathan added in a milder tone, "They were sent to a foster home when we had our accident. We were told we could pick them up when we got out."

Peter looked through their file, reading different details. After several sighs and grunts, he finally said, "I'm afraid you were misinformed. According to my records, you are both unfit parents, and we are instructed by the state to keep the children indefinitely."

"You what?" Linda shouted, holding nothing back. "You can't just take our children—"

Nathan placed his arm around her, trying to comfort her. "Look, there must be some mistake. We're good parents. We've taken real good care of our children. We've never harmed them in any way and besides—"

Peter interrupted, "We have several complaints filed against you stating you abused your boys sexually. I'm sorry, Mr. and Mrs. Daniels, but the state has taken your children."

Nathan stood up, still feeling the pain of his broken ribs when he moved. "Are you telling us we'll never see our children again? Don't we at least get a hearing or a trial or something?"

"In cases such as yours, there are no criminal charges being filed against you, so there is no need for a trial. In Colorado, the state can decide when parents are unfit. It is solely our decision as to where we place the children. All children are ultimately the state's responsibility. With the numerous complaints filed in your case, we decided it would be in the best interest of the children to place them permanently in a foster home."

Linda screamed, tears running down her face, "You can't take away my babies!" She lunged toward the social worker and began beating on his chest. "You can't take—"

Nathan pulled her away and grabbed her, hugging her tightly. "Honey, we'll get them back. Shh, it's okay. I promise you we'll get them back."

She became indignant. "Yeah, like you promised the IRS wouldn't take our house. Like you promised we'd be all right. Nathan," Linda was yelling and crying at the same time, "we've lost! Give it back to them. Whatever they want, give it to them. They can have our house, they can have our cars, they can take our furniture, and God knows they can have our money, but they can't have my babies."

Nathan could only hold her tighter. He asked Peter, "Can we at least see our boys, just for a few minutes?"

"I'm sorry, Mr. Daniels. I have explicit instructions not to allow that. It's better for the boys."

"Are they together, or were they separated?" Linda asked, trying to get herself under control.

Peter smiled. "We were able to keep them together. They're in a nice home, with some really good people. You really don't have to worry. Maybe after you have a new place and agree to some counseling, then perhaps someday we can give them back to you."

Nathan and Linda walked slowly to the car. They had not prepared for this. The morning Colorado air was cool, crisp, and a pleasant contrast to the cold, musty office. The sun had a cleansing effect on the soul.

Sitting in the car, Linda leaned her head into Nathan's shoulder. "What are we going to do? When is this nightmare going to end?"

Nathan didn't have the answer. He held her close. Tears filled his eyes as he tried to choke back the emotions. Linda began crying again. They sat in the car, holding each other, crying until they could cry no more.

Nathan placed the key in the ignition and started it. He drove straight to their home. As they approached the driveway, they couldn't believe their eyes. All the windows were boarded up. An IRS notice was nailed on the door. A notice-of-auction sign stood on the front lawn.

"They are going to hold the auction on Saturday. Do you want a good deal on a house?" Nathan tried to joke.

"I wonder what it will go for." Linda sniffled.

Nathan parked the car, and they both got out. Stepping on the lawn of their own home, they felt like criminals. A notice on the door stated that this was government property and warned people not to trespass.

Nathan took out his key, inserted it in the lock, and to his amazement, the door opened. They walked inside. The first thing Nathan noticed was the blood stains in the carpet where he and Linda had lain bleeding. As he stared at the spots on the carpet, he could hear Linda screaming, falling down the stairs. He shuddered as the scene flashed through his mind.

Everything in the house was tagged. Linda held back the tears. "I want some of this stuff. It's of no value to them." She walked into the garage, found a large box, and returned.

She went to various places, collecting pictures, memorabilia, and other items. In no time, the box was filled. They filled a second box, a third, and then a fourth.

They dug the suitcases out of the attic and packed as many clothes as possible into the four suitcases. When they were finished, they walked to the boys' room. As soon as the door opened, wonderful memories flooded their minds. They could hear the boys jumping on the beds, wrestling on the floor, laughing, and having a good time.

Linda walked over and picked up some of the clothes. She began folding them, straightening the room out of habit. She made the beds. "This room is filthy. We've got to clean the place up."

Nathan watched her move about the room, cleaning, folding, and straightening. "Honey." Nathan grabbed Linda by the shoulders. "We have to go now. We can't stay here."

"I've got to clean this place. It's a mess. I can't let anyone—"

Nathan grabbed her harder. "Linda, they're not coming back, at least not here. We have to go now."

Linda slowly looked up at Nathan, shaking her head. She exploded into tears again, sobbing uncontrollably. Nathan held her tightly, trying to comfort her, but he knew there was little he could do to make her feel better. He vowed to himself that he would make this right with her.

After the car was loaded, they locked up the house, turned, and looked at it one last time. They loved that house and would always cherish the memories.

****

Later in the evening as they sat in the living room with Maxwell and Judy, they shared the ordeal of the day. Max told Nathan and Linda about the phone call from Tom Haden and the death of Douglas Preston.

Max had his entire house and office scanned for listening devices and found several throughout both. They also discovered the hidden cameras. Judy was in shock to find out that someone had been watching them while they were in bed. It embarrassed her at first and then infuriated her. She was glad that they had not been intimate with each other in weeks.

At least now they felt like they could talk in their own home without being heard or watched. Security guards watched the house twenty-four hours a day.

"Why do you suppose they didn't kill us?" Nathan asked.

"My guess is that they need us until they get their documents back. I've given a copy to an attorney friend of mine in a sealed envelope with the instructions to open it and turn it over to the press in the case of my death or anyone in my family, accidental or otherwise. I sent Mr. Howard Baskins a note telling him this. I'm hoping this will protect us for a little while. I suggest you do the same."

Nathan changed the subject. "Did you check with the IRS about their illegal action against us?"

"Oh yeah, I almost forgot. They even gave me a copy of your notice." He walked into the den and retrieved his briefcase. "Here, look at this." He handed the notice to Nathan. "Check the date on top. According to them, you were given a thirty-day Demand Notice to Pay. From their records, they followed the law to the letter."

"But, that's a lie. They can't get away with this, can they?"

"We know it's a lie, but how do we prove it in court? That's the problem." Maxwell sat down on the sofa next to Judy. "They've covered their tracks like pros. We don't have a leg to stand on to pursue this case."

Nathan turned to Linda, placing his hand in hers. "What are we going to do now, Max? If we don't give them what they want, they continue harassing us, intimidating us. We don't get to see our children anymore, and we lose everything. If I do give them what they want, you say, they'll probably kill us. What are we going to do?" Nathan waited for a response, but Maxwell didn't have one. They all sipped their drinks quietly.

****

Big Al and Sergio sat in a van across the street from the Rosenthal's. Sergio continued adjusting the listening device to see if he could pick up the conversations. All he could hear was the blaring of the stereo outside all around the house.

"Why do you suppose they have the stereo playing outside?" Sergio asked.

Big Al gave him an unbelieving look. "Because they know we're probably trying to listen. He's a pretty sharp attorney."

"How long we going to sit here and listen to his music?"

"We'll wait around a little longer, till they go to bed. They have to turn it off sometime tonight," Big Al said as he laid his head back like he was going to take a nap.

"I hope you're right; this opera stuff is driving me crazy. I can't say much for his taste in music," Sergio said.

"That's just because you ain't got no class, Sergio."

"No, it's because I've got good taste in music." They both laughed.

CHAPTER THIRTY-FOUR

Howard paced the floor nervously. He would walk to one side of the boardroom then to the other. He stared at each director, looking him or her over. They all were talking to one another, waiting for the meeting to begin.

Finally, Howard spoke in his gruff, low voice, "Gentlemen and ladies, we are in a serious crisis. We must get the revenues up higher. The chief has asked me to call you all together to see what we can do. Congress needs more cash, and as you know, they can't very well raise taxes at this point."

Howard took a handful of change from his pocket and began pouring it from one hand to the other as he paced. He continued, "There is only one way to accomplish this, and that is to get the people who are not paying their fair share. We're going back through our records to 1985, looking for anyone who has not filed a return during those years. Once we find them, we're going to send them a notice to file or else. If at all possible, we will send them a bill for the amount owed. If they cannot produce proof that they filed a return and paid the taxes, then we'll charge them the tax, plus interest, plus penalty, plus a negligence penalty."

One of the directors raised his hand. "Sir, what about all the people who destroyed their records thinking they didn't need them anymore? Most people don't keep records for over five years—"

Howard cut in, "Precisely my point." He pointed his finger at the director. "Give this man a prize. You're catching on to our little secret. We have the greatest weapon available to collect these taxes, and that is fear. They'll pay because they're afraid to fight us. Most will not be able to prove they have paid even if they have, so we'll collect from them as well."

Howard continued pacing the floor, circling the conference table. "Are any of you opposed to this idea?"

The director from Texas lifted his hand in the air slowly.

Howard pointed at him. "You have a problem with this plan, Mr. Andrews?"

"No, sir. I was just wondering, what if someone can show a copy of the return but can't prove they paid the taxes owed, then what do we do?"

Howard grinned. "Well, Mr. Andrews, if they can't prove they paid, then they'll have to pay us again, now won't they? Plus, and this is the beauty of the plan, they'll owe us more than double the original amount because of interest and penalties. We have estimated that we can raise an additional one hundred billion dollars this year by using this method, and those estimates are conservative. Some have said we could go as high as a half a trillion dollars. Remember, this is over and above the current taxes we collect each year. This should help keep Congress off our backs for a while."

The director from New York spoke up, "Sir, speaking of Congress, what about this senator who has been in the paper lately? What is the story on this document, which he claims to have seen?"

Howard was taken off-guard by the question. He stopped pacing and put the change back into his pocket. "I'm glad you asked. This senator, Tom Haden is his name, is under investigation for misuse of campaign funds. Because of our investigation, he has fabricated some story to try to get us off his back. But it won't work; we're not going to drop the investigation. He has nothing on us, and there is no document that I'm aware of that would in any way harm the service. It's just a desperate ploy on the part of the senator to try to get the publicity away from him and focused on us. The press knows the true story. They're on our side. The truth will prevail."

The director from Colorado stood up. "Sir, you must be aware of a couple from our area who are also saying they have a document. A hearing was even held to try to stop the IRS from carrying out the plans that this document outlines. How do you explain that?"

Howard sat down in his chair at the head of the table. He leaned in toward the group. "Listen, we cannot go around chasing down every allegation that comes against the IRS. There is a simple explanation. This senator is a friend with the attorney who filed the suit in Colorado. The attorney is under investigation by our office as well; you know that, don't you, Mr. Jenkins?"

"Yes, sir, but that still—"

Howard interjected, "Well, put two and two together. They collaborated with one another on this whole issue. Even this Nathan Daniels, who owes us a lot of money in back taxes, is trying to use this same ploy. But guess who his attorney is?" Howard looked around the room almost gloating, "That's right, Mr. Maxwell Rosenthal. You see, they are all connected and coming up with the same fabricated story. Don't concern yourself with these false allegations. Focus on getting your revenues up. We'll be sending out a list to you of everyone we want notices sent out to by the end of this month. Getting those notices out is top priority. Where you have the manpower, serve the notices in person at their home or office. That always makes for a quick response from the people. Also, one last thing, don't be afraid to use your telephones. Again, where you have the manpower, get your people to call them on the phone to follow up on your letters. It will produce tremendous results and improve your collections by about 30 percent. Any questions?"

Several hands went up at the same time. Howard pointed to the man at the back of the room. "Yes, Mr. Jones, what is it?"

Jones stood up. "Sir, do we have the power to negotiate the amounts with the people and settle for a lesser amount?"

"If you think you can collect the total amount now, then yes. If it is a payout situation, then no. Cash in the hand is always better, so we'll be glad to take a lesser settlement."

Questions went on for another half-hour. Finally, Howard stood up. "Folks, it's three o'clock, and I know some of you have planes to catch. I thank all of you for coming on such short notice. I look forward to seeing your collection progress. Remember, don't stop doing what you're doing. Don't let your other departments drop the ball while you're getting this program off the ground. Let's get those tax dollars collected." With those last words, he sounded like a coach cheering his team on to victory. The directors stood up, shook hands with one another, and began saying their farewells. Most would be back on a plane that evening to return to their hometown. Some would stay the night, enjoying the nightlife of Washington DC at the taxpayers' expense.

When Howard returned to his office, he sat back in his chair, leaned back, put his feet on the desk, and placed a cigar between his teeth. Little did the directors know that they were moving into phase one of implementing the largest scam ever perpetrated on the American public in the history of the United States. Much of the money that would be collected through this program would be going to line the pockets of key officials in Washington DC, including his own.

All of the funds collected through this program would be moved through several private corporations created especially for this purpose, and these corporations would be taking out a very hefty percentage of every dollar that came in as a fee for collection services rendered. Originally, the Treasury was to receive 80 percent of the funds, but now they would be lucky to see half that amount. Howard Baskins had no idea how many people were involved in this conspiracy but knew his role would pay him well, and he would soon retire from public service a very wealthy man.

He had found out later that he had been groomed for this post and was hand selected by someone outside the service to fill his current position solely for the purpose of being brought into the network. The scheme had been years in the making, and he had no idea how many people were involved but knew that his direct orders came from someone called the Shark. He had already been paid handsomely for his efforts through the dummy corporations, but that sum was about to increase a thousand-fold if his estimates were anywhere near correct.

CHAPTER THIRTY-FIVE

Tom walked into the Blue Moon Diner. Elsie, the waitress, greeted him, "Long time, no see. Where have you been hiding out?" She smiled at him. "We missed your smiling face."

Tom turned to her in response. "You must not be reading the newspaper." He laughed then continued, "You just miss my big tips, and you know it."

Elsie threw a menu on the table as Tom sat down. "Do you want your usual, turkey sandwich on toasted wheat bread with lettuce and tomato?"

"Don't forget the mayo and pickle. Also, bring me a draft beer for a change."

Elsie yelled out to the kitchen, "One Thanksgiving special on hot wheat with all the trimmings."

Verlin walked into the restaurant. Tom caught his attention and signaled him to come back. Verlin shook Tom's hand and said, "Glad you could make it."

"I was surprised to hear from you. What do you have?"

Verlin leaned across the table to get close to Tom. "I'm not sure it's anything, but Tom, you'd better drop this whole thing and quick. It's hotter than you think."

Tom looked at Verlin. "Tell me about it. People's lives are being destroyed. Two people I know personally have been attacked; one has died, and the other almost died. My whole career is about to go down the tubes. I know this is hot. So, what else is new?"

Elsie walked up. "Do you know what you want?"

Verlin glanced over the menu quickly, then closed it abruptly, "Just give me the same as he ordered."

Elsie turned toward the kitchen and yelled, "Double that last order."

Verlin turned his attention back to Tom. "You haven't seen anything yet. These guys are dead serious about that document, no pun intended. They're playing hardball here. If you don't cooperate with them, you're going to be a dead man, just like your friend."

Tom was surprised by Verlin's tone. "What are you saying, that I should give up the whole matter and let the IRS do their thing?"

"I'm saying drop this whole thing before you end up in the morgue with your wife and family. You can't win this. It's bigger than any of us. Heck, it's bigger than the whole government. Why not give me the document, and I'll turn it over to them. That way, you'll be out of this mess for good. You can walk away clean."

"I don't know if I can do that or not. It's not in my character to give up a good fight." The senator smiled suspiciously.

"Don't consider it giving up; just consider yourself as cooperating with the authorities. It'll be better for you." Verlin's voice was insistent and almost threatening.

Tom didn't know how to take this new approach from Verlin. "Why are you doing this? A few days ago, you seemed to be in favor of pursuing this thing with me. What's happened to change your mind?"

"Nothing has happened. I'm only trying to save a good friend's life. This thing will get you killed if you don't drop it soon. They're not only going to destroy you politically, they're going to kill you if necessary."

Tom was now very suspicious. "Who have you been talking to since we talked last?"

Verlin became defensive. "I found out more about the document. You asked me to keep my ears open; well, I did. When I found out what happened to Molly Shanks, I began to fear for your life. That's all."

Tom leaned back in the booth to make room for his food. Elsie almost threw the plates on the table. "Hope you enjoy your Thanksgiving feast, boys. Can I get you anything else?"

Tom looked up and smiled. "No, I believe this will be fine. Thanks, Elsie."

They both ate quietly for the next few minutes. Finally, Verlin broke the silence. "Why don't you give me the document? I'll turn it over to the guys in our office, and they'll take it from there. We can do an internal investigation to see who's at the bottom of this thing. How does that sound?"

Tom chewed his last bite carefully before he answered, "What assurance would I have that once I turned over the document, I wouldn't end up dead on some country road?"

"I can't give you any assurances, but I believe that if you cooperate, you'll live. If you don't, then you will not stand a chance. You only have one option if you want to survive this ordeal. I don't know who these guys are, but I do know they play for keeps."

"Will you take the document public if I give it over to you?" Tom took a long drink from his beer mug, watching Verlin's expression, waiting for a reply.

"I'll say this, give me the document, and we'll make sure that whoever is responsible for it is taken care of and removed. We like to keep everything hush-hush in the service. We do have a reputation to uphold. We can't afford to have a scandal hit the media."

Tom put his beer mug down hard on the table. "I'll think about it and get back to you with an answer. I don't know what I should do. Give me a few days, okay?"

"You got it, pal." Verlin reached over to pick up the check. "Let me get this one. It was my invite."

"Great, I'll get the tip." Tom put a ten-dollar bill on the table.

Verlin almost choked. "The bill is only thirteen dollars; what are you buying from this gal?"

Tom laughed. "I have a reputation to uphold too. Besides, it's tax deductible." He gave Verlin a slight grin.

After Verlin paid the check, they walked outside together. "I'll call you in a few days," Tom said as they shook hands. "Thanks for the lunch."

"Don't wait too long. Time is running out. They're getting desperate."

Tom felt uneasy with the meeting and began going over it in his mind. *Something was not right about all this. Why did he suddenly change positions? How did he find out so much about a top-secret document?* He went over every part of the conversation, trying to find a clue, but came up with nothing.

Tom returned to his office and lost himself in his work, meeting with lobbyists, dictating letters, and returning phone calls. He didn't have time to worry about the IRS document or think any more about his options. With all the bad publicity lately, he would have to now fight for his re-election if he wanted to stay in office. But first, he would have to survive this crisis.

CHAPTER THIRTY-SIX

Peter Bonavich answered the telephone at Social Services, "How may I help you?"

"Yes, this is Stevens from the Internal Revenue Service. I need to get some information from you regarding the Daniels boys. We have reason to believe that the parents may try something foolish. I need to verify where they are located so we can send some men out there to watch them."

Peter scratched his head. "I don't know. I'm not supposed to release—"

"Mr. Bonavich, surely you understand the seriousness of this situation. If necessary, I'll go to your superiors."

"Uh, no, that won't be necessary. I'll tell you where they are. Just a minute." Peter began thumbing through his files. "Here we are. They are with a family by the name of John and Marlene Ackerman. Do you want their address?"

"Yes, please."

"They live at 2259 Butterfield Road in Denver, Colorado."

"Thanks a lot, Mr. Bonavich. You've been a big help. I'll let your superiors know how cooperative you have been."

Peter beamed as he hung up the phone and thought of the promotion he could receive with help from the IRS.

Maxwell Rosenthal turned to Linda. "It worked; I've got an address."

Nathan and Linda clapped with joy. "When can we go, honey?" Linda asked.

"Just as soon as we can get everything ready. You finish up the packing, and I'll take care of some other details."

Linda busied herself with the unpleasant task of packing all of their few possessions while Nathan made all the necessary preparations and loaded the car. He and Linda had decided between themselves what they must do. Max and Judy agreed with their plans but would purposely be kept in the dark of the details. Maxwell gave them several thousand dollars in cash as well as the title to his car so they wouldn't have to use any credit cards.

"I wish I could give you more."

"I'll pay you back some day. I promise." Nathan paused. "Thanks. I'll never forget this."

"I know you will, but that is the least of our concerns right now. The important thing is for you to get the boys back and to find a safe place to hide out until all of this is finally over." The two men hugged like two buddies who had been brought together in battle.

At six in the evening, Nathan and Linda drove out of the driveway and began their forty-five-minute drive to Denver. They would forever be grateful for all that Maxwell and Judy had done for them and didn't know how they would ever be able to pay them back.

At seven thirty, it was nearly dark. Nathan drove slowly up Butterfield Road, looking for the number. Linda shouted, "There it is!" and then added, "And there they are!" She pointed and began bouncing in the car seat. "There, see them?"

Nathan saw Matthew and Allen playing in the front yard. As the car eased slowly by the house, neither of them noticed the car passing by them. Nathan decided to drive on by as a precaution and to make sure no one was following them. Linda could hardly contain her excitement of seeing her two boys again.

The car moved close to the curb, and Nathan hoped that they would see them. Allen looked at the car, then suddenly recognized his parents. "Look, Matt, it's Mom and Dad!" Both boys came running toward the car.

Nathan grinned, and Linda opened the back door. "You boys get in; you're coming with us now."

"What about Mr. and Mrs. Ackerman? Shouldn't we tell them we're leaving?" Matthew asked.

"No, honey, it's better if you don't tell them anything. We have to get out of here and fast." Linda turned around, and putting her knees in the front seat, she leaned over and began hugging both boys, kissing them on the face. "I missed you guys."

Matthew closed the car door. Nathan stepped on the accelerator. He wanted to hug both of his boys, but right now his focus was to get as far away from this place as possible.

"Are we going home now?" Matthew asked.

"I can't wait to get home to my toys and computer games," Allen added. "Do you know these people didn't even own a computer, Dad?"

Linda turned around to face both of them. Her expression changed from joy to sadness. "Boys, I'm afraid we have some bad news. Our house has been sold and all of our possessions with it. We don't have anything left."

"Do you mean they took our baseball card collection?" Matthew yelled. "And all our clothes?"

"I'm afraid so, honey. We've been staying at some friends' house since we were released from the hospital. This is even their car. The IRS has taken everything." Linda's eyes filled with tears as she spoke. She fought the urge to cry, wiping her eyes quickly.

Nathan reached his hand over to hers and squeezed it gently. Matthew leaned forward and patted her on the shoulder. "It's okay, Mom. At least we're together again."

Allen sat up closer to the front seat. "Where are we going now?"

It was Nathan's turn to explain. "We're going on a long journey. I can tell you boys something right now. We'll probably not ever be returning to Colorado again. We're going far away to another country. But first, we have to make a few stops along the way."

Nathan turned onto the interstate. He felt relieved to be on the open road. His mind drifted, thinking about what the Ackermans would be going through when they discovered both boys were missing.

****

Mrs. Ackerman looked outside and could not see the boys playing in the yard. "Now, where did they go?" she mumbled to herself. She walked out the front door and looked up the street both ways. She began calling their names, walking closer to the street. *They're good boys. They wouldn't run off without telling me. Where could they be?*

She felt panic set in and began running up the street calling their names. Then she saw something on the ground. "Oh, no," she cried. Her heart beat faster. She bent over to pick up the object. It was the toy airplane Allen had been playing with in the front yard. "Allen! Matthew!" she yelled again and again.

There was no response. She ran to the house, picked up the phone, and dialed 911. The police arrived within minutes. Once they received the details and phoned in a report, the department suspected that the parents had kidnapped their children. An APB was put out for Nathan and Linda in a five-state area.

CHAPTER THIRTY-SEVEN

When Molly Shanks regained consciousness again for the second time, Tom and Lucy were by her side. "Hello there," Tom said. "Welcome back to the real world."

Lucy took Molly's hand in hers. "We were worried about you, thought you were never going to wake up."

Molly opened her eyes further and tried to sit up. She continued trying to focus and collect her thoughts. "Where am I? How long have I been asleep?"

Tom reached over to pour her a glass of water and offered it to her. "You're in the hospital. You were in a coma for several days. You came out of it yesterday but have been asleep almost ever since. Do you remember how you got here?"

Molly sat in the bed, drinking the water, looking bewildered. Water dripped down her chin, and Lucy reached over with a napkin to wipe it gently. Molly was puzzled by the thoughts that kept trying to come to the surface. She could only catch glimpses of events over the past few days. She couldn't separate her dreams from reality. She shook her head. "No, I'm afraid that I can't recall."

Tom decided to try something; it was a long shot, but he didn't have anything else. "Someone tried to kill you by making you take an overdose of sleeping pills. Do you remember anyone being in your home?"

Molly searched the depths of her mind. *Think! I've got to remember.* Then another picture flashed through her mind. *A man. There's a man in my room.* The picture went away.

Tom continued, "Molly, I believe you can remember. Don't force it. Relax and think back over the last time you were in your bedroom. You're getting ready for bed. Perhaps you heard a noise or saw someone.

Molly closed her eyes. The thoughts raced through her memory but were gone as fast as they came. *A man in my room, yes, there he is. He has a gun.* She shouted out loud, "The man has a gun!"

"So there was a man; what does he look like? Who is he? Have you ever seen him before?"

The picture was becoming more complete. Memories flooded her mind, and the pieces began to come together. "He forced me to take sleeping pills. He said he would shoot me if I didn't. Then he threatened to kill my cat." Her words were deliberate, almost forced.

Tom and Lucy smiled at each other. "That's good," Tom said. "Now, keep thinking. Do you know who did it? What did he say to you?" Tom took the note she had written out of his pocket. He had copied it the night she was found. "Do you remember writing this? Were you trying to tell us something?"

Molly read the note, and joy filled her being. "Yes! I remember now. Look at the first letter of the first three words of each paragraph. This guy, I'm sure, had something to do with the IRS, about that document."

"I knew it! I knew you were telling us something." He reached down and gave her a big hug. "You did good, Molly; you did good. You don't have to worry about anything. We have twenty-four-hour police protection watching over you. No one will come through that door who's not authorized and screened."

Lucy patted her hand. "You get your rest now. Can we get you anything? Juice? More water?"

"No. I'm fine now, thank you. It's so nice of you to come by and see me."

Tom's eyes watered. "We're just glad you're going to be okay. I feel responsible for getting you into this situation. I mean, if I hadn't found that document on your computer, then you wouldn't have—"

Molly reached up and put her finger to his lips to stop him. "I wanted to help. It was my choice, not yours. Now, I want to help more than ever. Where do we go from here?" Suddenly, Molly had a new burst of energy.

Tom looked at Molly. "Well, partner, I guess we'd better take our case to the FBI and let them begin working on it."

Lucy glanced at Tom. "Do you think they'll believe this story? It does seem a little farfetched, even to me."

"We won't know until we try. At least, we have a live witness instead of a dead one. We'll just tell them everything we know and let them go to work on it. Why don't we let you get some rest now? You've been a big help. I'll let you know what happens. And don't worry about a thing; there are two policemen outside your door. You'll be okay."

Tom and Lucy left the hospital. On the way back to his office, they stopped at a pay phone and made an appointment to see an the Director of the FBI in Washington. "Three o'clock will be fine. I'll be there." Tom hung up the phone and, out of habit, checked for change and found a quarter. He flipped it up in the air. "This must be my lucky day." He caught the coin and leaped into the air, clicking his heels together.

Lucy watched him from the car in amazement. "You look like you just won the lottery." She grinned.

"Nope, I'm just delighted to get this whole matter off my back, happy that Molly Shanks is alive, and besides all that, I found a quarter." He flipped it into the air again, catching it before it hit the ground.

"Wow, a whole quarter. Where are you taking me for lunch?" Then she quickly added, "And don't say the Blue Moon Diner."

"Okay then, how about a Big Mac from McDonald's?"

"That'll be better than that greasy spoon diner you call a restaurant." Lucy rolled her eyes and laughed.

****

Tom had been inside the J. Edgar Hoover Building many times and had even been to the Director's office before. But, today he felt different. *Why do I feel nervous? I'm not a criminal. I haven't done anything wrong,* he thought.

After waiting for almost forty-five minutes, the director came out and shook his hand. "Hello, Senator. I'm sorry to keep you waiting, but I was called away from my desk, and it took longer than I thought it would. I'm Frank Mitchell. We met once before, a couple of years back, when you first came to Washington."

Tom didn't remember him, but there had been a lot of people he had met over the years. He never was good at remembering names or faces. Frank led him into his office, a large office, with a beautiful view of the Capitol Building. One wall was filled with books from floor to ceiling.

Tom glanced around the office, admiring the fine wood furniture and leather chairs. "This is some office you have here. I can see I chose the wrong field."

Frank shrugged. "You know J. Edgar Hoover spared no expense to keep his boys happy. All of this was purchased back when he was director. I refurbished it a little. Now, sit down and tell me what's on your mind, Senator." Tom sat on the sofa while the director sat in a large leather chair.

He reached to the table beside him and flipped a switch. "You won't mind if we record this conversation, will you?"

Tom hesitated and then agreed. He wasn't sure where to begin, so he decided to go all the way back to the first phone call from Colorado. Forty-five minutes later, he paused then said, "So, that's when I decided to come to the FBI."

Frank had jotted down some notes during the course of Tom's account of what had happened. He glanced at his scribbling. "Let me make sure I understand you here. Your friend, Molly Shanks, is saying that someone from the IRS tried to kill her?"

"The person may not have been with the IRS, but it is my opinion that someone from the IRS hired him. I would stake my career on it."

"But, you don't have any proof, am I right?"

"Yes, but if you put all the pieces together, they fit. First a guy in Colorado Springs, a Raymond Phillips, gets shot, then George Shanks commits suicide by jumping out of his office building. After that, Douglas Preston, the man who helped me retrieve the document is killed in a bizarre automobile accident, and finally, Molly Shanks supposedly tries to commit suicide. The one thing each of these people has in common is that they all have seen the IRS document. This theory would not have worked had Molly Shanks died like she was supposed to, but now she is willing to testify that someone tried to kill her and make it look like a suicide. I believe Douglas Preston's death was made to look like an accident, and Phillips' shooting was made to look like a burglary."

Frank jotted another note on his pad. "But the fact remains, we still don't have any proof. If we are going to be successful, we have to have evidence. Being a former prosecuting attorney, you know that."

"Yeah, I know, but I also know that sometimes, when the evidence is lacking, you have to go with your hunches and follow your instinct. My instinct tells me that there is someone in the Treasury Department who is desperate and will stop at nothing to stop this from becoming public."

Frank stood up and walked over to his desk to look at his calendar and caseload. "Okay, I'll tell you what, Senator, we'll send a couple of agents to talk with Mrs. Shanks. I'll have our Colorado office check with this Maxwell Rosenthal and Nathan Daniels. Give us a couple of weeks, and we'll see what we can come up with."

"A couple of weeks?" Tom shouted. "We don't have a couple of weeks. All of us may be dead by then. These guys are playing hardball."

Frank leaned forward, placing both hands, palms down, on his desk, and spoke in a patronizing tone, "I understand, Senator, but we've got many other cases with real criminals, with real hard evidence, and with real live witnesses we are working to solve. As usual, we are shorthanded. I will do my best to do some investigation on this one, but we can't drop everything else to investigate the IRS." He paused for a moment then continued, "By the way, why haven't they tried to kill you? You've seen the document."

Tom stood up and walked toward Frank. "I don't know for sure. Maybe it's because I'm a senator and they're afraid my death will bring too much publicity. Or maybe it's because they know I have the document and they want it back."

"Speaking of the document, did you bring it with you?"

"No. I didn't want to chance carrying it around. It's in a safe place."

"Well, we'll want to see it sooner or later. I'll be in touch." Frank reached out his hand, and they shook.

Tom left the office not really feeling relieved that he had come but hoping that at least maybe they could get to the bottom of this whole situation.

CHAPTER THIRTY-EIGHT

Calvin Davis had never met the Shark. No one really knew who the Shark was or where he worked. The Shark was a code name for someone within the government who called all of the shots. When normal channels didn't work, the Shark, by hiring the right people, always got results. He was nicknamed the Shark because he was perceived as being vicious and cruel, and showed no mercy to his victims. He often used underhanded and even illegal means to collect what was rightfully due the IRS. There was nothing, it seemed, that the Shark couldn't get accomplished. He had contacts all over the world and could literally get a job done by the press of a button or as quick as a phone call.

For this reason, the identity of the Shark was top secret. He could be contacted only by certain individuals within the service and only through a closed computer system, which could be accessed only by a few selected officials. He could never be reached by telephone but would occasionally call in and discuss details about a particular case.

Calvin Davis had worked with the Shark on many occasions, but this case was the most complex. The Shark was on the phone. "Yes, sir, that is correct. We just received word from Colorado that Nathan and Linda have disappeared."

The Shark's voice sounded distorted as it passed through a voice scrambler. "I want you to get your men on the West Coast to put out an alert for them. We want them found. They have to surface somewhere. All other cases are to be placed on hold. This one is top priority. Now, what is the status of Molly Shanks?"

"Sir, she has recovered but so far hasn't remembered anything. Since our guy bungled the last attempt, they have put police guards around her."

"Surely, you can find someone on staff in that hospital who can help us. We have to get rid of her. She is our only witness that can link us to this case. We can't chance that she would be alive to talk."

The Shark changed his tone. "Davis, here's what we've decided to do. We must eliminate the three remaining couples, and I need your help. I'll have my guys in Colorado deal with the Rosenthals and Danielses if we can locate them. The senator and his wife must both be taken out on your end. If we can't get the documents back, then so be it. If they surface as they have threatened, we'll deal with that when it happens, but at least we won't have any witnesses. Baskins has been able to discredit these people successfully.

"Now, listen to me carefully. Each of these deaths has to be accidental and must be successful. We can have no more of these bungled jobs, is that understood?"

Calvin cleared his throat. "Yes, sir. I'll take care of it on this end."

"Fine, I'm counting on you."

"Sir, there is one other thing you should know," Calvin said, hesitant to reveal this new information.

"What's that?" the Shark asked.

"This afternoon, Tom Haden spent quite a bit of time in the FBI building. We don't know what was said, but we are confident it had to do with this case."

There was dead silence on the other end of the phone. Finally, the Shark spoke slowly, "This is why we must have no more mistakes. Make sure whoever you hire is a professional and will get the task completed. Pay whatever it takes to get the best man for the job. You have my list of contacts so just pick one. I'll talk to you later."

Calvin was relieved to get off the phone with him. His hands were sweaty, and he could feel the beads of perspiration on his forehead. He had been doing this for ten years, and he still got very nervous when he talked with the Shark. Calvin often wondered about the true identity of this man they called the Shark and was curious if he had ever met him. He often suspected Howard Baskins but could not be certain about his suspicions. He assumed he would never know for sure.

****

Calvin Davis sat alone in his car on a deserted pier in Baltimore. *Why did it have to be way up here? Why not in DC, closer to home?* he wondered to himself. He laid his pistol in the front seat, touching it for assurance. *He better not try anything with me or I'll ...* He interrupted his own thoughts and began arguing with himself, *Or you'll what, Calvin? Shoot him? You've never shot anyone in your life.* He countered back, *Yeah, but I could if I wanted to. I know it.* His fingers went around the trigger. His whole life had been a lie. He pretended to be this brave Vietnam vet who had been a hero. The truth was, he had been a coward. He ran in the heat of battle and had allowed his friends to be shot and killed without helping them. When he was discovered wandering through the jungle, he told a different story, one that made him sound like a real hero, a lone survivor.

The memory still haunted him. *You coward. You are a yellow-belly coward.* But, this time would be different. *I'll be brave, and I'll fight.*

A man in a dark suit strolled up beside his window and tapped on it. Calvin jumped out of his skin. He hadn't seen him approach. He rolled down the window. "You scared the crap out of me."

The man in the suit grinned. "Sorry about that. Did you bring the rest of my money?"

Calvin felt for the gun beside him before he answered, "Yes, but we have a problem."

"What do you mean we have a problem? I want my money. I've tried twice and deserve my cash."

"That's my point. You've tried twice, but you didn't accomplish it, now did you?" Calvin moved the gun toward the window and stuck it in the man's face, cocking the pistol at the same time. "Now, maybe you'll listen to reason."

The man put both hands in the air and began backing up from the car. "Hey, man, you don't have to shoot me. Watch where you point that thing."

Calvin opened his car door and slowly eased out. "You see, there is not going to be any money because you didn't complete your contract. This is my rule, and you have to play by it."

The man in the suit let out a whistle, and in a split second, three men appeared out of nowhere, all pointing machine guns at Calvin. The man in the suit put a big grin on his face. "I think you have met my friends before."

Calvin recognized them as the ones who had beat him up in the parking lot. "So those were your thugs. I suspected that but didn't know for sure."

"Yes, these are my thugs, and I suggest, Mr. Davis, that you present me with my money right now so you can be on your way. I don't want to shoot a federal agent, but I will if I have to, am I communicating?"

Calvin lowered his gun and opened the back door. "It's in here." He reached in and brought out a brown leather briefcase. "It's all here."

The man in the suit walked slowly to Calvin, took the briefcase, laid it on the car, and opened it. It was full of one-hundred-dollar bills, one hundred thousand dollars. "Looks good; call me if I can ever be of any assistance to you again. You have my number."

The man in the suit lifted up his hand to his partners, and they opened fire on the car … three machine guns blasting. Calvin hit the ground. They fired at the car, shattering the glass and filling the car with holes on three sides. Calvin lay on the ground, his face buried in the concrete screaming for them to stop. When they ran out of bullets, they laughed and walked away. One of them shouted, "Hey, Mr. Davis, you better stop driving government vehicles; you keep tearing them up." They all laughed and disappeared.

Calvin began crying, relieved he had not been shot but also remembering the days in Vietnam.

CHAPTER THIRTY-NINE

Matthew and Allen slept soundly in the back seat of the car. Nathan pulled into a parking spot. They had been driving all night, and it was a little after nine in the morning. "How about some breakfast?" he yelled, trying to wake the boys up.

"I'm starved," Linda responded.

The boys began to stir, rubbing their eyes, yawning, and stretching. "Where we at, Dad?" Matthew asked, still blurry eyed.

"We're in some little town in North Dakota, just south of the Canadian border. We'll stay here for a few days until we get some things settled, then we're going into Canada."

Nathan stood outside the car and stretched, doing a few deep knee bends to loosen up his muscles. The others piled out of the car, doing the same. They walked slowly toward the restaurant. The place was bustling with activity. The Daniels family stood out among the crowd as strangers, city folk, passing through, or so it seemed to them.

The waitress smiled with a big grin. "How are you folks today? Do you want a booth or a table?"

"Either will be fine," Nathan answered.

"Haven't seen you here before; where you from?" the waitress asked, trying to sound friendly but just wanting to be nosy.

"Uh, no. We have some business in town and will be here a few days."

"Business? What kind of business brings you way out here in no man's land?" She sat them at the table, laying the menus in front of them.

Nathan really didn't want to talk about it and decided to change the subject. "Where is a good motel in this place?"

"Well, I don't know how good it is, but it's the only one we got. It's just a mile down the road on your right, going toward the border. What did you say your business was again?" She stood there with a hand on her hip, bracing herself against the booth with her other hand.

Nathan smiled at her. "I didn't. What do you recommend to eat this morning?"

She finally took the hint. "You'll find that one thing is just as greasy and bad as the other. You want coffee?"

"Yes, please, two coffees and two milks."

"I want orange juice, Dad," Allen yelled.

"Okay, make it one milk and one orange juice."

"I'll be right back to take your orders." She sauntered back into the kitchen.

Allen jumped up on his knees and pointed across the room. "Look, Mom, there are real Indians in here."

"Shut up, you idiot." Matthew poked his brother in the ribs.

"Mom, Matthew hit me."

"Both of you calm down," Linda said softly. "Allen, keep your voice down; someone might hear you."

Nathan leaned in close and whispered, "Yeah, and they might come over here and scalp you."

Linda shot Nathan an unpleasant look.

The waitress came back with their drinks and took their order. She leaned over close to Allen and whispered, "Not only is he an Indian, he is a chief. But don't worry; he's at peace with the white man." She smiled and walked away.

Allen's eyes grew wider. "Wow, a real Indian chief."

Linda leaned on Nathan's shoulder. "I'm tired. I just want a hot shower and a warm bed. I feel like I could sleep forever."

Nathan hugged her. "I know what you mean. After we eat, we'll find the motel in town and see if we can get a room. We'll clean up, then we'll visit the courthouse."

Linda smiled. "I still don't understand fully what we're going to do at the courthouse."

"Don't worry about it. When we get there, I'll show you. Look, here's our food already. That was fast," he said to the waitress as she put the plates in front of them.

"Can I get you anything else?" she asked politely.

"We could use a warm-up on our coffee. Thanks."

They all began to eat as if they hadn't eaten in a week and were soon satisfied.

216

"Nothing like a good hearty breakfast to give you a whole new outlook on life," Nathan said to the boys.

After breakfast, they made their way to the motel. It certainly wasn't much to look at from the outside. There were fifteen little individual cottages in a semicircle, each with a little carport attached and in bad need of painting.

"Do we have to stay here?" Matthew screamed.

"They're ugly! Can't we go to a Holiday Inn?" Allen echoed. "They don't even have a swimming pool."

"No, I'm afraid this is it. Don't worry; we'll only be here a night or two. It won't be so bad. Pretend you're camping out." Linda tried adding a positive note to the situation.

"I'd rather sleep outside in a tent than in this dump," Matthew responded.

Nathan returned to the car with a key in hand. "We're in cottage number twelve, in the back."

The screen door creaked as it opened. Nathan put the key in the lock and opened the inside door, revealing a tiny room with two double beds. There was barely enough room to walk around the beds. A bare light bulb on the ceiling gave off the only light in the room. Linda walked into the bathroom, turned, and said, "Well, at least the bathroom is clean." She jumped back and screamed as a roach ran across the floor in front of her. "Oh, great, we have guests."

Nathan killed the roach. He and the boys brought the luggage in and sat them beside the bed. The boys flopped onto one bed, and Nathan lay down on the other. Allen reached up and turned on the old television set, turning the channel in search of a station. He found only two, and they were both fuzzy and full of static. He hit the television set with his open palm, turning it off. "Man, this place sucks."

"Believe it or not, man can survive without television," Linda remarked.

"As a matter of fact," Nathan added, "scientists have discovered that man can actually survive indefinitely without the use of television, radio, computer, or CD player." Nathan and Linda both laughed. Matthew and Allen just stared blankly at both of their parents.

"Are you going to shower before we go into town?" Nathan asked, still lying on the bed with his hands behind his head.

Linda gave him a sorrowful look. "After seeing the facilities, a hot shower doesn't sound as appealing as it did. I think I'll just go like I am. Do you boys want to stay here, or should we go with your daddy?"

Matthew and Allen looked around the room and then at each other and in unison shouted, "Go with you!"

They all piled back into the car and headed toward town. Nathan parked in front of the courthouse. "Why don't you boys wait for us right here inside the courthouse, while your mother and I take care of some business. We may be awhile, so sit here and read your book or something."

Linda looked around the room, reluctant to leave the boys alone. "I can stay here with them; you go ahead."

"I'm going to need you to help me. It will be faster. They'll be all right. The police station is right here. Nothing is going to happen."

Matthew and Allen sat down, both of them not too happy about being stuck inside an old courthouse.

Nathan and Linda walked down the hall looking for the sign that read *County Records*. "Here, this way," he said as he pulled Linda to the right. They opened the old wooden doors and walked to the counter. An older woman with large glasses worked busily at her desk, pretending not to notice them. Nathan cleared his throat to get her attention, but she continued working at her desk.

"Excuse me," Nathan said, raising his voice slightly. "Could I get some service?"

The lady laid down her glasses and looked up. "Yeah, what do you want?"

"I need to look through your records of births and deaths. I'm doing a story on someone and would like to browse through your files." Nathan could only hope she would buy this and not ask too many questions.

"Sure, help yourself. Just go straight down this hall; the third door on the right has all the records." She put her glasses back on and continued working, paying no attention to Nathan and Linda.

They found the room and slowly walked inside. Nathan didn't quite know where to begin, and Linda noticed.

"What are we looking for?" Linda asked.

"We need to find the records showing the deaths." Nathan was scanning the room, reading the various shelves. The room was filled with shelves from floor to ceiling, each about three feet apart. Located on the shelves were all kinds of records, including books recording every event of public record in the history of the county.

"There they are." Linda pointed at a group of shelves marked *Death Certificates*. Nathan began running his finger down the sides of the books then pulled one off the shelf. He turned page after page, reading the information. Linda watched closely over his shoulder, still not knowing fully what it was they were seeking.

"Here's one! Look at this." He pointed to an entry that showed the individual's name and date of birth.

"I don't get it." Linda shrugged her shoulders. "What does this have to do with us?"

Nathan explained, "Here is a male individual who was born about the same time I was, so he would be my age. But look at this." He pointed across the page to the other entry that showed the date of death just two years later.

Linda still looked puzzled. "I must be dense because I still don't understand what we are doing. What is so important about someone who died when he was two years old?"

"Simple. Public records are not computerized, at least not in these small towns, and they do not match birth certificates with death certificates. We are going through the death certificates looking for someone who was born about the same year we were but who died at an early age."

"Okay, that part I understand, but why someone who died when they were young?"

"That's the best part of my plan. If the person died as a child, there was never a Social Security number issued for him, so I don't have to worry about getting a duplicate. We order a copy of the birth certificate, use that to apply for a new driver's license and Social Security card, and presto, we have a new identity."

Linda stepped back, stunned. "A new identity? Do you mean ..." She paused.

"It's the only way to get completely away from our government and keep the boys. It is the only way I'll be able to get a job without the fear of being tracked down. It's the only way we'll be able to get into another country legally and alive."

Linda was puzzled again. "How will this get us into another country?"

"Simple. We apply for our passports once we have our new identities and fly away into the sunset."

"And I suppose we'll live happily ever after. Why didn't you tell me all of this before now?" Linda asked sounding irritated.

"To be honest, I was afraid to tell you, afraid you'd try and talk me out of it. When Maxwell gave me the idea, I was taken aback at first myself. But I've thought a lot about this plan, and believe me, honey, it's our only way out." Nathan took her in his arms and hugged her. "It's going to be okay." After a long period of silence, he continued, "We'd better keep looking."

Nathan turned the page in the binder and scanned it. Finally, after an hour, he yelled, "Here's one that's perfect; I could still use my first name."

"What's the chances we'll find someone with my first name?" Linda asked.

"I wouldn't count on that to happen. I'll just call you honey, like I always do, and the boys will call you Mom. Let's keep looking and see what we can find. Here, you take this." Nathan handed her another book. He wrote down all the necessary information from the record.

"Do we have to find one for the boys too?"

"Yes, but let's find ours first."

Linda continued reading the death notices, comparing the dates of death with the dates of birth. After going through several pages of records, she cried out, "Here's one! Will this work?" She pointed to the entry. "This would be perfect; I'd be two years younger."

Nathan looked over the entry and wrote down the information on his notepad. "Okay, let's go ahead and find another one for each of us in case these two don't work. Then we'll find the boys'."

They spent another forty-five minutes going through the records, locating two more names that would match approximately their own age.

"Now what do we do?" Linda asked.

"Now we write to the courthouse and ask them to send us a copy of our birth certificates, which we have lost."

"And they'll just send them to us without checking who we are?"

"That's certainly what I hope will happen if Max is correct."

Linda's face appeared puzzled. "But won't they cross check with the death certificates and find out we're dead?"

"It's my understanding that none of the courthouses really do a cross check. The death certificates are filed in one place and the birth certificates in another. What we have to hope for is that these two people were both born in this county. It is likely they were since they were so young when they died. But that's why I wanted to get a couple of other names, just in case."

As they continued their search for some names that matched the boy's ages, Linda smiled at Nathan and admired his expertise in this area. "Where did you learn about this?"

"I saw something on television about it a long time ago. It was a special on how people disappear and get new identities. Some detective was telling about this method. I had no idea at the time I'd ever be using it and didn't catch the whole thing. When I asked Maxwell about it, he confirmed that it would probably work. Let's go find our boys."

When they walked to the entrance, the boys were gone, and Linda's heart sank. They both began to run toward the doors and out of the courthouse, looking around as they did so. To their relief, Matthew and Allen were just outside sitting on the steps, hands propped up under their chins, looking totally bored. "Hey, fellows," Nathan yelled, "ready to go?"

Matthew stood up and walked slowly toward them. "We've been ready for a long time. This place is the pits."

Allen joined in, "Yeah, it's totally boring here."

Linda placed her arms around their shoulders. "Well, we can go now. We've finished our business. How about an ice-cream cone for a reward?"

Both boys' faces brightened with a smile. "Can I get a topping on mine?" Matthew asked.

"Yes, you can have a topping and a double scoop in a waffle cone." Nathan grabbed Allen and threw him onto his shoulders and began running toward the ice-cream parlor.

Nathan wasn't sure how he was going to explain all of this to the boys, but he knew that sooner or later they would need to know. He really didn't want to think about it right now. It felt good, at least for the moment, to be leading a normal life and having fun with his two boys.

CHAPTER FORTY

Janet gave her boss an update on what had been happening to their clients. Maxwell half-listened to what she was saying as he stared out the window. "Mr. Rosenthal, we've got to do something. Our clients are calling us one after another. The IRS is still harassing them and spreading lies about your firm. Can't we stop them somehow?"

Max sat quietly, not responding, lost in his own thoughts.

She continued, "We've lost over a dozen clients already, and I'm afraid we're going to lose more if something isn't done right away."

Maxwell turned slowly around in his chair to face her. "Come over here." Janet walked around to the other side of the desk with a questionable look on her face. Maxwell pointed down below. "Do you see the black sedan parked on the side street over there?"

Janet leaned toward the window to get a better look. "The one with the tinted windows? What about it?"

"Those guys are following me everywhere I go. I see them outside my house, at the office, when I go out at night. They are constantly watching and probably listening to what we say."

"I thought we had the office debugged."

"Oh, we did, but they still have devices. They can sit in their cozy little cars, aim microphones at us, and pick up much of our conversation." He placed his hands to his mouth and screamed at them in anger, "Can't you?"

"So that's why you've been playing the stereo so loud around the office."

"You got it, and that's why I installed outside speakers around my house that blast music. Of course, the neighbors are starting to complain."

Janet returned to her chair. "So what do they want? Why are they trying to destroy you?"

"They want their precious little document back, the one I tried to get made public. But now, I believe they want me. They won't be satisfied until I'm dead. That's why I never showed you the document. I didn't want to put your life in danger. We know for a fact that they have killed two people and tried to kill a third one."

"Who are they? Our government?" Janet raised her voice in alarm, trying to keep it quiet.

"Like any organization, they hire outside thugs to do their dirty work. There is no way to track it back to them, at least not yet. We don't have the evidence. But to answer your question, yes, it's our government or someone in our government doing this. And he's doing it to protect his own career."

"What can I do to help, Max?" Janet asked.

"The best thing you can do is to continue running this office as if nothing has happened. Do the best you can to keep up your day-to-day activities. I'll think of something. Meanwhile, I have to go to New York City on Friday, so make my reservations for me. Judy will be flying with me, and we'll be staying the weekend. Put us in the new Marriott on Broadway. She'll like that."

Janet stood up. She could always tell by the tone in his voice when the meeting was over. "Is there anything else?"

"Not right now. I'll be leaving for a while; I have an appointment across town. I should be back in two hours. Keep the clients happy if you can."

Janet returned to her desk, picked up the phone, and began dialing the travel agent.

Maxwell picked up the phone and called Judy. "Hi there; what are you doing?"

"I'm surprised you called. I just got out of the shower."

"Hmm, sorry I missed it."

"Still not too late, if you want to come by for lunch."

"Sorry, can't today. I only called to tell you to pack your bags. We're flying to the Big Apple for the weekend. I've got tickets to a Broadway play, and it'll just be the two of us."

"Just the two of us? Do you mean no business associates?"

"Well, I do have business on Friday morning, but I'll be free the rest of the weekend. I figured we deserved some time together. It's been a long time since we took a real vacation."

"Why, Maxwell, you're beginning to sound like a caring husband. What's the catch?"

"No catch. Just pack your bags; we're flying out Friday morning. I'll be home late tonight. I've gotta go, bye. Love you!"

Maxwell hung up the phone, grabbed his suit coat, put it on, and began straightening his tie. He stopped in front of the mirror and adjusted his collar and worked with his tie some more. He thought to himself, *I hope they heard all of that. At least you turkeys can't read my mind. There. That looks better. I look like a successful lawyer anyway.*

Janet was busy on the telephone as he walked by her desk, She acknowledged him leaving, and he waved. Maxwell stepped into the empty elevator. Standing alone inside, he had a terrible urge to scream at the top of his lungs. He did. The scream echoed inside the elevator, almost vibrating the plastic light covers on the ceiling. Just as he was at the height of the scream, the doors opened, and he realized the people standing there had heard him. He smiled awkwardly then mumbled an explanation, "I'm claustrophobic. Don't like closed-in places. My doctor said if I scream, it helps."

The other passengers slowly entered the elevator, ignoring him and standing to the other side. Max was laughing on the inside. *I feel like a real nut, but I feel so much better now.*

As Maxwell began walking down the street, the black sedan slowly pulled away from the curb. He caught a reflection in one of the windows and saw one of the men jump out of the car to follow him on foot. Maxwell decided to play a little game of cat and mouse. Instead of walking away from the men following him, he turned around and walked toward them. The one on foot tried to act inconspicuous and turned to gaze at a picture window. Maxwell walked up to him and said, "Hello there. Let me make your life a little easier."

The government agent in his dark-blue suit was caught totally off-guard. He was speechless.

Maxwell continued, "I'm going to my favorite restaurant to get a bite to eat. Could I buy you and your partner some lunch? That way, you won't have to try and keep up with me. Besides, I like to get to know those people who are following me. It gives me a better feeling. After lunch, I'm going to go get fitted for a new suit. You could join me and help pick it out. I just love your taste in clothes. Dark blue is in this year, you know."

The agent stared at Maxwell in disbelief. He tried to pretend that he had no idea what Maxwell was talking about. He turned and walked quickly toward the car, opened the door, and jumped inside. The car sped off, leaving Maxwell on the sidewalk laughing.

Upon entering the restaurant, Maxwell walked to the rear. He found the back door and slipped into the alley. Being careful not to be seen, he ran down several back streets until he reached an office building. He went in the side door and found the elevator. It was an old building, and the elevator jerked and groaned. When it finally stopped at the eleventh floor, he stepped off, relieved to have made it safely. *Maybe I'll take the stairs back down*, he thought.

He read the name on the door to be sure it was the right place and then opened it. The room was dark and musty. A florescent light hung over the desk in the reception area. The office was painted a pale-green color with dark wood trim. The furniture came right out of a 1920s movie. Magazines and newspapers were strewn all over the coffee table and chairs. Old coffee cups and Coke bottles sat around the room looking like they had been there for days.

Maxwell cringed with disgust and was greeted by a young blond wearing a bright-red, skintight dress that had a slit in it revealing her thigh. The office and the young woman reminded him of something out of one of those old detective movies.

"May I help you?" she asked in a pleasant girlish voice. Her eyes looked Maxwell up and down, making him feel most uncomfortable.

"Yes, I have an appointment with Mr. Blackwell."

She looked down at her calendar and pointed to an entry with her bright-red fingernail. "You must be Maxwell Rosenthal; just have a seat over there. I'll tell him you're here." She turned toward the office and yelled, "Hey, Barney, your one o'clock appointment is out here."

Barney Blackwell emerged from his office feeling embarrassed by his secretary's behavior. He wasn't anything like what Maxwell expected. He was short and overweight, and had a mustache that was in bad need of a trim. Maxwell couldn't believe that this was the same man who had come so highly recommended over the years by some of his colleagues though he had never personally used him.

Maxwell stood up to introduce himself. He held out his hand, but Barney ignored it, motioning him to come inside. "Sorry about the mess and my secretary. It's hard to get good help these days. She's my wife, so like Rodney Dangerfield says, 'I can't get no respect.' What can I do for you?"

Maxwell took a seat in one of the old wooden armchairs. It didn't feel very secure so he sat down lightly, listening to the wood crack. "I need you to do something for me. I'm willing to pay well for the service, but I can't explain much about it. I'll do the best I can."

After Maxwell had explained everything he needed done, Barney stood up. "That's it? That's all I got to do, and you'll pay me twenty-five thousand dollars for it?"

"That's all there is to it. I need your help, and I'm willing to pay you the twenty-five thousand dollars plus all your expenses. I'll give you half now and the rest when you complete the job."

"You got yourself a detective, Mr. Rosenthal." Barney reached out his hand to shake. This time, Maxwell ignored it and then reached into his pocket and pulled out the money.

"I believe you'll find it all there. One last thing, you can't tell anyone that I'm your client and be sure not to tell anyone what you're doing for me. Can your wife keep her mouth shut?"

"Jenny? Oh yeah, especially when you pay her to keep it shut." He picked up the bills and waved them in the air. "No problem there, trust me."

After all the arrangements had been made and gone over thoroughly, Maxwell made a quick exit. He decided to take the stairs. Returning to his office, he couldn't help but wonder if he would get away with it. *Time will tell. I'll know this weekend,* he thought. *Now all I have to do is explain all this to Judy.*

****

Judy was shocked at first but understood that it had to be done. She knew that there was no way to talk Maxwell out of going through with his plan, so she decided to support his decision.

****

On Thursday at exactly 9:00 PM, the Blackwells drove into the driveway in a rented Lincoln. Maxwell yelled to Judy, "They're here. The Johnsons are here."

Judy yelled downstairs, "I'll be down in a minute. It's been so long since we've seen them; I have to look my best. Give me a few minutes."

Maxwell opened the door and greeted them warmly, "Bob, Sharon, it's so good to see both of you again. How in the world have you two been? Neither of you have changed a bit, except Sharon here seems to have gotten prettier." He hugged each of them as he spoke, giving Sharon an extra squeeze.

"We've been great, just great. This is some place you have here. How long have you lived here?"

"Oh, it's been about five years. I can't believe it's been that long since we saw you two last. What brings you to town?"

Sharon kept quiet other than an occasional acknowledgment of a question. Bob did most of the talking. After drinks were served, Judy made her entrance. Neither of the two were what she had expected, but she knew her lines and recited them as she entered the room, "Bob, Sharon." She opened her arms to receive the total strangers.

Bob took full advantage of the opportunity, taking Judy into his arms and holding her as close to his body as he could. "Why, you are as beautiful as a cat on a Saturday night. You haven't changed a lick since I saw you last. How you been doing, honey?"

Judy was noticeably annoyed and turned to Sharon. "Look at you; I believe you've lost some weight."

Sharon faked it, "At least thirty pounds since we last saw you. I've been working out, and that's helped firm me up." She made a gesture, patting her stomach, while at the same time rolling her eyes at Maxwell.

Maxwell cleared his throat, turning quickly to Judy. "Could I get you a drink, honey?"

"Just plain soda for me, dear, thanks."

Maxwell went behind the bar to the small refrigerator and took out a can of soda. He placed some ice in a glass and poured it.

The four of them talked into the night. Most of what they discussed was fabricated lies, designed to make them sound like old college friends. Around midnight, Bob stood up to stretch and said, "Honey, we'd better go and let these folks get some rest."

Judy knew her line at this point. "Nonsense, it's late. Why don't you two sleep in our guestroom? You can leave out in the morning. We have a plane to catch tomorrow anyway."

"Well, we had planned on going to a motel tonight."

Sharon echoed, "We don't want to put you two out none."

Bob and Sharon continued to resist but then decided to stay as planned.

Judy added, "I've got some extra pajamas you can use."

Sharon spoke up, "Oh, that's okay; I usually sleep in the nude," as she gave Maxwell a seductive glance. "I find clothes so inhibiting and confining."

Maxwell tried not to feel embarrassed but knew his face was probably turning red. He simply grinned at Sharon then turned to Judy. "Well, then it's settled. Bob, you and I will go get your bags, while Judy shows Sharon to your room."

The guestroom had a private bath with a Jacuzzi tub. Sharon leaned toward Maxwell as he entered the room carrying her suitcase and grabbed his arm. "Ooo, I like bubbles. They tickle my body."

Judy almost lost it. Sharon was carrying this old friend game just a little too far for her comfort. When Max put down the suitcase, Judy took hold of his other arm and said, "Well then, I hope you and Bob enjoy it," emphasizing *Bob*. Then she pulled Max away. "Come on, honey, we'd better let these nice folks get to bed. We have a plane to catch in the morning."

Everyone said good night, and Judy was relieved to have the whole thing over with. She couldn't stand to have these two strangers in her home, especially Sharon.

The next morning, Maxwell was up before six making final preparations. The others began to rise after seven, and by eight, all were downstairs on the patio enjoying a breakfast of cereal, fruit, and coffee. They had given their maid the day off.

Judy came down dressed in her outfit. She wore a skintight dress cut very short, a low-neck blouse, and high heels. She also wore a short blond wig that looked like Sharon's hair.

Maxwell turned to her and gave her a sign, which indicated she looked good. He had never seen her in a miniskirt before, and she looked totally different. He was wearing a false mustache and slipped on the hat that Bob had worn the night before.

They all walked to the front door. Maxwell said, "It was good seeing you both again. I hope you don't wait five years to look us up."

"Now that we know where you live and how nice it is, I'm sure we'll be back," Bob replied. "Thanks for all of your hospitality."

Sharon cut in, "Yeah, and your Jacuzzi was great. Thanks for everything."

Maxwell opened the door, but instead of letting Bob and Sharon out, he and Judy walked out the front door, waving back toward the house. They climbed into the rented Lincoln and drove off. They could only hope that their plan would work.

Once Max and Judy had left, Bob walked over to the stereo and turned it on so that the music filled the house and the outside. He found a good oldies station and turned up the volume. Now, he and Sharon could talk freely.

Max and Judy drove toward the airport but not the one in Colorado Springs. They would drive to Denver and catch a plane out of there to Miami then change planes to Bermuda as Mr. and Mrs. Bob Johnson. "Let me see the envelope inside your purse," Max said to Judy.

Judy opened up her large purse and pulled out a nine-by-twelve brown envelope. She opened the clasp and pulled out the contents, which were two driver's licenses complete with photos of both of them and two passports under the names Robert M. and Sharon L. Johnson.

"How did you get these?" Judy asked.

"I didn't. Our friends from last night took care of all the details. They will be taking our place today on the plane to New York and spending the weekend out there while we make our getaway."

"So you never had a business trip to New York? All of this was just a setup?"

"Let's just say I've been planning for this ever since our press conference. I knew that we might have to make a quick exit out of the country and wanted to be ready."

"What are we going to do for money and clothes?"

"All of that is taken care of as well. We have suitcases in the trunk with our size clothes and money in a bank account in Bermuda under our new names. I've been feeding money to that bank account from a Swiss bank account we've had for years."

"It sounds like you've thought of everything. I hope you didn't have that bimbo pick out all of my clothes. I don't know how she can stand to wear these things." Judy tried to adjust her skirt as it rode up her thigh.

"I think you look pretty cute in that tight little outfit." Max smiled and reached over to pat her on her knee.

Judy's expression changed to one of agitation. "I'm sorry, Max, but this is just not me."

"You can buy yourself a whole new wardrobe when we get to Bermuda. Meanwhile, enjoy the new you. I feel like I'm running away with a complete stranger." He paused. "It feels good."

Judy shot him a dirty look. Max quickly added, "Just kidding!"

CHAPTER FORTY-ONE

Big Al and Sergio knew things were getting way out of hand. They had their orders and would follow them, but Big Al didn't like what he was feeling. Sergio was left to watch the Rosenthal house, while Big Al went to pick up the out-of-town visitor.

Big Al parked his car in the abandoned field. He watched the sky, looking for the plane. The white clouds touched the tips of the mountains. He heard an engine noise. Lifting his binoculars, he searched the sky until he saw the tiny object in the air.

The twin engine Cessna landed, bouncing several times on the rough runway, which had been deserted for years. The pilot taxied toward the waiting car and brought the plane to a complete stop.

The door opened, and a large-framed man, wearing a dark-black suit emerged. He carried a small briefcase and looked like a business executive. Big Al smiled to himself. *He doesn't look so tough. Actually, he looks like a wimp.*

The man opened the car door and, without saying so much as a hello, stepped inside and snapped his fingers, ordering Big Al to begin driving. Big Al had been warned that this person was not much of a conversationalist. He was a professional hit man and would do the job then be on his way by the afternoon, out of the state and out of the country.

Big Al thought of a dozen questions he would like to ask but decided it would be in his best interest to keep quiet. So they drove silently, not even looking at one another. The less he knew about this man, the better. Big Al would receive his ten-thousand-dollar bonus just for delivering him. He wondered how much the man was getting for the job.

When they drove up to the Rosenthals' home, the man spoke for the first time, "Does the house have a security system?"

"Yes, but it's no problem getting it shut down when you're ready to go," Big Al responded.

"How about a security patrol?"

"Nothing like that. An occasional patrol car comes by, but not very often."

Sergio walked over to the car and climbed into the back seat. "Their company left about thirty minutes ago."

The man in the suit opened his briefcase, never acknowledging Sergio's presence or his statement. He began assembling the pistol, attaching the silencer and checking the bullet chamber. He put it inside his holster underneath his coat, opened the car door, and said, "Let's do it!"

Big Al and Sergio jumped out of the car and walked with him toward the house. Sergio went straight to the alarm box and disconnected the alarm, while Big Al unlocked the front door. The man from out of town gently opened the door and eased his body inside ever so quietly.

"You two wait out here," he said as he disappeared into the foyer. He pulled out his pistol and crept through the house, looking around in all directions.

Barney and Jenny Blackwell were getting ready to play their second roles. Jenny was in the bathroom putting the final touches on her makeup. She wore a black wig and a conservative dress that came just below her knees. *How can Judy stand to wear these kinds of clothes? They look so ordinary*, she thought. *This dress does nothing for my body.*

Barney shaved off his mustache and dressed in a black pinstriped suit. "Are you about ready?" he shouted from the bedroom. "We've got to catch that plane in two hours. We should leave here in thirty minutes."

Jenny yelled back, "Yeah, yeah, I'm almost ready."

The man in the suit listened to the voices, discerning their location. He walked up the stairs, careful not to make a sound. The music blared in the background and would help to distract any sound he might make, but still he was cautious. He reached the top of the stairs and walked toward the bedroom. The door stood slightly open. Standing to one side, he eased the door open with his pistol, searching for his target.

Barney saw the door move from the mirror. When he turned around, he saw the man. "Who are—" The man fired two shots, each one hitting the target dead center in the middle of the forehead. Barney collapsed to the floor.

Jenny yelled from the bathroom, "Did you say something? Barney?" There was no response. She walked toward the bedroom. "Hey, out there, did you say something?"

The man in the suit took his position at three feet from the bathroom door. When Jenny opened it, he fired two shots. She slumped to the floor, never knowing what hit her.

In a matter of minutes, the man in the suit was out the door. Big Al and Sergio split up. "I'll meet you back at the office," Big Al said. "I've got to take our friend back to his airplane."

Sergio nodded and drove off. Big Al and the man in the suit drove quietly back to the airstrip. The man never spoke a word during their trip. The only words Big Al had heard him say during their time together was his asking about the security system and *Let's do it* when he got out of the car. This man was cold and heartless. Big Al hoped he would never be on the receiving end of this man's profession.

****

A message came over Howard Baskins' private terminal, which said:

To: Howard Baskins
From: Shark
Priority Code 1
Problem #1 eliminated.
Will begin working on #2 and #3.
Still have not located #2 but will
continue looking.

CHAPTER FORTY-TWO

Frank Mitchell was baffled by this case. He had been with the FBI for over twenty years and never once had the bureau been asked to investigate the IRS. He wasn't sure he wanted to get involved. His own tax returns were not that accurate. Like so many people did, he fudged on a lot of things, but mainly he inflated his expenses to reduce his taxable income. He knew that he would never be able to withstand the scrutiny of an audit, and he certainly couldn't afford to pay back any taxes. He was barely making ends meet now.

After interviewing Molly Shanks, he still was not sure if there was a case or not. As it turned out, she had no proof that the man who tried to kill her was from the IRS. She was only speculating that he was connected with them. But now he had just received word that Maxwell and Judy Rosenthal had just been murdered in their home. The police listed robbery as the motive, but Mitchell was suspicious.

Frank decided he would ask some more questions and do some more digging before he closed the case entirely. He made an appointment to see Howard Baskins that afternoon. If that didn't turn up anything, then he would drop the case.

He arrived early for his appointment. As he sat in the waiting room, Sheila came out several times to tell him that Mr. Baskins was still tied up, but he would be out shortly. "Are you sure I can't get you a cup of coffee or a cold drink?" she asked for the third time.

"Okay, you've talked me into it. I'll take a Coke if you have one."

"Sure. Do you want diet or regular?"

"No, I want the real thing, none of that diet stuff."

Sheila left and returned in a few moments with a glass of ice and a can of Coke. She gently laid a napkin on the coffee table and set the glass down. She proceeded to pour the Coke in the glass for him. "There you go. If you need anything else, just ask," she said and returned to her desk.

Frank was impressed with the service he was getting, although he was becoming very annoyed that he had been waiting now for over an hour.

Howard Baskins was not in a meeting. Nor was he in conference with anyone. He wasn't even on the telephone. He sat behind his desk, with his feet propped up, leaning way back in his chair. He puffed on his big cigar, and the smoke swirled around his head. He savored every second. It had been a long time since he had smoked a cigar. He was relieved that the wait was now over.

When Howard didn't want to see someone, he would use a ploy that always made him feel better. He would make the person wait unnecessarily, sometimes for two hours or more. If he were lucky, the person would leave. If not, the person was annoyed. Either way, Howard felt like he won and was in control of the person.

Howard looked at his watch as he inhaled another mass of smoke. He had succumbed to the temptation and had finally lit the cigar. *I guess an hour and a half is long enough to keep the FBI waiting. He'll at least think I'm overworked.*

He buzzed Sheila on the intercom. "Send Mr. Mitchell in now, please."

Frank walked into the office as Sheila opened the door. The room reeked of cigar smoke. He walked directly over to the desk. Howard had his head buried down in his desk, pretending to be busy at work. He glanced up. "Oh, Mr. Mitchell. Have a seat. So good to meet you." He motioned for Frank to take a chair but didn't bother shaking hands. He picked up his cigar from the ashtray, took another full drag from it, and blew the smoke straight toward Frank. "I hope the cigar doesn't bother you. Would you like one?" Howard lifted up a wooden box, displaying his expensive collection of cigars.

Frank lifted up his hand. "No, thank you. I don't smoke. You feel free to go ahead. I won't be but a few minutes. I just need to ask you a few questions."

Howard leaned back in his chair, clasping the cigar tightly between his teeth. "Why would the FBI be wanting to ask me questions? Is it one of our men? Is someone in trouble?"

Frank shook his head. "No, it's nothing like that. I'm investigating a case, the attempted murder of Molly Shanks. Her husband used to work here."

"George Shanks, of course; what a tragedy. He committed suicide, you know. Did you say attempted murder? I thought Molly tried to kill herself?"

"Well, that is what the police report said initially. However, since she came out of her coma, she's saying that someone from your office tried to kill her."

Howard forced a chuckle. "Don't tell me you believe her story. Surely you must know that we would have no reason to do harm to her."

"Well, we know for a fact that someone tried to kill her again at the hospital while she was in her coma. They would have succeeded if it hadn't been for Senator Tom Haden coming into the room. It seems he has saved her life twice now."

Howard blew smoke rings into the air then said, "Oh, yes, Senator Haden. We are well aware of him and his stories. Actually, they are outright lies. You shouldn't believe everything a politician tells you."

Frank leaned toward the desk. "I'm not saying we believe him or don't believe him, but you understand we must investigate these allocations against a branch of our government. It's in your best interest to clear this matter up as soon as possible."

"You're just doing your job, but believe me, there is nothing to all of this. It's ludicrous to think that someone from the IRS would have reason to kill, or should I say, try to kill, Molly Shanks. Senator Haden is a madman who is in deep trouble with the IRS and is trying everything he can to discredit us so the attention is taken off him. Well, I can tell you, Inspector, it won't work, not for one minute. We're proceeding with our investigation on Tom Haden, and trust me when I say you'll see him go down for tax evasion." Howard shouted his last tirade of words and was standing up, pacing the room. He took a handful of change from his pocket and poured it from one hand to the other. He continued, "Do you know how ridiculous all of this sounds? Do you have any idea? I'm afraid you're wasting your time. He has sent you on a wild goose chase."

Frank watched Howard pace nervously. He could usually tell when someone was lying, but this man was hard to read. He probed some more, "How about a document that Senator Haden discovered? Do you know anything about it? Is there a secret document?"

Howard stood still, facing the window. He stopped pouring the change and spoke with his back to Frank, "That document. The document is another one of his fabrications. We've heard rumors of a document for the past few weeks from as far away as Colorado, but we have yet to see a copy. If a copy does emerge, it will be a forgery. That I'm sure of, and you can quote me."

"So, you don't believe there is a document?"

Howard was curious now and turned to face Frank. "Have you seen the document?"

"No. I've only heard about it."

"There, you see? Everyone talks about this elusive document, but no one is producing it. How come? Because it doesn't really exist, that's how come." Howard sat back down in his chair and continued chewing on his cigar, which by now was only about a half-inch long. "If you want hard evidence, look at our records, where we are investigating these guys. We have documented proof they are evading taxes. We go after them, and they start hollering about some document. Hogwash!"

Frank looked puzzled. "You said 'they'; are you referring to Maxwell Rosenthal and Nathan Daniels?"

"Of course I am. They're all in this together. The story was created to divert attention from them to us. They both went to the media with it, but it backfired on both of them. Even the media wouldn't buy their story. Again, if they have the document, why not produce it?"

Frank glanced down at some notes on his pad. "Mr. Baskins, can you tell me anything about a Ray Phillips and a Doug Preston? How are they connected with this whole thing?"

Howard stared coldly at Frank. "I have no idea who those two men are. Why do you ask?"

"Senator Haden believes that they knew about this document and that they were killed because of it."

"Does he have proof?" There was silence. "I didn't think so. Do you really think the IRS is out there gunning down innocent taxpayers?"

Frank didn't answer the question but stood up and reached out his hand. "Thank you, Mr. Baskins. I believe I've taken up enough of your time. If I have any further questions, I'll get in touch with you."

Howard shook his hand this time. Frank turned and walked out the door. As soon as the door shut behind him, Howard grabbed the phone and dialed security. The door opened suddenly, and Frank stuck his head back inside, startling Howard. "Sorry to barge back in, but I do need to ask you one more question."

Howard slowly lowered the receiver back to the phone. "Yes, what is it?"

"Could you make sure I get copies of all those documents you have pertaining to your investigation of Senator Tom Haden, Maxwell Rosenthal, and Nathan Daniels?"

Howard was taken off-guard. "Huh, yes, I guess so. I'll have to check with procedures on this. I mean—"

"Oh, it'll be all right. I can give you a subpoena for them if that will help. I appreciate your help. Thanks." Frank smiled, waved goodbye, and then disappeared. Howard's fist hit the desk in frustration.

Frank didn't feel he had enough to continue an investigation, but something told him to keep going. He had been in the business long enough to know that sometimes you just have to follow your gut instinct. The facts don't always point you in the right direction. There was something about the way Howard responded to questions that made Frank suspicious. That's why he decided to get the IRS documentation on their investigations. It seemed strange that three people from across the country would come up with the same story even if they were friends. Frank decided he would give the investigation a little more time, maybe put a few more men on it, just for a couple of days, to see if it led to anything.

Power Unleashed

CHAPTER FORTY-THREE

Molly Shanks sat in her wheelchair. She wanted to walk out of the hospital, but they had their rules. Tom and Lucy pushed her down the hall to the elevator. A policeman walked in front of her and one behind her.

"I want to thank you two for coming to take me home. You didn't have to do this. I could have gotten someone else to come help me. My daughter offered to stay and take care of me."

"Nonsense," Lucy said. "What are friends for? We want to help. Besides, you're not going home. You're coming to our house to stay with us for a few days."

Molly turned around to look up at Lucy. "Oh, no, I can't impose on you two. No, take me to my own home. I must—"

"You must go home with us," Tom interrupted. "Lucy and I have gone over this, and it's the best thing for you. We'll have tighter security, and you won't be home alone. Besides, we've promised your daughter. Why do you think she was so willing to go back home?"

Molly thought quietly as she was rolled into the elevator. She knew they were right but felt like she was losing her independence by staying with them. "Okay, but it will only be until this whole mess blows over."

Tom smiled. "It shouldn't be too long now. The FBI is working on the case, and I believe they will get to the bottom of this soon."

Lucy bent over to whisper in Molly's ear, "Besides, it'll be nice having somebody around to talk to while Tom is gone all the time."

Standing in the elevator, the two police officers stood quietly, one on each side. Tom looked at each one but didn't recognize either of them. *They must be new*, he thought. Then he noticed something strange. One of the officers was wearing a pair of brown shoes. *Policemen always wear black shoes.* He glanced at the other one; they were black but had a casual look about them. Tom then began studying the uniform closer. *It doesn't fit well. It looks too baggy.* His heart began to beat faster. *These two aren't policemen. They are ...*

The elevator doors opened, and they all stepped out. Tom had to think of something fast. "Hey, Lucy, why don't you take Molly to the restroom before we start the long drive home?"

Molly started to say, "That's not—"

Lucy saw Tom signal her with his eyes and interrupted, "Yeah, that's a good idea. Let's find a restroom, Molly." Instead of moving toward the exit, they moved toward the lobby of the hospital.

Tom turned to the two policemen. "I believe you two can wait here. I doubt anyone will try anything inside the bathrooms. The officers looked at each other, and then struck a pose facing the restrooms.

As Tom, Lucy, and Molly moved closer toward their destination, Tom whispered, "Don't panic, but I don't believe our friends back there are cops. Stay in the restroom until I come in for you. Do you understand?"

Tom slipped into the men's room. He flipped out his little cellular phone and dialed 911. "Yes, this is Senator Tom Haden. I'm in the lobby of St. Andrews Hospital. There are two men dressed in police uniforms who I believe are going to try and kill us. Could you send several units immediately?"

"Where exactly are you located inside the hospital?" the operator asked.

"We are in the main foyer. We're hiding inside the restrooms, but they are standing outside. Hurry!"

He hung up the phone and called information for the number of the hospital. When the operator of the hospital answered, Tom said, "Yes, please connect me with security."

"This is Jefferson with security."

"Jefferson, my name is Senator Tom Haden. Listen to me carefully. There are two men in the main lobby of your hospital who I believe are posing as police officers. We are hiding in the restrooms on the first floor in the main lobby. I've already called the police. Could you and your men please come quickly? But be careful, these two are armed and may be dangerous."

After asking a few questions for clarification, Jefferson replied, "We'll be right up. Don't move, Senator."

Tom replaced the phone inside his coat pocket. Within minutes, he heard voices outside. He opened the door to peek out. There were at least ten security guards, with their pistols out of their holsters. One of them yelled to the policemen, "You two, put your hands in the air very slowly."

"We're policemen. We're escorting Molly Shanks and Senator Haden to their homes."

"We'll see about that; just keep those hands in the air where we can see them." One of the security guards walked closer, took their guns out of the holsters, and tossed them to the floor. Then he reached inside his pants pocket and pulled out his wallet. "What's your name?"

"Officer Morrell."

"What's your first name?"

"William, William Morrell."

"Give me your date of birth."

"It's December 11, 1956."

"Wrong, you missed it by a few years, pal."

The officers both held their heads down in disgust. Tom had stepped out of the restroom. Police cars swarmed the building, and at least twenty officers stormed the front doors with revolvers in hand.

Tom opened the door to the ladies' room and shouted, "You two can come out now. It's all over. We're safe."

Molly and Lucy came out together. "What happened? How did you know something was wrong?" Lucy asked.

"Those two guys weren't police officers. They are probably hired killers. I noticed that their shoes didn't match, then I looked at their uniforms closer, and they looked a little sloppy for DC policemen."

Molly looked concerned. "Do you think they were going to kill us?"

"I'm afraid so. They were probably just waiting to get us outside or to our house. We were lucky this time."

"This makes three times for me," Molly added.

"Any problem going home with us now?" Lucy asked.

"None at all; I want to be around people."

They watched the two men being placed under arrest and handcuffed. The police captain came over to Senator Haden and said, "We apologize for this. We found the real officers tied up in a linen closet wearing nothing but their underwear. I'm assigning four men to this detail for the next week. This will not happen again."

Tom shook the captain's hand. "Thanks for getting here so fast. Do I need to come downtown and answer any questions?"

"No, I believe we have all we need. If we need you, we know where to find you. We'll keep in touch."

"Any idea who these two are?" Tom asked.

"Not yet. We'll let you know as soon as we find out anything. At least with this episode, there is one thing we now know for sure."

"What's that?" Tom looked puzzled.

"We know that Molly Shanks isn't just paranoid."

****

Tom pulled the car into the driveway. Sitting on the front porch in a rocker was a stranger. "Who is that sitting on our porch?" Tom pointed toward the house.

Lucy looked. "I don't know. I can't see her that well. Who in the world could it be?"

The lady looked very old, maybe in her nineties. Her face was wrinkled and showed a life that had not been easy. She was short and tiny. It didn't appear that she weighed more than seventy-five pounds, but she looked spry for her age.

Molly looked from the back seat. "Oh my gosh, it's my mother. How did she find me here?"

Tom brought the car to a halt, and they all got out. The lady on the porch just kept rocking, pretending she hadn't noticed them. As they walked up to the porch, she spoke in her high-pitched voice, "Well, it's about time you got here. I've been waiting for nearly two hours. Where have you been? Why didn't you call me, young lady? I'm still your mother, you know. That never changes; I don't care how old you are."

Molly hugged her then cut in, "Mother, I want you to meet Senator Tom Haden and his wife, Lucy. They've been helping me a lot since I've been in the hospital. Tom and Lucy, this is my mother, Abigail Bishop."

"It's a pleasure to meet you." Lucy shook her hand.

Tom reached out and took her hand. "It's good to finally meet you. We talked on the phone." He was unconsciously talking louder.

"You don't have to yell. I may be old, but I'm not deaf. Why is it that people think old folks can't hear? My eyesight is going, my teeth are falling out, but I can still hear well. Thank you, Jesus."

"I'm sorry, I didn't mean to—" Tom stopped in mid sentence, not knowing what to say.

Lucy came to his rescue. "Why don't we all go inside and get something to eat. I'll make some lemonade and see what else I can fix up to serve."

Molly helped her mother out of the rocker. They all waited as she navigated herself toward the door. Tom took her by the arm to help her up the one step.

Abigail turned and swatted Tom. "I don't need any help from you or anyone else. I've been walking around fine by myself for nearly ninety years, and I intend to keep walking by myself. The day I need assistance to get around is the day I want to go to my grave. No, sir, you keep your hands to yourself. Help Molly there; she's been sick in the hospital. Do you know that I've never been inside a hospital in my entire life? It's my opinion that people get sick in hospitals. You think about it, that's where all the germs are. They put you inside with a bunch of sick folks, and before you know it, you get sicker and die. That's why I didn't visit you there, honey. That and I couldn't get a ride way over there to that side of town."

They all listened as she went on nonstop, watching her move slowly across the floor. Once inside, they sat around the kitchen table. Lucy began putting items on the table for a light lunch. Abigail continued talking.

"This whole thing is a conspiracy. George didn't kill himself. I don't believe it for a minute. They killed him just like they tried to kill Molly. I've never trusted the IRS. Back in the fifties when Arch, that's my husband, … He died in nineteen hundred and seventy-two. It was quick. He was outside mowing the lawn. When he came in, he complained about being hot and needing to lie down. He sat down on the sofa, closed his eyes, and never woke up again. They said he died of a heart attack."

She paused long enough to take a bite of her sandwich and a sip of lemonade and then continued with her mouth half-full of food. "Anyway, Arch had a business, and the IRS wanted to audit him. They didn't send him a notice; they just showed up one day at the store. They wanted to see his books, bank statements, and receipts. Well, Arch told them that if they wanted to audit him, they would have to make an appointment to come see him after store hours. He told them outright that he had nothing to hide, but he wasn't going to stop working just to accommodate their schedules. They tried to intimidate him, but he stuck to his guns. They made an appointment and came back in the evening."

After another half-hour, Tom excused himself. "I've got to make some calls. I'll be in the study if you need me, honey."

Lucy gave him a knowing look, which said, *Yeah, you get to leave, and I'm stuck here.* She smiled and waved him out. Abigail began talking on another subject.

CHAPTER FORTY-FOUR

Nathan studied the birth certificates, which had just arrived in the mail. He was now officially Robert Nathan Stillwell, and Linda was Mary Elizabeth Fontane. "I can't believe we got these so fast," Nathan said.

Linda sat at the desk, brushing her hair. "I can't believe we got them at all. It doesn't make sense that anyone can request a copy of a birth certificate and get it with no questions asked."

"Well, Mary Elizabeth, I must say you look totally different. I feel like I'm running away with a whole new woman."

Linda stopped brushing and turned to face Nathan. "Do you really like the color? Personally, I think it's too dark for my complexion."

"Nonsense, you look great. I like it … I really do. The only problem I have …" Nathan hesitated.

Linda turned to look at herself in the mirror again. "What? What's wrong?"

Nathan walked over and put his arms around her, bending over to hug her. "I just don't know if I can get used to calling you Mary. It sounds so foreign to me. I like Linda."

Linda moved her lips toward his, pulling his face toward her. They kissed, and Linda made sure it was passionate. When she released him, she said, "There, maybe you can get used to Mary kissing you like that, and maybe Mary will want to do even more than Linda ever did." Linda's voice took on a low sexy sound. "I mean, after all, I'm a totally different woman now." She grabbed Nathan and pulled him down to her once again. Nathan responded and gently lifted her to her feet. They held their passionate embrace for the longest time. Nathan began backing her toward the bed.

"By the way, where are the boys?" Nathan asked.

"It's okay; they're out playing at the playground. We'll be all right." She sat on the bed and pulled Nathan toward her, and they embraced once again and remained lost in their ecstasy. For a few moments, all of life's problems seemed to be a dream.

****

Calvin Davis sat at his desk in Washington DC. Things had not been going well for him at all. Nathan and Linda disappearing and the kidnapping of their boys would have been bad enough. Added to this, the escape of Maxwell and Judy and the killing of the wrong couple had moved Howard Baskins and the Shark to rage, accusing Calvin of total incompetence. And now, to top it all off, Molly Shanks was out walking around as a free woman. Calvin Davis needed a break.

The office door burst open. "Sorry to disturb you, sir, but I believe we found something on the Danielses. You might want to take a look at this."

Calvin jumped to his feet and followed the man down the corridor to a room full of computers, hoping this would be his lucky day.

The man pointed to one of the computer screens. "It's right here, sir. They used a credit card to charge some groceries in a town called Roundup, Montana."

"Are we sure it's the same Nathan Daniels?"

"Everything checks out. Do you want us to send some men up there to see what we can find out?"

Davis rubbed his chin for a moment and responded, "Yeah, send a couple of guys. This could be our lucky day. How soon can we get someone up there?"

"Probably by this afternoon. We'll let you know."

"Good, keep me posted. If they find anything, I want to know about it. They are not to make a move until they talk to me first." Calvin walked out of the computer room, feeling better. He thought to himself, *Now, all we have to do is locate the Rosenthals, and we can end this game of cat and mouse.*

****

Nathan and Linda had been in town a few days and were feeling comfortable. The town was very small and quaint. Nothing much to do except go bowling and to the theater or get involved in town politics, which most folks did. Nathan knew that they would not stay in Roundup,

Montana, but felt it was a safe place to lay low for a while until the search for them had calmed down.

They left the motel and took a drive into town. Parking the car along the main street, they visited the familiar stores that they had already frequented several times since there was nothing else to do. As they strolled along Main Street, the two boys ran ahead, playing little boy games as they walked, picking up everything in sight to investigate it closer.

Nathan watched Matthew and Allen, smiling at Linda. They held hands as they walked. Then Nathan spotted it. He stopped suddenly and just stared.

"What is it?" Linda asked.

Nathan didn't respond.

Linda could see from his expression that something was seriously wrong and began to get scared. "What is it, Nathan? What are you looking at?"

Nathan slowly lifted his finger and pointed without being conspicuous. "Do you see that car over there and those two men getting out of it?"

Linda looked. "Yeah, so?"

"So, I can spot a federal agent a mile away. I bet you anything that those two guys are from the federal government."

"Well, even in Roundup, Montana, they have government agents. Maybe they're here for another reason."

"Could be," Nathan said, "but it makes me nervous when I see one. Let's get out of here." He ran ahead and retrieved the boys, and they began walking toward their car.

The two men walked inside the local grocery and asked for the owner. They both flashed their identification and began asking questions. "Have you seen these people?" The agent showed four pictures of Nathan, Linda, Matthew, and Allen.

The owner scratched his head. "They don't look familiar, but we get a lot of folks coming in here from all over. Can't say as I remember them all. Could be that they were in here, can't say for sure. What did they do?"

The agent put the pictures away. "We have reason to believe that they used a credit card here at your store a few days ago. Could we go through your records, or could you see if you can find the charge slip on this transaction?" The agent opened his notebook and showed the owner what he needed.

The owner walked behind the counter and pulled out a shoebox of receipts and began going through them one by one. "Here it is, I think anyway. Is this it?" He handed the agent a charge slip. The signature matched Linda's exactly.

"They were definitely here. I don't suppose this rings a bell to you at all?" The agent was hopeful.

The storeowner looked over the items purchased, studying it carefully. "Yeah, I do remember her. She didn't have blonde hair though; she was a brunette. She had a little boy with her. The reason I remember her is because she seemed upset that she didn't have enough cash to pay for the order. When she pulled out her credit card, she was real hesitant handing it to me. I almost had to take it out of her hand."

The agent made a note in his book. "You say she had dark hair. Was it dark brown, dark red, or black?"

"I guess it was a blackish-red, but it was dark."

"Did you notice anything else? Did she say where they were going or where they might be staying?"

"No, she didn't talk much, not like a lot of our out-of-town customers. She was definitely not from around here though. We can spot city folks a mile away. They come out here trying to blend in, but they don't."

"You haven't seen her since this time?" the agent asked.

"No, can't say as I have. But we're not the only grocery store in town either."

The agents thanked the storeowner and turned to leave. Almost as a second thought, the agent turned around and handed him a card. "If you do see them again, give us a call at this number. We'd really like to know about it."

Nathan and Linda watched from their car as the agents strolled out of the store. "How could they have found us? How could they have possibly tracked us here?"

Linda's face turned pale. "I, uh ... I think I—"

Nathan turned to face her. "What? What do you think?"

Linda took a deep breath. "I think I know why they're here." Nathan looked at her, waiting for her to continue. "I used a credit card the other day."

"You what?" Nathan shouted. "Why would you use a credit card?"

"I didn't mean to. I didn't have enough cash and thought it would look more suspicious if I didn't buy it."

"That has to be the stupidest move you have ever made. Why didn't you just call them on the phone and tell them where we were located? Don't you know that is exactly what they were waiting for us to do?"

Linda got angry. "Look, I said I was sorry. I didn't mean to do it. It just happened, all right?"

Nathan raised his voice. "Tell that to your boys when they are taken away from you for good and they haul us off to jail."

Linda began crying. "I'm sorry. I just thought we were safe. It didn't occur to me that they could track us down this fast with our credit card. Besides, I thought we were leaving this town anyway and going into Canada. How was I to know that you would fall in love with this place and want to stay?"

"Oh, so now it's my fault. You're shifting the blame to me because I decided for us to lay low here for a while. Well, if I had known you were going to advertise our whereabouts, I would have moved on to another town."

They sat in silence in the car and watched as the two agents walked up and down the street in and out of stores. They couldn't hear what was being said but knew that the agents were showing pictures around town, asking if anyone had seen them.

Nathan started the car. "We'd better get back to the motel and check out. We have to get out of here and fast. These guys are going to find us shortly."

When they arrived back at the motel, they threw their clothes into the suitcases. Linda had never packed so fast in all her life. The boys carried the luggage to the car while Nathan checked out of the motel, and they sped away, headed west from town.

****

The two government agents flashed their badges at the motel owner and introduced themselves. He smiled at both of them and said in a slow western drawl, "My name is Clyde. You boys ain't from around here, are you?" Clyde didn't have much use for the U.S. government. He paid his taxes and kept his record clean, but as far as he was concerned, they were all a bunch of thieves. He lost thousands of dollars back in the seventies when the IRS put his business through a detailed audit. Clyde felt he had been treated unjustly but gave up his fight to get back his money. Now here they were on his doorstep, asking him for help.

One of the agents responded, "We're out of the Colorado office, temporarily assigned up here. Have you seen these four people before?"

Clyde looked at the pictures carefully. "No! Can't say as I have. We get lots of families traveling through here. I don't try to keep track of 'em. All I do is rent them a room. They mind their business, and I mind mine. Are they criminals or something?"

"We need to talk to them. It's official government business. Are you sure you haven't seen them? Some of the town folks thought they might be staying out here."

"As I said before, maybe they did, and maybe they didn't. I don't usually pay that much attention to our guests. They all look alike after a while."

"Could we take a look at your guest register for the past few days?"

"You got a warrant?"

"You want us to get one?"

Clyde thought for a minute, then took a box and laid it on the counter. "This would be this month's. All the people who have checked out are in the back alphabetically, and the ones in the front are still here. As you can see, we don't have a whole lot of business."

The agent thumbed through the cards, looking for something to give him a clue. He assumed they would not use their real name but was looking for a party of four. He turned up nothing.

The agents turned and walked out of the motel, thanking Clyde for his cooperation. Once they were in their car, Clyde reached down among the papers on his desk and picked up a registration card and looked at it: *Robert N. Stillwell, party of four.* He mumbled under his breath, "I hope they get away. They are a real nice family."

CHAPTER FORTY-FIVE

Maxwell and Judy sat on their patio watching the waves pound the shore. The sun was shining down on the crystal-blue water, making it sparkle. The breeze blew gently, bringing a refreshing coolness to the air. Judy loved the ocean. She could sit for hours reading a book, listening to the water roll onto the sand, and soaking up the sun. They sipped their morning coffee as they enjoyed the view from their villa. They couldn't believe that they had actually escaped the wrath of the government. They had read in the paper of their murder and then the subsequent discovery that it was not them but guests in their house. They felt bad for the detective and his wife. Maxwell would have never asked him to do it if he thought they would be killed. The newspaper had given the details that some intruders had broken into the house and killed them both instantly. There was speculation that it was a Mob killing.

Maxwell laid down his newspaper. "Well, at least we're not in the paper again today. Maybe they'll give up on us and leave us alone."

Judy opened her eyes to look at Max. "Right now, I don't want to think about it. I'm enjoying this paradise too much. Let's not ruin our one and only vacation by reminding me that the only reason I'm here is because we're being hunted down like common criminals."

"You're right, honey. I'm sorry. What's on our agenda today? Fishing, swimming, snorkeling, or boating?"

"How about taking me shopping down to that little village twenty miles south of here. It's a beautiful day for a drive."

"You got yourself a deal. We'll leave in an hour and a half. Can you be ready then?"

Judy stood up and walked around the table and put her hands on his chest. "No problem, big boy, as long as you leave me alone."

Max pulled her toward him, and they connected in a passionate embrace. She fell into his lap, almost sliding to the floor, but he held her tightly. "There will be more when we get back from our shopping trip," he teased. He helped her up and pushed her toward the apartment, slapping her fanny on the way. "Hurry up before it gets too hot to enjoy the day."

Maxwell's mind was not on shopping. All he had thought about since he had been here was to somehow contact Tom Haden to let him know they were okay. He knew, however, that contacting him would be dangerous and possibly blow their cover. *There has to be a way to do it*, he thought as they drove into the little village.

It was 10:30 in the morning, and the little town was already full of life. People were moving throughout the marketplaces, buying, trading, and selling. "Look over there," Judy exclaimed, pointing her finger. "Let's go in those shops first."

Maxwell found a parking spot in a crowded lot. When they climbed out of the little rental car, he said to Judy, "You go ahead and look around. I'm going to run a couple of errands, and I'll find you in one of those shops. Okay?"

"What kind of errands? What are you going to do?"

"Don't worry; I'll be all right. I just have to take care of some business." He kissed her on the lips, gave her a hug, then turned and walked away. He glanced back and noticed she was still watching him with a puzzled look on her face. He waved her on toward the shops.

Max made his way through the crowds to a lobby of a hotel. It was an old building but decorated nicely. The floors were marble, and it had huge pillars on each side. The ceiling was a hand-painted mural of bright colors, depicting different times of history. He spent the first few minutes staring at the ceiling and walking around in a daze. When he spotted the pay phones, he walked over to them. *I'll need change*, he thought as he reached in to pull out what he had. *This isn't enough.* He walked over to the clerk and handed him a ten-dollar bill. "Could I get this changed to quarters please?"

The clerk gave him a disgusting look but proceeded to count out ten dollars' worth of quarters.

Max sat down in the phone booth and closed the door for privacy. He dialed the operator. "Yes, please, Operator, I would like to place a person-to-person call to Senator Tom Haden." He proceeded to give her the number and waited as the switchboard operator passed the call to Tom's office, then his secretary answered.

"This is the overseas operator with a long-distance call for Senator Tom Haden; is he in please?"

"Yes, he's in, Operator; who may I say is calling?"

"A Mr. Jeffery Lockwood," the operator replied.

"Senator, you have a long-distance person-to-person call from a Mr. Jeffery Lockwood; do you want to take the call?" Tom's mind went blank and was taken off-guard. Jeffery Lockwood was the phony name he used from time to time. *Who would be using that name to call me?* he thought. Then it dawned on him. He shouted to his secretary, "Yes, Jeffery Lockwood, by all means put him through."

Max disguised his voice using a slight southern accent. "Tom Haden, you rascal. Do you remember me?"

Tom spoke carefully, "Sure, I know exactly who this is. How have you been doing? I've been thinking a lot about you lately."

A voice interrupted, "Please deposit five dollars and fifty cents for the first three minutes."

They both waited until twenty-two quarters had been deposited.

"I was just calling to let you know how things are going for us. We're all fine; my wife is doing well. We're enjoying our retirement. Hey, do you remember that bill y'all were working on the last time we talked?"

Tom thought of a response that would let Max know he knew. "You mean that government bill dealing with government control?"

"Yeah, that's the one. Whatever happened to it?"

"It died in the House. Nothing has happened really since then. I'm just glad it died in the House and not in the Senate, if you know what I mean?"

Max did. "Yes, I think I do. Have you heard from our mutual friend, the one we played golf with so much?"

"No, I haven't heard from old bear. He seems to have disappeared off the face of the earth. But I can tell you this much, I heard from his wife a while back. Said she and the boys were doing fine."

The nagging voice came over the telephone, "Your three minutes are up; please deposit additional quarters if you care to continue talking."

"Well, Tom, it was good chatting with you. When I get back in town, I'll look you up. Say hello to your lovely wife for me."

"I'll do that, and you do the same. Write this number down and call me tomorrow."

Maxwell knew Tom was up to something and scribbled the number down.

"Call me at three o'clock tomorrow. And, Jeff, take care of yourself. Be careful."

255

As Tom hung up the phone, he could only hope that if anyone was listening, he or she didn't know it was Maxwell Rosenthal. He was glad to know that they were doing well and hoped that Maxwell would call him tomorrow. *This will be the final segment of my special surprise*, Tom thought. *I only hope he will call me.*

Maxwell had felt nervous about calling Tom but was now glad he had followed through. He made his way back to the marketplace and found Judy enjoying the shops. "Did you find anything yet?" Max asked.

"Just a few things." Judy pointed to the clothes draped over her arm. "Do you like this?" She held it up to her face.

Max gave his standard reply, "It's okay. Sure, it looks fine."

"I know it looks fine, but do you like it personally?"

Max thought a minute. "Well, not really. It doesn't look like you. It's ... it's too old looking."

Judy replied, "Finally, a little honesty. Thank you very much for your opinion." She took it back to the rack and replaced it where it had been.

CHAPTER FORTY-SIX

With the police surveillance on their house, Tom and Lucy didn't have to worry about being watched all the time. The IRS had called off their watchdogs, at least for the time being. Tom still suspected that they were listening in on conversations, though his constant inspection of the house, cars, and office turned up no bugging devices of any kind.

Lucy and Molly spent a lot of time together while Tom worked. They had become close friends and enjoyed each other's company. Life had returned to normal for Molly, except she still could not get herself to go back home. Even with police protection, she was too scared, fearing that whoever had tried to kill her three times would not give up. Tom and Lucy gave her a portion of their house, and she felt secure staying with them.

Tom stayed busy working on the most important project of his career. He hit upon an idea, which he hoped would work. It was important to keep it top secret until the release date to prevent being bombarded with negative publicity. The project was a one-hour prime-time special that would be aired on all four networks plus some cable channels. He was able to put it together using his connections in the White House. All of the networks thought it was a press conference from the president of the United States.

So far, he had secured airtime from three of the networks and was waiting for an answer from the fourth. In order to keep it quiet, all of them signed confidentiality agreements stating they could not publicize the upcoming broadcast until the day of airing. It was a big gamble, but Tom felt he had nothing to lose at this point.

The special would be aired in one week; the final taping would take place today. He had one more stop to make before he went to the studio. Pulling into the parking lot, he looked at his watch. It was five minutes before three. He walked into the mall and approached the pay phone from which he had called Max several times before. Someone was using the phone. He paced nervously waiting for her to hang up. It was two teenagers who were laughing and carrying on a senseless conversation. He waited two more minutes, and it seemed that the two girls were going to talk forever. Finally, he could wait no longer and approached the girls.

"Excuse me, but I'm expecting a very important phone call on this telephone any minute now. Could I convince you to take your call somewhere else?" He handed each of them a ten-dollar bill.

They stared at the money and smiled. "Sure, mister, whatever you want." They grabbed the money, hung up the phone, and walked away giggling to each other.

Tom opened his bag and pulled out a tape recorder. He plugged one end of the cord into the microphone jack and placed the other end with a suction cup device onto the side of the mouthpiece. The phone rang.

Tom grabbed the phone. "Hello?"

"Is that you, Tom? This is Ma ... Jeffery Lockwood."

"It's okay, Max; I think we're okay. Listen, this is important. I know you don't have much time. I'm recording this conversation, and with your permission, I want to use it on my special, which will air next week during prime time. Is that okay by you?"

"Sure, anything that will help. Are you going to ask me questions, or you just want me to talk?"

"I'll ask a couple of leading questions, but then you go ahead and talk freely. Tell as much as you can about this whole mess and why you had to flee the country."

Maxwell was nervous. He took a deep breath and said, "Okay, let's do it."

Tom pressed the record button and for the next fifteen minutes listened as Maxwell explained how he had gotten involved in the case, what the IRS had done to him and his clients, and finally how he had left the country fearing for their lives.

"I guess you might say that I'm a fugitive from a system that is so powerful you can't fight it."

"Thanks, Max. I appreciate your input into this program. If you can pick it up wherever you are, we should be on the air next Wednesday between eight and eight thirty."

"It was my pleasure, Tom. I just hope this works. Good luck. I would love to be able to come home again, although I must admit, it's pretty nice down here."

Tom hung up the phone, put his recorder back into the briefcase, and headed out of the mall. Now he was headed for New York City. He glanced at his watch and figured he would be at the studio by 7:00 PM. He decided to take the train and then he would catch the subway to the studio, or he might walk the few blocks from Grand Central Station, depending on how he felt and what time he arrived. Lucy and Molly were going to meet him at the studio. They drove up earlier in the day to spend some time checking out the stores in New York City.

Tom arrived in the city by six and decided to walk the few blocks to the studio. The sidewalks were packed, and the streets were jammed as millions of people poured out of the towering offices, trying to get home from work. Tom couldn't help but wonder, as he watched the mass of people, just how many of them would be affected by the IRS document if the plan was carried out. A panhandler approached him and tried to get a dollar out of him. Finally, Tom reached into his pocket and gave the man five dollars. He was a sucker for a story.

As he walked, a drunk bumped into him, and he heard the crash of a bottle breaking. The drunk looked up at him and said, "You broke my bottle of wine!" Tom tried to ignore him, but the drunk followed after him and began yelling, "Hey, you! I said you broke my bottle. You owe me twenty bucks."

Tom didn't have time to argue. He reached into his billfold and pulled out a twenty-dollar bill and handed it to him. "Here, go drown yourself in liquor and buy yourself a meal while you're at it."

The drunk took the twenty dollars and smiled, giving Tom an okay sign. Tom knew he had just been duped by the oldest trick in New York City. A drunk carries around a bottle of water and watches for an unsuspecting tourist. He bumps into him or her and drops his bottle, making it crash to the cement. It works almost every time as people are in a hurry and the drunk usually threatens to call the police.

Tom arrived at the studio near Fifty-Second Street and took the elevator to the studio. Inside, the producer and associate producer greeted him. "You must be Senator Tom Haden; come right this way. Your wife and friend are already here. Just have a seat in here, and I'll send them in. We're putting some touchups on their makeup, and we'll put a little on you as well. It'll give you a little glow, if you know what I mean."

Tom walked into the open studio and watched as the crew walked around adjusting, calling out orders, and testing their equipment. He had expected a bigger and more elaborate studio than this. It was really nothing to look at, almost drab. Television had a way of making things look better than they were. *That's ironic*, he thought. *Television makes things appear better than they really are, and I'm appearing on television to show the American people that things are worse than they really are.* He chuckled to himself.

"Senator Haden," a voice called out from across the room.

Tom looked up and saw the familiar face, with that famous mustache, walking toward him. Tom walked toward him, extending his hand. "Gerald, it's good to see you again."

"It's nice to see you, Senator. I'm glad you're early. There are some things I would like to go over with you before we begin taping. Let's have a seat over here."

Gerald Harris led Tom to a couple of chairs off the set. He opened his notepad and began going through some modifications he wanted to make. Tom agreed with them all then said, "Gerald, there is one more thing." He reached inside his shirt and pulled out a tape. "This is a recording of a conversation I had just a few hours ago with that attorney I told you about, the one who disappeared. It's about fifteen minutes long. I don't know if we can use any of it or where it will fit in, but there is some good information on here."

Gerald took the tape. "Let's hear what's on it."

As they listened to it, Gerald turned to his producer. "Let's record about five minutes starting right here. I don't know if I'll use all of it, but let's have it ready." He looked at his notes again. "I believe it would work perfectly right after our segment with Molly." He jotted the information in his notes and told his producers to do the same. "Okay, let's get the senator in makeup. We'll start taping in about thirty minutes."

Lucy and Molly were in the makeup room, finishing up. They greeted one another. "Did you two have a good shopping trip?" Tom asked.

"We had fun. Didn't buy anything, but enjoyed the day here. We've been here about forty minutes. How did your day go?" Lucy asked.

"I spoke with Maxwell today. I've got a recording of him, and Gerald may use it on the show."

"That's great; so they're all right then?"

"Yes, but I sensed that he wouldn't mind if this whole thing would get solved so he could come home again."

"Let's pray that your program will be the beginning for getting this whole matter resolved once and for all."

"I'll go along with that."

Tom was told to take his place in the chair, and they began putting makeup on his face. "Do I really need this?" he asked.

"You do if you don't want to look like you are dead," the makeup artist responded. "Besides, we women do this every day. Think about that the next time you're complaining about how your wife is always late." The women laughed.

****

This was the kind of story that Gerald Harris was drawn toward. He not only had agreed to host Tom's special and ask the leading questions, but he had also booked Tom onto some other talk shows the day after the first airing of Tom's special. Gerald wanted to tape more than needed so he would have some exclusive coverage with Tom Haden that had not been aired. He had also told his producers to be prepared to do two days with Senator Haden if this thing was as hot as he thought it would be. The IRS document would be the focal point of all the programs, and he had his copy locked up in a safe spot. All of this was being done with every member of his staff being sworn to secrecy. No one was to leak to anyone, especially the press, what they were working on in the studio after hours. His staff was used to the idea of keeping secrets. This is what had made him and his show that used to be on cable so successful and how he had been able to scoop the networks on many news stories. He wondered, as he sat in his office, where this story would lead and how it would turn out in the end.

Tom had also warned him about the dangers, both to his life and of opening himself up to a thorough investigation by the IRS. This didn't bother Gerald; he loved the excitement of being in the heat of controversy. A lot of people could criticize Gerald Harris for a lot of things, but it would never be that he was afraid of danger. On the contrary, he thrived on it and longed for it. That was why he took this assignment in the first place.

CHAPTER FORTY-SEVEN

Howard paced the office in his usual style, pouring change from one hand to the other nervously and chewing on an old cigar butt. He was smoking nearly five a day now and didn't care who he offended with his smoke.

He walked to his desk and pushed the intercom button. "Sheila, get me Calvin Davis on the phone."

"Yes, sir, right away," Sheila replied. She knew that tone and knew that Howard was irritated about something. She dialed security.

"Sir, Calvin Davis is on line one."

"Calvin, Howard here. What in the sam hill is going on down there? I've been waiting for you to report in on our little problem. What's happening?"

"I'm afraid that we're not making any progress. We still haven't located the Rosenthals. The Danielses were found, but they slipped away from us."

"They what?" Howard yelled.

"We believe we only missed them by about an hour. Somehow they got word we were in town looking for them, and they skipped. We've put an alert out in the surrounding states but have heard nothing so far."

Howard grew angrier. "I'm beginning to believe that all of you are totally incompetent and unable to carry out the simplest plan. How about our senator?"

"He's out of town right now. I don't believe he's doing anything else since his FBI friend has pretty much dropped his investigation of the matter."

"Where did the senator go? Or did he give your boys the slip again?"

"No, sir, we know where he is; we just didn't see a need to follow him there. He and his wife are spending the weekend in New York City, playing tourist."

"What about Molly Shanks?" Howard's voice dropped lower.

"She's with them on the trip. We have it set up to take care of all of them when they return. That's all I can say on the phone right now. Trust me, sir, we have this one under control."

"Your men had Daniels and Rosenthal under control and look what happened. I'm telling you right now, you have five days to get me some results, or I'll have you playing security guard on the nightshift of this building. Do I make myself clear?"

Davis nodded in agreement and mumbled, "Yes, sir, perfectly clear. I'll be in touch."

****

The man worked alone. Armed with only a small toolbox and flashlight, he moved around the house with ease. He worked in the basement preparing the furnace. He had been told to make it look like an accident. Because he was a professional, there would be no signs of tampering. There would be no dynamite or other explosives. All it took was some very simple rewiring procedures.

He crept upstairs in the dark. When he found the thermostat, he checked it. It was set on sixty-five degrees. He turned it up so the furnace clicked on, and the blower began to blow. He ran downstairs to check the furnace. *Perfect. This should do the trick, and no one will ever suspect anything*, he thought.

He ran back upstairs and clicked off the furnace. Making sure everything was as he left it, he crept out the back door and disappeared into the night.

CHAPTER FORTY-EIGHT

When Linda woke up, she rubbed her eyes. "Where are we?" she asked as she looked around, trying to make out the images passing by.

Nathan turned to her, ignoring her question. "Good morning. Welcome back to our world. Are you hungry?"

"I'm hungry, tired, and in desperate need of a bathroom. I could also use a hot shower and a change of clothes. Where are we at now?"

"We'll stop up here in a few minutes. We can get a room and take some time off driving. How does that sound?"

Linda smiled, still looking around. The sights looked familiar, but her mind wasn't kicking in yet. "Are you avoiding my question? Where are we?"

"Don't you know? Look around and see if you notice anything."

She wasn't in the mood for games. She raised her voice. "Look, if I knew where we were, I wouldn't be asking. Just give me a straight answer and find me a bathroom."

Nathan knew when to stop and quickly responded, "We're on the outskirts of Colorado Springs."

"Colorado Springs? Are you crazy? Why are we back here? They're looking for us here."

"Exactly, and the last place they would expect us to be is right back where we started. We'll only be here for a few days. There is some unfinished business I have to take care of before we disappear permanently." Nathan pulled the car into the restaurant and motel area, parking in the circle drive. "I'll see if we can get a room. You get the boys up, and I'll meet you in the restaurant."

The Danielses spent the whole day in the motel room. The boys watched television while Nathan and Linda slept. Finally, about seven in the evening, Nathan woke up.

Yawning and stretching, he slowly stood up. "I'm hungry; how about you guys?"

They all yelled yes in unison.

Linda looked in the mirror. "Give me a few minutes to get ready. I have to do something with my hair."

They entered the restaurant at seven thirty. After they finished their dinner, Allen asked, "Can we go swimming?"

Matthew echoed, "Yeah, can we? Please."

Linda smiled at both of them. "Okay, I guess. Why don't you two go on up to the room and get your suits on, and I'll meet you out at the pool."

Both boys jumped away from the table and ran toward the lobby. Nathan yelled, "Don't go in the water until your mom gets there. Do you hear?"

They both waved their hands in the air as they disappeared out of the restaurant.

Nathan turned around to face Linda and took another sip of his coffee. "I'll be going out tonight, and I'm not sure when I'll be back. It may be very late."

"Do you want to tell me what you're up to and why we're back here or not?"

"I believe it's better that you don't know, and I'll tell you after it's all over. You really need to trust me on this one, honey."

"Oh, I trust you. I would just like to know what you're doing … you know, in case you're hauled off to jail, I'll know why. You're not going to do something stupid, are you?"

Nathan reached across the table and took her hand in his. "I love you, and I'm sorry that I got you into this mess. I'm sorry you lost your home, and I'm sorry we almost lost our kids. I'm sorry that we have to be on the run. I have one chance to make things right, and I have to see if I can or not. It may not even work, but I have to try." He stood up, walked around the table, bent over, and kissed her goodbye. "Don't wait up for me. I'll be late. I love you."

"I love you too. Be careful." She kissed him again and then watched him as he walked out of the restaurant.

****

Nathan pulled up to the gates of Micro Tech. He wasn't sure if his card would still work or not. He wasn't sure of anything at this point, but he knew he had to try. He placed the card into the machine, and to his amazement, the gates swung open. "One down and three to go," he mumbled to himself.

After he parked his car in his usual space, he sat and looked around. Memories flooded his mind as he thought back over the years of dedicated service he had given this company and how good they had been to him. He thought about Ray Phillips and the time when they first saw the document on the computer screen. *Why didn't we just leave it on the computer and forget about it?* he thought to himself. *If only we had known then what we know now. No, I guess I would do it again just to show those …*

He grabbed his briefcase. It wasn't unusual for employees to come in and work at night, especially computer programmers. He often worked fifteen-hour days to get things done. He placed the card into the slot. A buzzer sounded. He opened the door. *I guess they haven't changed any of the codes since I left. They must still have me on medical leave.* He walked through the corridors, making sure he avoided seeing people or being seen. His goal was to get inside the computer room and hope no one else was working in there tonight.

He took the elevator to the fourth floor. As he stepped off the elevator, two men turned toward him. He quickly turned to get a drink of water and pretended to take a long drink. They both ignored him, too busy with their own conversation to even notice. When they disappeared behind the elevator doors, he straightened up and walked to his old office. It wasn't actually an office but rather a large room full of computer equipment. It was more like a lab. He stood in front of the door and looked at it, once again thinking back over all the days he had spent there. He slowly placed his card in the slot, and the doors opened.

Once inside, he sat down at the computer terminal and began hitting the keys, attempting to crack the encryption code. He wasn't sure if he would be able break them to get in the system or not, but he held his breath. He typed his code word and waited. The computer hummed, then suddenly he saw it, the familiar screen. He almost yelled out loud, but caught himself and whispered it, "I'm in, yes!"

For the next four hours, he entered endless access codes and attempted to access the IRS main database known as IDRS. Once inside that system there would be no limit to what he would be able to accomplish. Nothing seemed to be working. *I really thought I could get into the IRS files, but I guess not.* He stood up and stretched. His eyes were getting heavy. He looked at his watch. *One o'clock. I've only got about five more hours before I need to be out of here. Maybe I should call it a night and come back tomorrow. No, I mustn't give up. It's early yet. I'll keep trying.*

He opened his notebook, which listed phone numbers of various government agencies and departments. He picked up the phone and dialed out. Someone answered, "Operations, this is John."

Nathan's voice became authoritative. "Yes, this is Harold in Systems Analysis. How are you doing this evening?"

"Tired, but I'm okay. Who is this?"

"Harold Simmons. I'm working on the new computer systems, and I'm needing your help tonight. What did you say your name was?"

"I'm John."

"John, before I go any further, I need your employee number and your security clearance code. It's protocol, you know."

John understood and proceeded to give him the required information.

Nathan continued, "We're running a test on our computer equipment; could you help me out by doing some testing for us while I'm with you on the phone?"

"Sure, what is it you need?"

"Are you in front of a computer?"

"Yes, I'm at my terminal station."

"First, I need the IP address for the computer you are working on."

John quickly looked it up and told him what it was. Nathan punched in the number on his computer. Within seconds, unbeknown to John, Nathan was able to see John's computer screen on his screen and yet remain invisible. He also had a program running that would record every keystroke made on John's computer.

"Now, John, you do have access to the IDRS, don't you?"

"Yes, of course!"

The IDRS stood for the Integrated Data Retrieval System and held the records of all taxpayers throughout the country. It was accessible to those higher up in the service as well as revenue officers. Using last name, Social Security number, or document number, one could pull up anyone's file, and this was the system used to make changes and update clients' records. This system was monitored and checked to make sure no unauthorized person accessed it. Someone in this system was only a few keystrokes away from generating millions of dollars in false refunds.

Nathan continued, "I need you to access the IDRS if you don't mind."

John did as he was told. It never dawned on him that someone from outside the service was calling him, as he knew that the IRS had been working on updating software for years. "I'm in the system; what do you need now?"

"I think we're almost finished; hold on a second." Nathan had recorded every stroke that John had made on his computer and was able to capture the user name and password. When he was sure he had the information, he continued, "You can log out now. I think that will conclude our test."

"That was easy." John was surprised that it was over so fast.

Nathan typed in the password on his computer, and the program began running. In a few seconds, the screen lit up with a message: **"WELCOME TO THE IRS SERVICE CENTER. PLEASE ENTER YOUR PERSONAL ID."**

"I need to complete my report. Let me verify your personal identification number." Nathan repeated the number John had given him earlier. He put in the ID, and he was into the system.

"We are finished with our test. Everything checks out. Thanks for your help."

"Sure, anytime," John replied.

Nathan had counted on reaching someone who wasn't too alert but wanted to be helpful. He felt sorry that John would probably be called on the carpet in a couple of days for accessing the system, but he couldn't worry about that now. He searched file after file until he finally found what he had hoped to find. On the screen before him was a file, the one he had wanted all along, *Howard L. Baskins.* Nathan smiled a broad grin. He knew what he would do now. "Mr. Baskins, you deserve everything you're about to get. I hope you enjoy it."

Nathan continued pressing the keys like a master at work. He was able to plug into the IRS's files, which recorded audits, tax due notices, levy notices, and other pertinent information. He typed in Howard Baskins' Social Security number and added his name to the delinquent taxpayer list. He typed "lien" in the proper field to show a tax lien had been filed against him. Under the column that asked for the date of notice, Nathan typed in tomorrow's date. *This ought to get your attention, Mr. Baskins.* Under the amount owed, Nathan typed in a figure of $179,000. After the computer automatically computed the interest and penalties, the figure jumped to over $424,000. Nathan was almost laughing out loud as he watched the computer do the calculations.

Suddenly, the door flew open, and the lights came on, flooding the room with light. Nathan turned and saw a security guard standing at the door with his hand still on the switch. The guard was startled. "Oh, I'm sorry. I didn't know anyone was working in here."

Nathan didn't recognize the guard. He was relieved but still shaking. "Uh, yeah. I should be finishing up in here before too long. I like working with the lights off though. You must be new here. I've been out on medical leave and am just returning."

The guard stretched taller and put his thumbs inside his belt. "Yep, I've been here about two weeks now. I'm just part-time, but hey, it's a start."

"Well, I'm sure I'll be seeing more of you. Thanks for checking on me." Nathan turned back to his work.

The guard turned the lights off. "No problem, take your time. Just let me know when you leave."

Nathan turned his attention to the computer screen. He breathed a sigh of relief, but his heart was still racing. He opened up his own file. He couldn't believe it. There it was on the screen, information regarding the amounts owed, notices sent, and taxes levied. He decided to try something and went to another screen. Under the amount paid, he input the amount that was owed. The balance at the bottom of the screen quickly changed to zero. "There, at least I'll disappear without owing the IRS money," Nathan whispered to himself. "And who knows, maybe we'll even get our house back, assuming of course this all works."

Nathan knew that what he was doing was illegal, but he rationalized it, knowing he was innocent. He wasn't sure what kind of bells and alarms were going off at the IRS computer center, but he was hoping that no one was paying attention. *What are they going to do, arrest me? I'm already a fugitive from the United States government. They are already trying to kill us.*

Nathan worked until four o'clock in the morning. He stood up and stretched then reached down and turned off the computer. On the way out the door, he saw the security guard who had come in earlier. He waved to him and said, "Good night. It took me a little longer than I thought. I think I'll sleep in tomorrow."

The security guard waved at him. "You look like you could use some sleep. Have a good night."

After Nathan opened the door to the motel room, he crept in quietly. Linda stirred in bed and turned over. She sat up and whispered, "What time is it?"

"Shh, go back to sleep. It's too early to get up." He slipped off his pants and climbed quietly into the bed. Linda curled up close to him and fell back asleep.

Nathan lay in bed with his eyes wide open staring at the ceiling, wondering what would happen to them and thinking about what he had done that morning. He finally fell asleep.

CHAPTER FORTY-NINE

Lucy and Molly spent the weekend in New York City and were glad to get back to Alexandria, Virginia. Tom decided to go to the office and catch up on some work.

Lucy opened the door. "Brr, it's cold in here. I'll turn up the heat." She walked to the thermostat. "No wonder, it's only sixty-three degrees in here." She turned the dial until she heard the furnace click on, and the blower began blowing cold air through the vents at first. After a while, the air began to turn warm then hot.

Molly carried her suitcase up the stairs. "I think I'll take a hot shower and lay down for awhile," she yelled down to Lucy, who was now in the kitchen.

"Are you hungry?" Lucy yelled back.

"No, I'm still full from breakfast and lunch. I really don't need anything, just a hot bath and a warm bed."

"Okay, have a nice rest. I may do the same." Lucy walked out toward the street to check the mailbox. The mail had stacked up in the couple of days they were gone, and the box was full. She carried it back to the house and went to the kitchen, sat down at the table, and began sorting through it.

The telephone rang. "Hello, Haden residence."

"Is this Lucy?"

Lucy recognized the voice and cringed. "Yes, how are you, Abigail? You probably want to speak to Molly."

"I don't care; I was just calling to see if she was all right. I had one of my feelings again. You know where I get a funny feeling when something is wrong. I guess everything must be all right."

"Yes, we're just fine. We just got back from New York City and were—"

Abigail interrupted, "I went to New York City one time, and that was all I needed. How can those people stand to live in that crowded place? When we were there, the streets were filthy, and there were criminals everywhere. You could tell they were the criminal type by the way they stared at you. No, sir, I don't need to go back to that city no more."

Lucy began to yawn then cut in before Abigail could start another sentence, "Well, Molly is in the shower. I'll tell her you called when she wakes up from her nap. I think I could use one myself."

"Well, I'm just glad she is fine. I'll call back tomorrow, and we'll chat. You lay down and get some rest."

"Thanks, I think I will. Goodbye now." Lucy hung up the phone and laid her head down on the kitchen table. She yawned again and fell asleep.

Molly finished her shower, put a robe around her, then lay down on the bed and closed her eyes. She fell asleep quicker than she had thought she would.

****

Tom looked at the stack of papers his secretary had piled on his desk. He wasn't sure he could face them but began to plow through them one by one. He was glad that he had decided to return to the office. *At least I won't have to face this in the morning. I can start off clean.* As he signed papers, looked over proposals, and shuffled through the stacks of mail, his mind continued thinking about the special, which would be aired this week. It was difficult to concentrate when his career as a United States senator was in jeopardy.

After he had gone through the entire stack of paperwork, he looked at his watch. *It's eleven o'clock already. I better get home and get some sleep.* He cleared off the rest of his desk, placing most of the papers back on his secretary's desk. He turned out the lights and headed for his car.

When he drove up to the house, he noticed all the lights were still on, both upstairs and down. *They must still be up*, he thought.

As he opened the back door, the house was unusually quiet. "Lucy, I'm home. Lucy?" There was no response. He walked into the kitchen and saw Lucy with her head lying on the table. He touched her shoulder and immediately knew something was wrong. "Lucy, wake up." He shook her harder, but there was no response.

He ran out of the room and ran through the house. "Molly, Molly, are you awake?" He ran upstairs to her bedroom. He knocked loudly. Hearing no response, he opened the door slowly. Molly was lying on the bed. Tom yelled at her. He went over and shook her violently, slapping her gently on the face. "Molly, you have to wake up. What's happened?" Molly didn't respond.

Tom grabbed the phone beside the bed and dialed 911. He told them the situation, gave his address, and hung up the phone. He then ran back downstairs to Lucy. He laid her on her back on the floor and began to give her CPR. It seemed like hours, but within ten minutes, he heard the sirens pull into the driveway. He ran to the door and opened it, waving them inside.

They worked feverishly on Molly and Lucy. Within minutes, they had them on a stretcher, taking them to the ambulance. The house was full of firemen, and several police officers had also arrived on the scene.

The senator yelled to the chief, "I'm going to the hospital with my wife. You don't need me here, do you?"

"No, Senator, go ahead."

A fireman came up out of the basement. "We found the problem, sir."

The chief looked up to make sure the senator was still there. "What is it?"

"The furnace had a loose connection on one of the pipes and was throwing carbon monoxide all through the house."

Tom walked slowly toward the fireman. Anticipating Tom's question, the fireman added, "It doesn't look like foul play. It looks like an accident, plain and simple."

The chief turned to Tom. "It happens a lot with these old houses. We see it all the time. You run along to the hospital, Senator. We'll take care of everything on this end."

Tom walked out the door and climbed in his car. He couldn't shake the feelings he was having that somebody had just tried to kill him and his family. He didn't believe that it was any accident.

He followed closely behind the ambulance to Mt. Sinai Hospital. When they pulled into the emergency entrance, the hospital doors opened immediately, and doctors and nurses came pouring out to meet the ambulance.

It only took a few minutes to get Molly and Lucy inside. Tom watched the expression of the paramedic as he explained the situation to the doctor who was taking over. One of the nurses walked over to Tom. "Are you Senator Tom Haden?"

"Yes, I am."

"Please come with me, Senator. You can wait in the private lounge area. We'll get word to you as soon as we know something."

"Can't I go in with her? I need to—"

"No, Senator. It's best if you wait out here. We can work better that way. She's in good hands. Dr. Snyder is one of our best ER doctors."

"Is she alive?" Tom's voice quivered.

"I don't have any news on her condition, but we'll let you know just as soon as we can. Could I get you a cup of coffee or anything?"

"No, I don't think so. Thanks. Just let me know something as soon as you find out."

"I will." The nurse closed the door.

Ten minutes had passed, and there was a knock on the door. Before Tom could say anything, a young man walked in and introduced himself. "Good evening, I'm Mike Dahman. I'm the chaplain on duty. I understand your wife has been brought into the emergency room. Would you like some company?"

"Sure, come on in. Do you have any word on my wife yet?" Tom asked hopefully.

"They don't tell me much. I know her condition is serious, but that's all I know so far. How did it happen?"

Tom spent the next few minutes reliving the past hour, bringing the chaplain up to date. The chaplain listened, only asking questions that would allow Tom to talk freely. There was a knock on the door, and a doctor opened it. "I'm Doctor Snyder. Senator, I'm afraid I have some bad news."

Tom turned white. He was expecting the worst, but he had hopes that somehow she would pull through. He sat down in the chair.

The doctor continued, "Your wife died. We believe she was dead on arrival. I don't believe we ever had a chance, but we tried our best."

Tom broke down and started crying. The chaplain leaned in close to Tom and placed his arms around him to give him some support.

"I'm sorry, Senator. We truly are sorry. Would you like to see her now?"

Tom nodded his head to indicate he would. The chaplain asked, "Would you like for me to go with you?"

Tom again acknowledged that he would. In the military, he had seen death firsthand, but now, he was weak. His legs felt like they were made of rubber. As they approached the room and opened the door, he saw his wife lying on the table. He ran to her side and fell on top of her, crying uncontrollably. "Lucy, my darling Lucy. Why? Why did you have to leave me?" He felt her hand, lifting it up. It was cold. It didn't feel the same as it once had. He looked at her face and continued crying.

The chaplain patted Tom on the back and whispered, "She's okay now, Senator. She's in God's hands. He'll take care of her."

Tom barely heard the words of the chaplain. He didn't want her in God's hands; he wanted to feel her in his hands. He cried out again, "Lucy, I love you. Please come back to me. Lucy, honey, I can't live without you. Please … please … please."

The doctor and chaplain tried to comfort Tom but knew there was very little they could do. They knew from experience that in time, he would face the reality of her death.

Thirty minutes later, when Tom regained his composure, he remembered Molly. "What about Molly Shanks? Is she dead also?"

"I'm afraid so. She evidently died before your wife. Do you know if she has any relatives we can notify?"

Tom straightened up. "Just her mother, here locally. She has some children who live out of town. I'd contact them first. Someone needs to be with her mother when she's told. I guess I could go tell her. I don't know anyone else who knows her. What do I need to do here?"

Doctor Snyder answered, "We have some forms to fill out and need for you to sign. We'll need to know what funeral home you want us to contact, then they'll take care of everything else."

Tom finished up what he had to do. When he left the hospital, it was almost two o'clock in the morning. He stood in a daze staring up at the sky, looking at the stars. He didn't quite know what to do next. *I guess I'll go see Mrs. Abigail Bishop and get that over with*, he thought. *That will probably take the rest of the night.* He wasn't looking forward to this at all. He had to make some calls first, so he stopped by the house. He was so tired, he didn't know if he would make it through the night or not, but he knew he had to try. He picked up the phone to call his in-laws and children. *They will need to know tonight before the news media begins telling the world*, Tom thought. *They're going to miss their mom. She was the center of their world, when she was there with them.* He replaced the receiver as he began to cry again.

CHAPTER FIFTY

Howard Baskins stared at the notice he had received. He couldn't believe his eyes. "How did they come up with this figure?" He screamed to himself for the fifth time, "And why wasn't I notified before this? I can't come up with this kind of money."

His thoughts were interrupted when Sheila paged him on the intercom, "Mr. Calvin Davis is on your private line, sir."

"Thanks, Sheila." Howard picked up the phone. "You better have some good news for me."

"Well, sir, we were two-thirds successful. Lucy Haden and Molly Shanks died this morning at Mt. Sinai Hospital. Senator Haden is still alive."

"Maybe that will work for us. Maybe now he'll be more willing to give up that document. Any word on our other missing persons?"

"Nothing new since we talked last time. Daniels has disappeared, but we're still looking. We believe he may be headed for Oregon or Canada. We're watching the border crossings as best we can."

"Good. Let me know if you find anything on either Daniels or Rosenthal."

"Yes, sir. I'll talk to you later."

Howard hung up the phone. He wasn't proud of the accomplishment but was at least glad that two more people were out of the way. He turned his attention back to his personal problems.

The intercom buzzed again. "Sir, the chief wants to see you in his office immediately."

"Call him back and tell him I'm busy and—"

"Sir, he said he didn't care what you were doing; you were to drop everything and come to his office now."

Howard couldn't imagine what was so important that it couldn't wait a little while. "Okay, tell him I'll be right up." He walked to the mirror and straightened his tie. He put on his suit coat and brushed through his hair, what little there was left.

He walked into the receptionist's office, and she smiled at him. "Good morning, Mr. Baskins. You can go right in; the chief is expecting you."

Howard walked in and shook hands with the chief. They made small talk for a minute, and then the chief spoke, "Howard, I've called you up here because I received some distressing news this morning. I understand you are under investigation by the IRS and owe nearly half a million dollars in back taxes. Is this true?"

Howard stammered, "Well, uh, sir ... I just received the notice—"

The chief interrupted, "Just tell me, Howard; is it true?"

"Well, yes, sir, it's true but—"

"There are no buts in the service. You know the rules. If you owe money to the IRS, you must pay it immediately or forfeit your job. We can't have our own people owing us large sums of money and not paying their taxes. It doesn't look good for the service. Do you understand?"

"Yes, sir, I understand perfectly, but there's a problem here."

"What's the problem?"

"I don't believe I owe the money. I've never been audited, and my returns have never been questioned."

"Now, that's not what my records indicate. They say you've been given ample notices that the tax was due, and you ignored them. Furthermore, it indicates that a Notice of Levy was sent to you thirty days ago, and you ignored that. Now we have received a garnishment notice, which we must honor. That's the problem. Do you have the money to pay this notice?"

Howard looked at him in disbelief. "How many people do you know working for the service who could come up with nearly a half-million dollars? That's ridiculous. Of course, I don't have the money."

"I'm putting you on suspension until this matter is cleared up. At least if the media gets a hold of it, I can say we have dismissed you. Turn over all your work to your assistants. I'll have a meeting with them to bring them up to date. Meanwhile, you go out and get this taken care of and paid. You can fight it later, but if you want to keep your job, you'll have to get it paid. That's the rules."

The chief stood up to indicate the conversation was over. Howard walked out of the office, almost slamming the door behind him but catching himself just before he did. He returned to his office and told Sheila the news. She was shocked. He called a meeting of his staff and by noon was out the door returning home. He had no idea where he was going to come up with that kind of money in such a short period of time.

Power Unleashed

CHAPTER FIFTY-ONE

Nathan needed to make one more trip to Micro Tech. He had been working diligently all night, every night, for the past three nights and sleeping during the day. This would be his last trip. He had no idea if what he was doing would accomplish anything, but at least he felt like he was fighting back. It gave him a sense of accomplishment and a feeling of pride to know that he was using the same system that had brought him down to retaliate and get his revenge.

He sat at the computer terminal and contemplated his next step. He called up his Swiss bank account and looked at the balance. It had been opened the week before with only one hundred dollars. Now it was time to do some major transfers. He plugged into the account for Howard Baskins. The balance showed an amount of over $5 million dollars. Nathan had opened the account in Howard Baskins' name and had been making transfers into the account for the past few nights using funds from the dummy corporations that the group had set up for themselves and had already ripped off millions of dollars in their test runs. He obtained this information from the document and was able to track down the bank accounts and hack into them. He left a trail that Howard would never be able to explain and that the FBI would surely find. Hopefully this would be the end of the corporations and the money would be returned to the government.

Now he was ready for the final step of his plan. He hit the keys and made the transfer: two million dollars from their corporate accounts into a personal Swiss bank account. He figured this would replace everything the IRS had taken from them plus some of the heartache and loss of earnings. He justified his actions by telling himself that he was only taking back what had originally belonged to him in the first place.

He called up his bank record, and there it was, a new balance of $2,000,100. *This looks like a lot of money, but it has to last us the rest of our lives. Besides, they owe it to us for ruining our lives.* Now, they were free to go anywhere in the world. He would have the funds transferred into ten smaller accounts in banks all over the world, which he would set up once he arrived at his final destination. The trail would be so long and confusing no one would be able to find it, at least he hoped that would be the case.

Nathan turned off the computer, leaned back in his chair, and let out a long breath. His task was done. He looked at his watch and saw it was only one o'clock in the morning. "I'm done early tonight," he yelled to the security guard on the way out the door. "You have a good evening." The guard waved to him as he left.

The night air was cold and crisp. Nathan felt like hitting his heels together in the parking lot. Now all they had to do was get out of the country. He had plans for that as well, but first he had to break the news to Linda. He wasn't sure how she would take to the idea of living in a foreign country for the rest of her life. He was about to find out.

****

Nathan woke up feeling like someone was watching him. He slowly opened his eyes and saw four eyes staring at him. It was Matthew and Allen. He rolled over, rubbing his eyes to wake up. "Good morning, boys. What are you doing?"

"Waiting for you to get up," Matthew responded.

"Yeah, Mom said we had to wait for you to get up before we could go eat breakfast, and we're hungry."

"So, you were going to stand over me and watch me until I woke up? Is that it?"

"No, we were going to throw a glass of water on you if you didn't wake up." Matthew laughed, exposing a glass of water he had been holding behind his back.

"It seems a shame to let it go to waste." Matthew held the glass up to his mouth like he was going to drink it, then without warning slung the glass of water toward his dad, hitting him square in the face.

Nathan jumped out of the bed, while Matthew screamed, "Mom! Help me, Mom!"

Before Linda could get out of the bathroom, Nathan grabbed Matthew and threw him on the floor. "Get me a glass of water, Allen."

"I can't. Matthew will kill me."

Linda walked out. "What's going on out here? It sounds like you guys are wrecking the place."

Nathan stood up, letting Matthew go. "No, it's just a little fun for us boys. Good morning, sweetheart."

"Good morning. You got back early last night. Are you through now?"

"Yep, we're going to check out today. We'll talk more about it over breakfast. I need to get into the bathroom for a minute." He leaped into the bathroom and shut the door behind him.

Forty minutes later, they sat in the restaurant ordering breakfast. Nathan thumbed through the morning paper. On page two he saw a story that struck his attention.

Senator's Wife and Friend Die in Accident

Lucy Haden, wife of Senator Thomas Haden, was found unconscious in her home in Alexandria, Virginia. She and a friend, Molly Shanks, had just returned from a trip to New York City. Officials on the scene attribute the death to carbon monoxide poisoning. There were no signs of foul play, and suicide has been ruled out. A faulty furnace system is to blame, and the deaths were ruled as accidental in the police report. Both were pronounced dead upon arrival at Mt. Sinai Hospital.

The article went on to name the survivors. Nathan leaned over and showed Linda the article. After she read it, they looked at each other. "Do you really believe it was just an accident?" Linda asked.

"I don't care how they died; I would bet you anything that it was no accident. Somebody got paid big bucks to make it look like an accident." Nathan folded up the paper and laid it down. "This makes a good introduction to what I need to talk about this morning."

"What about the boys?" Linda asked.

"They'll be all right. They need to hear this. It concerns them as well. I've been making some arrangements for us to leave the country."

"Leave the country? But, Nathan, we can't just up and leave this—"

Nathan put his finger to her lips. "Hear me out first. We have to get out of here. As long as we're in this country, we're in danger. Look at what they did to the senator's wife. I can't take a chance of letting that happen to you or the boys. They won't stop until they get rid of us. We're getting our

285

passports in Phoenix, and then we're on our way to a small island in the Caribbean. I've got it all worked out. We'll stay there for a while, maybe a year or so until we find the exact place we want to go and settle down."

"What will we do there? How will we survive?" Linda raised her voice.

"I've got that all figured out as well. You'll have to trust me on this one, at least for a little while. We'll be okay financially for many years, especially down there where the cost of living is cheaper."

"But, Nathan, we don't have much money left. How in the world are we going to be able to afford airline tickets?"

"That one's easy. Before we left, Maxwell gave me the title to his car. We'll sell it and use the money to get us there. It should bring us over twenty thousand easy."

Linda was skeptical, but both boys thought it was a neat plan. They liked the idea of going to a foreign country; at least they thought they did.

"It's all settled. We leave here today, and we'll drive to New Mexico. We'll sell the car there and catch a plane to Miami tomorrow. I've already made the reservations and everything."

Linda still looked unsure about the whole plan but managed to get out the words, "Okay, I guess." Both boys were excited about the new adventure.

They left the restaurant to pack their suitcases. Nathan would be glad when they were finally out of the country. Until then, he would remain nervous and cautious.

Later that same afternoon, as they drove toward Albuquerque on Interstate 25, Nathan could not help but wonder what was going to happen with Howard Baskins and how all of this was going to end.

CHAPTER FIFTY-TWO

It was ironic that Tom Haden's hour-long television special fell on the same day as the funerals for Lucy and Molly. It was scheduled to be aired at eight o'clock in the evening, Eastern Standard Time. The fourth network had agreed to air the broadcast, and it would be aired simultaneously on all four. In addition to the networks, several cable channels were carrying the show as well as some national radio stations. After tonight, Tom Haden would be a household name.

The president of the United States had agreed to start the evening and introduce the subject. The networks had all given up an hour of their time thinking he was giving an address to the people and an update on economic conditions of the government. He would then introduce Gerald Harris, who would take over from there and introduce the evening's topic. Gerald decided to start off the segment with a live shot of himself to bring the viewing audience up to date on the events that had taken place during the week. Tom would join him by satellite, and they would then introduce the different segments that had been taped earlier that week. There would be three live broadcasts: one in the beginning, one in the middle, and one at the end. Gerald would ask the questions and keep the show rolling. Tom was told that all he had to do was respond to Gerald with appropriate answers.

The countdown was about to begin. There was a live shot of the president in the Oval Office. "Fellow Americans, good evening. I come to you tonight with some very special news about something that has been going on in our government that even our senators and congressmen do not know about. As you know, the Internal Revenue Service has operated for years now under their own authority pretty much making their own policies. They are, for all intents and purposes, a self-governing body.

However, lately, some things have come to my attention, and I want to do everything in my power to bring them to your attention so we can put a stop to their actions. To explain all of this in detail, I've asked Gerald Harris to take over. Please watch and listen."

The president finished up his introduction and was about to turn over the live feed to New York City. A voice off camera yelled, "Get ready out there, people. Five, four, three, two, and one." He pointed his finger at Gerald to give him the cue.

The camera shot was wide, with Gerald sitting on a stool. Behind him was the emblem of the United States of America. To his left was the American flag. As the camera zoomed closer, Gerald stood up off his stool and began walking toward the camera. "Good evening and welcome to this special program. Mr. President, we thank you for making this happen tonight, and the American people will thank you also. I can assure you that tonight's program will be unlike anything you have ever seen before. You will be watching history in the making. You will be watching the news as it is happening, before it has even become news. This show is about power. This show is about corruption in the system. This show is about how power unleashed can be overused when corruption enters the system. This show is about what is happening in your country right now."

The script scrolled across the screen in front of him, each word carefully chosen. The cameras that were run by remote control by a single man in a booth off to the right of the studio followed Gerald closely as he strolled across the stage area. In the far background was a picture of Washington DC with the Capitol quite visible. The camera pulled away from Gerald as he walked, getting a full body shot of him and the Capitol Building behind him.

"I am joined tonight live from Washington DC by Senator Thomas Haden, who is responsible for this event. Good evening, Senator, and welcome."

"Good evening, Gerald. It's good to be here tonight to be able to tell my story." Tom was nervous. He had never enjoyed live television appearances. The camera picked up the senator's face on a large television screen behind Gerald.

"I'll start tonight, Senator, by asking you to briefly explain why you've chosen, at great personal expense I might add, to get your message across in this manner."

"I'd love to elucidate that to the American people. What we are about to witness on this program tonight began taking place several weeks ago. I originally tried to tell the people what was happening by holding a news conference. You may recall that I was scoffed at, and the media had been leaked lies about me by the government. There were false rumors spreading through Washington and around the country that I was being audited and charged with misuse of campaign funds."

Gerald cut in, "And recently there have been some new developments to this story, is that correct?"

"Yes, Gerald, that's correct. The same people in government who are responsible for the deaths of several other people murdered my wife and our good friend, Molly Shanks, this week. That's why this show is so vital to me." Tom began to choke up on camera.

Gerald showed sympathy and spoke in a quiet voice, "And you just buried your wife today. Our sympathies go out to you, Senator, and thank you for taking the time from your own tragedy to be with us tonight."

The camera backed off of Senator Haden and showed Gerald in a close-up. "What you are about to see may shake your faith in the American system. It will certainly wake you up to the need for reform in our system. It shows what can happen if the wrong people get into power. It illustrates in a way you never dreamed what happens when power is unleashed with no controls. Watch closely."

The program continued, showing the footage that had been taped a few days earlier. Gerald walked off the stage toward the camera crew. The executive producer called over to him, "Gerald, you have an urgent call on line one."

Gerald ran over to a phone, pressed the button, and said, "Hello, this is Gerald."

"I'm glad I found you. I don't know if you can use it or not, but I have some more information on your story. I saw the first part of the story and knew I had to try and find you. I'm Nathan Daniels."

Gerald was ecstatic. He motioned for his producer to come over and whispered to him while Nathan talked, "Get this call on a recorder and hurry." He spoke to Nathan, "Don't say anymore until I get a recording device on you. I may be able to use this on the next segment. We're tight, but I think I can work it in by cutting down some of my dialogue."

The producer gave Gerald the sign indicating he was hooked up. "Okay, now we're recording you. Go ahead and tell me everything you can."

The conversation lasted only ten minutes. Nathan was cautious not to give any indication of their present whereabouts or future plans. He stuck with the facts about how they had discovered the document and how the IRS harassed them and took all of their possessions, including their children. Gerald listened intently. He had heard some of this from Tom, but it was different coming firsthand from the source.

Gerald interrupted Nathan, "I'm going to have to go now for our next live segment. You hold on, and I'll be back to you."

Gerald ran back onto the stage, and the production manager began the countdown while makeup people swarmed around him giving him a last-minute touchup. "And five, four, three, two, one." And the finger pointed toward Gerald.

"I know as you watched this first segment, you are as shocked as I was. This is not a fabricated story. This is not something that happened years ago. This is an event, which is taking place right now, even as we speak. I just received a call from one of the other victims. He has disappeared but chose to call in to tell his side of the story. We'll talk with him in just a few moments, but first let's talk with Senator Tom Haden again. Senator, you mentioned several times in this first segment about a document. We'll hear more about it in the next segment, but could you tell us briefly just why this document is so dangerous?"

Tom cleared his throat. "Yes, Gerald, I'd love to. This document outlines a plan to collect taxes from unsuspecting taxpayers who have already paid their fair share. What it outlines is this: The IRS would begin destroying old tax records from as far back as twenty years ago. Then they will send notices to those people telling them that according to their records, these people never filed nor paid their taxes. If they can't produce the cancelled checks and proof they paid the taxes due, then they will have no choice but to pay the additional taxes, plus penalties and interest."

"But, isn't there a statute of limitations, like three years, Senator?"

"Well, you see, that's the beauty of this scheme. The statute of limitations does not apply if a person has never filed. The person at the IRS who concocted this scheme is counting on the fact that most people do not keep records beyond four or five years. Thereby, when they receive the notice, they will not be able to produce proof that they filed and paid the taxes due. With the IRS, the burden of proof is always on the taxpayer. If the IRS says you haven't filed, the current law says there is no statute of limitations. Therefore, a person who cannot prove he has filed will have no recourse other than paying the amount the IRS says is due or attempt fighting them, which usually is in vain. With the court system, a person is innocent until proven guilty, but with the IRS, a person is guilty until he or she proves himself or herself innocent. It's totally reversed, and this needs to be changed also."

"It sounds like we need to change the entire system. Senator, I'll get back to you in just a moment. But first, we have with us, right now on the phone, the man who first discovered this document, Mr. Nathan

Daniels. We are delighted you called, and I want to thank you personally for your bravery and your willingness to take a stand on this issue. But tell me, why didn't you just turn this over to the media when you first found it? Why did you wait until now?"

"Gerald, we knew as soon as we read this document that we were in over our heads. This was big, but we had no idea how big. The first thing that my friend, Ray Phillips, and I did was to go to an attorney friend for help and legal advice."

"You're speaking, of course, about Maxwell Rosenthal, who we'll hear from a little bit later in the program," Gerald added.

"Yes, we took the document to him. He advised us to sit tight while he made some phone calls. He called Washington DC and spoke with Senator Haden, and the next thing we all knew, everything hit the fan. Our houses were bugged, we were followed, kept under surveillance, and I was audited. All of Maxwell's clients were being audited, and I don't know what all happened to the senator. Anyway, by the time we tried to go to court and the press, the IRS had gotten to both, and we were labeled as traitors and tax evaders. My wife and I were beaten up in our own home by what we believed to be Treasury agents, and everything we owned was confiscated by the IRS without due course. When we woke up in our hospital room, we found out that even our children had been permanently taken from us. All of this happened because we failed to give back this document that we had found."

"I'm receiving a cue here that we have to move on to the next segment. This next video portion will give you detailed information about the document that Nathan discovered. You won't believe what you see, but remember, these are the undistorted facts."

The production manager gave a cut sign across his neck, and Gerald breathed a sigh of relief that they were off of live television again. He walked back to the phone and spoke some more with Nathan.

On television screens across America, Tom Haden showed the world the document that had been discovered. It outlined a plan of systematically and knowingly destroying a taxpayer's tax records that were in the system and then sending out notices showing the taxpayer had never filed returns for five to ten years earlier and that he or she owed the back taxes plus penalties and interest. Tom also showed where this had been tested in a pilot program in the Northwest. Sixty-five percent of the people who received such notices ended up paying the amount due or settling for a lesser amount because they had not kept any records dating that far back. This pilot program was all the ammunition that Howard Baskins needed to implement his nationwide collection efforts to get revenues up over the next few years.

Tom also outlined how the head of collections, Howard Baskins, was doing this to promote himself in the eyes of his superiors and how the document explained that part of the proceeds would be funneled into his and some others' personal bank accounts. At the end of the video, Tom Haden looked right into the camera and said, "This man and those conspiring with him must be stopped. The government tax system should never be abused in this manner. This is why I've chosen to spend my own money to get this message out to you, the American people. I am also setting up, along with some attorneys, an advocacy group to help anyone who has IRS problems at no cost. This group will intercede on your behalf and fight for you. What can you do? Go to our Web site and get a copy of this document today. There, we have outlined your rights as a taxpayer. Get to know them. You do not have to be intimidated by the IRS into paying something you do not rightfully owe. Secondly, write to your congressmen and tell them to change the IRS system to reduce some of their powers. We've been reluctant in the past to dictate to the IRS what it can and cannot do. This must stop. They work for the people. The Gestapo tactics, intimidation, and threats must stop. This is still a free country, and the last time I checked, a person was innocent until proven guilty in a court of law.

"Third, write to the media. Send a letter to your newspaper, the television stations, as well as the radio stations to let them know you want them to stand up and fight for the truth. In the past, they have been easily swayed by the press releases from the IRS. The politicians are also intimidated by the IRS, afraid of being audited and harassed if they don't say what the IRS wants them to say. Finally, if you don't have access to our Web site, write me at the address, which will be shown on the screen, and I'll send you a copy of this document and a copy of the Taxpayer's Bill of Rights so you'll know how to proceed if something like this were to happen to you.

"I thank you for watching this program this evening and trust it has been an eye opener to all of you. I look forward to fighting this fight with you. Together, we can win against this corrupt system. Thank you and good night."

Gerald was back on stage, and the camera moved in to a close-up shot. "We are live once again, and Tom Haden joins me by satellite. We also have Nathan Daniels on the phone, who has been involved in this case from the very beginning. Tom, you believe that your wife and friend were both killed by the IRS, is that correct?"

"Well, I wouldn't say by the IRS directly, but I believe that somehow they were responsible. So far, everyone who has been connected with this case is either dead or on the run. We have Ray Phillips, who first discovered the document, died of gunshot wounds from a supposed burglary. Douglas Preston, who helped me obtain the document out of Molly Shanks' computer where her husband had stored it, he died from an auto accident. George Shanks supposedly committed suicide, but now we're wondering about that. We have documented proof that someone made three attempts on Molly Shanks' life, and of course, the final one succeeded. Then we have my wife, Lucy, who is an innocent victim. In addition, Maxwell and Judy Rosenthal have disappeared, and two people were killed in their home, which we believe were mistaken for the Rosenthals. Then finally we have Nathan Daniels, who has had to disappear to survive."

"We have Nathan on the phone right now. Nathan, do you concur with the senator's conclusions?"

"There's no doubt, Gerald. There are just too many coincidences to ignore. I believe that my wife and I would be dead now if we hadn't fled when we did."

"I understand that you also have kidnapped your own children from their foster home, and they are with you. Is that correct?"

"Yes, it is. The state took our children and declared us as unfit parents. We're fighting back in the only way we know how. We've taken our children back, and we'll go somewhere else to live out our lives, hopefully in peace and without ever being harassed by the government."

"Well, gentlemen, our time is up. This has been a most informative hour. I thank each of you for sharing your story with us and pray that this nightmare will soon be over for you both. If you want to see more of this, Senator Haden and I will be on several talk shows over the next few weeks. Consult your local listings and program guides as to which ones. We were unable to get Nathan Daniels' story on the air in its entirety, but if you go to the Web site on your screen, we will have the full recorded version posted on there in a few hours as well as a rebroadcast of this show. Until then, this is Gerald Harris reminding you to stand up for your rights. If you would like to comment on tonight's broadcast, dial 1-800-555-4700 and tell us what you think."

The producer and a few other crewmembers applauded as they signed off the air.

A slide showed on the screen the address and Web site address where people could go to get more information. Credits began to roll thanking all of those who had helped put the broadcast together in record time.

Gerald thanked the crew for their dedication and hard work. All of them gathered around him and began bombarding him with more questions.

CHAPTER FIFTY-THREE

Frank Mitchell stood on the doorstep with two other FBI agents, ringing the doorbell. A woman's voice came over the intercom. "Yes, who is it?"

"This is Frank Mitchell; I'm with the FBI. I need to talk with Howard Baskins. Is he in this morning?"

"Just a minute please."

In a few moments, Howard opened the door. He had a puzzled look on his face when he saw the other two men standing there. "Good morning, come on in. Would you like a cup of coffee?"

The three men remained on the steps and made no movement into the house. Frank spoke in a monotone voice, "Howard Baskins, we have a warrant for your arrest. You have the right to remain silent. You have the right to have an attorney present during questioning. If you give up your right to remain silent, anything you say can and will be used against you in a court of law. Do you understand your rights?"

"What is this all about? Why am I under arrest?"

"Mr. Baskins, please answer the question; do you understand your rights?"

"Yes, I do; now, what is this all about?"

One of the agents turned Howard around, pulling one arm behind his back. He adjusted the handcuffs to fit comfortably.

Frank began to explain, "You are under arrest for conspiracy against the United States government and embezzlement."

It was the last part of the charges that Howard heard. "Embezzlement? I've never—"

"Perhaps you can explain to a jury how you suddenly accumulated over five million dollars in a Swiss bank account on a salary of one hundred ten thousand per year."

"Five million dollars? I don't know what you're talking about. I've never … I don't have five million dollars."

The agent gently shoved Howard toward the door while Frank continued to speak, "Well, you can explain all of that to the judge. I'm sure you'll have a good explanation of why you opened a Swiss bank account and how you obtained this sudden wealth."

They placed Howard in the back seat of the car and sped off toward headquarters.

****

The evening news carried a teaser ad, which said, "The IRS is rocked with a scandal as one of its high officials is arrested. More arrests are expected in the next twenty-four hours. Details at six."

Senator Tom Haden's popularity was soaring. Since the airing of his program the night before, calls and telegrams to his office were pouring in from all over the country, thanking him for his bravery and his stand against the deceptive ways of the system. The president of the United States called him to personally thank him for his fight and vowed to the senator that he would support legislation to clean up the IRS.

He appeared on two talk shows that morning; his picture and name were in every newspaper across the country; and he would be the main topic on all the news programs.

In every story, there was mention of two other couples that were yet to be located, the Danielses and Rosenthals. Their pictures were splashed on every newspaper across the United States.

CHAPTER FIFTY-FOUR

Maxwell Rosenthal watched the stateside news and read every newspaper he could get his hands on. They sat out on their patio listening to the waves gently roll onto the shore.

Judy finished one of the articles. "Does this mean we'll go back home now?"

"Do you want to go back home?"

"Not really, at least not yet. I'm enjoying it here. This is like one long vacation. I feel like we're actually getting to know each other for the first time."

Maxwell smiled. "I know. I was thinking the same thing. I've not really missed the hectic schedule, the late nights, and the screaming clients. I've enjoyed the leisurely pace of the Tropics."

"Can we survive, I mean financially?"

"Are you kidding? With the cost of living here in Costa Rica, we have enough to last us the rest of our lives. Who knows, maybe I'll write that novel I've always wanted to write."

Judy cuddled up closer to Max. "That sounds romantic, sitting in a tropical paradise, writing a novel. What will it be about?"

"How about a novel about how one couple almost got killed by IRS agents who were after them because they had stolen a secret document?"

Judy laughed. "No. I don't think that will work. No one would ever believe it. You'd better write a romantic novel."

Maxwell pulled Judy toward him and gave her a passionate kiss on the lips. She returned the kiss. As they held the embrace, Judy thought, *I hope this never ends. It's so romantic.*

Max released Judy and whispered, "If I'm going to write a romantic novel, I'll need some passionate love scenes. What do you say we go practice some?"

Judy smiled, grabbing him by the hand. "Sounds great to me. Where do you want to start, on the beach or in the room?"

"Tell you what, I'll follow you."

CHAPTER FIFTY-FIVE

Nathan and Linda sat in the Miami airport waiting to board their plane. They had watched the broadcast from their hotel room. Their pictures appeared on every station as the media repeated segments of the broadcast over and over again. They could only hope and pray that no one would recognize them. Neither of them could believe that this nightmare was finally coming to an end.

Matthew and Allen occupied themselves by strolling around the waiting area, putting their faces up against the glass, watching the planes come and go.

Linda broke the silence. "Wouldn't it be safe for us to stay here now?"

Nathan stared off into space for a moment and then replied, "It's hard to say. It's possible that with time our names could be cleared and we could get everything back, but I really have my doubts. And do you really want to take the chance?"

"Why? We're innocent."

"Well, don't forget, we did kidnap our boys. The IRS could still say we owed the back taxes. We have no assurance that the taxes we owe would be forgiven, and we certainly don't have any proof that we don't owe them. What do you want to do?" Nathan hadn't told her about hacking into the computers and changing their tax statements.

Linda sighed. "What I really want to do is go back to our house and pretend none of this ever happened. That's what I really want to do, but I know that realistically, it's probably impossible."

"I think you're right. I believe we should proceed with our plan and get out of the country. We can always come back in a few years if we want. We have enough money to last us."

"By the way, that reminds me, how did we suddenly get all of this money?" Linda sounded like a reporter.

Nathan looked at her, paused, and smiled then said, "Gee, you know, I'm really looking forward to living in the Caribbean. I hear the people are friendly, and the climate is beautiful year round."

"Are you avoiding my question?"

"No, dear, I was just making conversation."

A voice came over the loudspeaker. "Flight 427 is now ready for boarding at gate twelve. Please have your boarding passes ready."

"We better go," Nathan said. "Matthew, Allen, come on over here."

As they gathered up all of the carry-on baggage, Linda teased him, "You're not going to tell me, are you?"

"Let's just say that right now it's better that you don't know. Now, let's go before we miss our plane."

Once settled onto the plane, it seemed like only minutes before the captain announced that they would soon be leaving Miami. Nathan reached over and gently placed his hand inside hers. She squeezed it.

Nathan closed his eyes. As the plane began to taxi backwards, there was a sigh of relief as thoughts of freedom flooded his mind. *How nice it will be to not have to hide anymore. We can stop running.*

Linda thought about her home and her family she was leaving behind. *Will I ever see them again? Will we ever come back here again?* Tears welled up in her eyes as the plane soared into the air. She knew, as she watched out the window, that she might never see the United States again. The tears streamed down her cheeks. She wiped them away, trying to force them back. *At least I have my family, and we're all alive.* She squeezed Nathan's hand as she reached across the aisle and grabbed Matthew's hand.

Nathan read her thoughts and whispered, "We can start over again. We'll have a new life. You'll see. Everything will be fine." He reached over and wiped one of the tears from her cheek. He put his hand on her shoulder, whispering in her ear, "I love you, and I'm just glad we're all together again."

Linda let go of Matthew's hand and placed her hand on Nathan's cheek, looking directly into his eyes. "I love you too, and I'm glad we're together. It's just that I'm going to miss …" She began to cry again.

"I know. I know. So will I. But we're safe, and we have each other."

The plane climbed higher until it soared through the clouds. The ground below disappeared. Nathan and Linda looked out the window and saw the sun shining brightly. It symbolized to both of them that their lives were just beginning again. In a way, they both looked forward to what the future held.

Nathan leaned his seat back, closed his eyes, and for the first time in months, felt really relaxed. He smiled as he thought of Howard Baskins and couldn't help but wonder what he was thinking at this very moment.

****

A well-dressed man stood in the terminal watching the plane soar into the air. Suddenly, there was a flash of light in the sky, and the large 727 exploded in midair. People watched in horror as the plane nosed downward toward earth and came crashing to the ground, leaving another ball of fire in its path.

The well-dressed man took a piece of paper from his coat pocket, mumbling to himself, "Now there are only three people left who can testify against Howard Baskins. The Shark will be pleased." He crossed four names off the list. He headed for his gate to catch the next plane to Washington DC.

It was unfortunate that so many innocent people had to die, but it was for a higher cause, and nothing or no one could stand in their way for the success of this operation.

****

Nathan jumped forward suddenly, grabbing the seat in front of him. Linda was shaken from her restful state. "What is it?"

"I don't know." Nathan took a deep breath. "I saw our plane." He stopped, not wanting to tell her the rest of his dream. "I must have been dreaming. I'm okay now."

Linda stroked his arm, smoothing the hairs that were standing on end. "Go back to sleep. You need to rest. You're just on edge." She snuggled up closer, laying her head on his shoulder.

Nathan's heart was still pounding hard. He laid his head back in the seat, feeling certain now that he had made the right choice to double book their flights and change plans at the last minute. He tried not to think about the past few months and forced his mind to think only about how they were going to spend the rest of their lives in their new home. Pulling his wife closer, he whispered, "I love you."

She kissed his lips gently. "I love you too."

"What's the first thing you want to do when we get to our little island?"

"Oh, that one is easy. I want to take off my shoes and run along the blue waters and feel the sand beneath my feet." Linda smiled just thinking about it. "How about you?"

"Me? I'm going to throw off my shoes and chase you down the beach."

They both laughed and snuggled closer to each other.

EPILOGUE

The man known only as the Shark to some sat in his large office staring out the window. A sound came from his computer signaling him of an important high-priority message. He turned to his computer, pressed some keys, entered his password, and read the text that flashed on the screen.

To: Shark
From: Calvin Davis
Target #2—nowhere to be found.
Trail has been lost.
Will await further orders.

Suddenly, his office door opened, and his secretary entered the room. "Mr. Chapman, you have an appointment to see the president in an hour. Do you need anything else?"

Verlin Chapman turned to face her. "No, Connie, I think I have everything ready. Send for my car please."

"Yes, sir. It is already scheduled for 11:00 AM."

"Thank you. That will be all."

Verlin glanced at his computer screen and smiled, thinking to himself, *Everything will proceed as planned with a few minor adjustments. This is only a temporary setback. The president will be glad to see our new projections for next year and will be delighted that our plan has not been thwarted. His pretending to uncover our scam was a brilliant move and should guarantee his second term. By the time he leaves office, we'll all be very, very rich.*

He wasn't sure what he was going to do about his old friend Senator Haden, but knew for the time being, they would need to back off. He could only hope that the senator would do the same now that all of this had been made public. Maybe he would call his old friend to arrange another lunch. As he had already discovered, it never hurt to keep your enemy close.

Verlin stood up and hit a key on his computer, and the message on the screen disappeared. He walked outside, where his limousine was already waiting. He climbed in, and the car drove up Pennsylvania Avenue to the White House.

THE END

ABOUT THE AUTHOR

Mickey P. Jordan is an entrepreneur and currently owns several businesses in Austin, Texas. He has over thirty years experience in the income tax preparation field working with the largest companies in the industry. This is his second of three novels. He lives with his wife, Diane, in Leander, TX. They have two grown children, Christina and Mikki.

Printed in the United States
25959LVS00001B/160-177

9 781418 491734